Open Circle

STACY MONSON

Scripture is taken from the New International Version of the Bible.

ISBN: 978-1-7323990-6-8 (print)

WELCOME TO THE MOSAIC COLLECTION

We are sisters, a beautiful mosaic united by the love of God through the blood of Christ.

Each month The Mosaic Collection releases one faith-based novel or anthology exploring our theme, Family by His Design, and sharing stories that feature diverse, God-designed families. All are contemporary stories ranging from mystery and women's fiction to comedic and literary fiction. We hope you'll join our Mosaic family as we explore together what truly defines a family.

If you're like us, loneliness and suffering have touched your life in ways you never imagined; but Dear One, while you may feel alone in your suffering—whatever it is—you are never alone!

Subscribe to *Grace & Glory*, the official newsletter of The Mosaic Collection, to receive monthly encouragement from Mosaic authors, as well as timely updates about events, new releases, and giveaways.

Learn more about The Mosaic Collection at
www.mosaiccollectionbooks.com

Join our Reader Community, too!
www.facebook.com/groups/TheMosaicCollection

If you'd like to find out about monthly launch team
opportunities, sign up at
www.mosaiccollectionbooks.com/launch-team

BOOKS IN THE MOSAIC COLLECTION

When Mountains Sing by Stacy Monson
Unbound by Eleanor Bertin
The Red Journal by Deb Elkink
A Beautiful Mess by Brenda S. Anderson
Hope is Born: A Mosaic Christmas Anthology
More Than Enough by Lorna Seilstad
The Road to Happenstance by Janice L. Dick
This Side of Yesterday by Angela D. Meyer
Lost Down Deep by Sara Davison
The Mischief Thief by Johnnie Alexander
Before Summer's End: Stories to Touch the Soul
Tethered by Eleanor Bertin
Calm Before the Storm by Janice L. Dick
Heart Restoration by Regina Rudd Merrick
Pieces of Granite by Brenda S. Anderson
Watercolors by Lorna Seilstad
A Star Will Rise: A Mosaic Christmas Anthology II
Eye of the Storm by Janice L. Dick
Totally Booked: A Book Lover's Companion
Lifelines by Eleanor Bertin

DEDICATION

To those who are challenged by the many forms of dementia including Alzheimer's Disease, Frontotemporal Degeneration (FTD), Lewy Body, MCI, and Parkinson's, as well as other diseases that seek to rob them of their identity, their place, and their dignity—thank you for fighting the good fight. Your courage is inspiring.

To those who provide countless hours caring for their elders at home, I pray for God to provide the strength, patience, resilience, humor, energy, and funding you need each day. You are truly the unsung heroes.

To those professionals who honor our elders by caring for them through housing, daily cares, and providing services, thank you for showing up each day to make life better for those in your care.

And to those who tirelessly raise funds, campaign to change laws, and spend their lives doing research to find the cause and cure to save the next generation, my gratitude and heartfelt thanks.

It takes a village to care for the elderly, the weak, the confused, the tired, so we each must play our part to make our homes, our communities, and our world a better place to live out our golden years.

Update: Since the initial release of Open Circle in 2018, dementia has become very personal for me as my husband was diagnosed in early 2020. As you can imagine, much has changed in our lives; dementia causes long-reaching ripples across so many lives. I've shared more of my story at the end of Open Circle.

Even to your old age and gray hairs I am He, I am He who will sustain you. I have made you and I will carry you; I will sustain you and I will rescue you.

Isaiah 46:4

CHAPTER ONE

"Ashes to ashes, dust to dust." The pastor sprinkled a handful of fine dirt on the mahogany casket and Mindy Lee "Minnie" Carlson closed her eyes, drawing a slow breath. Why did roses smell so different at a funeral than they did in the backyard?

"We commend our brother, Frank, to his eternal rest."

The too-familiar words burned into her heart. Frank shouldn't be in that casket. He should be peeking over her shoulder waiting to taste a fresh-baked oatmeal raisin cookie. Or standing outside the adult day center, binoculars in hand, explaining the difference between a goldfinch and a canary. Better yet, he should be home caring for his beloved wife, Helen.

Her gaze ran across the headstones in the tiny Lawton, Minnesota cemetery, anger prickling under her skin. Frank's death could have been prevented if someone had listened to her. She'd sounded the warning daily for the past two weeks. But no, what did the small-town social worker know?

Her jaw ached from clenching. She wouldn't let this

happen again. To anyone. Next time she would— Warm fingers touched her bare elbow and she jumped.

Nick Butler looked down at her with a solemn expression. "Minnie, stop by my office when you get back, please."

Lips pressed against the outburst that threatened, she nodded, and he moved away. At least he had the decency to look sad, whether he felt it or not. While he was the administrator of both the Crosswinds Care Facility and the Open Circle Adult Day Center, she didn't report directly to him, which could explain why he'd ignored her warnings. She'd have to wrestle her roiling emotions under control before facing him or she'd be out on the street. Losing her job wouldn't save the rest of her seniors.

Her attention drifted over the mourners as they dispersed, stopping on Dorothy. Heat surged through her chest like a blowtorch. Responsibility for Frank's death rested on Dorothy. The adult day center director had insisted she had Frank's health issues under control, even berating Minnie for being "obsessive."

Gray-streaked black hair piled on her head like a bird's nest, Dorothy paused beside Helen, Frank's widow, said something with an appropriately sad expression, and then hurried away. Nothing in her demeanor spoke of actually caring about Helen, or even Frank.

Minnie threaded through the remaining mourners to where Helen now sat alone on a white folding chair, gazing at the casket. In poor health for months, she'd relied on Frank's unwavering devotion to get through each day. Minnie settled beside her. "Hello, dear Helen."

Helen's yellow raincoat seemed two sizes too big, swallowing her tiny frame. Tears trickled down softly wrinkled cheeks as wiry gray hair lifted and fell in the gentle May breeze.

Minnie reached for her hand, grasping the cold, frail fingers warmly. "I'm so sorry about Frank."

"Wasn't he wonderful?"

Throat tight, Minnie nodded. "The best."

"I can't believe he's gone." The limp hanky she pressed to her face muffled her sobs as she crumpled toward Minnie.

Holding the trembling woman, Minnie squeezed her eyes shut against a fresh surge of outrage and grief. When she returned to the office, Nick had better be prepared. The seniors of Lawton deserved better than this.

Helen sat up, mopping her face as she pulled in a shaky breath. Two women took the seats on her right and she turned toward them. Minnie stood and paused beside the casket, pressing a hand against the cool wood. The fragrance of the white rose spray made her heart ache.

"We'll take care of Helen, Frank," she said. "And I promise I won't let this happen to anyone else. I'll make them listen next time." She set her shoulders and left the cemetery.

Half an hour later, standing in her tiny cubicle in a corner of the adult day center, she checked the mirror. She couldn't look much worse. Dark circles under puffy eyes, mussed brown curls framing a ghostly face. She smoothed her hair and lightly pinched her cheeks, then walked across the parking lot to the adjacent care facility.

The door to Nick's office was open, as usual. She paused to whisper a prayer for control and then knocked.

Nick swung around in his chair and motioned her in, phone to his ear. "Mmhm. Right," he said. "That's what I thought. How much time do you need?"

She wandered along the back wall, looking at framed photos lining the credenza. Nick shaking hands with an older gentleman while accepting an award. Sprawled on the grass with several children crawling on him. Surrounded by seniors of Open Circle, wearing plastic leis and holding cups of lemonade with paper umbrellas.

He ended his call and she faced him. *Stay strong for Helen and Frank.*

"Thanks for coming, Minnie. Close the door and have a seat."

She did as he asked and settled across the desk from him, hands clenched in her lap. Moisture touched her hairline as she prepared to fight for her seniors.

He studied his fingernails, a frown gathering his dark eyebrows together. "We should have listened to you."

Her eyes widened then narrowed. "Yes, you should have. There were enough signs. His weight loss was obvious, the growing confusion a huge red flag. Yet Dorothy let him cancel both of the doctor appointments I'd made."

The memory of the argument added to the fire in her stomach. She flung her hands up. "We should have worked together to get the infection treated, not against each other."

He opened his mouth then closed it and nodded.

"If Dorothy had listened, if *you* had listened, we wouldn't have had a funeral today and Helen wouldn't be a widow. We can't make decisions for our clients based on what fits our schedule or our budget. That was Frank's life that got pushed to the back burner."

His expression darkened. "Minnie—"

"Too many decisions lately have been based on budget constraints." She grasped the chair's black metal handles to keep from leaping to her feet. "I understand some of our funding has been cut, but up to now we've always put our seniors' welfare above everything else. If that's no longer true, I can't work here anymore."

The words reverberated in the silence. Where had that decision come from? She forced herself to hold his gaze, chin up. He looked away first and sighed, his face drawn, tie loosened.

"I'm sorry we didn't move on your suggestions," he said finally.

The unexpected apology threw water on her fury, and her shoulders lowered. He pushed abruptly to his feet and she jumped. While he stood at the window, she studied his profile. He'd run the 64-bed care facility for almost five years, and was highly respected by the staff and residents, and as well as most of the town of three thousand. He also oversaw Open Circle, the adjacent adult day center where she'd been the social worker for three years.

As the silence stretched, she looked across his desk. Papers neatly stacked. A silver travel mug, a stapler, a round desk caddy. It wasn't fair to blame him for Frank's death. Not entirely. He'd proven his passion for Lawton's seniors over the years in the long hours he kept, the many times he joined in activities at the care center and at Open Circle, and his natural affinity for the older generation.

"Minnie, I want you to run Open Circle. Starting Monday."

Her attention flew back to his face. "Excuse me?"

"Dorothy is taking a...leave. I want you to take her place."

"But..." Thoughts and questions collided in a kaleidoscope of confusion. "What about Cheryl? She's the assistant dir—"

"I want you to run it." His firm tone silenced her protest. "I've seen your work with the seniors and the families. I like your vision and your work ethic. Frank's death might have been prevented if your warning had been taken seriously."

She stared at him, an erratic pounding beneath her ribs. She wasn't a leader. She didn't want to be in charge; she'd simply wanted someone to hear her concerns.

He returned to his chair, his expression softening. "I hoped you'd jump up and down saying yes."

"Well, I..." She blinked and shook her head. "I don't know what I expected you to say, but that wasn't it."

His partial smile faded as he leaned his forearms on the desk and clasped his hands. "I want you to run this program however you see fit. I trust your judgment. But there's something you need to know before you give me the answer I want."

She waited.

"The Board of Directors wants to close the center for financial reasons, but in light of Frank's death, I wrangled a four-month stay to not upset the community even more. If you can get things turned around by September first, we might not have to close."

Four *months* to fix five years of mismanagement? Staffing issues, program concerns, rebuilding the community's trust, meeting the seniors' needs—in four months? *Lord? Is that even possible?*

"Who will handle my position?"

He cleared his throat. "I think you'll be able to handle the most important parts."

She frowned. "Wait. You want me to be the social worker *and* the director?"

"I'm sure it feels like a lot, Min, but I wouldn't ask if I didn't think you could handle it. Only for a few months. You already know how Open Circle runs, so I'm confident you'll pick up the extra duties easily. We'll certainly compensate you for that."

The earlier panic threatened. *God, you know I can't do this on my own.*

Letting the statement sail upward, determination straightened her spine. If taking on the director role enabled her to uphold her promise to Frank, she'd do it. With God's help, she'd make sure every senior in Lawton got the care and respect they deserved. "Okay. I'll do my best."

Nick grinned and stood, offering his hand. His six-foot-four frame dwarfed her by almost a foot. She met his warm grasp, heartbeat ramping as reality spun through her like a summer tornado.

He was her new boss. *She* was the new director of Open Circle Adult Day Center. And she had a promise to keep.

⁓ℓ⌀

Jackson Young propped his elbows on the picnic table and refocused his lens on the red cement wall in front of him. Another cloud dimmed the brilliant Chicago sunshine and he bit back a sigh of frustration. Lighting had been iffy throughout the shoot, conspiring to keep him from that one perfect shot. Or even a nearly perfect shot. Sweat trickled down his back as he waited.

Male voices floated over him as the skateboarders got into position again at either end of the ramp. He drew a steadying breath as the smooth sounds of approaching wheels set his nerves tingling then silence as two young men lifted off the cement. They passed in midair, arms spread, their backflips a mirror image. Jackson snapped a rapid succession of shots, heart pounding. Man, these kids were good.

The skateboards rattled to a stop amid whistles and clapping. Jackson relaxed and checked the shots. Far more promising than most of the earlier ones but until he could pull them up on a decent screen, he wouldn't celebrate.

"Hey, man." One of the boys dropped on the bench opposite him, cap on sideways, necklaces glinting in the light. "Get one that time?"

"Definitely." *Hope so, anyway.* "Amazing work, bro."

The teen grinned. "Thanks. We've been workin' on that for a while. Hoping to put it in the show this weekend down on the pier. You gonna be around to see it?"

Jackson zipped his camera into the padded case. "Wish I could, but I'm heading home tomorrow." It'd be a great opportunity for more photos, but if he didn't get today's shots processed over the next few days, he'd be late on the assignment. Even after three years of a perfect record, the compulsion to be on time every time hadn't waned. Did he have to spend the rest of his life making up for the Big Blunder?

"Where's home?" the boy asked as he popped a stick of gum in his mouth and propped his elbows on the table. The talent Jackson had photographed all day hardly seemed possible in such a scrawny kid.

"Sacramento. I hate to miss the show. You guys'll rock it."

"Bobby G is an amazing dude. I jus' hope I can keep up."

"I bet you can. Thanks for letting me in on today's practice, Jimmy." Jackson reached out a fist and the boy bumped it. "I've got your email, so I'll get the photos to you in the next week."

"Great. Sorry the weather didn't cooperate."

Jackson shrugged. "It's all part of the job. I think I got some great shots."

Joining the young men now relaxing along the cement wall, Jackson thanked them, praising their work and determination, then headed out of the 'hood. After a grueling day filled with inconsistent lighting, a few skateboard crashes, and humidity that sapped his energy, he needed a shower.

Thirty minutes later, he let himself into Noah Russell's apartment, grateful he could crash at his best friend's place whenever he came through Chicago. With Noah traveling on a photo assignment, Jackson had the small apartment to himself.

A whistle from the living room corrected the thought. He and Ima had the place to themselves. "Be right there, lovely lady."

He set the camera case on a kitchen chair, dropped the pile of mail he'd collected on the table, then let his backpack slide to the floor. Rubbing his aching neck, he sorted through the envelopes. On the road for a month, he'd had his mail forwarded from Sacramento. He shook his head. Even the junk mail had followed him.

A stark white envelope at the bottom of the pile stood out against the others. His eyes widened at the return address. Lawton? Why would someone from his hometown contact him? Especially Daniel A. Benson, Attorney-at-Law? Probably looking for permission to use a photograph.

Stuffing the envelope in his back pocket, he retrieved a can of soda from the refrigerator and went into the living room to greet Ima. The cockatiel whistled and chirped as he approached her cage, nodding her head in the goofy dance that always made him laugh.

Leaning close, he whistled softly. "How are you, Miss Ima Bird?" She fluttered white wings and tossed her green-tufted head. "Yes, you look ravishing as always."

He dropped onto the old leather couch and pulled off his boots, massaging his feet as he watched her preen. Stretching out, he focused on relaxing his knotted neck muscles, loosening the strain between his shoulder blades, letting the day's frustration seep out.

After a long swig of soda, he opened the envelope and pulled out a crisp sheet of paper. He scanned the opening and bolted upright. *What?!*

He read the first line again, aloud this time as if that would make it clear. "Emily Young has requested we contact you regarding several family matters needing resolution as soon as possible."

Emily Young was dead. She'd died five years after his parents abruptly uprooted him from Lawton and moved to Milwaukee. At least, that's what they'd told him. He stared blindly across the room. They'd severed their relationship with his grandparents when they moved away. No amount of begging on his part had convinced them to let him go back for a visit.

At fifteen, when they'd told him Grandma Em had died, he'd grieved deeply for her. If she were indeed still alive and living in Lawton, his parents had lied to him. Deliberately. He scanned the rest of the brief letter that requested his presence as soon as possible in the tiny town. Twenty years. He'd lost two decades with her! No, his parents had stolen them.

"Why?" He pushed off the couch and paced. "Why would they lie about that? What was the point?" Apparently, she hadn't died—although his dad had, of suicide eight years ago. His mother had quickly remarried and moved to Europe. With no siblings or even any cousins to check with, he'd have to track his mother down if he wanted an answer.

Grandma Em is alive. His heart pounded the message. Grandma Em is *alive!* "But it doesn't make sense, Ima. Why hasn't she contacted me before now? I'm not hard to find."

She flapped her wings, heading bobbing as if in sympathy.

Memories tugged at him. "She gave me my first camera, you know. And she always wore cowgirl boots." He glanced at his own boots, a private nod to his childhood. "I need some answers, Miss Ima."

She whistled. He pulled his cell phone from his back pocket. "Let's give Daniel A. Benson a call. Maybe it's all a big joke." A big rotten joke.

Dialing the number, he almost hoped it was. Then hoped it wasn't. Since rebounding from his Big Blunder of three years ago, his schedule had gone crazy. How could he fit in visits with his grandma? How could he not? His stomach twisted. And at some point, he'd have to confront why his parents lied to him.

As the attorney's phone rang a second time, Jackson lightly tapped the birdcage. "I have a feeling life's about to change, Ima. Hang onto your perch."

CHAPTER TWO

Minnie paused in the doorway of Dorothy's office—*her* office now. *How do I do this? Where do I start?* From the messy desk to the half open file drawer, and the tattered curtains keeping the room in shadow, the director's office near the reception area screamed chaos. Cleaning would have to be first. She couldn't work in this disaster.

She strode into the room and set her computer bag beside the desk, then relocated the stack of papers from her chair to the meeting table. Throwing the curtains wide, sunlight splashed across her face, and she closed her eyes to soak in its comforting warmth. A fresh start—

"Minnie?" Her name ended in a stunned question mark.

The sun's gentle warmth vaporized under the cold frown of Cheryl Post, Dorothy's second-in-command. "Hi, Cheryl. Come on in."

The short, squat woman didn't move. "*You're* Dorothy's replacement?"

Minnie's smile faded. "Nick didn't tell you?"

"Only that Dorothy had gone on leave." She folded thick arms, pale blue eyes narrowed.

Thanks, Nick. Minnie stood straighter and swept a hand toward the chair across the desk. "Come in. We have a lot to talk about. I'm going to need your help if we want to get things turned around."

The sharp lift to Cheryl's chin sent heat into Minnie's cheeks. Bad choice of words. Cheryl would take any criticism of Dorothy personally, as would half the staff.

Minnie settled in her chair, praying for words to soften the unintentional slam. "You know these seniors, Cheryl. And you know Lawton. Your expertise is vital to keeping Open Circle the amazing place it's always been."

The older woman's stare didn't waver as she silenced her beeping pager. "I have to go. Without a social worker, I'll have to pick up some of that slack. You'd better fill your position soon."

"Well, I'll still—" Her words trailed as Cheryl stalked away. Staring at the empty doorway, her heart took up a disjointed pounding. So much for a smooth transition. She wouldn't mention that for now she would cover both jobs. Dorothy hadn't seemed all that busy anyway.

She dropped her head into her hands and squeezed her eyes shut. What did she know about running a center? Hiring people, supervising? *What was I thinking?* Her phone rang, and she jumped.

One step at a time. You can do this. For Frank. She lifted the receiver. "This is Minnie. How may I help you?"

"Minnie? What happened to Dorothy?" The loud, scratchy male voice was familiar.

"Dorothy is on leave. I'm filling in for her."

"Oh. Well, this is Clarence Johnson."

Clarence, that's right.

"Dorothy said she'd be sending someone out to give me and Martha a ride to Bingo on Wednesday. That gonna happen?"

"Of course we'll get you to Bingo, Clarence. I'm so glad you're getting Martha out of the house." She pulled a yellow notepad closer and jotted a reminder. "Are the new meds helping her arthritis?"

The knots in her shoulders unravelled as she chatted with the older man. She'd accepted the position for people like Clarence and Martha, Francis, Bertie. And Helen. Two more phone calls followed. Staff members filed in and out with questions about getting Phyllis' new glasses picked up, why the coffee pot was making a strange noise, and who should unplug the toilet in the ladies' room.

Minnie answered what she could or sent them to Cheryl. She managed fifteen minutes at the mid-morning sing-along before another phone call dragged her back to the office. The next time she had a free moment, her watch showed one-forty-five. No wonder her stomach growled.

A search for her lunch bag came up empty. *Great.* With a grunt, she leaned back in the chair and closed her eyes, a hand over her rumbling stomach. It certainly wouldn't kill her to go without a meal.

"Sleeping on the job already?"

A smile filled Minnie's face and calmed her heart. "Come in, come in. How's my favorite Bunco player?"

The bright blue tin in Emily Young's hands matched her eyes. "Apparently a lot better than you."

"Em" settled into the chair across from Minnie. Her red hair was windblown, cheeks pink, eyes sparkling. While many of the seniors in Lawton were dealing with the physical and mental effects of advanced age, Em seemed more like sixty than eighty-one.

She held the tin out across the desk. "Mindy Lee, you look like something my old Elmer Fudd dragged in from the woods."

Minnie snorted. The monstrous Tom cat probably

could drag her, if he ever decided to expend the energy. She lifted the lid off the tin and inhaled deeply. Em's famous, fresh-baked chocolate chip cookies. "Mmm. They smell wonderful."

"There's no better smell on God's green earth than cookies right out of the oven."

Minnie bit into one and closed her eyes with a sigh. "Exactly what I needed." Except...something was different, like maybe a missing ingredient. She chewed slowly. Or something new. Opening her eyes to ask, she encountered a frowning gaze. "What?"

"I thought I'd find you dancing on the ceiling. Instead, you look like they backed the bakery truck over you. Rough first day?"

"You could say that."

A smile tipped the corner of her mouth. "What made our handsome young director finally give old Dots the boot?"

"Em! Shh."

Glancing at the open doorway, Em leaned forward and whispered loudly, "Trust me. this is the best thing Nicholas could have done for this place. The next best thing would be for him to ask you out."

"You're impossible," she whispered back, heat blazing up to her eyebrows. "I don't want to date my boss. But that has nothing to do with Dorothy going on leave."

"Leave, schmeave." Em waved brightly manicured fingers and rolled her eyes. "Nobody believes that story, dear. Dorothy was simply taking up space until her retirement. With you in charge, things will turn around."

Not if this first day was any indication. Tears sprang to the surface, and she turned her gaze toward the window, blinking rapidly. Crying on day one would hardly inspire confidence in the staff. Or herself.

Em reached across the desk and rested a hand on Minnie's. "Look at me, honey."

Jaw clenched, she did.

"You are exactly where God wants you, doing what you've always wanted to do. Don't try to fix everything all at once. Slow down and listen. Let Him lead, and it will all work out."

Minnie held her gaze, drawing strength from the smiling love and encouragement of her favorite person in the world. They were family, all that either had left.

"You're right." Her shoulders lowered. "I need to trust He has a plan."

"Darn tootin', darling." She stood, then put a hand to her forehead as she swayed.

"Em?" Minnie jumped up and reached toward her. "What's wrong?"

Color had washed from her face but as she blinked and steadied herself, a light pink returned. "Forgot to take my blood pressure pill this morning. I'll go home and do that now." She winked before heading to the door. "Don't worry. I'm fine. Toodles, dear heart."

Minnie lowered back into her chair and took another cookie, then swiveled to look out the dirty window. She needed to let God lead on this journey. But that didn't mean she shouldn't be ready for battle, at least where Cheryl was concerned. Whatever his reasons, Nick had picked *her* for the job. Cheryl could posture all she wanted, but it wouldn't change anything.

She dusted cookie crumbs from her hands and turned to the computer. With September looming like thunder clouds over a corn field, there wasn't time to feel sorry for herself, or even waste energy fighting with an angry assistant director. She had work to do and a promise to keep.

Finally back in his Sacramento apartment after a long month of photo shoots, Jackson studied the Chicago photographs on his computer screen, searching each for that one flaw that would make him toss it out. Intently focused on taking these last shots, he hadn't realized the sun had peeked out, casting perfect lighting over the boys on their skateboards. The colors of their hoodies and hats blended into a vibrant blur. Eyes narrowed, lips pursed, arms outstretched—they were the picture of concentration as they passed each other in midair.

He sat back and rubbed his eyes, then stretched his arms overhead and smiled. He loved the thrill when a shot came together like this. And he'd thought his time in Chicago was a bust. Now he could head to Lawton on Monday with nothing hanging over his head.

Lawton. Since the phone call with Daniel A. Benson last week, he'd replayed the conversation in his head a hundred times. One simple sentence changed his life.

"Yes, your grandmother is very much alive and doing remarkably well here in Lawton."

Stunned by that revelation, all rational thought had fled. He'd stammered through the rest of the call, asking the same question several times. "And we're talking about Emily Young who was married to Richard Young, right? They had one son, Tony. And one grandson?"

The thought of seeing his grandmother made his heart spin like the kid on the skateboard. The urge to hang up on the lawyer and call Grandma Em immediately had surged, but he'd flattened the idea. Their reunion had to be done in person. No awkward phone call, just one long hug. And maybe a tear or two.

He headed to the kitchen for more coffee, but the ring

of his cell phone sent him back to his desk. Noah Russell's name made him smile. "Hey, man. Does my girl miss me back there in the Windy City?"

"Not that she's mentioned," Noah replied. "I'm glad you answered your phone for once."

Jackson grunted. "If you didn't always call when I've got a camera in my hand—"

"When *don't* you have a camera in hand?"

"Right now. That's why I answered the phone."

Noah chuckled.

"So, to what do I owe the honor of you yammering in my ear, Russell?"

"Got an offer I think you'll like."

"I'm listening." He propped the phone against his shoulder and filled the coffee carafe with water.

"Pierre New York wants to do a feature on global humanitarian work."

"Pierre Guillaume's art gallery? Cool."

"Your name came up."

The pot thumped onto the counter, cold water sloshing over his hand. "How would he know who I am?" Pierre Guillaume was *the* name in art studios. World-renown.

"Everyone knows who you are, pal."

This had to be another of Noah's pranks. "You spreading rumors about me again?" He emptied the carafe into the coffeemaker and pushed the button.

Noah laughed. "Pierre is planning a feature on humanitarian work for this August."

"I see you're on a first name basis with him." Definitely a joke.

"You will be too. He wants to feature you in the show. There'll be a few others there, like me, and Paul Branton, but he wants *you* to have top billing. I'd be jealous if I didn't think he was spot on."

"Very funny." He grunted. "You, me, and Branton in New York City. Right. People would flock to see our show. Good one."

"I'm not kidding, Jack." The laughter had vanished. "Dead serious here."

"Well, your friend 'Pierre' didn't call *me* so I think somebody's yanking your chain."

"Have you checked your phone lately? You were in Chicago all last week, and I *know* you don't answer your phone when you're working."

Jackson stared out the kitchen window. There'd been several missed calls from unfamiliar numbers, but no messages.

"Jackson?" Noah rarely called him by his first name. Only when—

Jackson's heart leaped into his throat.

"I've played some good jokes on you, Jack, but I wouldn't joke about this. You still there?"

"Yeah. I'm just..." He shook his head. "Why me?"

"I know you're still beating yourself up over the blunder, Young, but people respect your work. Nobody highlights the forgotten people better than you. So?" A grin returned to his words. "What do you say? You in?"

"Of course I'm in! When? How?"

When the call ended, Jackson dropped onto a stool at the breakfast bar, smiling stupidly across the kitchen. He had three weeks to get his life in order before heading to New York to meet with Pierre Guillame to plan his show. *His* show!

He jumped to his feet, letting the stool crash to the floor as he pumped his fist in the air. "Yes! It's about time."

If he believed in God, he'd either thank Him or ask what took so long. Instead, he would celebrate his own grit and determination. For three long years, he'd taken every assignment lobbed his way, no matter how small, logging thousands of miles around the globe, taking pictures of anything and everything. Whatever it took to get his career back on track.

Hands on his hips, he studied the sparse studio apartment. His favorite old chair, a TV and a desk, a few dishes in the cupboard, a bed. He lived like a nomad because home was wherever the camera took him. When loneliness threatened, he packed a bag and headed back out into the world.

In the space of a week, his life had spun 180 degrees. He had his grandma back from the dead, and a major showing set for New York City. He had time to visit Lawton, then he'd be off to New York. There might even be a few days of downtime. He poured a fresh cup of coffee, chuckling. *Who am I kidding? I hate downtime.*

He settled back at his computer and set the steaming mug to the side. Then he leaned back and laced his hands behind his head, heart still hammering against his chest. "Look out, world. Jack Young is back. For good this time."

CHAPTER THREE

Minnie settled in at her desk at six-thirty Monday morning. She'd spent her first week trying to get a handle on her new duties, to understand what needed attention and what could wait. And avoiding Cheryl. Not anymore.

In the silence of the empty center, she closed her eyes and pulled to mind her dream for the program: this old building resonating with conversation, laughter, and wobbling voices raised in off-key song. Daily activities designed to honor and celebrate the uniqueness of each person, staff included. Respect and dignity offered to all.

"Lord, I know we can make it happen." Her quiet prayer filled the office. "Help me focus on what's going right today. And where change needs to happen."

Fear formed like the dark clouds outside, threatening to drown her. David must have felt like this when he faced Goliath, although one of her giants looked a lot like five-foot-two Cheryl Post. "And *please*, keep me from looking too far into the future."

Though her heart still trembled, she opened her eyes and turned resolutely toward the computer. Time to step up and make Open Circle the program she'd dreamed it could be. The program Nick had asked her to restore.

She blasted through the backlog of emails. The morning staff arrived, turning on lights and music, starting the coffee, voices muted as they met with Gail, the activities director, to review the day's schedule.

At seven-fifteen, Minnie stationed herself in the reception area as the first client, flamboyant former storeowner Bertie, swept through the front door.

"There you are, you sweet thing." Bertie tossed a tattered white boa over her shoulder and gave Minnie a peck on the cheek. "I asked the girls where you've been."

Minnie smiled, the sticky imprint from Bertie's red lipstick clinging to her skin. "Buried under paperwork. You look wonderful this morning. I love that pink sweat suit."

"Someone bought it for me. My daughter, I think." She leaned close and whispered loudly, "I don't think I like pink, but I didn't want to hurt her feelings."

Minnie squeezed her hand. "I know pink isn't your favorite color, but it brings out the lovely color in your cheeks. I'll see you in Bingo, okay?"

Bertie blew her a kiss before adjusting her grip on the walker. She shuffled down the hall toward the large activity room where Cheryl stood guard over coffee and donuts.

The front door opened, and Minnie turned toward it. "Well, if it isn't my favorite Lawton police chief."

"*Retired* police chief," Ronald reminded her gruffly. "But I could still take on any of those young'uns."

"I know you could, but that wouldn't be good for their morale, now, would it, Chief?"

"It'd get 'em off their duffs," he grumbled and marched away.

Immensely proud of his law enforcement career, Chief groused non-stop about the young guys who seemed far less prepared. Some of the Open Circle staff called him Mr. Crank, but Minnie loved his passion for the community.

"Well, lookee here. It's sweet little Mindy Lee!" boomed a familiar voice.

She turned with a smile. "Jerry! How are you?"

He caught her hand between his meaty ones and pumped vigorously. "The sun is shining, the corn is growing, and the cows are giving milk. What could be better?"

She giggled and retrieved her hand. "Sounds perfect to me. You're looking very spry today."

The former Lawton mayor loved nothing more than glad-handing his way through the center telling war stories. Some were true. Others, she suspected, were a bit exaggerated. Or fabricated. "There's lots to be done to keep this town in good shape. Never a dull moment, you know. Being mayor keeps me young."

One of the aides took his arm and encouraged him toward the activity room. Minnie sighed, still smiling. This was where she belonged—greeting these dear people, setting the tone for the morning. Her smile vanished when Em arrived looking strangely rumpled and pale, the sparkle missing from her smile.

"Em? Are you okay?"

Leaning against the front counter, she waved off Minnie's concern. "I slept wrong and my neck is a little sore. I took a few ibuprofen before I left so I'll be fine in a bit. Now, I'd better get a donut before Cheryl decides to pack them up." She straightened and blew a kiss Minnie's direction before heading down the hall.

Minnie watched her through narrowed eyes. Em's

usually energetic stride wobbled. She seemed to be leaning slightly to the right. Minnie took a step to follow but the center's van arrived to deposit six more seniors. Making a mental note to check on Em during Morning News, she turned to greet the group.

For the next thirty minutes, Minnie stayed near the front door, welcoming the seniors, noting who looked better or worse since their last visit. She would chart her questions for Linda, the center's nurse, about Bertie's gout and Moses' broken finger.

Humming the hymn that filtered down the hall from the activity room, she closed the trash bag sitting beside the front desk and took it out to the dumpster behind the center. Rounding the corner, she stopped short. Two teen-aged aides jumped and held their cigarettes behind them.

Her cheerful mood dissolved as she approached them. She hadn't been impressed with their attitudes or their work ethic since Dorothy hired them six months ago. The fact that Wade was Chief's grandson and Justin was Wade's friend from the next town over shouldn't give them special privileges.

"Hey, Wade. Justin." She set the garbage bag at her feet and crossed her arms. "How come you're both out here and not with the seniors?"

They exchanged a glance before Wade shrugged and crushed his cigarette under a ratty tennis shoe. Neither met her gaze. "Cheryl said we could take a break."

"You know we need the right staffing with the seniors all the time, right? We can't have more than one staff out of the room at a time."

"Dorothy never cared."

"*I* do. The safety of our seniors is our number one priority." She threw the garbage bag into the dumpster.

"So, you've had your break. I'm sure Cheryl needs you in there."

They slunk toward the rear door without looking at her.

"And guys?" She waited until they turned back. "I'll get a break schedule set up so you'll have a chance to get out here for a cigarette, but only one person at a time. Got it?"

They glanced at each other. "Sure. Whatever."

As they disappeared inside, she released a long sigh. She had more damage control to do than she'd expected. *Lord, give me patience. And wisdom. I have no clue what I'm doing.*

⁂

Jaw clenched, Jackson rested his forearm against the overhead bin and closed his eyes, fighting the urge to push his way off the plane. People were taking forever to gather their things and file off. The flight to Minneapolis had taken three very long hours.

He had returned to Minnesota after a twenty-year absence. When his parents wrenched him from his idyllic childhood, it had ripped his ten-year-old heart out. In the lonely months that followed in Milwaukee, he'd told himself they'd return to Lawton any day. That had kept his hope afloat. When they moved to St. Louis, the hope started to fade. Ohio had snuffed out what remained.

The line of people finally started moving and he hoisted his duffel over his shoulder, following the memories that beckoned. He'd loved going to his grandparents' house every day after school. As an only child, he'd always been able to amuse himself. The old farmhouse had plenty of nooks and crannies for exploring, a window seat where he'd play with Legos, and a big, warm kitchen he'd loved.

Striding off the jetway into the airport, the aroma of fresh bakery items welcomed him. He breathed deep, a smile touching his mouth. Grandma Em had made amazing things. Fresh bread with slabs of melting butter, homemade apple sauce and hand-cranked vanilla ice cream. Golden apple pie, and sheets of cookies right out of the oven.

Following signs to the baggage claim, his mouth watered. She'd always insisted he take the first cookie. Nothing better than warm cookies with gooey chocolate, and a glass of cold milk. No doubt he'd been spoiled. No kid in Lawton had a better grandma.

He paced around the baggage carousel. Once he picked up the rental, he had a two-hour drive southeast to Lawton. He'd be there after lunch, meet Daniel A. Lawton at his office, and then surprise Grandma Em. Hopefully she wasn't too old to remember him. Or so frail that his sudden appearance gave her a heart attack.

His camera case strap tugged at his shoulder. How many thousands of flights had he taken headed for places unknown? Yet he couldn't remember one time when his knees had knocked like this. This flight had brought him home, to the only family member he still cared about, to resurrect a relationship he'd been forced to give up long ago.

"Buck up, Young." He yanked his suitcase off the conveyor belt. "You're not a kid anymore. It's time to step out from behind the camera and meet your grandmother."

⁓

The office door flew open and an aide beckoned frantically. "Minnie! It's Emily!"

Her wide-eyed fear yanked Minnie out of her chair and

into the hallway where a small crowd gathered, heads bent over something on the floor. Her heart lodged in her throat. *Dear God, not Em!*

She shouldered into the circle and dropped to her knees. Emily lay on her back, wild red hair framing her ghostly face, her blue eyes darting back and forth.

"Who called 9-1-1?" Minnie barked.

"Mary," Cheryl said.

Minnie enclosed Emily's hand between hers, forcing a smile. "Hi, Em. The ambulance is on the way. They'll get you checked out in no time, okay?"

The darting gaze fastened on hers, fluttering in and out of focus. The right side of her face sagged toward the floor, her right hand limp in Minnie's grasp. The left side of her mouth moved but the sounds were gibberish.

Minnie shoved the terror away as Mary, the center's nurse, knelt at Emily's other side. They exchanged a tortured glance before Minnie looked up at the confused, frightened expressions looming above.

"She's going to be fine, everyone." She forced the words over the knot in her throat. "How about backing up to give her some air? It's pretty stuffy down here." Feet shuffled, walkers pulled back a few inches. "Thank you. That helps a lot."

"The ambulance is here." Cheryl's calm voice from somewhere above them.

Minnie gave a quick nod. "Em? They're here already. They'll have you fixed up lickety-split, okay?" She glimpsed two pairs of shiny black shoes threading through the circle of legs, and squeezed Emily's frail, icy fingers. "Here they come."

Cheryl clapped her hands firmly. "Everyone, let's go to the activity room and let the paramedics do their jobs. Come on, Moses. Bertie, you come too. Chief, you stand watch and keep others out of the way, please. All right, everyone. Let's go in the other room. Emily is going to be just fine."

Minnie scooted around to kneel at Emily's head and gently stroked her hair. Two men in starched white shirts and black pants joined them on the floor, smiling reassuringly at the older woman. One glanced at Minnie. "Her name?"

"Emily Young. She's eighty-two and—" Emily's sharp grunt cut her off. "Sorry. She's eighty-one. She'll be eighty-two in a few weeks." Dear Em was in there fighting. *Please, God. I'm not ready to lose her too.*

The men spoke gently, working in tandem to take her vitals, hook up a bag of clear fluid, and prepare her for transport. Minnie stood alone in the parking lot as the ambulance pulled away, praying disjointed words.

This same scene had played out in her own house five years ago, but it had been her mother being swept away. Her mother who'd had a heart attack and never came home.

"Grab your purse, Min. I'll drive you to the hospital." Nick's voice came from beside her.

The thirty-minute ride to the hospital in Rochester felt like slow motion. At the Emergency Room counter, the clerk assured her Emily was in the very best hands. "We have fabulous staff with her. Someone will be out shortly to give you an update."

The wait was intolerable, prayer impossible. Minnie paced, asked again for an update, then continued her trek from the dusty windows to an aquarium of listless fish, to the empty corner bookshelf and back to the windows. The squeak of shoes on linoleum made her jump. With every ping of the intercom, she spun toward the doors that blocked her from Em.

Nick sat quietly watching her, occasionally checking his phone, offering an encouraging smile when she focused enough to look at him.

Please, God. The plea pounded with her heartbeat, matched her steps, and fended off the fear of life without Emily Young.

Ninety minutes passed before a doctor emerged through the automatic doors and headed toward them. Minnie rose on wobbling legs, fists clenched at her sides. Em was gone. She knew it. Nick stood beside her.

The doctor's smile seemed inappropriate for the news he was about to deliver. "You got her here in good time. I think we caught the stroke early enough to prevent extensive damage."

Minnie stared at him.

He patted her shoulder. "I think she's going to be fine, but we'll keep a close eye on her over the next few days to be sure."

"She's not...gone?" *Thank you, God. Thank you.*

"Only as far as her room on second floor." He nodded, eyebrows raised. "She's a fighter. I'm hoping she'll come out of this with minimal issues. We'll know more after a day or two."

It took every fiber of control not to throw herself into his arms with a burst of tears. "Thank you," she croaked. "I'm..."

"Grateful," Nick said, giving Minnie's shoulders a squeeze. "Thanks, Dr. Knox. When can we see her?"

Twenty minutes later, Minnie dashed down the long hall toward Room 212, Nick's long strides keeping pace. She swung into the room and stopped. Em lay still in the bed, her hair a dull red against the white bedding. Minnie approached with silent steps, afraid to wake her, afraid she'd never wake. A nurse finished checking the monitors, then turned and greeted Minnie with a reassuring smile.

"She's doing fine," she said. "Her prognosis is good, but it will take time for her to come around."

Nick spent a few minutes beside Minnie, then left with a promise to check back once he'd visited with the hospital staff. After the hours of panic, Minnie welcomed time alone with Em. She sank down in the chair and took Em's limp hand between hers, tears unchecked as she studied the beloved face.

"You gave us quite a scare, you know." Her attempted smile failed. "Even your unflappable Nicholas has been worried. But they say you're going to be fine, so you work on getting your strength back, okay? I need my favorite cheerleader to help me get Open Circle turned around."

She released a long breath. "I'm not ready to let you go, Em. I don't want to be alone. And it's all about me, you know," she added with a choked laugh. "So be prepared. I'm going to push you to get back to your old self."

The monitors beeped evenly in the silence. Minnie watched the screen for a moment, then looked at Em. "You're all the family I have," she whispered, "and I'm all you've got. I'll do anything and everything to keep you with me. You're stuck with me, kid."

She pressed Em's cold hand to her cheek. "I wouldn't want it any other way."

CHAPTER FOUR

Jackson drove slowly through Lawton, memories skipping along the street ahead of him. The old bank where he'd gone with Grandma Em to turn in his pennies stood empty, weeds sprouting along the side of the building. The Lutheran and Catholic churches still faced off across the next intersection. It seemed God hadn't gone out of business in Lawton, judging from the neatly cut grass and the flowers planted along the sidewalks.

The grocery store he and his buddies had biked to for gum and Slurpies had apparently closed long ago. A smile touched his mouth even as he sighed. That store had kept them sugared up through long, hot summers. The old hardware store looked as mysterious as it had when he was a kid.

The smile resurfaced as he passed Scheid Park. Kids played on brightly colored playground equipment, but he could still envision the old metal swing set, the rickety slide that had seemed a mile high, and the monkey bars where he'd fallen and broken his arm.

The familiar aroma of farmland and flowers floated in through his open window. The car seemed to steer itself from the park to the elementary school that had a new wing, past the nursing home that looked more tired than twenty years ago, to his old neighborhood.

Gravel crunched beneath his tires as he drove past Billy's dingy white house on the corner, then Micky's brick rambler that sported a new roof, and then...what's-his-name's blue house that looked abandoned. The big kid who'd bullied him at school. The guy had probably ended up in jail. Or maybe he'd turned himself around and become the CEO of a big company. He chuckled. Doubtful.

A small rambler at the end of the cul-de-sac sat tucked back from the road as if hiding from its neighbors. Jackson pulled the rental car to the curb and looked at the lifeless house. Scraggly, overgrown bushes leaned against faded siding. A pot with a single yellow flower sat on the front step. Blinds were closed in every front window.

The sad little house tugged at his heart. His childhood hadn't been idyllic, but it held happier memories than this neglected place. He checked his watch. Ten minutes until the lawyer appointment. Plenty of time to get from one side of Lawton to the other. At least, that's what it used to take. Hardly a thriving metropolis, but no longer the sleepy little town of his early childhood. He'd seen three stoplights so far. While empty storefronts revealed the toll of a depressed economy, signs of hope reflected in the glass of new buildings, and the bustle of activity on Main Street.

How much had Grandma Em changed over the years? His heart rate followed the increasing speed of the car. He couldn't wait to find out. His phone rang as he approached the next intersection, and he answered on speaker.

"Hey, Daniel. I'll be at your office in five."

"Jackson, I just talked to Open Circle, the senior center

your grandma goes to." Concern edged the words. "Emily had a stroke."

The car lurched to a stop. "What? When?"

"Before lunch apparently. I called to make sure she was there today for your visit."

The pounding in his chest made it hard to breathe. "Is she..."

"Holding her own. Do you know where St. Mary's is in Rochester?"

"No. Wait." He couldn't think. "In Rochester, you said. What's the address?"

Trembling fingers entered the information into his GPS, then he thanked Daniel and screeched around the corner heading toward the highway. *Hang on, Grandma. I'm almost there.* He pounded the steering wheel. She couldn't die, not before they saw each other one more time. At least once more.

Thirty minutes later, he stood in the hospital room doorway watching a dark-haired young woman, tears on her cheeks, speak quietly to the older woman in the bed. He stepped back into the hall to check the room number, then frowned at the intimate scene. Why would an aide be crying over his grandmother? At least Grandma wasn't alone. He should have gotten here yesterday.

He moved into the room and the girl looked up, their gazes meeting in the silence. Dark eyebrows pinched upward over tear-filled eyes.

She stood, still holding his grandmother's hand, and brushed the wetness from her cheeks. "Can I help you?"

"I'm Jack."

"Minnie."

Minnie? As in Minnie Mouse? A corner of his mouth twitched.

Her expressive eyebrows lifted as she waited for him to

say more. She was tall and slender, dark hair brushing her shoulders. Pretty. Maybe a neighbor? He looked at his grandmother, then back at the young woman.

When he remained silent, her mouth curved up. "Maybe you have the wrong room?"

He gave himself a mental slap, cheeks warm. "No. I'm here to see Emily. Emily Young."

She glanced at his grandmother with an affectionate smile. "She's sleeping, as you can see. How do you know her?"

"I'm her grandson."

The smile vanished as her eyes went wide. "You're *that* Jack?"

"Uh...yeah?" Was there another one? He glanced down at his travel-wrinkled clothes. "I just got into town. I got a letter from her attorney a few weeks ago."

"Ah." She nodded. Mouth in a tight line, her chin lifted. "You're a bit early to collect on her millions. They think she'll pull through fine."

His gaze swung to his grandmother's placid face. She had millions? From where? He opened his mouth, but Minnie Mouse spoke first.

"Nice of you to show up now. Where've you been the last twenty years?"

The hostile words poked him in the chest like a long, accusing finger. His defenses shot up, stiffening his spine. He didn't owe her an explanation. "Who are you, anyway?"

Pink spots formed on her high cheekbones as she wrapped both hands protectively around his grandmother's. "I'm all the family she's had for decades."

Family? He stopped a snort. Probably after the supposed millions. The idea was laughable. His family had never had money. He met her challenging gaze and lifted an eyebrow. "Since you're not related, I find that interesting. Especially when you talk about the money she supposedly has."

She pulled back as if slapped.

A twinge pinched his heart. *What are you doing?*

"So, how's our sweet Emily?" A young nurse bustled into the room, shooting a smile at Jackson as she passed. She stroked Emily's forehead. "Hi, dear."

Minnie Mouse turned away, standing in stiff silence as the nurse checked the monitors, and the bags of fluids hanging on the pole beside the bed. "You're doing fine, Emily."

"When will she wake up?" The girl's voice was pinched.

"She's sedated for now, but she'll be more awake tomorrow. She's doing fine, really. You did a good job getting her here as quickly as you did."

She brought his grandmother here?

A corner of her mouth flickered upward. "I have a great staff. Everyone loves Em."

Em? His eyebrows shot up. She called his grandmother by the nickname he'd used as a child? How ingrained was she in his grandmother's life? He moved to the side of the bed. "I'm Emily's grandson, Jackson Young. How can I find out more about her condition?"

A frown flickered across the nurse's face. "Her grandson? I didn't know she had one."

Ouch.

She glanced at Minnie Mouse. "I thought Minnie was her only family."

"She isn't family," he said, more sharply than he'd intended. "I'd like to talk to the doctor as soon as possible."

"Of course. Come with me and I'll page Dr. Wilson."

Jackson glanced at his grandma then at the young

woman beside her. She glared back. He nodded before following the nurse from the room. She'd just have to get used to him being in his grandmother's life. He'd never let go of his only family, ever again. No matter what Minnie Mouse or anyone else thought.

⁓

Minnie sank back into the chair, staring at the empty doorway. What was he doing in Lawton? A famous, globetrotting photographer with time to travel the world but never to visit his grandmother.

She straightened in the chair. How dare he show up now? Did he think he could waltz back into her life pretending he hadn't ignored her for two decades? Did he have *any* clue how much pain that had caused her?

She brushed a shaking hand over Em's unruly red hair. Only a few months ago, Em had shown her a photo spread in a magazine, proud to point out her only grandchild's name beneath the stunning photographs. Gnarled fingers ran gently across the pages as if trying to touch him through the pictures. Her wistful expression had made Minnie's anger flare.

"Minnie?"

She jumped. Nick left the doorway to stand across the bed from her. "How's she doing?"

"The same. Sleeping quietly anyway." She released a long breath. "She's a tough cookie but...I wish I'd paid closer attention."

His frown met hers. "You couldn't have predicted a stroke."

"She hasn't been herself the last week. She's looked tired, not as sharp as usual." She managed a short, broken laugh. "Even her cookies haven't been as good."

He moved around the bed and set a hand on her shoulder. "Minnie, that wasn't enough for any of us to think stroke. Besides, you'd have had to hogtie her to get her to the doctor."

"I know. But...I made a promise not to let this happen again." She lifted her gaze to his. "A promise I have every inten–"

Jackson appeared in the doorway, hesitating when he saw Nick. Then he moved forward, hand extended. "I'm Jackson Young. Emily's grandson. And you are?"

His superior tone sent spears of irritation through Minnie.

"Ah, the long-lost grandson." Nick reached across the bed to shake his hand. "Nick Butler. I work at the Crosswinds Care Center in Lawton."

"The nursing home? I see. Well, she won't be needing your services."

Minnie stared up at him. "What's that supposed to mean?"

He shrugged. "When she's released from here, I'll move her to a nearby rehab."

"*You'll* move her?" She shot out of her chair. "What are you talking about?"

Nick put a hand on her arm. "Minnie—"

She shook him off, glaring at Jackson. "How dare you strut in here after twenty years and start making decisions on her behalf!"

"She's my grandmother."

Nick's voice cut firmly between them. "Emily doesn't need to hear this. Take it out to the hallway."

Jackson looked from Minnie to Nick, then stalked out of the room. Minnie closed her eyes, seething from his pompous announcement.

"Minnie, take it easy. You don't know that he'll act on

anything."

"Oh, yes, he will. He's obviously a very important person." She walked on stiff legs into the hallway, spotting him in the family waiting room at the far end.

He stood with his back to her, facing the window, hands in his jeans pockets. When she approached, he glanced at her. "I'm sorry. I shouldn't have said that in front of my grandmother."

"You shouldn't have said it at all." She folded her arms. "What gives you the right to walk into her life and take over? You haven't seen her in twenty years."

"We're family. She needs someone to make decisions for her until she's back on her feet."

"That's what I've done. She's more my family than yours." She ignored the frown that darkened his face. "Do you know what her favorite candy is? How about her favorite color? Does she like the Vikings or the Packers? What flowers does she plant every year on Mother's Day?"

His silence goaded her. "Do you know what church she attends? Come on, Mr. Grandson. You must know something about her since you're *family*."

Their gazes held as her sarcasm echoed in the stony silence. He blinked first and looked away. "You know nothing about me but you're awful quick to pass judgment."

"How is stating the truth passing judgment? Em and my grandmother were best friends their whole lives. She's been part of my life since before I was born. You're right—I'm not blood family. But you haven't taken time out of your world travels to visit her, or acknowledge her birthday, or even Christmas." She angled her chin. "Not one time."

Something flickered across his face before his jaw set. "I'm here now. And I plan to make sure she gets the absolute best care possible, which I doubt she'd get in Lawton."

"Of course not. What would a small town have to offer her, other than the love and support of lifelong friends? But that probably doesn't count in your world."

"What would you know of my world?"

"I know you're a very busy, very important photographer. And heaven knows why but she's been proud enough of you to show everyone when one of your photographs shows up somewhere."

His eyebrows lifted as if in surprise.

"I also know you travel all over the world for your precious photos, while your lack of interest in your grandmother caused immeasurable heartache. So if you think I'll step out of the way just because you've finally shown up, you can think again."

The angry words pouring from her mouth were as foreign as the young man facing her. She'd never spoken like this to anyone, but she couldn't let him sweep Em away from everything she'd known. She wouldn't.

Tears crawled up her throat and she turned away, squeezing her eyes shut. Em's stroke had scared her half to death. She couldn't lose her. Especially not to this arrogant man who didn't care one whit about his "grandmother."

"I can assure you I have only the best of intentions where she's concerned." Restraint colored his quiet words. "There's a lot you don't know about me and my relationship with my grandmother."

She looked over her shoulder. "You don't know anything about *us* either. If you did, you'd know Lawton is where she belongs. Not in Rochester or anywhere else."

As silence pulsed between them, nauseating exhaustion making her legs wobble. "It's been a long day. I'm going home but I'll be back in the morning." She skewered him with a glare as she passed. "Assuming you don't move her between now and then."

After a silent ride back to Lawton with Nick, she made it through the back door of her house before the torrent was loosed. Sinking into a kitchen chair, she laid her head on her arms and sobbed.

CHAPTER FIVE

Minnie pulled open the front door of Open Circle and stepped into an unusual quiet. At ten o'clock, the center usually hummed with activity. Jody, the receptionist, and Gail, the activities director, looked up from their conversation.

"Welcome back," Jody greeted her. "How's our Emily this morning?"

Minnie leaned heavily against the front counter. "Better. She recognized me and squeezed my hand." She managed a tired smile. "It was so good to see her awake."

"We've been praying for her." Gail hugged her warmly. "I'm sure the whole town is now."

"Thanks, hon. She needs it." The embrace brought tears to the surface. A recent college graduate, Gail's perky blonde sweetness contrasted Jody's dark spikey hair, tattoos, and growing pregnancy. The seniors loved both young women. Gratitude swelled in Minnie's heart. "It's quiet here this morning."

"I think they're waiting for an update," Jody said.

"Ahh. Well, I'll drop off my stuff and let them know she's doing great."

In her office, Minnie unloaded her bag, stashed her purse in the drawer, and then rubbed her burning eyes.

"How's Emily?" Cheryl stood in the doorway, concern replacing her usual antagonism.

"Better. Alert and following commands."

"What's the prognosis?"

Minnie booted up her computer. "Good, at this early stage anyway. She didn't try to speak, so I'm not sure how that's been affected. The doctor said we did great getting her to the hospital so quickly." She met Cheryl's gaze. "Thanks for stepping up to run things after I left."

Cheryl's concern faded into indifference, and she shrugged. "Nothing I haven't done before. I have to get the Morning News started."

In the silence, Minnie's shoulders drooped. She'd been the director for three weeks now. Would Cheryl be this cold forever? The phone rang and she sat up straight, pushing the question aside. She had enough to worry about.

The center atmosphere remained subdued through the morning. Without Emily's cheerful, energetic presence, conversations were muted, laughter at a minimum. Minnie stayed in the background and watched the interactions.

After lunch, Gail's sparkling enthusiasm provided the only energy in the room. Most of the staff members slouched in their chairs or whispered amongst themselves during the trivia game. At the late morning sing-a-long, many of the seniors tried to sing along but struggled with the pages of lyrics. Only two staff, Laura and Cheryl, bothered to help. The other three seemed more interested in biting their nails or twirling their hair. Minnie circulated through the group, pointing out words, singing with gusto even as she cringed. She hadn't been hired for her musical ability.

When the group gathered for the afternoon snack, Minnie returned to her office and sat frowning out the window. Why had Dorothy hired people who didn't like spending time with seniors? No wonder the center struggled. It couldn't thrive under a cloud of lethargy and indifference. But she couldn't make it profitable in four years let alone four months without major changes. Staff changes. Programming improvements. Attitude adjustments.

But why bother? Half of the staff will quit, and I'll just drive the center into the ground faster.

"See you tomorrow, Minnie."

She swung around at the cheerful farewell and motioned Gail into her office. "Hey, do you have a minute?"

"Sure." Plopping into the chair, she smiled. "What's up?"

Minnie studied her for a moment, an answering smile lifting her mouth. Gail epitomized the perfect staff person. Happy to be at work, eager to make a difference in the lives of the seniors. "We haven't had a chance to chat much over the past few weeks."

"The schedule's been crazy," Gail agreed. "How are you doing in your new position? Getting settled?"

"Learning on the fly, but I'm getting the hang of things."

"You're a natural. The seniors love you." Her smile faded, and she averted her gaze. "I couldn't say that about Dorothy, so I'm glad Nick put you in charge."

The unexpected affirmation silenced Minnie's earlier doubts. "Thanks. Tell me how you're feeling about your job."

"Great. Well, pretty great." Her head bobbed as if to convince herself. "It's good."

"What would take it from good to great?"

She shrugged and picked at powder blue fingernails. "Well, I think good is...good."

"Gail, you can be honest with me." It would be devastating if she quit out of frustration. "I want you to enjoy coming to work. How can I make things better for you?"

After a moment, Gail lifted her head and met Minnie's gaze. "I could use more help from the staff. Sometimes I have to tell *them* what to do more than I have to tell the seniors. I don't think...Well, I don't think a lot of them like seniors."

Minnie blinked. "That's what I've been thinking."

Gail relaxed in her chair.

"You're doing a fabulous job, Gail, but the staff isn't stepping up like they should. I plan to address that issue in the next few days."

"Really? That'd be great. Putting a little energy into the activities would really help."

Minnie nodded. "People are going to have to step up to the plate or—" Or what? She'd fire them? Her stomach twisted.

"That's awesome. I'm so glad you had me stop in." She glanced at her watch and stood. "I'm teaching yoga at the studio in thirty minutes, so I'd better get going." She paused at the door. "What do you think about a Zumba class for our seniors?"

"Well, I'm not sure I can see too many of them doing the salsa around the room."

Gail laughed. "Not the full-out Zumba. There's a new version that's been developed for seniors and people with restricted movement, getting the blood flowing without the crazy dance moves. Maybe I can teach you and the staff and see what everyone thinks."

"Sounds fun. Keep those ideas coming."

As Gail left the office, Minnie swung back to the window, smiling. Those were the conversations she wanted to have with the staff. Throwing ideas around, thinking of new ways to add quality to everyone's day.

The smile faded as Cheryl's voice floated in from down the hall. It wouldn't be quite as upbeat with her senior staffer. She shook her head briefly and reached for the phone to call St. Mary's for an Em update. Cheryl needed to ramp up her energy and enthusiasm, or... A shiver ran down her spine. Or things would get ugly fast.

～

Jackson leaned against the wall outside his grandmother's hospital room, listening to the nurse chat with her. Grandma Em's response was too soft to hear. It might not be smart to surprise her with her health compromised. Maybe he shouldn't go barging in there without clearing it with the doctor. What if his appearance gave her another stroke? Or a heart attack? A cold sweat chilled him. What if—

"Oh, good. You're back." The nurse's voice startled him.

He pushed away from the wall. "I didn't want to interrupt. How is she today?"

"She's alert, following commands, tracking—all good signs. Her speech is off, but that's not necessarily permanent. She's got some movement on her right side, but the doctor is hopeful she'll regain her gross motor skills with therapy. Go on in and see her."

"Well, I—I'm not sure..." Maybe if he were holding a camera he'd be more coherent. "I'm afraid my visit might upset her."

She cocked her head, frowning. "Why would it upset her?"

"We haven't seen each other in a while. She'll be surprised to see me."

"Ahh. Emily is a tough character. I think she'll be glad to see you. If she gets agitated, push the call button and I'll come in."

"Okay." He'd stay close to the button. "Thanks. By the way, has Minnie Carlson been by today?"

"Early this morning. Those two are like peanut butter and jelly. She's such a dear, and Minnie is so good to her."

Great. Jackson faced the door and squared his shoulders. He'd traveled across the world, even into war zones without blinking. He could do this. He forced his feet to take him into the room, then paused to study Grandma Em propped up in bed, looking out the window.

She certainly wasn't the healthy, vibrant grandmother he remembered, but she was also twenty years older. She still had that crazy red hair, which had been calmed with a brush this morning, and tucked behind her ears.

Her head turned against the pillow, and their eyes met. He waited a moment, heart in his throat. She blinked several times before the left side of her mouth lifted. She raised a thin hand in invitation, and a rush of tears burned his throat.

He approached slowly and took her fingers in a gentle grip. "Hi, Grandma. I'm Jackson."

Her gaze clung to his. The half-smile deepened. "Cam. Ra."

Relief dropped him into the chair at her bedside. "Right. I'm your grandson with the camera."

She continued to smile at him, clutching his hand, and he grinned back, not sure what else to say. It would be easier if the conversation were two-sided. Tears sparkled in her eyes.

"We have a lot to catch up on. I'm sorry I've been away so long." He looked down at their clasped hands. "I didn't know... We left in such a hurry I barely got to say goodbye. Then Mom and Dad told me—" He shrugged. Her smile had faded but her eyes remained locked on him. "Anyway, I'm really glad Daniel, your lawyer, found me. Now we can get caught up."

Her head bobbed as the smile returned.

"I have some great news." Excitement pushed him to the edge of his chair. "I'm having a show of my photos in New York. And the best part is I get to run the whole thing. I've got a ton of ideas. The hardest part will be narrowing them down to the ones with the greatest impact."

A recent conversation with Noah floated to mind and he smiled, looking past her out the window. "I work with great people, Grandma, like my best friend, Noah. You'll have to meet him. He's quite the character."

He chuckled and turned his gaze back to her. Now asleep, the half-smile remained on her face. He scooted closer, keeping a gentle hold of her hand. This first visit had gone well, considering. That smile, though crooked, was the smile he remembered.

Facing Grandma Em's brown-eyed protector didn't seem so daunting now. From this moment on, he'd make whatever decisions were needed because that's what family did for each other. Real family.

Once Grandma Em got her strength back, they'd have lots of time to talk. He gnawed the inside of his cheek. Then she could explain what happened to the family, why his parents left Lawton so abruptly. He needed to understand why his past was such a mess.

CHAPTER SIX

Minnie glanced at her watch and rolled her chair from her desk. Two-thirty? The endless director duties could easily swallow her entire day if she didn't get out of her office occasionally. Greeting the seniors each morning and helping serve lunch were marked in red on her calendar, but that didn't provide enough face time.

Stretching her arms overhead, she wandered into the small reception area, a space that had desperately needed updating. She'd challenged Gail to create a decorating activity that would involve staff and seniors, as cheaply as possible. The results so far had been amazing.

Red, purple, orange, and brown prints of gnarled, arthritic-swollen hands mingled with the strong prints of family members and staff. The colorful handprints created a vibrant sense of community and welcome.

Minnie leaned against the front counter. "So, what do you think of the decorating, Jods?"

"It's turning out great!" The receptionist leaned back and ran a hand over her growing tummy. "I'm amazed Gail got everyone, even Chief, to participate. And I love having names painted below each print."

"I wondered how people would react," Minnie said, "but leave it to Gail to get everyone involved. We're so fortunate to have her on staff." She turned back to the young woman seated behind the waist-high counter. "As we are with you."

Jody grinned. "We're a great team, aren't we?" Her spunky persona enlivened the front end of the program. Minnie loved her stories of breeding golden retrievers and raising three-year-old twin boys on a hobby farm.

A new voice broke into their conversation. "...because fishnet stockings are all the rage." Bertie's cigarette-strained voice echoed from the hallway. She toddled into view, Chief prodding her toward the door. "Honestly, men know nothing about style."

"My gun is enough style for me," he grumbled.

Minnie and Jody exchanged a smile. He handled his "assignment" of getting Bertie out the door with focused intensity, just as he had his law enforcement career.

"Chief," Jody chimed in, "don't you think fishnet stockings would be an interesting addition to the uniform?"

Life was not a laughing matter to Chief, but he had a soft spot for the receptionist. She could regularly coax a smile to his craggy face. The corner of his mouth crooked upward briefly as he glanced toward her. "Don't need deputies in skirts trying to catch lawbreakers."

"Maybe the lawbreakers would slow down to take a look."

He muttered something unintelligible and directed Bertie toward the door. As he and Bertie were next-door neighbors, his granddaughter drove them to and from the center each day. Minnie held in a giggle as she watched the police officer try to get the flighty woman closer to the door, feathery red boa floating behind her. Keeping Bertie focused resembled herding one cheerfully confused, neon colored cat.

Minnie hugged the tall, thin woman and shook Chief's hand before they headed out to the waiting car, then shared a wink with Jody as Frances wandered into the reception area. A school cook for forty years, she loved nothing more than rearranging the pots and pans in the center's small kitchen.

"Hello, dear Frances." Minnie sidestepped in front of the tiny woman before she could reach the door. "Where are you off to?"

"It must be time to serve lunch, isn't it?" She craned her neck to look around Minnie. "The kids will be waiting."

Dementia had crept into Frances' life near the end of her school kitchen reign, forcing her into early retirement. It had been three years since leaving the job she loved, and Minnie knew she still grieved the abrupt departure.

Minnie glanced at the clock over Jody's desk. "Not quite time, Frances. We'll let you know, okay?"

Frances wrung her hands, glancing around the reception area. "Shouldn't we start making the sandwiches? It takes two hours to make four hundred and eight sandwiches."

"We'll get them started very soon. We don't want the bread to get stale, so we'll wait a bit. You've always done such a great job making sure all of the kids get something to eat."

Minnie no longer hesitated over the use of what the aging industry called therapeutic fibbing. She'd seen what happened when staff tried to force reality onto a confused senior. Normally mild-mannered elders could quickly turn belligerent, even combative when someone contradicted what their confused brain told them.

Cheryl had been slow to accept the idea, but when Chief pulled an unloaded gun on her and threatened to arrest her for interfering with police work, she'd finally embraced the concept. Chief and the rest of the seniors were happier and more cooperative when the staff incorporated their perception of reality into the day.

Minnie guided Frances back toward the main activity room with a gentle arm around her shoulders. "You're the best head cook Lawton Elementary has ever had. How many of the students do you know by name?"

Her face brightened. "All of them," she said proudly. "This year there are three hundred and eighty-eight. I know every one of them."

The youngest of the clients at merely sixty-six, Frances' cheeks were barely wrinkled.

She'd been known for a keen memory of each student who passed through the elementary school doors, making the diagnosis of Alzheimer's at age sixty-three that much more devastating.

"There's Justin and Robbie and Caleb," she recited as they walked. "And Hannah, Emily, and the Stinson twins. Oh, what are their names? The boy is a bit naughty, but I know he can do better. His sister is an angel."

Minnie directed her back to a chair at the Bingo table and settled beside her. Cheryl presided over the game with an aura of boredom that had put several of the seniors to sleep in their chairs.

"Let's see how you're doing in this game, Frances," Minnie said. "Oh, look! You have both O-72 and O-75. You're getting close to a Bingo." She leaned across the table and tapped George's arm. He startled and sat up, straightening his glasses. "George, it looks like you almost have Bingo too. Only a few more numbers for you."

With Frances focused on the game, Minnie got up and

circled the table, helping the seniors find the right numbers. She looked around the spacious room for the rest of the staff. Ward leaned against the kitchen counter chatting with Patty, a high school aide. Laura emerged from the bathroom pushing Arlice in her wheelchair. Minnie returned Arlice's wave.

Arms folded, Minnie waited until Ward glanced toward the Bingo game, satisfied to see him give a start when their gazes met. He said something to Patty, who blushed and returned to filling saltshakers, and sauntered over to take a seat at the end of the table farthest from where Minnie stood. He leaned toward George and pointed out the number Cheryl called.

When programming ended and the last of the seniors had departed with family members or on the Open Circle bus, Minnie returned to her office to finish writing employee reviews. She'd scheduled brief meetings with every staff member through this week and next. The growing tension in the center made her hair stand on end. Whispered conversations stopped when she entered a room. Cheryl spent more time glaring at her than smiling at the seniors.

With guidance from Sue, the human resources director, Minnie had, with a quaking heart, put two people on notice for insubordination after they ignored her requests —simple requests to benefit the seniors. Tempted to add Cheryl to the list, she squashed the idea, hearing Em's advice to move slowly and let God lead.

Stacking the folders neatly, the name on top made her smile. Laura had been the last review of the day, a pleasant way to wrap up what felt like the Inquisition. If only she could have ten more Lauras. *Please, God?*

What she needed now was dinner and a brisk walk, then a quick trip to see Em again. She locked the folders in the cabinet, grabbed her purse and started out of her office. Cheryl's lowered voice made her pause in the doorway. The woman stood in the reception area with two of the aides, all with their backs to Minnie, who took a silent step back.

"What do you mean she put you on notice?" Cheryl hissed.

"She told me I'd better start doing what she says, or she'll can me."

Minnie winced. Hardly the wording she'd used during the girl's review.

"She can't fire you. She needs a good reason like you stole something or hurt somebody. Your work is fine."

"Not according to her highness. She said we have to make sure the seniors are safe." She released a noisy sigh. "Like they could get hurt sitting in a wheelchair. It's not like they're going to run away or anything."

The other girl ran a hand through waist-length black hair. Minnie had repeatedly asked her to tie it back as a safety precaution. "If she finds out I wasn't sick when I called in last Friday, I bet she'll fire me on the spot."

"How would she find that out?" Cheryl's was a stage whisper. "It's not like she has time to follow up on our calls. She's running harder than Dorothy ever did."

The girls giggled. "Dorothy couldn't run with a bear chasing her."

"But at least she stayed out of our way," the first girl said. "Minnie seems to be everywhere. I liked her better as the social worker. She wasn't here half the time and spent the rest with the oldies."

"Even then she was in our business," Cheryl said, "but at least Dorothy could shut her up. Now she's out to save the world. Don't know how that's going to happen since they'll be shutting us down come September anyway."

Eyes burning, Minnie slid another step back. Cheryl's anger and disdain would have been a physical slap if she'd gotten close. How could she work with that kind of attitude?

She straightened with a scowl. She should fire her right now! She could, according to Sue. She could march out there and— Reality deflated her stance. Whether she had the right or not, if she fired Cheryl, half of the staff would quit.

How do I work with people who don't even like me? Maybe I'm making things worse.

She lifted her chin. No. Em would never let her quit. She'd tell her to buck up and listen for God's guidance; get over the pity party and focus on the people who needed her. She'd do whatever it took to turn the program around.

Setting her shoulders, she bustled out of her office. Cheryl was no longer in view, and the other girls broke apart when they saw her, bumping into each other as they tried to get away.

Minnie smiled at them. "Have a great evening, girls."

"You too."

Climbing into her beloved old Buick, she set her computer bag on the floor, buckled herself in and pulled out of the lot. Only when she had turned the corner did she allow the smile to slide from her face.

Her new, painful mantra—whatever it took. She'd do whatever it took for her seniors and for Open Circle. For Bertie and Chief, Frances, Helen. And especially for Em.

"Whatever it takes, Lord," she whispered into the silence.

CHAPTER SEVEN

Jackson pulled out of the hospital parking lot and pointed the car toward the attorney's office. Sitting with his grandmother every day the past week, telling her about his life and sharing his dreams gave him the oddest sense of... something. Belonging, maybe. Or importance.

He wanted to make sure she got the best care once they released her, which meant doing research. The Crosswinds Care Center in Lawton wasn't an option. Too run down, too old. She deserved the absolute best place to recover. He'd ask Daniel for suggestions, and then to do his homework and get the paperwork signed before Minnie Mouse could raise a ruckus.

An hour later, he choked on the turkey and Swiss sandwich Daniel's secretary had ordered in. Grandma Em had named *him* as her financial power of attorney? "But you said she has all her mental faculties."

Daniel, a balding middle-aged man with a cheerful smile, threw back his head and laughed. "Oh, trust me. She's definitely got all her faculties. She picked you for a reason."

"And that would be?"

"I have no idea. When Emily gets something in her head, there's no talking her out of it. But I have to say, she's right pretty much all the time. She knows her mind, knows what she wants and why, and she goes for it." He popped a potato chip into his mouth and chuckled. "If that woman had decided to run for mayor, she'd have run unopposed."

"Because she's tough?"

"Because everyone loves her. Nobody would run against her because they wouldn't get a single vote."

Jackson sat back, an ache filling his chest. So much wasted time. He could have been part of her life all these years. Instead, she'd filled that hole with Minnie Mouse.

"It still doesn't explain why I'm her POA."

"Financial POA," Daniel corrected.

"Is there another kind?"

"Medical. That person makes her health care decisions. It can be the same person as the financial POA, but sometimes that's not the best idea."

Like a balloon with a slow leak, air seeped out of his lungs as he stared at Daniel across the table, knowing the answer. He forced the words out. "So her medical POA is..."

"Minnie Carlson."

Of course. The one person who would fight him on every decision out of spite.

"It's essential for Emily's welfare that the medical and financial POAs work together," Daniel continued, "to make the best decisions for her. Minnie is almost as big of a fixture in this town as Emily." He smiled. "I've known that girl since she was a baby. Did the financials for her parents when they owned the grocery store."

The smile faded as he shook his head. "Darn shame her

father died so young. But that Minnie, she's gold, especially where Emily is concerned. I can introduce you—"

"We've met. At the hospital." This could get ugly.

"That's great. I'll set up a meeting for the three of us to discuss what the plan will be when Emily's released. Make a smooth transition for her. She's such an independent old gal, I imagine she's fighting mad about the inconvenience of having a stroke."

Jackson nodded and wrapped up the rest of his sandwich. He needed to get busy researching so he'd be prepared for that meeting. He gave a silent snort. Brawl would be more like it. Minnie Mouse wasn't going to be happy when she found out he controlled the money. Well, he'd be so prepared she'd have no possible argument, and he'd get his grandma the right kind of help.

ᴕᴇᴏ

Em sat propped up in bed when Minnie arrived before dinner on Friday. With her hair lightly brushed and fresh red lipstick on, she didn't look like she'd had a stroke. Minnie pressed a kiss to her forehead before dropping into the chair next to the bed. "So, are you behaving?"

Em waved her left hand and rolled her eyes. "Pish."

"I'll take that as a yes. Dr. Wilson said you're starting therapy tomorrow. They'll have a schedule ready when you get out of here in a few days."

"Yes. I'll be. Okee."

Tears tightened Minnie's throat. "I know you will because you're going to do whatever the therapists say."

Em held out a frail hand and Minnie grasped it, forcing a smile. "You sure gave me a scare, Em."

Sympathy flashed in her blue eyes. "Sor. Eee."

"Don't apologize, silly. It's not your fault." Minnie

cleared her throat. "Okay, I need some advice. Up to listening to my woes?"

At Em's nod, Minnie settled back in the chair and shared the events of the past week, including her plan to pare down the existing staff. Though Em couldn't participate in the conversation in her usual blunt way, it was a relief to share the burden.

"We'll see how things shake out this next week." Minnie sighed. "I don't imagine it will be pretty, but Nick put me in charge so I'm going to do what I think is right."

Em gave a nod. "Yes. Good."

"So." She hated to ask. "Have you had any...visitors today?"

Em's tired expression brightened, a half-smile lifting her mouth. "Cam. Ra."

So much for hoping Jackson Young had realized his mistake and left town without bothering Em. "Jackson came by?"

"Day. Each day. Nice."

Every day? He'd been careful not to cross her path when he visited. "I'm glad it didn't upset you."

A sparkle lit Em's eyes as she lightly squeezed Minnie's hand. "Cute."

Minnie frowned, trying to picture him clearly. She'd seen him through an angry haze. Tallish. Brown shaggy hair. That cheesy shadow of a beard. What color were his eyes? It seemed his looks had been overshadowed by his audacity. Maybe cute in a bohemian sort of way.

She forced a smile and stood. "Well, he's your grandson, after all. Now, I hear the dinner cart in the hallway so I'm going to head out. I have a meeting in thirty minutes." She loved Daniel but knowing Mr. Sneaky Grandson would be there curdled her stomach.

Em blinked slowly and nodded. "Thu."

Minnie pursed her lips. Thu? "I love you too."

A frown shadowed Em's pale face. "No."

"No?" Had she already been replaced by Mr. Bigshot Grandson? *Don't be ridiculous.*

Em's mouth worked to form the right words. "Th-h-han. Coo."

Ahh. "You're welcome. And I know you love me." She kissed Em's cool forehead then leaned back to wag a finger at her. "Remember what I said before. You've got work to do, Miss Emily. I need you back on your feet as soon as possible so get some sleep. Tomorrow's a big day."

With surprising strength, Em kept hold of her hand. Eyebrows tented, chin quivering. Her fearless Em was afraid? Minnie flinched at the ping in her heart.

"I'm teasing. You're doing great." She rested her cheek against the top of Em's head for a moment then straightened. "Whatever you do will be enough for me. I'm just so glad you're still here."

A smile softened Em's face and she released her grip. Her slow wink brought a rush of tears up Minnie's throat. "Enjoy your dinner. I'll see you tomorrow. Love you." Outside the room, Minnie paused. *Please, God. Heal her. Bring her back to me. To all of us.*

She swung her purse over her shoulder and headed for the elevator. Now to meet Daniel and Mr. Grandson. *One more thing, Lord. Could you help me be civil? For Em's sake?*

⁓

Settled in the reception area at Daniel's office, waiting for Minnie Mouse to arrive, Jackson called Noah. Maybe discussing the plans they'd been emailing about would distract him for a few minutes.

"We're off and running, my friend," Noah said, "Pierre is already getting a huge response to your show."

He smiled at the enthusiasm in his friend's voice. "*Our show.*"

"The noise is all about you as the headline. I told you, Young. People have been waiting for you to surface. This is a smart decision on Pierre's part."

Jackson couldn't stop the grin. "I agree. Having you, me, and Branton in one show is gonna be amazing. Speaking of which, what did Branton say about our ideas?"

"Loved 'em. I sent you an email about ten minutes ago with a few things he threw into the mix."

The door opened, and Minnie Mouse stepped in. Her gaze swept over him and landed on the receptionist. The blatant dismissal stung.

"Jack?"

"I'm here." He turned away, dismissing her as well. "Did he like the theme we came up with?"

"Totally. Wait 'til you see the artwork he sent. One more reason I'm glad he's part of this circus. And we're both glad you're the ringmaster."

Jackson forced a laugh. "Remember that wasn't my idea. What day are we meeting in New York?"

From where she stood chatting with the receptionist, Minnie Mouse's cheerful voice drowned out Noah's response. Jackson wouldn't have thought her capable of laughing—especially with him in the vicinity.

"Got that?" Noah's words startled him.

"Sorry, what?"

Noah chuckled. "You're sounding a little distracted. Maybe you're spending too much time in that speck of a town."

Daniel entered the reception area and gave the Mouse a long hug. When they turned to look at him, Jackson held up a finger. Minnie rolled her eyes and said something to Daniel that made the older man chuckle before they headed for the meeting room.

"Noah, I've gotta run. Looks like my meeting is about to start. Thanks for sending that stuff from Branton. I'll look it over and get back to you."

"Don't get too distracted out there," he added with another chuckle. "We need you focused and in top form for the show."

"You got it."

Jackson turned off the phone and put the show out of his mind, ready to head into battle with Minnie Mouse. The visual would be funny if it weren't about his grandmother.

"Jackson, glad you could join us." Daniel grinned and indicated the third chair at the round table.

"Sorry. Going over a few details about the new show."

Daniel turned to Minnie, who still hadn't looked directly at Jackson. "This young man is planning a big deal in New York City to show off his work. Emily will be thrilled when she hears about it."

She nodded, throwing a tight smile in Jackson's general direction. "Very exciting."

Daniel looked from her to Jackson, then gathered his papers together. "So, I hear Emily is doing better, which is wonderful news. I didn't think this would keep her down for long. When will they release her?"

"The doctor told me early next week," Jackson said, then felt a chill from Minnie's withering glance. Maybe he should have let her answer.

Daniel shifted in his chair, eyebrows raised. "That what you heard too, Minnie?"

"Yes."

"Okay. Good. That's good." He fidgeted, glancing

between them again. Minnie's expression remained stony. "I'm assuming she'll head to Crosswinds for therapy?"

"That would make the most sense since this is her *home*," Minnie said, still not looking at Jackson. "She'll only need a short time there, and then she can go home to continue her therapy. You know how much she hates any kind of doctoring."

The moment had arrived. Jackson drew a silent breath and plunged in. "Actually, I've been doing some research and I think the place she'll get the best therapy is at St. Matthew's Rehab in Rochester. It's a private residence with 24-hour attendants, one-on-one therapy, customized diet. The works."

Minnie turned her head toward him. The frost in her eyes curled the hair on his arms. He'd expected an outburst, not silence. He fought back a squirm.

"Rochester, eh?" Daniel said. "Why there? What've they got that's better?"

Great. He'd offended both of them. "Well, it's not that there's anything wrong with Crosswinds, but St. Matthew's offers more extensive and personalized help." He flipped open his folder and pulled out the comparison chart he'd created. "I'm sure the therapy here would be fine, but the program in Rochester will get her back to normal quicker. It was designed by Mayo Clinic therapists and it's cutting-edge treatment for stroke victims."

His phone conversation with one of the therapists had convinced him the award-winning program would give Grandma the best treatment possible. They'd have her back on her feet before the Lawton nursing home could even develop a plan of action.

In the silence, he lifted his gaze to Minnie who studied him like he was from another planet.

"I'm sure you want her home as quickly as I do," he said. Weren't they all on the same team here?

"This *is* her home, Mr. Young. Her friends are here. Her church, her pastor. Me." Her gaze impaled him. "The best therapy in the world can't fix a broken heart."

"Oh, come on. We're talking therapy for a brief time."

"And part of the therapy process is being surrounded by friends and family. It's not just about making sure she can walk again. It's about healing her spirit as well."

He held back an eye roll. Was she a hippie too? Any minute she'd pull out a tambourine. "I'm sure they take that into consideration in Rochester, Ms. Carlson. And it's thirty minutes from here, not across the country."

"It might as well be across the country. Since you haven't lived here for decades, you wouldn't know that most of her friends no longer drive." She clasped her hands on the table. "Do you have any other family?"

He raised an eyebrow. "What does that—"

"It's a simple question. Yes or no."

"No."

"Neither does Emily, aside from me. But what she does have is community here in Lawton, something you probably haven't experienced in your world travels. Love and support will be as important, if not more so, for her recovery as having Mayo Clinic therapists." Pink spots appeared on her cheeks. "You might want to put that consideration on your chart."

Did everything have to be touchy-feely with her? "I don't think a bunch of old people standing around her bed singing Kumbaya will be as effective as world-class therapy."

Her eyes went wide. Something inside him flinched. *Incredibly stupid, Young.*

Daniel cleared his throat. "Well, this has been an

interesting discussion, but we need to make a decision about where Emily will go when she's released."

Minnie pushed away from the table and turned her back on the men, rolling her shoulders slowly. A deep exhale filled the silence.

"So. Jackson, you want to move her to the facility in Rochester, correct?" Daniel asked.

"Correct."

"Minnie, you want her rehab at Crosswinds, correct?"

She remained still. "Yes."

"Okay. Well, we seem to be at an impasse here. Minnie, as Emily's medical power of attorney, you have the right to decide where and what her treatment will be, since she's unable to communicate her wishes clearly at this time."

She turned. Daniel held up a hand. "However, Jackson is her financial power of attorney—"

"*What?*" Mouth agape, she stared at the attorney. "Since when?"

He perched reading glasses on his long nose and shuffled through his papers. "For the last three years."

Minnie blinked several times as if he'd physically slapped her with the words. Her mouth opened and closed before her gaze swung to pin Jackson to his chair. "How did you do that?"

He lifted his hands in self-defense. "I didn't do anything. I just found out the other day."

She looked at Daniel then back at him. "Why would she pick someone she hasn't seen in twenty years to handle her finances? That makes no sense."

"I agree," Jackson said.

"Then unappoint yourself."

"I'm afraid only Emily can do that," Daniel said.

"Wow." She shook her head slowly, hands lifting then dropping to her sides. "This is so...wow."

Jackson felt like he'd sucker-punched her somehow. "This whole thing is confusing, but for now we need to decide what's best for Grandma Em. I think, looking at what the different programs offer, the best thing would be for her to spend a week or so in Rochester. She'd be home much quicker."

"So you want to believe."

He slid the folder toward her. "Look over the reports yourself. Emily deserves the best, and I want to make sure she gets it. I won't settle for less."

She shot him a contemptuous glance before looking at Daniel. "Will Medicare cover the place in Rochester?"

"No. It's private pay," Jackson said then pressed his lips together. Did he have a death wish?

She glared down at him. "She doesn't have that kind of money."

"Actually, she does," Daniel interjected. "Emily has done very well with her investments. But don't let that affect your decision, Minnie. Do what you think is best for her."

"So, I can decide where she goes but he holds the purse strings."

"That would be correct."

Jackson chewed his lip. A long evening loomed. "What if we can't agree?"

Daniel sighed. "I suppose I could appoint someone as her guardian, someone other than you two, and they would make the decision. But that could get pricey. I think we can work it out here, don't you?"

Folding his arms, Jackson leaned back in his chair. He'd done his homework and had considered the situation rationally. The Mouse apparently couldn't. He would hold his ground for as long as it took.

"Her time at Crosswinds would be covered by

Medicare so she wouldn't have to touch her own money," she said to Daniel.

"But at-home care isn't," Jackson countered. He'd done that homework as well, figuring it would be part of her argument.

She turned back to the window, shoulders stiff. She didn't seem to be breathing. Silence enveloped the room. Finally, her rigid posture drooped. "Fine." The word was barely audible. "Move her to Rochester."

When she turned to look at him, the defeat in her eyes pinched his heart. He wanted her to believe in the idea as much as he did. "I think it's the right decision. She'll be back here in no time."

Minnie looked at Daniel. "Do you need me to sign anything?"

"No." The older man's eyebrows lowered. "You're sure this is what's best for Emily, Minnie?"

"No, but he is." Her chin quivered. "I just want her well." She slid her purse over her shoulder. "I haven't been home yet today, so I'm going home to eat. Thanks, Daniel."

"All right. We'll get things set up and I'll call you with the details." He stood and wrapped her in a hug. "Go home and rest, young lady. This has been a tough week for you."

Without looking at Jackson, she left the room. Daniel settled in his chair and sorted through the paperwork, making notes on several pages. Jackson took a long swig from the plastic water bottle. The cold silence reminded him *he* was the outsider.

He shifted his gaze to the window and watched Minnie trudge across the parking lot toward a battered old car. The preparation had served him well. It was the right decision. So why did he feel so lousy?

CHAPTER EIGHT

Minnie awoke Saturday morning determined to make the move as painless as possible for Em, though the very thought of it splintered her heart. In moments like this, she missed her mom more than ever. The sense of being truly alone wrapped cold tentacles around her, squeezing away every breath.

Coffee in hand, she settled in the rocker and pulled the colorful prayer shawl around her shoulders. Em had knit it for her three years ago, a birthday gift that continued to wrap her in warmth and love.

She pulled her Bible onto her lap. How could she prepare Em for the move? "God, it's yet another thing I am totally unprepared to do. Help me figure out how to tell her."

Arriving at the hospital two hours later, she stopped at the nurse's station and told the nurse where Em would go on Tuesday. Even as the woman nodded and made a note in the chart, the simple lift of her brow made Minnie want to blame the heartless, egotistical grandson. But she'd agreed, which made her as guilty as him.

Minnie peeked into the room. Em sat up in bed, hair in disarray, holding a red ball out in front of her. Her left hand covered the right and seemed to be doing most of the squeezing. Her frown of concentration lifted Minnie's aching heart. If anyone could come back one hundred percent from a stroke, it was Emily Young.

She entered the room. "Well, look at you. Hard at work on your therapy already."

Em gave a short nod, focused on her hands. Minnie perched on the windowsill and watched. After four more squeezes, Em dropped her hands to her lap and rested her head back against the pillow. A bead of sweat rolled past her ear.

"Hard work, hmm?"

Em turned her head and managed a partial smile, holding out her left hand. Minnie grasped it and pressed a kiss to the bony knuckles. "You look better this morning. Stronger. Did you have breakfast?"

"Egg." She wrinkled her nose. "Code."

Minnie laughed. "Cold eggs? Yummy. How did you sleep last night?"

Em sighed. "Code."

"Did you ask for another blanket? I bet they'd have gotten one out of that blanket warmer thing."

"No. Tough."

"Yes, you are. And I'm glad. That stroke might have taken a lesser woman out. But it's not a sign of weakness to ask for another blanket, you know."

"Worker." She frowned. "I will. Work hard."

The full sentence sent Minnie's heart soaring. "I know you will. And you'll be back home in record time. Everybody at Open Circle sends love and hugs. They miss you." She squeezed Em's hand. "*I* miss you. I can't wait until you're back."

"Hard?"

"Much harder than I expected. But I keep remembering what you said. God put me in this position so I'm going to do what I can and remind myself He'll be there with me." She sighed. "It's just easier to do when you're there."

"Well, good morning!" Jackson's voice crashed between them like a sledgehammer against one of Em's porcelain cups. "You're looking beautiful this morning, Grandma." He crossed the room and gave her a quick kiss, taking her right hand in a familiar gesture.

Em's smile was wider than the one Minnie got when she arrived. Maybe she should set up a visitation schedule so she wouldn't have to run into him. *My, aren't we cranky today.*

"Good morning, Minnie." His tone held a note of caution.

Aware of Em's gaze on her, she gave him a toothy smile. "Good morning, Jackson."

His eyebrows lifted. She turned her attention back to Em. "I heard you'll be getting out of here on Tuesday. I'm assuming the doctor already told you that?"

"He stopped in yesterday afternoon and told her."

Minnie bit her lip, keeping her gaze on Em. *God, could you give him a really long photo assignment somewhere? Like Siberia?* "Wow. You're a ventriloquist! Your voice sounded just like Jackson."

"Sorry." Irritation colored his apology.

Em's eyes crinkled at the corners. Still holding their hands, she looked slowly between them.

"Along the lines of getting out of here," Minnie continued, "your grandson wants to tell you his plan." She settled back on the windowsill and leveled her gaze on him.

His smile faded as his Adam's apple bounced. Clearing

his throat, he sank down on the chair beside Em. "The doctor says your prognosis for a complete recovery is really good, Grandma. And the way to ensure that is to get the best possible care. There's the normal kind of physical and occupational therapy, and then there's state-of-the-art therapy that has a proven record of a faster, more complete recovery."

Em's brow had lowered during his set-up. Minnie pressed her lips together. Mr. Grandson was about to get a taste of the real Emily Young.

"You'll love this." His words picked up energy. "We did some research—"

Minnie cleared her throat.

"Actually, I did the research. Minnie was too busy."

Her fingers curled around the window ledge.

"I found a really great place," he continued, with the tone of someone trying to talk a four-year-old into taking her medicine. "It's amazing. Cutting edge, Grandma. It's got a warm water exercise pool. One-on-one therapists. They'll fix any kind of meal you want. It's the new trend in stroke rehab and, thanks to the Mayo Clinic, we have it right here in Minnesota."

Em pulled her hand from his, a spark of independence lighting her eyes. If she had her speech right now, she'd be blasting Jackson's shaggy hair off his head. "Where."

Jackson's smile widened. "Right here in Rochester."

"No."

"But Grandma, it's a great place." The enthusiastic smile wobbled. "I've checked it out myself. We want you home as quickly as possible so getting the best care will ensure that."

"Home."

"You *will* go home. Very soon." He nodded. "The doctor thinks maybe a week or ten days, tops."

"No."

Jackson's gaze lifted to Minnie who looked back at him, eyebrow raised. She dipped her head slightly to encourage him to continue.

His face darkened. "Minnie thinks it's a great idea."

Em's head swiveled toward Minnie, a lopsided frown on her pale face.

Minnie slid off the windowsill and perched on the edge of the bed, taking Em's hand in hers. "What *I* think is a great idea is getting you home as soon as possible. You're a fighter, and I know you're going to work hard to get back on your feet."

Em's blue eyes widened and locked on hers. "Go?"

Help, God. "I know you'd get very good care at Crosswinds." She pursed her lips, summoning the courage to continue. "But...I think Jackson's right. This new place is even better."

Em awkwardly folded her arms and lowered her chin. "Stay."

"I know you want to stay in Lawton. I *want* you to stay." She sighed. "I miss you so much, and I want you better as soon as possible. So if this new place can make that happen, let's give it a try. Please?"

Jaw clenched, clutching the exercise ball in her left hand, Em stared down at her rumpled covers. Thankfully Jackson remained quiet. A long exhale relaxed her shoulders, and she looked sideways at Minnie. "Don't want." Fear darkened her eyes again.

"I know you don't. How about this? I'll go with you and we'll talk to the people together. We'll make sure it looks good before we decide. And if you really don't like it, you won't have to stay. Okay?"

Em held out her left hand and Minnie grasped it.

"Okee." She looked at Jackson, her frown still in place. "Don't want. Okee."

"That's great, Grandma." He smiled like a child who'd gotten his way.

Minnie had never disliked him more.

⁓

Jackson pushed through the front doors of the hospital, intent on catching the Mouse. He wanted to set things straight after what she'd said to Grandma Em. There. She crossed the street, dark hair flying in the breeze, her stride long and determined. He jogged after her. "Minnie!"

Her pace quickened. He broke into a run and caught up to her mid-block. "Minnie, wait."

She kept walking.

"We need to talk."

"No, we don't."

He took her arm but she yanked away, whirling to face him. The tears on her cheeks were a stark contrast to the blaze in her eyes.

"What is your problem?" she demanded.

"Well, I—" He stepped back, hands raised. It seemed to be his usual position around her. "We should talk about...the..."

"You got your way. Now leave me alone." She turned and strode away, wiping her face.

He jogged to keep up with her anger. "Why did you tell her you'd check it out before deciding?"

She stopped and pulled in a short breath, looking upward as if for help. "News flash, Mr. Young. She hates hospitals. She hates going to the doctor, for that matter."

"Once she gets there—"

"She'll hate it! She doesn't care about cutting edge anything. She agreed only because I gave her an option. Stop treating her like she's some frail old lady who's unable to use her brain. She deserves to be part of the decision-making."

Jackson's cheeks warmed under her fiery blast.

Eyes narrowed, she set her hands on her hips. "And for the record, while I agreed she should go there, I will not *make* her go. I've never for one minute treated her as anything other than the intelligent, independent, wonderful person she is, and I'm not about to start now." She lifted a trembling hand to brush the hair from her cheek.

His heart clenched. He shoved his hands into his pockets and dropped his gaze. It hadn't occurred to him to ask Grandma Em what she wanted. *What an idiot.* "You're right. I should have involved her in the decision. She deserves that."

"Yes, she does." There was a long silence before she sighed. "I'm sure you're trying to do what you think is best, but maybe you should get to know her first."

Ouch. He nodded, relieved to see the fire in her eyes fade. "You're right." He lifted his shoulders. In his rush to claim his place in his grandmother's life, he'd walked right over her. "I guess I have a lot to learn."

After a long pause, Minnie said, "I'm praying that the rehab center is as good as you think, and that she'll settle in fairly easily."

He pressed his lips together. She could pray all she wanted but it wouldn't do any good. He knew that from past experience. "Me too. Well, I guess I'll see you here on Tuesday when she's ready to go, if not before."

She stepped back. "Okay then."

"Okay." She wasn't yelling at him. This was progress. He

stepped back as well and gave an awkward wave. "Have a good weekend."

The distrust that usually shadowed her face faded as she turned away. Watching her head toward the parking lot, he itched for his camera. Her posture touched him. An aura of strength and sadness. Determination and...defeat?

The camera lens would see beyond the protective, bossy wall she kept in place, like it would reveal his own insecurities if he turned it on himself. Behind the images they projected were battered, lonely hearts, which explained his focused determination to rebuild a relationship with his grandmother. And why Minnie guarded hers so fiercely.

It was the one thing they had in common.

Tuesday morning, heart rattling against her ribs, Minnie gripped Em's cold hand as the aide pushed the wheelchair through the doorway. Squinting against the sunshine, she shook her head. Why had she ever agreed to this? Em hadn't spoken since Minnie arrived an hour earlier with Nick, who'd wanted to wish Em well before his meetings at the Mayo Clinic. While Em had seemed pleased by his visit, she'd remained subdued.

Even her grandson couldn't elicit a smile out of her. Minnie glanced sideways. He didn't look as cheerful today. Maybe he had second thoughts as well. She stopped a snort. Doubtful.

The short, beefy MediVan driver approached with a broad smile that revealed a wide expanse of teeth. "Miz Emily? I'm Rufus. I'm gonna drive you just across town to your new place." He patted her hand. "You is gonna be very safe with me."

Em looked up at him with a faint smile. "Okee. Careful."

He released a belly laugh that made Minnie smile. "I be very careful. I hear you are a special lay-dee."

Em waved her left hand at his declaration, her half-smile widening a fraction. "Pish."

Minnie extended her hand, thankful God had sent this cheerful man to make the trek with them. "She's definitely special, Rufus. I'm Minnie Carlson."

His meaty hand engulfed hers. "Nice to meet you, Miss."

"And I'm Jackson, Emily's grandson."

Minnie looked away. Was that the only way he could introduce himself?

Within minutes, Rufus had the wheelchair strapped into the van with Minnie settled beside her. When they pulled out of the hospital's circle drive and onto the highway, Minnie glanced out the back window. Jackson followed in his rental car, sunglasses on, hair blowing in the breeze from the open sunroof. She turned forward. Maybe he'd get lost on the way.

The winding drive through Rochester flew by as Rufus told stories of growing up in Jamaica, the tenth of twelve kids. Em chuckled, then laughed outright when one outrageous tale outdid the last.

They rumbled down a shaded street to a cul de sac. The smile faded from Em's face. Her frown held a sadness Minnie had never seen before. Heart aching, she reached for Em's hand and held it firmly then turned her attention to the house Rufus pulled up to. Mid-morning sunlight shone off the dark green roof of a tan single-story building with green shutters. A riot of flowers lined the front walk and cascaded from ceramic pots near the door. An expansive, perfectly manicured lawn stretched around both sides of the building, a silver maple shading the driveway and front door.

"Here we are, Miz Emily." Rufus hopped out and hurried around to fling open the side door of the van. Busily unstrapping her chair, he continued his chatter. "I bet you be back home before you know it."

Minnie nodded at the wink he shot over Em's head before he lowered the platform where he'd placed her wheelchair. Jackson parked behind the van and strolled toward them, whistling. Minnie clenched her fists to keep from wiping the smile from his face. This wasn't the time for celebration.

A dark-haired man in khakis and a navy polo shirt emerged from the house. A young woman in similar attire but with a bouncing blonde ponytail followed him.

"Hello!" he called as they neared the group beside the van. "This must be Emily Young." He squatted next to the wheelchair and extended his hand. "Mrs. Young, I'm Robert, the director of the New Life facility. This is our assistant director, Kerry." He stood and smiled at Minnie. "And this must be your lovely granddaughter."

Accepting his hand, Minnie quietly corrected him and introduced Jackson. Em had greeted the directors and now sat staring at the house. Minnie followed her gaze. It could be anyone's sprawling home if there were a basketball hoop in the driveway and bikes on the grass.

She knelt beside the chair and looked into Em's pale face. "Holding up okay?"

Fear flashed in her eyes before she lifted her chin in stoic Emily fashion and nodded. "Okee. Work hard. Come home."

Eyes burning, Minnie smiled. "I cannot wait until you're home. I'll be praying it's sooner than anyone expects."

"Ready for a tour, Mrs. Young?" Kerry asked.

Rufus, who had been chatting with Jackson, bid Em and Minnie a boisterous farewell, climbed back in his van and roared off as they started up the walk. When Em reached for Minnie's hand, she clasped the cool fingers in a reassuring grip.

Lord, I don't know which of us will take it harder when I have to leave her here.

CHAPTER NINE

Jackson followed behind Grandma Em and the Mouse as Kerry pushed the chair toward the building. He wanted Grandma to be happy here. And he wanted Minnie to see that he could make the right decisions for his grandmother, with or without her help.

Staff clad in khakis and hunter green polo shirts offered a cheerful welcome as their small group entered through the wide front door. Grandma Em lifted a frail hand in response, a half-smile brightening her face.

"Let's take a quick tour, Mrs. Young," Kerry said, as the director excused himself to take a call, "and then we'll head to lunch."

Grandma Em shrugged and Jackson exchanged a nod with Kerry. Hopefully the stay here would bring back the grandma he remembered—full of spunk and life.

As they moved from room to room, the Mouse peppered Kerry with questions that made Jackson flinch. Couldn't she ask that stuff out of Grandma Em's earshot?

"So, what percentage of people recover fully from a stroke?"

Jackson rolled his eyes.

"Good question," Kerry said.

Of course it was.

"It really depends on the level of severity, whether it's a mild stroke, a TIA or—"

"TIA?" Jackson asked.

"Transient ischemic attack," the Mouse explained. "Like a mini-stroke."

He frowned. "How do you know that?"

The withering glance she shot over Grandma Em's head sent heat crawling up his neck. "I work with seniors. All day, every day. It's my job to know these things."

Kerry led them through several rooms filled with equipment and machinery. Floor to ceiling mirrors lined the walls. Racks of various sized dumbbells stood at the far end of one room, green weights on the bottom, blue next, pink on top. Jackson smiled. The pink ones couldn't even be a pound each.

Several therapists held clipboards where they stood close by their patients. Looking like high school gym teachers, Jackson expected them to be wearing whistles as well.

Kerry led them to the side of the room. "The right exercises, targeting the right muscles, will rebuild strength and coordination." Her gaze moved to Grandma Em. "And that will get you out of that wheelchair faster."

Grandma Em looked around the room, frowning. Patients were huffing through exercises, faces pink. No one looked strong enough to move without assistance.

Squatting to meet Grandma Em's gaze, Kerry laid a hand on her arm. "Your stroke wasn't as severe as many people's, Mrs. Young. I expect you to make a fabulous recovery. Attitude is half the battle and from what I hear, you have an awesome attitude toward life."

Jackson nodded. The grandma he remembered certainly had.

"I've yet to see anything knock Em down for very long," the Mouse said.

Kerry directed them to the next room, and Jackson slid forward to Grandma Em's side and reached for her hand before the Mouse did. Childish, maybe, but he was tired of being an after-thought on the tour.

"Why all the mirrors?" he asked as they stopped in the middle of the room.

"They're used for posture checks," Kerry said. "Good posture is essential in strengthening core muscles, relieving stress on the neck and spine, and providing a sense of health and wellness."

He nodded, glad the Mouse didn't respond. *I suppose she knew that.* She barely looked at him. After their conversation outside the hospital last week, he'd been determined to ask more questions. She seemed as determined to make him look stupid.

"So that's a quick tour of some of our work rooms." Kerry smiled at Grandma Em. "How about after lunch you and I talk about the issues you're facing, and set a few goals? I know you want to get home as fast as possible," she added with a wink, "so that will be goal number one. But we'll set exercise, speech, and daily living goals—a mixed bag designed to get you up and moving as fast as possible. Sound okay?"

Grandma Em studied the pretty blonde with focused attention. "Yes. Go home."

Kerry nodded. "Exactly. Mmm. I smell something wonderful. Let's finish the paperwork and head to lunch, shall we?"

Jackson set his hand on his grandmother's thin shoulder. Kerry exuded confidence in the program. He hoped Grandma Em felt it too. "Sounds like a good plan to me."

⁓

Returning to the front room, Minnie rolled Em's chair away from where Kerry and Jackson chatted, and parked it beside a plush couch near the windows. Settling next to her, Minnie raised an eyebrow. "So, what do you think? Want to give it a try?"

Blue eyes clung to hers for a long silent moment. Em's right eyelid drooped a bit, her hands limp in her lap. She leaned slightly to the right. Minnie wrestled back the urge to call Rufus to take them home.

Finally, Em nodded. "Yes. Come. Home?"

Minnie gave a firm nod. "Of course you can come home if you don't like it. I promise."

Jackson joined them, keeping his distance from Minnie as he lowered onto the couch. "We won't make you stay if you don't want to, Grandma."

Minnie stared at him, mouth open.

"I'm impressed with everything they have to offer, aren't you?" he continued. "The best technology. Top-notch therapists. And lunch smells great."

Minnie thrust her hands under her legs to keep from smacking the back of his head. How quickly he managed to undo his kind words. It was all about his big idea.

A tentative smile lifted Em's mouth as she looked at him. He always managed to get a smile out of her. Clearly, she loved this man she hadn't seen in decades. And it was equally clear to Minnie how he didn't deserve that adoration. She bit her lip and looked away.

"Okee. I can. Do this."

Jackson stood and pressed a kiss to the top of her head.

"I know you can, Grandma. I'll get you all signed in, okay? Then we'll have lunch."

Halfway through the meal, Minnie straightened in her chair beside Em. She'd been so focused on helping Em through this transition, she hadn't planned beyond the arrival. She'd ridden here in the medi-van with Em. Now she had no way home!

"Minnie? Is there something wrong with your food?" Kerry asked from across the table. Conversation stopped as the others turned their attention to Minnie.

She shook her head quickly. "Not at all. It's delicious. You have an amazing chef."

The young woman nodded. "We're so fortunate to have Geno. He's a favorite with the staff and the residents." She beamed. "I'll pass along your compliments."

"Please do." As conversation resumed, Minnie pushed the food around her plate. She had two options. She could call for a very expensive cab ride back to Lawton or... Without moving her head, she glanced toward Jackson who chatted with Robert.

What were you thinking? Obviously, she hadn't been.

As Jackson pulled away from the curb, the Mouse looked at the New Life building, jaw clenched, chin trembling. He had the sudden urge to take her hand, assure her Grandma Em would be fine. An image of her slapping him squelched the desire and he focused on driving.

"I'm impressed with how the staff treated Emily," he said eventually.

She nodded.

Merging onto the highway, he tried again. "She's a pretty tough gal, isn't she?"

"Mmhmm." Her gaze remained straight ahead, hands clasped in her lap.

Jackson released a quiet sigh and settled back in the seat. Grandma Em seemed to really care about this girl, but he struggled to find something likable about her. She was cold, cranky, and borderline rude. Except with Grandma Em. Then she became a different person.

He glanced at her. Shoulders slumped, she looked surprisingly vulnerable, as if she'd lost her best friend. He frowned. Maybe she had. Didn't she have any girlfriends? Was the Suit he'd seen with her at the hospital her boyfriend? He shook his head. If so, he stunk at it, leaving her to visit Grandma Em by herself all the time.

"Em doesn't follow orders very well." Her words startled him.

"Oh? Why's that?"

Their glances met, and a smile lifted a corner of her mouth before she looked away. "She knows her mind. And she's never been afraid to express it. So, if someone tells her to do something she doesn't want to do—"

"They'd better duck," he finished for her, enjoying her smiling nod. "But she'll do what the therapists at New Life tell her to do, won't she?"

The Mouse pursed her lips. "I think so because she wants to come home." A sigh escaped. "It killed me to leave her there."

Jackson ignored the pinch of guilt. "Yeah." His mind filled with questions about his grandmother's life, what he'd missed. He tried to sort them into order, so he didn't overwhelm Minnie with his aching desire to know Grandma Em.

As he opened his mouth, she rested her head back and closed her eyes, turning her face toward the window. Jackson felt the door slam on his questions, once again closed out of his grandmother's life. The Mouse excelled at dismissing him without a word, making him feel like a nuisance in her life.

Fingers curling around the steering wheel, he glared at the ribbon of highway stretching before him. Fine. He'd get his questions answered elsewhere. Once Grandma Em had recovered, they'd have all the time in the world to get reacquainted. Without the Mouse running interference between them.

CHAPTER TEN

"Come on in, Justin. Have a seat." As the teen dropped into the chair, she folded trembling hands on her desk and focused her thoughts. "Open Circle is successful because we work as a team."

Justin looked at her blankly.

"That means we work together to make this the best place for staff and seniors alike. We make sure every shift is covered so the seniors are always safe. When someone takes an unscheduled break, it puts undue pressure on the rest of the staff."

He rolled his eyes and picked at his jeans.

Minnie flipped open a file and shifted through the papers. "Justin, this is the third time you took an unscheduled break. After the second one last week, I put you on notice and made it very clear that if it happened again, you'd be terminated. That was the form you signed the last time we met, remember?"

His head lifted abruptly, shaggy blonde hair hanging over one eye.

"Because you were out of the building unexcused again this morning, I have to let you go."

"Let me go where?"

Lord, I hate this. "You're fired. As of right now. You'll receive your final paycheck in a few days. Please collect your belongings, and I'll walk you out."

"Wait. What?" He sat up, back straight. "I need this job. My dad'll kill me if I get fired again!" The first true burst of energy she'd seen out of him. "I only left for like ten minutes."

"I'm sorry, Justin, but I need staff I can depend on."

"Okay, okay. I won't do it again."

Hardly inspiring. "That's what you told me the last two times." She stood and locked her knees. "I have a meeting in a few minutes, so please collect your things now."

He jumped to his feet. "You're firing me for having a cigarette? You can't do that!"

"I'm not happy about it, Justin. It's not how I hoped things would work out."

"You stink as a boss."

Even from a seventeen-year-old, it stung. "I've made myself as clear as possible about our policies."

He straightened to his full height and glared down at her. She met his gaze, praying for strength and protection. As sullen as he usually was, he'd never looked threatening, or even capable of anger.

"Fine. Whatever." With an expletive, he flung open her office door, and stomped toward the activity room.

She followed at a distance. He snatched his oversized sweatshirt from the closet, muttering loudly, then stormed into the kitchen to retrieve a greasy lunch bag from the refrigerator. He swiped his arm toward an empty can on the counter. It bounced across the tile floor.

As they headed back down the hall, Ward emerged from the bathroom. "Hey, man. What's up?"

"She fired me," he said, flinging an arm toward Minnie.

"What?" Ward turned a glare on her. "You fired him?"

"Justin," Minnie said, "please finish collecting your things."

"You can't fire him." Ward stepped between her and his friend. "You gotta have good reason."

"This doesn't concern you, Ward," she said quietly. Nausea rose from the pounding of her heart. "However, both Justin and I know the reason. Please go back to work."

"I ain't goin' back without Justin. Either you unfire him or I'll quit right now."

This explained why Dorothy had never fired anyone. Well, she wouldn't be bullied by a couple of teens. "That is, of course, your choice, Ward, but I'd hate to see that happen."

Jaw clenched, his eyes darted from her to Justin and back. "I ain't workin' for someone like you."

"I see." Her voice remained surprisingly steady as she faced down the mutiny. "Then you'll need to collect your things as well, and I'll escort both of you out."

"What, now?"

She nodded. "If I'm that terrible to work for, then it would be best for you to find another job. Now."

Justin started toward the front door as Ward blustered in indecision, then turned sharply to follow. "This place is nuts," he declared. "Workin' anywhere would be better than this."

Minnie followed them to the front door, focused on the swaggering young men so her legs didn't buckle. *Safety first. Meltdown later.* She flinched when they slammed open the front door, then watched them disappear down the block, willing the tears back.

"Boss?" Jody's voice from behind the desk.

Swallowing hard, Minnie turned. "Well, that didn't exactly go as planned."

"You were great."

Not so much. "Thanks." The simple praise bolstered her flagging spirits.

She headed toward her office to fill out *two* sets of termination papers, then paused. "Keep an eye on the front door, okay? In the heat of the moment, they might come back for more grandstanding."

Jody gave a firm nod and pressed the button that locked the front door. "Got it." Her expression softened. "Need a cup of coffee?"

Her kindness loosened Minnie's stranglehold on her emotions. "Not right now, thanks. I'd better get the reports done."

She closed the door and sat at her desk, staring at Justin's paperwork. Being short one staff member wasn't ideal. Two was pretty much disastrous. Biting her lip, she jotted a few notes on the report, then pulled up a second set on her computer.

Okay, God. Now I'm the director, the social worker, and an aide. I could use some help.

A life preserver might be better.

⁓

Thursday morning, Minnie pulled her hood over her head, dashed across the pockmarked parking lot, and thrust her key into Open Circle's front door. Inside, she shook the water from her jacket. A flash of light preceded a heavy roll of thunder, and she paused to look back out into the downpour. She loved a good thunderstorm, especially once she was snug inside.

Flipping on the reception area lights, she went into her office, letting the peacefulness warm her. Arriving every day at six-thirty gave her a half-hour head start before the morning staff arrived. Thirty minutes to get settled, to wander through the building turning on lights and praying for the staff and the seniors.

After booting her computer, she headed toward the kitchen to start a pot of coffee. Halfway across the activity room she paused, head cocked. A splat, followed by another, then another. She turned in a slow circle to locate the dripping.

"No!"

A dark brown stain on the top of the old upright piano revealed an overhead leak. She dashed across the room and pushed against the piano. It slid an inch. She shoved again. A quarter inch. Stepping back, she scanned for a problem. The brakes. Releasing them, she rolled the piano toward the middle of the room, then dashed into the kitchen for towels, grabbing an orange bucket on her way back.

From the condition of the piano lid, the leak had obviously started overnight. Water slid between the keys. Heart aching at the damage, she dried the beloved instrument as best she could. Music was integral to Open Circle, to minds clouded with dementia. While the seniors might not recall someone's name or what they ate for lunch, they could sing the songs of years past. Minnie paused, wet rags in hand, hearing warbling voices raised in song, seeing the spark of joy on wrinkled faces as music brought them moments of clarity.

The fun of singing around this old upright brought life to the activity room. As a volunteer played with gusto and more than a few wrong notes, the seniors stood or sat side-by-side sharing memories of a time when they were in the midst of life, not bystanders watching days slip by.

Tears in her eyes, Minnie patted the top of the piano, then went to the kitchen to start the coffee. Heading back to her office on silent feet, she listened for more leaks. One in the small meeting room had soaked the worn carpet. She retrieved another bucket.

She'd gone through half of her emails when the two early morning staffers dashed in from the downpour. Briefed on this latest issue, they gathered umbrellas and towels, and prepared to greet the first seniors.

Moses arrived with the early group. Still living in the farmhouse where he was born, he told everyone he'd predicted this storm over a week ago. He confided to Minnie that because of the winds and the way the wheat blew, he'd known a change of weather approached. Minnie assured him she remembered and thanked him for his concern for the group. He beamed under her praise.

The day sped by as Minnie filled in during Minnesota Bingo and drew laughs as she fumbled along in Gail's first Elder Zumba class. She helped serve and clean up lunch, and finally dropped into her chair at two o'clock to finish a report she'd started last week. Five minutes later she retrieved yet another bucket to catch the new leak behind her desk. Releasing a tired sigh, she contemplated the growing stain on the ceiling overhead. Roof repairs were not in the budget. Every penny needed to go toward hiring new staff.

"Got a minute?" Cheryl's terse words came from the doorway.

Minnie hid her sigh with a nod. A minute with Cheryl felt like a lifetime. "Of course. Come in."

Cheryl perched on the edge of a chair and met Minnie's gaze with a frown. "You need to hire more people."

"I realize that."

"If you don't get at least three more people hired next

week, I think the rest of the staff will quit. We're wearing out from this schedule."

Was that a threat? "I understand. I didn't anticipate people quitting after I let Justin go. Losing three has been a challenge." After Justin and Ward's dramatic exit, Patty had given her notice. It had been a long week. "I really appreciate everyone jumping in to take up the slack."

"There wouldn't be slack if you hadn't decided to fire Justin."

"Our seniors deserve more than people simply collecting a paycheck, Cheryl. They've worked their whole lives to make this town what it is. Don't we owe them the best we have to offer?"

"Oh, please." Cheryl rolled her eyes. "Being under-staffed is hardly offering our best, Mindy Lee. At least we had enough people here to cover the shifts."

"There's no point paying staff who spend more time hanging out behind the building than inside where they're supposed to be."

"Well, while you hide out in here playing on your computer, the rest of us are working our tails off to fill every shift. A little regard for the staff would be good for morale."

The resentment in Cheryl's words pushed the air from Minnie's lungs. Playing on the computer? She opened her mouth, but no words came out.

"Excuse me. Is this a bad time?" Jackson stood in the doorway, his dark gaze swinging from Minnie to Cheryl.

Oh, great.

Cheryl stood, smoothing her work apron. Her face lit with interest, she stepped toward him, extending her hand. "Please come in. I'm Cheryl, the assistant director."

"It's a pleasure to meet you, Cheryl." He shook her hand, offering a pleasant smile. "I'm Jackson Young."

"Are you related to Emily, by any chance?"

"I'm her grandson."

"Ah. The famous photographer." Her smile deepened, pink filling her cheeks.

Minnie watched the exchange, wide-eyed. She didn't know either of them could be so courteous.

Jackson shrugged. "I don't know about famous but yes, I'm a photographer."

"Emily is always delighted to show us your photos. I'd love to hear more about your job. It sounds fascinating— traveling the world, taking pictures in exotic places, seeing your work in Life Magazine and National Geographic."

All of which had kept him so busy he hadn't cared that his grandmother lived alone. Jaw clenched, Minnie swung back to her computer and blindly pulled up an email. Anything would be better than watching Cheryl swoon over him.

In the silence, she glanced back, surprised to see color seeping into Jackson's face. Hands in his pockets, he squirmed under the woman's smiling gaze.

"I've always wanted to be a photographer," he said finally, "but only because there's so much to be said through pictures that can't be put into words."

"You obviously have a lot to say since your photos are so amazing."

Minnie rolled her eyes.

"Thanks, Cheryl. I appreciate that."

Ignoring the plink-plink of raindrops behind her desk, Minnie typed random words.

"So, I'm hoping Ms. Carlson has time to give me a tour."

"She's very busy doing...director stuff," Cheryl responded quickly. "I'd be more than happy to oblige."

"I don't want to bother—"

"Oh, it's no bother at all. I'm the assistant director so I do lots of tours."

Minnie turned to face them, biting her lip as Cheryl bounced on her toes, her round face glowing, eyes pleading. "Thanks, Cheryl," she said. "That would be great. I need to get these reports finished and over to Nick before I can go home." She moved her gaze to Jackson's. "I'm sure Cheryl can answer any questions you might have."

"This is perfect timing," Cheryl said. "We finished lunch and Gail, our activities director, is playing music trivia with the group. We might be able to catch the end of the game."

"Okay. Sure. Thanks." Jackson sounded strangely reluctant.

Minnie turned back to her computer as their voices faded. Staring at the screen, she ached for Em's presence at Open Circle, seeing her stricken face as they'd gotten into the Medi-van. Why hadn't she fought harder to move her back here? Why had she let him take over?

Plink-plink.

Tears burned the back of her throat and she squeezed her eyes shut. After a brief tour of their simple facility, weaving around orange buckets, she could imagine what he'd think. Not only would he not see Open Circle as the best place for his grandmother, he'd see it and the adjacent care facility as bottom rung.

Plink.

She wouldn't care about his opinion if it weren't about to cost her the only person she had left.

⁓

Jackson struggled to keep his passive photographer face on as Cheryl led him down the hall. From the outside, Open

Circle was a tired looking building that had experienced one too many harsh Minnesota winters, in desperate need of a fresh coat of paint. Overgrown, scraggly landscaping, a rutted mess of a parking lot. Inside, mismatched and battered furniture. Orange buckets caught water dripping from the ceiling.

He wrinkled his nose. And the smell. While he'd endured the stench of third world countries, he hadn't expected to encounter such a strong aroma here. An overpowering blend of perfume, powder, and urine.

They stopped in the back of what Cheryl called the activity room to watch the seniors gathered in a half-circle facing a young blonde. Perched on a stool, guitar in hand, she enthusiastically sang about daisies and marriage or something.

With one last strum, she asked. "Who remembers the name of that song?"

Standing behind the old people, half of whom were asleep in their wheelchairs, Jackson watched the girl work the disinterested crowd. A woman in the front row sang the first line of the song again, waving a red boa.

"That's right, Bertie," the girl chirped. "Daisy, Daisy. It's also called Daisy Bell. Can anyone guess when it was written?" She spread a smile around the group. "Here's a hint—long before any of you were born."

Jackson's eyebrows lifted. They looked ancient.

"Bertie, what do you think?"

The feather boa woman pursed her lips. "May twelfth?"

The blonde smiled. "Good guess. What *year* do you think?"

"Purple," a man in the second row said.

This isn't where Grandma belongs. These people were nuts.

The girl laughed. "Maybe they wrote it in purple ink.

Good guess, Bill. Daisy Bell was written in 1892. Isn't that amazing?" She repositioned her guitar. "Okay, we have time for one more. Sing along if you know the words."

Jackson folded his arms, itching to bolt from this depressing place. How did the staff stand it? His gaze wandered the room. There were about thirty old people but only two aides, looking bored out of their minds—a teen-aged guy and a middle-aged woman. For so many old people, shouldn't there be more help?

He turned to Cheryl. "Is this all there is for staff?"

She looked around the room then lifted her shoulders. "For today. Minnie fired three of our staff recently."

He frowned. "Isn't there a specific ratio that needs to be in place? Like one staff to so many old people?"

The woman pursed her lips and looked away. "Well, yes. But don't tell anyone. We could get in trouble." She glanced at him, eyebrows pinched together. "Minnie might even get fired. She's trying hard, but to be honest, she's in over her head with this job. I'm hoping she doesn't drive the center right into the ground."

And *this* was where the Mouse wanted his grandmother to be instead of in Rochester getting award-winning care? "It seems like a good thing I got here when I did so my grandmother gets better care. No offense, of course."

"Oh, none taken. Our wonderful seniors deserve dignity and respect. But like I said, this job is a little too much for Minnie. Emily is in a good place there in Rochester. That's where I would take my grandmother if she needed care."

Jackson rubbed the back of his neck, watching the blonde wrap up the useless singing activity. A burst of activity followed as the aides stood and started wheeling and leading some of the old people toward the front door.

"That's the end of our planned activities for today," Cheryl said. "I'll take you back to the front desk."

Following her down the hall behind several shuffling seniors with walkers, Jackson marveled at Cheryl's upbeat attitude working in a setting like this, for someone like the Mouse. They were fortunate to have her. As they reached the front reception area, she left him at the desk with an apology and a comment about having to be everywhere since they were so under-staffed.

Minnie stood near the front door, chatting with the feather boa woman. They shared a laugh and a hug before a serious looking old man took the woman's arm and almost pushed her out of the building.

Jackson leaned back against the wall. From this vantage point he could watch the Mouse in action. Cheryl's apologetic tone when she talked about Minnie made him think she'd been reluctant to share her real thoughts, but he needed to know the truth.

"Hello, dear Frances," Minnie said to a short, stout woman. "Did you have a good day?"

"I don't know," the woman said, hands lifted. "Did we get enough sandwiches made?"

"We did." Minnie helped her into a droopy sweater and buttoned it with a surprisingly gentle touch. "You did a great job today, dear."

"Do you think so?"

The childlike question drew a hug from the Mouse. She looked different, relaxed and happy. She seemed to really enjoy chatting with the oldies. Their faces lit up when she hugged each one of them. The small woman sang some of the daisy song. Minnie joined in as Frances shuffled out the door.

He frowned, watching the Mouse tease one of the old men who said something that made her laugh. This was like seeing her twin—completely different from the testy, cold woman he dealt with. This one had a beautiful smile.

As the last old person went out the door, she turned and hesitated, apparently seeing him for the first time. The smile disappeared behind a curtain of distrust. She lifted her chin and approached him. He pushed away from the wall.

"Done with your tour, Mr. Young?"

"I am. Your assistant was very helpful."

Uncertainty flashed in her eyes before she smiled tightly. "I'm glad. Are there any questions I can answer for you?"

He'd rather deal with the warm, happy woman than this one. He obviously didn't bring out the best in her. But then, she hadn't brought out his best, either. "Actually, yes. I'm wondering how often my grandmother comes to the program."

"Every weekday. She's the life of the party."

I'll bet. He nodded. "I see."

She stood silent before him, eyebrows raised. "Anything else?"

"Not at the moment."

"Then I'll let you be on your way. I have some paperwork to finish up before heading over to see Em this evening." She took a step toward her office.

He started toward the door, then turned back. "Actually, I do have one more question."

She paused.

"Why do you call her Em?"

Her eyes narrowed as if debating an answer, then her expression softened. She gave a tiny shrug. "She's been Em as long as I can remember. As a child, I had trouble saying my L's. I guess she told me to call her Em since that was a letter I *could* pronounce." She tilted her head. "Why do you?"

A corner of his mouth lifted. "For the same reason. Thanks for your time." Outside, he pulled in a deep breath of fresh sunshine and climbed into the rental car. Make that two things they had in common.

CHAPTER ELEVEN

Caught in a whirlpool of thoughts and emotions, Minnie heard only snippets of Pastor Karl's sermon Sunday morning. If she couldn't find qualified people to hire, the center wouldn't last another month. If the center closed, what would happen to her seniors? She'd have failed in her promise to Frank after barely four weeks.

Her fingers curled around the worship bulletin. She would *not* lower her standards. If she did, she might as well hire back the workers she'd let go. *God, where will I find the right people?*

The pastor's pleasant voice broke into her prayer. "So those are today's announcements, unless anyone else has something?"

After a brief silence, a woman's voice came from behind Minnie to the left. "I do, Pastor Karl. This is...hard to do but..."

Minnie shifted and craned her neck to find the person behind the wavering voice. Kim Raynes, the quilt shop owner, stood in the back row, tissue clutched in a white-knuckled grip. Pink blotches spread across her face as both chins quivered. Minnie's heart went out to her.

Pastor Karl moved down the aisle to stand beside the short, round woman, putting an arm around her shoulders as he held the microphone close to her. "Tell us what you need, Kim."

"Okay. Well, I own the Busy Bee Quilt Shop on 4th and Main. Or...I did." A tear slipped down her cheek. "Some of you know I closed the doors last week."

A murmur ran through the crowded sanctuary, heads shaking slowly. Minnie sighed. The cutest shop on Main Street.

"I couldn't...I wasn't bringing in enough money. And with Jim out of work because of his back, well..." She dabbed under her eyes then swallowed hard and straightened. "So I'm looking for work. I enjoy working with people. That's what I'm good at, but I'll do anything. I'm dependable and hard working. And Jim says I'm funny. Which I guess I am. Sort of."

The congregation gave a gentle chuckle. Heart leaping into overdrive, Minnie stood. "I have an opening, Kim."

Another murmur rippled around the room.

Her red-rimmed eyes went wide. "You do?"

"You'd be perfect for it. In fact," Minnie turned her gaze to encompass all two hundred people, "I have several. At Open Circle Adult Day, we offer a good salary and ongoing, extensive training, but there's one thing that's non-negotiable. You have to love working with seniors."

"Tell us about Open Circle, Minnie." Pastor Karl winked at her over the heads that swiveled back and forth.

She jumped on the unexpected opportunity, a tingle running down to her toes. "You all know many of our seniors. For most of you, they played a part in raising and educating you. That's certainly true for me. They served this community through their businesses or fed us from their farms. They protected us, provided entertainment, and donated endless hours of volunteering to keep Lawton thriving."

The congregation looked back at her, smiling, more than a few eyes shiny with tears, heads nodding.

"I'm so blessed to be part of their golden years. To offer them the dignity and love they've showered on this town is a privilege and a responsibility I don't take lightly. This job isn't for everyone," she added. "We all know that aging can bring changes and complications. Many of our clients are wrestling with dementia which makes them say or do things..." She lifted her shoulders. "Out of the ordinary."

Laughter as more heads nodded.

"We offer a safe place for them to spend their days, with fun and stimulating activities, nutritious meals, and lots of love. It's the least I can do for them. I hope some of you will join me." Looking back at Kim, she smiled. "Let's talk later."

The woman nodded, her face crumpling as she put the tissue to her nose.

Abruptly aware of the soapbox she'd stepped up on, Minnie dipped her head toward the congregation. "Thank you." Sinking back onto the pew, she knotted trembling hands.

A person near the front of the sanctuary started clapping. Within seconds, the room filled with applause. Heat scorched her cheeks as she looked around, touched by the smiling, enthusiastic response.

"Thank you, Minnie," Pastor Karl said, striding to the front of the sanctuary. "I know that those seniors fortunate enough to spend time with you at Open Circle are indeed grateful. I hope some of you will take her up on that offer and jump in to care for our elders. Now, let's close with prayer."

Minnie spent a half hour after the service chatting with Kim and several other women who were interested, or thought they knew someone who might be. Leaving the church, her feet barely touched the asphalt. As she climbed into her old car, her heart burst into song. Tears overflowed, making it difficult to see the road. *Thank you, thank you.*

She couldn't wait to get to New Life to tell Em about the unexpected morning.

Jackson stood on the front walk, studying the familiar white two-story with the wrap-around porch. Relieved to see it looking well-cared for, his gaze roamed eagerly from window to window—the living room in front, his grandparents' bedroom above on the left, his on the right. The big old kitchen in the back. He closed his eyes, smelling fresh bread, hearing his grandfather's snore, feeling the cool wood floor under his feet.

Unlike his parents' home, this one breathed life into the neighborhood. Wildflowers sprouted along the porch, waving in the breeze. The maple tree towered over him. He'd spent hours in its branches taking pictures of whatever passed below. By second grade he'd loved cameras, even the single-use disposables, his knack for photography the one interest he shared with his grandfather.

He climbed the wide porch steps and turned to look over the neighborhood, seeing it through the eyes of a ten-year-old. The Murphy house across the street. Old Man Johnson's duplex next to it. He squinted down the block toward the little blonde girl's house. Amanda? Alyssa? The girl with long pigtails, freckles decorating her nose. His first crush.

He turned his attention back to this familiar front yard. The trees were tall and strong, stretching up to a cloudless sky with long limbs that invited climbing. A smile creased his face. He'd have to climb that maple to take pictures before he left town. Maybe he really could see all the way to California.

Standing on the freshly painted porch with the double swing at the far end, warmth stole up from his toes. The first sense of home he'd felt since arriving in Lawton. It would be perfect if Grandma Em came out the front door wearing her ever-present flowered apron, a plate of cookies in hand.

His shoulders dropped. That wouldn't happen for a few more weeks at least. She'd made slow but steady progress these first days at New Life, but she had a long journey ahead of her. He sighed and turned toward the front door.

Daniel had encouraged him to check on Emily's house, to stay there if he needed to. The key hid where it always had, under the front mat. He shook his head. Only in small town America could you do that. The shiny brass key in his fist, he squeezed his eyes closed and wished he could find words to pray. It would be a prayer for Grandma Em's complete recovery, so she could come home and sit with him on the swing.

Loneliness loomed and he opened his eyes, pushing the sadness away. Since he didn't pray anymore, he'd do what came naturally—act. He'd told Daniel he would check on Grandma Em's old cat that the neighbor had been looking after. Run the lawnmower if the yard needed it. A glance over his shoulder showed neat trails across the grass.

Someone already cared for his grandmother's home in her absence.

He let himself into the house. Much as he hoped it would smell like his childhood, no lingering aroma of baking greeted him, no flowery grandmother smell. Instead, it was a bit musty, the silence magnifying his footsteps across the hardwood floor.

"Here, kitty, kitty." What had Daniel called the cat? Something strange like Edward or Elijah. "Ed? Alfred? Mr. Cat?"

He slid the curtains aside and opened the front windows, pausing to enjoy the summer warmth that sweetened the room.

"Brrrrow?" The deep voice made him turn. And laugh. The biggest Tom cat he'd ever seen sat on the braided rug beneath the mahogany dining room table, squinting as if he'd been woken from a deep sleep.

"Hey, kitty." He squatted and held out his fingers. "Why am I not surprised Grandma would house a cat like you?" The creature lumbered over, sniffed the outstretched fingers, and then flopped onto his side with a thud, purring loudly.

"I can take a hint," Jackson said with a chuckle, running a hand over the wide back before scratching his white tummy. "Wow. I bet you'd win a contest for being the largest feline in captivity."

The cat closed his eyes, content to be handled where he lay in a stream of sunshine.

Jackson stood and wandered through the house, smiling as he got reacquainted with each room. Little had changed. Returning to the living room, he stretched out on the couch and turned on the television. Mr. Cat jumped up and slammed his bulk into Jackson's stomach as he settled in. Stroking the soft fur, Jackson had the sense of being right where he was supposed to be. He closed his eyes with a sleepy smile.

"Who are you and what are you doing here?"

The loud demand, that seemed only moments later, startled him to his feet, sending the cat to the floor. Flattened ears and squinty eyes spoke volumes.

"Sorry. I must have dozed off." Jackson rubbed his eyes and forced his mind to clear.

"Most burglars don't take naps in the houses they're robbing." The tiny elderly woman in a navy running suit and gleaming white tennis shoes challenged him from where she stood inside the front door.

"I think you're right." Jackson retrieved the remote from the floor and clicked off the baseball game, then crossed the room, hand extended. "I'm Jackson Young, Emily's grandson. You must be one of the neighbors?"

She ignored his hand, her gaze running the length of him. Lips pursed, she folded her arms and harrumphed, obviously a sound of disapproval. "Her grandson, eh? Where've you been all these years?"

Here we go. He shoved his hands into his pockets and lifted his shoulders. "In California."

"You could have at least visited on a holiday."

He nodded over a swell of defensiveness. "I certainly would have if I'd known she was alive. My parents had a disagreement with my grandparents when I was young. After we moved away, my folks told me she died. I only recently found out she's alive and still living in Lawton."

The woman's faint eyebrows jumped up, then lowered into a scowl. "What kind of parents would do that?"

Good question. "I don't know what their reasons were."

"You know she had a stroke?"

"I arrived that afternoon." A deep sigh. "Not a good way to meet for the first time in so many years."

115

"Not at all. And now she's stuck over in Rochester for rehab." Her pale blue eyes darkened. "That your harebrained idea? She would have been fine staying right here where her friends are. And where Minnie could get to her every day. They're as close as blood relatives, you know. Have you met Minnie?"

"I have."

Smiling fondness replaced the frown. "Darling girl. She's been Emily's pride and joy all these years."

Darling girl? Irritation burned his throat.

"Don't know what Emily would've done without her. And now the poor girl is trying to run the adult center *and* run back and forth to see her grandmother."

He bit his lip, hard. Did everyone consider *her* the rightful grandchild?

"Too much for such a sweet little thing, in my opinion." She shook her gray head. "Dumb idea to move Emily, if you ask me."

His spine stiffened. It would be over his dead body that he'd let *his* grandmother get dragged to that old nursing home. Or the fun house they called a senior center.

He opened his mouth, but the woman moved past him toward the kitchen. "Better get some food out for Elmer Fudd."

Elmer Fudd! No surprise she'd name the beast after a cartoon character. Trailing the woman and the lumbering cat, he asked, "Are you her next-door neighbor?"

"To the east. My husband and I moved in eighteen years ago, right before your grandfather died. Emily sold off most of the farmland not long after that."

She pulled a can from the refrigerator and removed the plastic lid. His nose crinkled at the aroma as she dumped the contents into a ceramic bowl.

"I don't remember my grandfather talking much."

"Richard didn't waste a lot of words. He and Emily were as opposite as could be, but he sure doted on her." She set the bowl of brown mush on the floor. Elmer attacked it with gusto. "She missed him terribly after he died."

Pain seared through his chest. How could his father have walked away from his aging parents like that? There'd been a brief mention of his grandfather's death, and then the lie about his grandmother's. What had been the point?

"Are you planning on staying around here long?"

He blinked his attention back to her. "I'll be here another week or so, then I have to be in New York for a few days. I'll be in and out over the summer. I want to spend as much time with my grandma as I can."

The woman's wrinkles relaxed slightly as she nodded in what seemed to be approval.

"I'd like to stay here in her house. Would that be okay with you?" Why was he asking her permission?

"That's a fine idea. Old Elmer is pretty lonely here by himself. I come as often as I can but with my husband having Parkinson's, I can't leave him for long."

"I'm sorry to hear that. Is there anything I can do to help? I could run some errands for you, mow the lawn?"

An actual smile tilted her thin lips upward. Success!

"That's very nice of you. I just might have a few things you could do. What did you say your name was?"

"Jackson."

"That's right. The photographer. Emily is always quick to show us the magazines with your pictures in them. She's quite proud of you. I'm Audry. No e."

Warmth filled his chest. "It's a pleasure to meet you, Audry. I'm glad to know my grandma has such a good friend close by."

She paused at the front door and looked back at him, her thin, veined hand resting on the doorknob. "And I'm glad to know Emily's grandson isn't the scoundrel we'd thought. You seem like a fine young man. Goodbye."

He stood looking at the empty doorway. He had a lot of work to do to prove to Lawton he wasn't a "scoundrel." With a snort, he looked down at the cat cleaning his sizeable paws.

"There's one person who won't ever believe differently, Elmer. No matter what I do." For some reason, the idea stung.

CHAPTER TWELVE

Tuesday afternoon, Minnie stood at the front door and waved as the three women left Open Circle, new employee packets in hand. A grin plastered on her face, she did a spin and posed *a la* Michael Jackson, giggling when Jody applauded from behind the front desk.

"Well, aren't you happy this afternoon."

"I'm not happy," Minnie insisted. "I'm ecstatic. We've added three wonderful ladies to our staff."

"Isn't it great? So how's our sweet Emily? Is she behaving at the rehab center?"

Leaning against the counter, Minnie propped her chin in her hand. "Surprisingly, she is. Last night she showed me how she can already lift a two-pound weight with her right arm. Her speech is clearer too."

Jody relaxed in her chair, hands folded on her rounded stomach. "That sounds like our Emily." She wiggled pencil-thin black eyebrows. "Do you get to see her hunky grandson much?"

Hunky? "Not really. We make sure one of us is there every day. We're her cheering section."

"What a blessing he showed up when he did."

Minnie bit her lip. Not the word she'd use, but she had to admit Em seemed happy to have him back in her life. She straightened. "Well, back to work. I want to get all of the new ladies' paperwork processed this afternoon, so they can start training tomorrow."

"Hey, Min?"

Halfway to her office, she turned. "Hmm?"

"I'm glad you're the director now. It feels better coming to work every day. Everyone seems happier."

For a moment, Minnie couldn't breathe over the lump in her throat. She blinked quickly and offered a wobbly smile. "Thanks, Jody. I'm glad to hear that."

In her office, Minnie plopped into the chair, the smile still playing at the corners of her mouth, and closed her eyes. "Thank you, Lord," she whispered. "We make a good team, don't we? As long as you're leading."

Now if Em would fully recover, life would be perfect. Well, with one exception.

An hour later, Jackson jogged up the Open Circle steps and pulled open the front door, glad for the brush of cool air against his skin. At least Minnie could afford air conditioning for this run-down shack.

"Hi, Jackson." The pierced and tattooed receptionist welcomed him with a bright smile.

"Hi. Wow, I'm amazed you remember me." He stopped at the desk, waiting until the girl looked away before glancing at her nameplate.

"We don't get too many famous people here in Lawton, so it's pretty easy to remember you."

"People might remember my photographs, but they

don't usually have a clue who I am. Is Minnie in her office?"

"She is. She's talking to a roofer about getting repairs done. I think they're wrapping up. Have a seat and I'll let her know you're here as soon as they're finished."

"Thanks, Jody." He settled in a chair and thumbed through a *Reminiscence* magazine, listening to the muffled rumble of the roofer's voice followed by the Mouse's.

A moment later, the door opened slightly.

"So, what do you think? Friday night work for you?" The man's voice had a personal note that brought Jackson's head up. Who did roofing on Friday night?

"Ted, that's not—"

"C'mon, Mindy Lee. You'll get a good discount on the repairs and," the tone turned suggestive, "we'll have some fun."

The door banged shut. Jackson looked over at Jody who scowled at the closed portal. While the words were muffled, the Mouse's biting tone came through clearly and he pressed his lips together. Apparently, the roofer didn't understand who he was dealing with. Or he liked living dangerously.

When the door crashed open, a lanky young man in overalls, cheeks blazing pink, strode through the reception area and straight out the front door. Jackson dropped his gaze to the magazine in his hands while the Mouse slammed drawers in her office, muttering loudly.

"Can you believe him, Jody?" She emerged from her office, face flushed. "Like I would even consid—Jack!"

He peeked over the top of the magazine. "Hi."

"What are you doing here?"

She certainly had a way with men. "I want to compare notes about Grandma's progress."

Her eyes narrowed. "Compare notes. With me."

He nodded.

"Well...okay." She rubbed her temple with two fingers, then waved a hand toward the front door. "That was—"

"The roofer," he said. "I heard."

She bit her lip and glanced sideways at the grinning receptionist. "I suppose you did." Pulling in a deep breath, she lifted her chin. "Jody, we'll be just a few minutes."

"Sure thing."

Jackson followed her into the office, glancing at his watch; she'd made it clear this would be a short visit. Settled in the chair across from her, he waited while she stacked papers and rearranged items on her desk. When she finally looked up, the color in her face made her eyes a golden brown.

"So," she said, then dropped her gaze and pushed her hair behind pink-tinged ears.

Without the usual armor in place, she seemed suddenly young and vulnerable. He smiled to himself. He'd never expected to think of her in those terms. "So, I wanted to get your impression on how you think Grandma is handling the rehab."

She leaned back and folded her arms, studying him from under a lowered brow. "Does it really matter what I think?"

He held back a sigh. Did she have to make everything a battle? "Of course."

She turned her gaze toward the window, lips pursed, her reply slow in coming. "Well, I think it's actually going pretty well. I had supper with her last night. Her speech is improving. She showed me how she's using the walker now." A smile softened her expression. "I don't know which of us was prouder."

The smile vanished as her gaze swung to his. "How do you think she's doing?"

"Good. Really good. But…"

A dark eyebrow lifted.

"It's just… She gets confused sometimes. She'll forget what we're talking about in the middle of the conversation. Or she forgets my name. That seems weird."

Minnie nodded. "Weird but not unexpected."

"Was she like that before?"

"Not in the slightest."

He blinked. "So why aren't we worried?"

"Confusion can be caused by a whole host of issues. The stroke, of course, but also by having the daily routine disrupted, being in an unfamiliar place, even an infection. If there's dementia, some of the confusion can be permanent, but most of the time it improves when they return to their normal routine."

His heart skipped a beat. "She has dementia? Shouldn't we do something? There must be medication she can take. Or brain exercises? I hear those are important to keep things working right." He wanted to reach across the desk and shake her out of her calm. "Maybe we should have her seen by a specialist in…brains." *Brilliant.*

"Not at this point."

Gazes locked, his fingers curled around the arms of the chair to stay anchored. He itched to leap to his feet, shout at her, get her to react. Pulling in a silent breath, he forced his heartbeat to slow. Okay, he could play this game. He settled back. "So, what do *you* think should be done?"

"Nothing."

"*What?*" So much for calm.

"Nothing at the moment."

When she leaned forward and clasped her hands on the desk, he lowered his chin. The wise social worker was about to enlighten the clueless photographer.

"It's not at all unusual for seniors to become confused

after a traumatic event like this. I'm praying it's temporary and that once she's home, where everything's familiar, she'll get back to normal."

Ahh. The push to move her back to Lawton.

"In the meantime," she continued, "we focus on getting her strong enough to function on her own. I've spoken to the doctor and the D.O.N about it."

"D.O.N?"

"Sorry. Director of Nursing. They're keeping an eye on her, of course."

"But what about medications? I've heard of different Alzheimer drugs. What about that?"

Mouth tugging down at the corners, the Mouse shook her head. "We can't load her system with meds right now. She's had a really nasty experience. The more active she becomes, the stronger she'll get and the better her brain will function.

"I'm seeing more and more of the old Em coming out," she added. "But it's hard to watch the struggle, isn't it?"

The fight drained out and he dropped back in his chair. "Yeah. Really hard."

They sat in silence for a moment, then Minnie straightened and met his gaze. "So, anything else?"

And just like that, she dismissed him. He folded his arms. "You've hired a roofer?"

She glanced away, lips pressed in a tight line. "No, I haven't. That was the first of several contractors. And he bid himself right out of a job."

Grinning, he nodded. "I heard. Good for you for not letting him push you around."

Her chin lifted. "I'm not someone who gets pushed around, Mr. Young." She held his gaze. "By anyone."

With the sting of that reminder, he stood. "I've learned

that the hard way. Thanks for your time. I appreciated hearing your thoughts about my grandmother."

The challenge left her eyes and she opened her mouth, but he turned and left the office before she could fire another shot.

"Have a nice afternoon, Jackson," Jody said.

He managed a tight smile before stalking out of the claustrophobic building. Distance. He needed lots of distance between him and the Mouse.

"It's not about her," he told his reflection in the rearview mirror, backing out of the parking spot. "It's about Grandma Em. That's all that matters."

With a satisfying squeal of tires as he rounded the corner, he pointed the car toward Rochester. As a photographer, he knew how to put his focus on the right place, which was Grandma Em. As he did, the Mouse would fade into the background. Where she belonged.

CHAPTER THIRTEEN

After a morning spent training the new caregivers on safety precautions, Minnie arrived for Saturday brunch at New Life thirty minutes later than she'd planned. She paused outside Em's room to smooth her hair and calm her racing heart, then put on a smile and pushed the door open.

Jackson relaxed in a chair next to the bed. Em was dressed in a new black sweat suit, hair combed, lipstick on. Seeing Minnie, she sat up straighter and, with a beautiful, full smile, held out both hands.

"Here's my girl," she said.

Minnie's heart soared at the full sentence spoken with no hesitancy. "Sorry I'm late. Don't you look beautiful this morning?" She pressed a kiss to Em's forehead. "I love the new outfit."

Em's left hand grasped hers tighter than the right. "From Jack," she said.

Jack? Minnie glanced at him. "He has good taste."

"Yes. Good."

Jackson got to his feet and presented his arm. "Shall we go to the dining room, Mrs. Young?"

Em chuckled as she clasped his arm. Following them from the room, Minnie matched her stride to the older woman's short steps, pushing away the sting of Jackson's dismissive attitude. Of course she wanted him to be good to Em, but watching them grow closer made her feel shut out. *She'd* been the bright spot in Em's life for decades. She rolled her eyes at the childish attitude.

The aroma of bacon, coffee, and pastries beckoned them down the hall. As they neared the dining room, Em and Jackson exchanged a smile. Minnie looked away. Maybe she should come back later. After Mr. Grandson left.

"Here comes our beautiful Emily. And without her walker." In a starched white shirt and black pants, the portly young man at the double doors beamed at her. "Good for you."

"No walker. Anymore." Her pale face glowed under his attention. "Time to walk."

"More like strut," he teased. "You look about ready to dance." He winked at Minnie. "All right, then. Three of you for brunch? Let me show you to your table."

She'd make a break for it now. "Em, I think—"

Em turned toward her, a hand extended. "Dear heart, I'm so glad. You're here. Hungry?"

Familiar fingers wrapped around Minnie's, warmth enfolding her heart. She smiled past the burn in her eyes and nodded. "Always. Let's eat."

During the meal, Jackson entertained his grandmother with stories of his travels, photos he'd taken, people he'd met. Minnie listened without comment. He had one story after another from decades of work, building his reputation one photo at a time. It explained why he'd never returned to Lawton. What did their small town have to offer a world traveler, other than his only relative who had desperately missed him?

From under a lowered brow, Minnie studied his animated face as he and Em laughed over his story about a curious baby giraffe in Tanzania. Focused on her halting conversation, quick to hold her hand, he seemed to truly care about his grandmother. Minnie dropped her gaze to the eggs she'd pushed around her plate.

Em glowed under the attention, asked questions about his life, laughed easily at his stories. She seemed to prefer his presence over anyone else.

Orange juice slid hard over the knot in her throat, and Minnie turned her attention to the crowded room. Laughter and conversation floated over the clink of silverware on china. Family and friends of all ages relaxed at linen-covered tables. Elders in wheelchairs, or with walkers or canes nearby, seemed to soak in the energy.

Much as it pained her to admit it, this had been the right choice for Em. The focused plan of action, the constant encouragement from trainers and aides alike had coaxed the weak, frightened woman of two weeks ago back to the smiling, engaged woman Minnie adored.

So why wasn't she dancing on the table? Her glance moved to Jackson as he placed his hand on his grandmother's. Maybe she would after he went away. And he would. His busy, important life would call him from their sleepy town and he would leave Em behind. Probably with promises to return soon, but he wouldn't.

"How about we sit out on the patio for a bit?" Jackson's voice cut into her angry thoughts.

"Yes. In the sun," Em agreed. "Cold in here."

They strolled out to the back patio and settled her under a green umbrella. Minnie scooted her chair to Em's left and lifted her face to the sunshine, delighting in the touch of warmth against her air-conditioned skin. "Mmm. This is perfect."

"Yes. Very perfect."

"This weather is a lot like Sacramento's," Jackson said from her right side. "Blue skies, mild temps. It doesn't get any better than this."

"You don't live here?" Em asked.

He glanced at Minnie. "Not anymore. I live in Sacramento, remember?"

"Oh." She frowned. "Do you like it there?"

What if Em decided she should live closer to her globetrotting grandson? Ridiculous. She wouldn't leave Lawton. Minnie's gaze slid toward Mr. Grandson again. He'd obviously cleaned up for the visit. Shaggy hair brushed and shining under the sun, clean shaven, a starchy blue cotton shirt. She caught a glimpse of the man Jody referred to as "the hunk." The warmth in his smile, which had certainly never been directed at her, seemed genuine.

Minnie's eyes narrowed. He'd never answered her initial question about why he'd stayed away, or what brought him to Lawton now. There had to have been a catalyst of some sort. Maybe he really did think his grandmother had money. She obviously had more than Minnie knew about if she could afford to pay for her rehab at this swanky place. Maybe "Jack" knew more than he let on.

His cell phone rang, and he excused himself to take the call. Em settled back in her chair, still smiling. Minnie wrestled the anger under control. She wouldn't let his presence rob her of enjoying her limited time with Em.

"How are you?" Em's inquiry pulled her from the dark swirling thoughts.

She slapped a smile into place. "Good. Remember the

new caregivers I hired this week? They're turning out to be fabulous. It's really a God-thing, Em. I thought I'd have to close Open Circle since I couldn't find anyone to hire, but He provided the perfect women. Even Cheryl thinks they're okay, and she doesn't like anyone. Especially someone I like.

"And then a few days ago," she continued, intent on sharing all of her news before Jackson returned, "Ted came in to do an estimate on repairing the roof. Remember Ted? The tall, skinny redhead? We went to high school together and—"

"Mindy Lee." Em reached for her hand, leaning forward in the patio chair. "What's wrong?"

The piercing blue eyes rested steadily on her. This was the Em she knew, cutting through the blarney to the real issue. The woman who had supported her through teenage angst, arguments with her mother, and the fear of leaving home for college.

"Tell me."

Minnie turned her face away, willing the tears back. Em's fingers tightened on hers. "Oh, Em," she sighed. "I miss seeing you every day, having lunch with you. Eating your cookies."

"I'm sorry."

With a sniffling laugh, Minnie waved a hand at her. "Don't apologize. You've been working so hard here. I'm being a baby."

"What else. Is wrong?"

Jackson stood at the far end of the manicured lawn, still on his phone. Minnie watched him, fighting the sudden urge to throw something at him. What could be so important that he'd make his grandmother wait while he talked? Maybe a girlfriend. Right. Who would put up with him?

"I have. Room."

Minnie swung her gaze back. "What?"

"In my heart. For both of you."

A tear slipped out. Did Em always have to know what she was thinking? "I know."

"No." Em shifted in her chair and clasped Minnie's hand with both of hers. "Dear heart, look at me."

She did, slowly. The love shining on the lightly wrinkled, beloved face flooded her aching heart with soothing warmth.

"I can love you. Both." Em glanced at Jackson. "He is an answer to prayer. But you." She lifted a hand to Minnie's face. "You are my heart."

The words were like a spigot, releasing the tears. "Oh, Em." She pressed the thin hand to her cheek. "I'm so afraid he's going to hurt you again. I don't understand where he's been or why he came back. And I'm afraid that when he leaves, I won't be able to mend your heart."

"We will know. Later. He will tell us." She smiled. "I love you. With everything I am. He can't. Stop that."

Minnie held her gaze, seeing the sparkle she'd desperately missed these past weeks. Then she laughed, brushing at her tears. "Am I that obvious?"

"To me." She patted Minnie's cheek. "We are connected."

Minnie soaked in the declaration. "Yes, we are."

A clearing throat broke into the moment, but this time Minnie didn't care. Em's gentle words had calmed the tormenting fear.

"Are you two ladies okay?"

"Yes." Em patted his empty chair. "Sit."

Jackson's gaze shifted between them before he settled beside her. "That was my friend, Noah, with some news about the New York show."

"Good news?"

"Very. Pierre, the gallery owner, has come up with some new publicity ideas that are amazing. Unfortunately, it means I have to run to New York to look over the drafts."

Minnie looked past Em at Jackson. "You're doing a show in New York?" After Em's reminder, she would focus on being interested rather than irritated.

"I signed on right before I came to Lawton." His green eyes sparkled in the sunlight. "It's an amazing, totally unexpected opportunity. Pierre, who owns the studio, wants to highlight humanitarian work around the world, and he decided he liked my photos enough to build a show around them."

"*You* do humanitarian work?" The words were out before she could censor them.

He shifted and gave a partial shrug. "I photograph the life-changing work that's being done. To help spread the word."

She leaned back in the patio chair. That put him and his work in a completely different light. But even that didn't excuse his absence of two decades. "So, the show is all your work?"

He shook his head. "Several good friends will be part of it too. They're amazing."

"My Jack is a star," Em said proudly, patting his hand.

Minnie ignored the ping in her heart. "How long will you be there?"

"This time? A couple of nights. I'll have to go back for more extensive planning, but this will be a quick visit." He grinned at his grandmother. "I don't want Minnie to have to carry all the weight of keeping you in line any longer than she has to."

"Pish." She waved a hand at him, smiling. "I'm doing great."

"Yes, you are." Jackson lifted his gaze to Minnie's. "And we're proud of you."

A heartbeat of hesitation, then she nodded. She didn't trust him but maybe someday they could be on more friendly terms, in a distant sort of way. Depending on what his excuses were. Maybe. In the meantime, she would warn him against dropping out of Em's life again. And make sure he got the message.

CHAPTER FOURTEEN

Pierre Guillaume Finest Arts. Jackson stopped, jostled by people hurrying along the sidewalk, and stared at the elegant signage. A tingle raced up his body, and he burst into a smile. It was truly happening. He'd had plenty of shows over the years but nothing on this scale. Nothing in New York City.

"Hey, Young! You gonna stand out there grinning like a baboon, or come in and get to work?" Noah's voice floated over the hum of traffic. Standing on the front step of the studio, hands on his hips, a wide, welcoming grin filled his face.

"Russell, you sure know how to give a compliment." Jackson weaved through the crowd and threw his arms around his friend. "I'll bet the women go wild when you whisper those sweet nothings in their ear."

Noah returned the backslapping hug and laughed. "Of course they do. Now get in here. We've got work to do."

The studio was more incredible than the photos he'd seen. Parquet flooring gleamed beneath spotlights, and white walls provided a clean background for the oversized paintings on display. Jackson paused before a colorful painting that covered most of the back wall.

"I think that's called 'Leftover Paint,'" Noah whispered loudly.

Jackson grunted in agreement. Wild strokes of reds, yellows, purples, and blues extended from one end of the canvas to the other. He tilted his head, following a long stroke of blue. Maybe it signified a road? A pathway? A mistake?

"Ahhh, here he is." The unmistakable French accent spun Jackson around. An elegant man approached, arms extended, thick white hair brushed back from a tanned and wrinkled face. Blue eyes sparkled below bushy brows. "The artiste we have been waiting for, no?"

He grasped Jackson's shoulders firmly and welcomed him with light kisses to each cheek. Pierre Guillaume was an icon in the art world, a giant in both photography and sculpting, though not in stature. To be welcomed into the master's studio set Jackson's heart pounding.

Pierre leaned back. "You had no troubles arriving here?"

"None at all, Mr. Guillaume."

"*Mais, non!*" Strong fingers squeezed his shoulders before releasing him. "I am Pierre. No monsieur. Come, let's talk with this crazy friend of yours in my office. We have a show to plan. And I know it will be the best of the season, yes?"

Propelled by Pierre's arm around his shoulder, Jackson glanced at Noah who fell into step with them. His friend grinned and winked.

"You are caring for your grandmother, I hear. That is a good thing. Tell me about the lovely woman."

As they crossed the studio toward a back hall, Jackson told him about his long-lost grandma and her journey back to health. In the back of his mind, he waited to awaken from this amazing dream.

At dinner in the hotel bar that evening, Noah leaned back, sipping a diet coke as he studied Jackson. "So, tell me how it went with your grandma."

Jackson smiled. "You'll definitely have to meet her."

"Is she impressed with your work? Did she ask where you've been for twenty years?"

"Her stroke has made talking a little challenging, so we haven't had any in-depth conversations. I've told her a lot about you, though."

"Me? Why?"

"Because you're a lot more interesting than me."

Noah threw back his head with a laugh. "So you've been making things up."

"Maybe. But you gotta admit, we've had some crazy adventures, Russell."

"Yeah, we have, haven't we?"

Jackson pulled out his phone, smiling as he showed photos of Grandma Em in the garden area of the rehab center, at dinner, and playing cards. "She's really doing great. Getting stronger every day. If our show goes well, and my name gets back out there, I hope I'll have a more normal schedule. I want to spend time with her, which is impossible with the way I've lived the past few years."

"Your name's already out there," Noah said absently, scrolling through the photos. Whoa." He sat up. "Who's the looker with your grandma?"

"What? Oh. That's Minnie."

"Minnie? As in Minnie Mouse?"

He cringed. It sounded awful aloud. "Her real name is

Mindy Lee. I guess Minnie is a nickname. She and my grandma are family friends."

Noah gave a soft whistle. "I'd like a family friend like that."

Like Minnie? He leaned over and looked at the photo—Minnie and Em sitting on the rehab patio last week. He'd caught her in an unguarded moment. Sunlight on brown waves, pink cheeks, dark eyes laughing at the camera. Too busy ducking from her barbs, he rarely had time to admire her looks.

Noah flipped through more photos. "These are great, man. Only you can find beauty like this amidst wrinkles and missing teeth." He chuckled. "Love this woman with the feather boa." He typed something then handed the phone back and asked, "So is it serious?"

"Is what serious?"

"You and Minnie Dee."

Jackson's eyebrows jumped to his hairline. "No! Well, if you mean is she serious about hoping I'll drop dead, the answer would be yes. Let's just say I'm not one of her favorite people."

"She's gorgeous, my man. You'd be an idiot to let her get away."

Jackson slid his phone into his back pocket, shaking his head. "At this point, I'm happy when we can have a civil conversation. And with this show to plan, I wouldn't have time even if she *didn't* hate me."

He planted his elbows on the table and leaned forward. "We've got to make this show work, Russell. After the Blunder, I was blacklisted. This is my chance to remake my name and get back on the request lists. I don't have a lot of time left with my grandma."

A clock ticked in the recesses of his mind. Not nearly enough time.

Em wiggled her fingers out the car window. "This is wonderful. I haven't been on a ride. Forever. Thank you."

"It's my pleasure." Minnie pulled into the McDonald's parking lot. "How about some ice cream as we explore Rochester?"

"Perfect."

Minutes later they slid back into traffic, chocolate shakes in hand. They shared comments about the weather, the variety of colors blooming in yard after yard, and how much they loved summer.

Minnie parked at a neighborhood playground where they finished their ice cream. Having Em all to herself made her heart sing. "I'll be so glad to get you home."

"Me too. Soon." Em stuffed a napkin into her empty cup and smiled. "Mmm. Good." She looked so much healthier now—cheeks pink, the familiar sparkle back in her eyes.

"The doctor said your progress has been amazing."

She shrugged. "I have had good help. I am ready to go home."

Minnie reached over and squeezed her hand. "I'm so proud of you."

"Can't keep me down for long."

"Ain't that the truth," Minnie agreed with a laugh. Soon life would be back to normal. And then perhaps Jackson would go back to wherever he came from.

"Let's walk," Em said.

The suggestion spoke volumes. Grinning, Minnie opened her door. "Race you to the swings!"

Em laughed as she climbed slowly out of the car. When Minnie reached her side, Em took the proffered arm. "I don't ever want to use the walker. Again."

"Well, don't start running laps quite yet, okay? Let's get all of your strength back before you slide into your tennies and take off down the road."

Ambling along the smooth asphalt path, Minnie lifted her face to soak in the afternoon sun. "What a glorious day."

"It is." Em walked quietly for a moment, her gait still slightly uneven. "I miss Jack."

Minnie pressed her lips together, the soft declaration dimming the sunlight. How did that man manage to weasel his way into the conversation from halfway across the country? "He'll be back tomorrow."

"I know. He's a good man. Don't you think?"

"He certainly seems to love *you*," she said evasively. Good men didn't ignore their family for decades.

"Do you like him, Mindy Lee?"

Her cheeks warmed under Em's direct gaze. "I hardly know him. I haven't spent time with him like you have."

They stopped walking and Em faced her. Even having regained a few pounds, she still seemed fragile. "You would like him. If you took the time. He's interesting."

Minnie raised her eyebrows. "What am I, chopped liver?"

Em laughed. "Sometimes."

"You'd better watch it, young lady," Minnie warned. "I might leave you stranded here."

"No, you wouldn't," she said with smiling certainty.

"Well, you'd still better watch it."

Em took her arm again and squeezed it as they continued their stroll. "I am blessed."

Minnie's eyes burned at the simple statement. With all she'd been through in her nearly eighty-two years, Em still found the bright spot in everything. She wanted to be like her when she reached eighty. It wouldn't hurt to try to be like her now actually. She pressed the fingers that grasped her arm. "Me too."

When Minnie arrived for dinner the next day, Em sat perched on her bed chatting with Robert.

"Uh oh. It's the boss man. This looks serious." She turned a mock frown toward Em. "Have you been sneaking out at night?"

Robert laughed and straightened from where he leaned against the wall. "We caught her again," he said, reaching out a hand in greeting. "Good to see you, Minnie. You're just in time for the announcement."

She shook his hand. "I'm all ears."

"I asked Miss Emily how she felt about going home on her birthday."

"Tuesday?" A smile bloomed as she looked at Em. "And I'll bet she said it would be the best birthday ever."

Em beamed, hands clasped below her chin. "I did. Isn't it wonderful. News?"

Settling beside her on the bed, Minnie wrapped her in a hug. "Absolutely. I'm so proud of you!"

"We all are, Miss Emily," Robert said, then turned his attention to Minnie. "Dr. Wilson gave her the all-clear to head home with a few provisions."

Holding Em's hand, she nodded. There would no doubt need to be help until Em was steady on her feet and able to live independently. "And what would those be?"

He held Em's gaze. "Some in-home help for a bit, to make sure there are no falls that might land you right back here. Continued therapy to keep increasing your strength and stamina. And regular trips to the ice cream shop in Lawton."

Em laughed. "I can do that last one. For sure."

"I'd better go with you," Minnie said, bumping against her shoulder, "to make sure you're okay." Jackson would be off running a show somewhere or taking photos deep in a jungle. Or so she hoped.

Robert laughed with them. "That sounds like a good plan. We have a list of occupational and physical therapists in the area who have excellent track records with stroke patients. I'll get a copy to both of you tomorrow." He glanced at his watch and headed toward the door. "Now I'd better get home for my own dinner or my wife will have my head. We'll keep the discharge discussion going over the next few days to get all of your questions answered."

"Thank you," Em said. "This has been good. For me."

"Wow," Minnie said. "That's high praise from a woman who hates anything medical. That might have to go on your next brochure, Robert."

"I definitely want that in writing, Miss Emily. Have a good evening, ladies."

In the silence that followed his departure, Minnie leaned her head against Em's. "I'm so excited you're coming home. This has been a long journey."

"Yes. But it's time. To go home. I will do my therapy and keep getting stronger. But," she shifted to look at Minnie, "do I really need someone. With me?"

"They must think so since it's one of the conditions of being released. At least for a bit." Expecting this, Minnie had prayed for ideas on the drive over. "How about this? Remember Kim from the quilt store downtown?"

Em pursed her lips, nodding slowly. "Round?"

Minnie giggled. "Yes, she's a bit round. She's one of my new caregivers, and an absolute delight. What if she came in the mornings to get you up and going for the day, and then between Jackson and me, we can cover the rest. I can help you get ready for bed too."

Em sat quietly for a long moment, frowning, then her thin shoulders lowered. "I like Kim. I can do that. For a bit."

Yes! "You won't need help for very long. Just until you've got all your strength back. Like Robert said, we don't want you falling and ending back here, right?"

"Right. Not coming back. Ever."

"That's my girl." A flash of concern tempered the tingling joy of Em coming home. Jackson still held the purse strings. Since he'd driven the decision for Em to come here, he'd no doubt want to make the home care decision.

He could argue all he wanted, but she knew the people in Lawton, the amenities, and she knew seniors and caregivers. Mr. Grandson didn't have a leg to stand on if he wanted to debate this decision. Thank goodness Em still had use of both of hers. Minnie would make sure she received the best of everything, even if it meant getting less sleep as she balanced Open Circle and caring for Em.

She was family, whether he liked it or not.

CHAPTER FIFTEEN

The nearly two-hour drive from the Twin Cities airport had taken forever. Finally in Rochester, Jackson parked beside Minnie's battered Buick at the rehab center, climbed out of the car and jogged up the sidewalk to the front door. "Get a grip on yourself, Young. You've been gone all of three days."

Inside, he greeted Lindsay at the front desk and headed down the familiar hall toward his grandmother's room. A burst of laughter welcomed him as he entered. "Well, look at these beautiful card sharks."

"Jack!" Grandma Em beamed at him as she set her cards down and pushed out of the chair. "Welcome home."

He gave her a gentle hug. Aside from Ima Bird at Noah's, there'd never been anyone to welcome him home. He leaned back and smiled down at her. "It's great to be back. And look at you practically jumping out of your chair. You look wonderful."

"I feel wonderful."

He dropped a kiss on her head, then released her tiny frame and turned toward Minnie, who stood beside the table. Her smile seemed warm and genuine. He clenched his fists at his sides to hold back the ridiculous urge to hug her. "Hey, Minnie. You look good. Apparently, she didn't get too out of control."

"Not too much." Her cheeks wore a pretty pink as she smiled. "If I didn't know better, I'd say you missed your hometown."

"Well, I missed my family, that's for sure." He folded his arms over the goofy dance in his chest. "I'd say you two held up pretty well in my absence."

Minnie dropped back into her chair and flung a hand across her forehead as she exclaimed, "How ever did we manage before you came along?"

He chuckled at her lousy Southern drawl. "I've wondered that myself." He retrieved a chair from across the room and settled beside his grandmother. "So, have you behaved yourself?"

"Pish." She waved a hand then laboriously picked up her cards. "I always behave."

"Ask her to define behave," Minnie added, without looking up.

Grandma harrumphed as she focused on arranging the cards in her hand. Jackson stuck his hands under his thighs to keep from reaching out to help her. The strength and control of her right hand still lagged.

She lifted her chin and looked down her nose at Minnie, then played a card. "Spades."

"Oh, sure." With a sigh, Minnie selected a card from the pile. She had double what Em held. "You picked that because you know I don't have any."

"Of course. Why play if not to win?"

"Good point, Grandma." He winked in reply to Minnie's good-natured scowl. "I seem to recall that even when I was little, she never, ever let me win. I had to work for it."

"Hollow is the victory. You didn't work for."

"Wise words from Lawton's card shark," Minnie grumbled. She played an eight with an exaggerated flourish. "Diamonds. So, are you going to tell Jackson your good news, or shall I?"

⁓

Jackson opened the passenger door as Minnie came down the sidewalk in a bright pink T-shirt and black capris, clutching the colorful ribbons of the three mylar birthday balloons dancing behind her. "Good morning, Miss Carlson."

"Good morning, Mr. Young. My, such service." She smiled and slid into the car, gathering the balloons into her lap. "I'd stash these in the back but..." She glanced over her shoulder at the mass of balloons, then raised an eyebrow at him. "Did you buy out the party store?"

"Pretty much. I'll stuff you back there on the ride home," he said before shutting the door. He grinned at her laughter as he went around to the driver's side and climbed in. Turning the key in the ignition, he looked at her. "Let's go get our favorite girl."

"We can't get there fast enough."

He steered them through town and onto the highway that pointed toward Grandma Em, relieved Minnie had remembered to bring her smile. He'd hoped the drive to Rochester wouldn't be a repeat of their drive home when they'd left Grandma at the rehab center.

The trip to New York had been a good break for them both. She seemed a thousand times more relaxed around him now.

"I'm so glad we're bringing her home on her birthday," she said.

"Me too."

"How are plans going for your show in New York?"

"Great. I've had other shows, but none this size, and none with two other amazing photographers. It's more work than I expected but also more fun."

"What all is involved?"

"A lot more than I would have guessed." As they zipped over miles of highway, he shared details about the planning, the assignments that produced these particular photographs, and a little about Noah and Paul. He steered the car off the highway into Rochester and the conversation back to her. "So how are things at your work?"

"Wonderful." Her smile deepened. "I hired three new caregivers who've worked out beautifully. I had worried about bringing the staffing numbers back up after I had to let a few go, so I'm thrilled with how God worked it out."

"Cheryl mentioned that you were short staffed," he said, "so I'm glad you like the new people."

She went still, the earlier smile now a frozen replica as she looked at him.

"Did she?" Ice edged the words. "What else did she mention?"

Of all the topics you could have picked, Young. "Only that some people had been let go. She said you're new to the job, so you've been, you know, getting used to running the place." His voice trailed.

Minnie stared out the front windshield. "I see."

I see what an idiot I am. "I'm sure it's hard to try to run a place like that."

"Meaning?"

"Well, you know. With needing more staff, and the

building in sort of rough shape." Winding through town, he glanced at her rigid profile. "I'm sure you're doing a great job. It's just...you know, you're young and new to being in charge so you're bound to run into some difficulties. But everyone can see how much you love the old folks." *Stop talking!*

The final blocks to the center were silent. Even the balloons had stopped their incessant squeaking. It didn't seem Minnie was even breathing. Apparently, she didn't like Cheryl being right about how she ran the center. Next time he'd talk about Elmer Fudd.

～ぃ℘

Minnie kept her lips sealed as Jackson parked at the curb. She'd been right. Cheryl had shared her misgivings about Minnie's leadership with Jackson, and he'd bought into it. She climbed out with her balloons, waiting as Jackson removed his dozen from the back. Hers tangled in the breeze, bounced off her head and wrapped around her arm. His floated behind him in perfect, color-coordinated order.

She followed him into the building and down the familiar hallway. *This is Em's day. You can pout when you get home. Right now, toughen up.*

Em stood by the window in her black running suit, red hair combed, smiling up at the cloudless sky. Minnie paused in the doorway to absorb the happy sight, Jackson beside her.

"She looks ready to go," he whispered.

She glanced up and managed a smile. "Let's do it."

Laughter and fanfare filled Em's send-off as one staff person after another stopped her in the hallway to say goodbye. From the dining room wait staff and Chef Paul, to housekeepers and therapists, each shared kind and encouraging words.

More people lined the sidewalk to Jackson's car, with Robert and Kerry standing beside the open passenger door. Em smiled, hugged, and waved until the car finally pulled away from the curb, then dropped her hands into her lap and sighed. "I'm glad to leave. But it was a good place. To get strong."

From her seat in the back, Minnie watched Em turn a smile toward Jackson. "Thank you for choosing it."

Minnie looked out the window to avoid Jackson's gaze in the mirror. While she'd admit it had been the right decision, she couldn't face his gloating in the reflection.

"It was a team decision," he said.

Two hours later, with Em settled in her rocking chair by the front window, Minnie handed her a small bowl of raspberry sherbet with chocolate chunks sprinkled on top, then perched on the arm of the couch. "Sorry you're stuck with only us for your birthday. We'll celebrate big when you're stronger."

Em's crooked smile filled with love. "This is all. I need. My family and ice cream." She focused on taking the spoon in her right hand and scooping out a bit of the treat. Her sigh of satisfaction relaxed Minnie's shoulders. It took all of her willpower not to offer help. Em would have pushed her right off the couch.

Jackson settled on the other end of the couch with a large bowl of the dessert and turned his attention to his grandmother. "Thanks for letting me hang out here, Grandma. I've enjoyed getting to know Audry and her husband. And Elmer and I are buddies now."

"I'm glad."

"It's good to be home," he said.

The dessert stuck in Minnie's throat. Home. Even after

a 20-year absence, this was more Jack's home than hers. She swallowed the frozen lump with difficulty.

"You'll always stay here when you come?" Em asked.

"If it's not a problem."

Her pale face lit. "Never. I want you here."

Minnie took their empty bowls to the kitchen, then paused to lean against the counter, tears stinging. Em had said she had enough love for both her and Jackson. While her adult brain knew it was true, her child's heart ached at the thought of being left out on holidays, of Jackson whisking his grandmother away to exotic locales. Of being alone.

"Minnie?"

Jackson's voice yanked her from her pity party. Without looking at him, she rinsed her hands. "I'll be right out."

"No rush. She fell asleep in the chair." He leaned back against the counter and folded his arms. "Man, I'm glad to have her home."

"This old house must hold wonderful memories for you." The words nearly choked her.

"Mmhmm. But you know what? The memories come from my time with her."

Irritation flared, and she turned. "So why—"

His phone rang, and he held up a finger. "Hold that thought. I've been waiting for a call from the studio."

Minnie wiped the counter as he chatted, then returned to the living room, relieved the call had cut off her demand for answers. She wouldn't have it out with him today—not on Em's birthday, and not in her house. But eventually she'd find out the truth. She prayed it didn't break Em's heart.

Jackson finished the call, then resettled on the couch, Grandma still snoring softly in the rocker. Minnie flipped through a magazine in the corner chair, feet tucked under her. She didn't look up.

"So, we should talk about getting care lined up for her," he said softly, glancing at his grandmother who didn't stir.

Minnie closed the magazine and lifted her gaze to his. The pinch to her eyebrows looked more sad than mad. "There's a wonderful woman at the center who's already said she'd be happy to help Em."

Of course she'd decided on a plan already. "Shouldn't we talk about it together before a decision is made?"

She glanced at Emily before responding in a loud whisper. "Do you know anyone around here?" She might as well have shouted at him.

"Not yet, but—"

"I've lived here my whole life. I've known this woman for years, and I've worked with her at the center. She's got the perfect temperament to work with our strong-willed Emily, and she'd love the extra hours. Do you have a different suggestion?"

Her arched eyebrows were like a waving red flag. "No, but it would have been nice to be consulted before the decision was made." If Grandma weren't sleeping, he'd be yelling.

"I'm open to ideas, questions, whatever."

He released a silent snort. Maybe Grandma felt sorry for her because she was alone, but he couldn't imagine *choosing* to share life with her. "Have you talked with my grandma about this arrangement?"

"Of course." The angle of her chin lifted a fraction. "I would never make plans *for* her."

Zing. "Does she know the girl you want to employ?"

"Yes, she knows the *woman* who will be helping her get up and dressed, and practice her therapy exercises."

"And she approves? Or didn't she have the option?"

"I approve." His grandmother's voice cut in clearly. She held his gaze steadily. "I don't want help. But I will. Let Kim help if the doctor says I need to."

She pushed slowly from the chair and looked from him to the Mouse. "I need you to get along. Stop fighting. Over me. I will make my own decisions."

She shuffled out to the kitchen, using the back of the dining room chairs to steady herself. Jackson watched her go, then closed his eyes for a moment. He'd try not to argue with Minnie in Grandma's presence, but get along? Dang near impossible.

CHAPTER SIXTEEN

Jackson set his bowl on the table, poured two glasses of milk, and then settled into his chair. He waited as Grandma Em bowed her head and said a simple grace before asking, "So what is it you like about Open Circle? Why is it so important to go back?"

Grandma Em crumbled saltines over her bowl of tomato soup. "It's home."

"This is home. That's…a mess."

"Be nice, dear." She took a careful sip. "That mess is my friends."

Who could be friends with people who didn't act normal? He pursed his lips. "But…they aren't like you. So many of them are…have…issues."

Serious blue eyes met his. "I have issues."

"Not like them. You aren't…" Crazy. Nuts. Out of it.

She went back to her soup, obviously willing to let him dig a deeper hole.

"You have all your faculties," he said finally. That was a better word than crazy.

"Questionable right now," she said, a smile tugging at the corner of her mouth.

Leaning back in his chair, he tossed his napkin on the table. *Just say it, Young.* "Some of them can't even complete a sentence. Some are pretty nutty, actually."

"They're still my friends."

The simple words punched the air from his lungs.

She set her spoon down and looked up, hands resting in her lap. "Do you have friends, Jack?"

"Sure." A few.

"Would you still be their friend if they had cancer?"

"Of course." His argument was about to go up in smoke.

"When they get old?"

"I'll be old then too. But that's—"

"Even if they have Alzheimer's?"

A tremor shot through him. She didn't have it. And he'd do whatever he could to make sure it stayed that way. Including keeping her out of that loony bin. "You don't."

"But some of my friends do. Should I not be their friend. Anymore?"

From the corner she'd backed him into, he frowned. "I don't want you to get it. And if you keep hanging around them…" It sounded ridiculous.

The smile that crinkled her eyes sent heat rushing into his face. "It's not contagious, Jack."

"I know that." He pushed away from the table and went to stand at the window. From the research he'd done, he knew she couldn't "catch" it, but it was incurable. Terminal. And they didn't know what caused it. "Everything I've read says we have to keep our brains active. Stay stimulated."

"Yes."

Turning, he leaned against the window frame. "You

won't be if you spend your days with people who can't...
who don't..."

"Of course I will." She took a bite of her half-sandwich
and chewed slowly. "Staying here alone would be worst.
Worse. I want to be with my friends. I belong there. We all
do." Her calm smile clashed with his frown. "Together."

The idea she would become like some of them scared
him far more than taking photos in the roughest
neighborhoods or most isolated villages ever had.

"I love Open Circle," she said. "I bake for them. I sing. I
help lead Bible study. It's good for me." She waved at his
chair. "Sit so I don't have to shout. Please."

He trudged back like a dutiful ten-year-old and slid
into his seat.

"I want to go." She sipped at her soup. "Minnie needs
me there."

He closed his eyes to hide the roll. Minnie needed to
shut the firetrap down. "Cheryl told me it's going to close
down in a few months."

"Cheryl is sour grapes."

"Cheryl?" The helpful, devoted assistant director was
probably the only thing holding that place together. "She
loves her job. She said she'll be devastated when it closes."

Grandma Em studied him for a long moment.
"Nicholas chose Mindy Lee. To be the director. She is
doing her best, but she needs help. From everyone." She
shifted to face him. "Minnie is a wonderful social worker.
She has a gift. For people. Intuitive. And she's hard work."
She frowned. "A hard worker."

Jackson held in a snort. Hard work was more accurate.

"She can make changes but not alone. This community
needs Open Circle. I do what I can." She reached a thin
hand toward him. He took it automatically. ""Why don't
you come," she said. "Spend time there."

The sudden sparkle in her eye set off warning bells. What did she have in mind?

"They said I need help for now. A helper. Right?" She cocked her head. "You come with me. Be my helper."

He wanted to pull his hand away, fold his arms and refuse. But he'd do anything for her. And darned if she didn't know it. "For you, I'll try to suspend judgment."

"And you'll come along? To help?"

He sighed. "Fine. If Minnie will let me in the door." He managed a tight smile. "I'm not high on her list of favorites, you know."

She squeezed his hand. "You are on mine. Now, I think I need a nap."

Helping her to her temporary first floor bedroom, he covered her with a blanket and left her with a kiss to her cool forehead. Much as he doubted Minnie could keep the center open, he'd do what he could to support her. Because Grandma Em had asked. It seemed like wasted energy.

⁓

Minnie and Jackson stood in the Open Circle reception area watching the staff happily greet Em Monday morning.

He crammed his fists into his pockets, brow drawn down. "This must be what it feels like when your kid goes off to school."

She glanced sideways at him. "Just remember she's not five. And she won't appreciate it if we hover."

He waved a hand at the commotion. "I know, but I don't want her to overdo it."

"We have an amazing staff here, Jackson. They'll keep an eye on her." *Like they did long before you came on the scene.* "She's surrounded by people who adore her."

"I'm glad for that. She asked if I'd stay to keep an eye on her. Would you mind?"

"If you're going to interfere with the staff or the programming, then yes, I mind."

"I have no intention of interfering." He held her gaze. "She was so determined to get back here, I want to know why it's important to her."

Minnie opened her mouth then snapped it shut. "This is home to her," she said. "You're welcome to make it yours, as well. But please let the staff do what they're trained to do."

"Yes, ma'am."

She curled her fingers against the urge to smack the condescension off his face and turned toward the front door. So much for thinking they could be friends. "I'm glad we understand each other." A smile loosened the clench of her jaw as she greeted Frances. "Good morning, dear Frances. Ready for another big day?"

Thirty minutes later, Minnie closed her office door and dropped into her chair, turning toward the window. So far, Jackson had stayed in the background, chatting with Cheryl, watching as the center's energy moved from the front door to the activity room.

Resting her head back, she closed her eyes. "Lord, how much longer do I have to put up with him? He thinks so poorly of Open Circle that he has to stay to make sure Em is okay. Can't you send him away?"

The ping in her heart made her cringe. "Sorry. I suppose that's the wrong attitude. But still..." She released a deep sigh. "Well, if you won't make him go away, give me patience when he starts questioning everything we do. And keep my hands busy so I don't throw something at him when he suggests Em would be happier elsewhere."

She turned toward her computer. It promised to be a long week.

—⁓—

Jackson watched Minnie disappear into her office. The quiet click of the door felt like she'd slammed it in his face. She couldn't be more obvious that she didn't want him here. What was she hiding?

"We're heading in to Bible study, Jackson." Cheryl's voice broke into his thoughts. "Would you like to join us?"

He pushed away from the wall and met the woman's hopeful gaze. "I sure would." *I'll be checking out every aspect of this place.*

Following Cheryl around the corner and into a meeting room, his eyebrows lifted. Only a handful of seniors were gathered in a circle.

"Jack! Are you joining us?" Grandma Em patted the empty chair beside her. "Sit here."

He gestured toward the corner. "I thought I'd just be a mouse in the corner—"

"Nobody is a mouse in God's eyes, young man." The thin, gangly man on her other side waved him into the group. "We could use a younger perspective on the Word."

Perspective? He hadn't opened a Bible in years. "Oh, I don't think—"

"Don't be shy, Jackson. Everyone is welcome here." Cheryl's hand at his back propelled him into the circle.

Slinking across the worn carpet, he settled beside his beaming grandmother. "I didn't bring a Bible."

She winked. "We have plenty."

The gangly man bowed his head and the group did likewise. Jackson lowered his chin but kept his eyes open.

The simple prayer slowed his racing heart, releasing the breath he'd unknowingly held.

"So, Jackson, is it?"

He started and looked toward the man who was apparently the leader. "Yes, sir."

"How about you read today's passage. It's Psalm 23." He smiled. "You might have heard it once or twice."

"I don't think..." He took the Bible Grandma Em held out, frantically digging through memories of Sunday School. Where was Psalms? *What* were Psalms? He let the book fall open and hid a grin. There, right in the middle. He lifted his gaze. "I'm sorry, sir. What part?"

"How about the whole part?"

The group chuckled. Jackson's ears burned. With Grandma Em leaning lightly against him, he held the heavy book so she could see it, cleared his throat, and started reading. The familiar words relaxed his shoulders. A hush fell over the room as he finished the passage and he closed his eyes, hoping he wouldn't be called on to say something wise.

"Thank you, Jackson. Those are mighty powerful words. Helen, what do those verses mean to you?"

A tiny woman with sad eyes ran her hand lightly over the page. "It's a reminder that God walks beside me every day as I miss my Frank," she said softly.

A gentle murmur ran through the group.

"He's right beside you, Helen," Cheryl said, taking the woman's hand. "That's a message straight from God to remind us we don't go through trials on our own."

Jackson held back a snort. God had left him high and dry after the Big Blunder. If that wasn't a trial where he could have used some heavenly help, he didn't know what was.

"Jackson, what do you think?"

He blinked to the present and found eight pairs of eyes resting expectantly on him. He glanced at Grandma Em and bit down on the sarcasm that threatened. Rubbing his nose, he searched for a kinder answer. "Well, I think that life is...full of trials."

Graying and balding heads nodded around the circle, faces wrinkled from decades of life turned toward him, waiting.

"I think maybe the verses are meant to give comfort. And hope. Without hope, I think there are times when we'd give up." Such as three years ago. "But if we're surrounded by people who care about us, we can get through whatever it is." *Or we can plow through on our own.*

"With God leading the way," a man across the circle added.

"Exactly." *Or not.*

The conversation moved on and Jackson hid a sigh as a line of sweat trickled down his back. He hadn't sounded like a complete idiot anyway. Grandma Em spoke up, the gangly man responded, and the group laughed.

Jackson moved his gaze slowly around the circle. These people seemed sane and intelligent. With walkers or canes nearby for most, it obviously wasn't their brain that needed help. A corner of his mouth twitched. This kind of spirited conversation seemed much better for Grandma Em than hanging with the loony bunch in the other room.

As the study wound down, his phone vibrated. He excused himself and went out to the reception area to answer. "Jackson Young."

"Hey, Jack. It's Dave Emerson in Minneapolis."

"Dave! Great to hear from you. How are things in the Cities?" He leaned against the wall outside Minnie's office.

"Good. Did I catch you on a shoot in Africa? Or atop Mount Everest?"

Jackson laughed. "Actually, I'm about two hours south of you. In Lawton, my hometown."

"That's pretty tame for your kind of photo shoot."

Night and day different. "I'm visiting my grandma. So what's up?"

"Well, I've had a cancellation and I'm hoping you can give me some names of people who might want a free spot for a show."

"Okay, give me the details."

"I have a great year of shows lined up between well-known local artists, a few new ones, and a few you probably know. But my August person just cancelled due to a family crisis. They forfeited their payment, so I've got a weekend open. Unfortunately, it's short notice. Any ideas?"

Jackson straightened. Dave's gallery was mid-size, classy, and well known for showcasing premier artists. His heart kicked into a gallop. "Yeah. How about me?"

"What? That'd be awesome!" Excitement rang through the phone. "I heard from Noah that you've got a show in New York City later in August. Could you do one here too?"

"I think it'd be a great way to promote the NYC show. We could bill it as an off-Broadway kind of thing. I've got photos already being printed."

Minnie passed him and went into her office.

"If you take care of the publicity," he added, "I'll get the rest of the prints ready."

"Man, that would be great. I'd love to have you back. It's been what—four years? Or maybe longer?"

"Four sounds right." His last show before the Big Blunder.

"You're sure you can swing this? It's seven weeks from now. Not a lot of time to prep."

"A lot of it's already in process."

Minnie emerged from her office, glancing at him as she hurried back down the hall. He turned and followed her progress until she disappeared around a corner.

"Wow." Delight filled Dave's chuckle. "I never considered *you'd* step in. You're always a huge draw."

His old friend's words sent warmth through him. "Can't guarantee what size crowd you'll get, but I'd love the opportunity."

Jackson clicked off the call, shaking his head. Interesting how the unexpected opportunity presented itself right after reading the verses about God presence in daily life. *Don't get all mystical, Young. It's simply a coincidence.*

He headed toward the music in the activity room, his step light. More exposure. Another opportunity to rebuild his career. He could only hope someone showed up.

CHAPTER SEVENTEEN

From her office window, Minnie watched Jackson help Em ease into his car, wondering who was more exhausted— Em after a busy first morning back at Open Circle, or herself after seeing Cheryl whisper nonstop to Jackson. She doubted Cheryl's sweet nothings in Jackson's ear were sweet. Probably more about how Open Circle had floundered under her watch.

"We are *not* floundering," she said aloud, pulling up the financial pages on the computer. The numbers knocked the indignation from her lungs. "Or maybe we are."

The center's income had dropped after Frank's death and the departure of three clients to nursing facilities. They'd added one new client but only two days a week. She released a long sigh. Hardly a drop in the leaking financial bucket.

She leaned back in the chair, rocking gently. The atmosphere of Open Circle had dramatically improved over the past month. The new aides were energetic, focused, and happy to be working. Bonds were quickly forming between them and the seniors. Even Chief now had a favorite—gentle Ruth.

"Lord, how can we keep running without money?" she whispered. In the silence, she mentally handed the center over to God, as she'd done daily since stepping into the new position. "I can't do this alone."

She sat up and studied the numbers again. She'd hoped to hire one more aide, but that wasn't feasible for now. So...she'd cut her pay and pick up the slack. It was the only logical option. In her social worker role, which constantly took a back seat to the director role, she needed to stay involved in activities to assess the seniors. And she'd do paperwork at home after dinner.

"Please let this be enough to keep us going. And could you send us a few more clients? Soon?"

A short-term fix for a long-term problem, but the decision filled her with fresh determination and reminded her of the mantra—whatever it took. She'd do whatever was necessary to keep Lawton's seniors healthy, happy and loved. Even if it meant Em spent more time with Jackson than with her.

On Friday, Grandma Em declared she would stay for lunch to celebrate the end of her first week "back in the real world."

Jackson frowned at her across the table during coffee. "I don't know. I think it might wear you out."

She smiled through the steam rising from her cup. "Dear Jack. Thank you, but I have to eat. Somewhere."

"But—"

Grandma Em looked past him and beckoned, her bracelets jingling. "Mindy, dear."

Jackson felt a presence behind him.

"Yes, ma'am?" Minnie's cheerful voice.

"I would like to stay for lunch. Today. Would that be okay?"

"Of course, silly goose. You must be feeling stronger."

"Very much."

Jackson wanted to argue the point. While she didn't look nearly as exhausted as she had the first few days, that didn't mean she should spend another hour or so at the center.

A hand lightly touched his shoulder. "What does your grandson have to say?"

He glanced up in surprise and opened his mouth.

"My grandson can stay too, if he wants," Grandma Em said.

Minnie giggled—giggled!—so he closed his mouth. Meeting Em's smiling gaze, he sighed dramatically. "Whatever Mrs. Young wants is fine with me."

"I'll tell Bill to add two for lunch."

Jackson glanced back as she turned away. She wasn't glaring at him anymore. If he didn't know better, he'd think he even earned a few points when he joined in the trivia game on Wednesday and helped serve coffee yesterday. The cease fire might not last long but being in her good graces felt like a victory. Of sorts.

He'd learned quite a bit about Open Circle and dementia this week. And Minnie Mouse. Little was what he'd expected. Once he got used to the occasional outbursts of a few seniors, he relaxed and enjoyed the activities. The quirkiness of each person had become more entertaining than irritating. A few times he'd had the strangest sense of being part of something, not watching through a lens.

When coffee time ended, he headed to the kitchen.

Minnie lined clear plastic pitchers on the counter beside the sink.

He cleared his throat. "Since we're staying for lunch, what can I do to help?"

Minnie glanced at him, filling a pitcher with water. "I can run her home later, if you'd rather leave."

Earlier in the week, he'd have taken her up on the offer. "I'd like to stay." He lifted his shoulders. "I'm hungry."

She set the full pitcher on the counter and turned to face him. "Okay. How about you help serve?"

He met the challenge in her gaze then reached toward the box of serving gloves. "At your service, Madam Director."

As she turned away, he caught the twitch of her mouth. "Bill, put this man to work so he stays out of my hair."

"Shall do," came the chuckling response from the large bald man at the stove. He turned and nodded at Jackson. "Bill Nordine."

"Jackson Young."

"Ahh. Emily's storied grandson."

Jackson flinched as Minnie exited the kitchen shaking her head.

"Welcome to my humble kitchen. Now let's get to work. That hungry bunch out there will be banging their silverware if we don't get the food out on time."

Tucking his camera case under the counter, Jackson washed his hands before snapping the gloves on. Following Bill's direction, he filled the water pitchers, set the tables, retrieved serving utensils.

Bill filled plates with steaming vegetables, roast beef, and mashed potatoes, handing them to Jackson and two other staff to deliver to the tables. It was organized chaos with a constant hum of voices and movement. Jackson took plates to clients, poured milk and water, and assured several seniors they could start eating. More than once he served the wrong thing, grateful Cheryl kept an eye on him to correct the mistake.

Moses ate a gluten-free diet so he couldn't have the roll. Bertie didn't like potatoes of any kind on her plate. Chief was lactose intolerant and not happy about it. He informed Jackson he'd been the police chief for twenty years so if he wanted milk, he should get it. Cheryl slipped into the conversation to remind the disgruntled man, in graphic detail, what happened when he had milk. Jackson swallowed hard and returned to the kitchen.

"So, Jack," Bill said as they wiped down the stove and counters, "how goes the photography business?"

"Great. Lots of interesting assignments and freelance work lately."

"Do you work for any particular studio or magazine?"

"Nope." Jackson sprayed the serving counter with disinfectant. "I've been lucky enough to make a living as a freelancer. I get calls for specific shoots, or I do my own work and hope someone will buy the photos."

"And that brings in enough to live on?"

"Usually." The scarcity of jobs after the Big Blunder flashed through his mind. The most recent assignments from repeat customers still felt tenuous, like the art world waited for him to screw up again. "I've done it long enough that my name is fairly well-known among editors, which helps."

"So you must travel a lot."

"Quite a bit, although I can pretty much create my own schedule. Like now. I've put off a couple of assignments for a month or two so I can spend time here with my grandmother."

"How did the famous photographer work out in the kitchen, Bill?" Minnie's voice came from behind and

Jackson glanced back. Her smile, directed at the cook, seemed to include him as well.

"Like a champ." Bill winked at Jackson. "I think he has a career as wait staff if he ever gives up his camera."

Jackson laughed. "I'll keep that in mind." He turned to look at Minnie. "I enjoyed it, but I don't know how your staff keeps it all straight. Cheryl had to follow me around to make sure I didn't kill off clients with the wrong food. Or step on Frances."

Her smile faded as she gave a nod. "Thank goodness for Cheryl."

"Is Grandma ready to go?"

"I think so. Much as she would like to stay for the afternoon, she's wiped out. She's sitting with Jody at the front desk."

Jackson retrieved his camera and then extended a hand to the cook. "Bill, thanks for letting me crash around in your kitchen."

"You're welcome back anytime, Jack."

Leaving Minnie and Bill chatting, Jackson headed toward the reception area, letting a wry smile emerge. Bill might welcome him back, but he doubted the pretty director with the fiery disposition would be happy about it.

Sunday evening, Minnie arrived at Em's with a chicken dinner in a picnic basket. Parking beside Jackson's rental, she gathered the basket and reading materials she'd collected for Em and headed toward the house.

Jackson stood on the front step, holding the door open. "Mmm. That smells great. Chicken?"

The unexpected courtesy brought a flush to her cheeks

as she approached. "And potatoes. A little salad and rolls."
She passed him, glancing over her shoulder. "You're
welcome to join us, if you want."

"Thanks, but this is your time with her. I grabbed
something earlier."

As Em emerged from the kitchen, the smile that lit her
face warmed Minnie's heart. "Dear heart! Do I smell
chicken?"

"Your favorite. I hope you're hungry." She set the basket
on the dining room table and quickly went into Em's
waiting hug.

"I'm off to the gym, ladies. Enjoy your evening." Jackson
gave a short wave and headed out into the warm
summer air.

Minnie offered Em a crooked smile. "He's going to be
pretty buff when the summer is over if he keeps up these
workouts."

"Buff?"

"Fit. In good shape." After they'd brought Em home
from rehab, Jackson had suggested she have dinner with
Em whenever she wanted while he went to the new fitness
club. The offer had come out of nowhere, and she'd been
waiting to discover his ulterior motive. Apparently, he
didn't have one.

She unloaded the basket. "Let's eat. I'm starved."

Lawton news filled their dinner chatter, along with
how delightful Kim was as a morning helper, and
upcoming events at Open Circle. They cleared the table
and settled in the living room with tea and brownie bites.

"Are you more settled now. In your job?"

Minnie nodded. "I think so. I adore the new staff we've
hired. They're full of energy and ideas, and they love all of
the seniors. Even Chief." She sipped her tea. "I couldn't ask
for more."

"Cheryl is better?"

She grimaced. "Well, I guess I could ask for more from Cheryl. She isn't as hostile as before, but she won't be happy until she's the director." Meeting Em's sympathetic gaze, she shrugged. "I'm doing better at ignoring her comments, but occasionally she gets in a zinger that makes me want to— Well, let's just say they're hard to ignore."

"She is jealous."

"She'd love to see me go down in a flaming wreck."

Em chuckled. "You won't. You are too good."

"Too stubborn."

They sat quietly for a moment, Em rocking gently in her chair. She looked at Minnie and raised her eyebrows. "Have you gotten used to having Jack there?"

Minnie bit her lip, struggling to keep her expression neutral, and studied the vase of fresh wildflowers on the coffee table. "Sure."

A pause and then, "Mindy Lee."

"Really. I'm so busy I hardly see him."

"He is behaving?"

She grinned. "He *is* a grown-up, you know. I don't think his behavior is a problem."

"So what is?"

The stroke hadn't affected Em's perception. Minnie sighed and turned her gaze to the window. "I feel like he's waiting for me to screw up. I'm pretty sure that whatever Cheryl has said makes him think we're the next Titanic." She turned back, lips pursed. "Doesn't he have work to do somewhere else? Like Siberia?"

Em's crooked smile emerged. "I think he likes being here."

I wish he didn't. Wasn't it enough she had Cheryl watching her every move? Now he had to, as well?

169

"Well, there isn't enough going on around here to keep him busy taking pictures. He'll have to leave eventually."

Em took a bite of brownie and chewed slowly. "But he will come back again. We're family."

The simple statement burned into Minnie like a branding iron, marking them as family and her as...not. She released a long sigh. "I'm sorry, Em. I know he's your grandson, but I have enough pressure trying to turn Open Circle around without people who want it closed breathing down my neck."

"He doesn't want the program to close."

"So he wants you to think."

"Mindy Lee." She waited for Minnie to look at her. "Have you tried liking him?"

Ouch. She had *dis*liked him from that first moment in the hospital. "He doesn't make himself very likable where I'm concerned." Nor did she, if she were honest. "If he's not a supporter of Open Circle, I can't like him. Ever."

"He's learning. He hasn't had family or friends. Around him."

"I can tell." The acidic response burned in her stomach. "Sorry."

Em smiled sadly. "Jack's dad, our son Tony, was very much like *his* dad. My husband, Richard. Tony said little but had big dreams. Too big for real life. He got angry with us so they left. I didn't know where they went." Her gaze fluttered out of focus as pain crossed her face. "I missed them. Jack especially."

Minnie's heart pinged. "I know you did." So if she truly loved Em, why would she want Mr. Grandson to go away? It would break Em's heart. And that would break hers.

"To have him back is..." Em lifted her gaze heavenward. "God heard my prayers." She met Minnie's gaze. "And He

170

hears them now. I hope you will give Jack a chance. He is trying. To get along. He wants to be part of our lives."

"Part of *your* life," Minnie corrected.

"Both of us. He likes having a family. You are the quarrelsome sister he never had."

A laugh slipped out. "I most certainly am not. He's a bossy older brother. And a know-it-all."

"See? Like brother and sister." She held out her hand. "Will you keep trying to get along? For me?"

Minnie took her hand. Why not ask for the sun and moon to switch places?

Em squeezed her fingers. "God will help. If you ask."

A sigh rattled deep within Minnie's chest. "I know. So I'll ask." She grinned. "It will be a miracle if we can get along."

With a wink, Em took another brownie. "That's His business, you know."

CHAPTER EIGHTEEN

During coffee and donuts Tuesday morning, Bertie patted Jackson's cheek. "You are a nice man," she said. "I have a granddaughter you should meet."

He laughed and wagged a finger at her. "I've heard about your matchmaking, Miss Bertie. Right now, I don't have time to date."

"There's always time for love," she said with a smile. "Let me tell you about my George. He didn't think he had time for love either."

Bertie had become one of his favorites. While she couldn't remember what she ate for breakfast, she told countless, funny stories about raising six kids, running the Five & Dime for forty years, and life after retirement. And she was Minnie's greatest cheerleader. Right after Grandma Em. And Moses. And Chief.

In his second week of visiting Open Circle, Jackson had gotten to know the seniors, astonished to find many of them far more lucid than he'd originally thought. He visited with them and watched the daily routine, wanting to know why they loved Minnie so much. Why most of the staff enjoyed working with her, with the exception of a very few. For a center supposedly going downhill, these were happy, engaged people.

"No! I don't want to. I need to get back to the farm. Get out of my way."

Okay, most of them. Jackson looked past Bertie to the newest participant in the center, ninety-four-year-old Elwin. After four days, he was no happier than his first day at Open Circle. He told anyone and everyone he had crops to plant, equipment to fix, and horses to shoe. He didn't have time to sit around playing Bingo.

Minnie squatted beside Elwin's chair and spoke quietly. His shoulders relaxed slightly as he focused on her, the edge slipping from his bushy-browed frown.

Still listening to Bertie's tales, nodding occasionally, Jackson pulled his camera from under his chair. First he focused on Elwin's craggy profile, leaving Minnie blurred in the background. Then he focused on her as she looked up at Elwin. He zoomed in on her slender fingers where they rested on Elwin's faded red flannel shirt.

When he captured the exchange of their smiles, he couldn't stop his own. Minnie stood and helped Elwin to his feet, strolling beside him as he shuffled to the table where a group worked on several oversized puzzles. Jackson kept shooting, taking in the colorful scene—

sunshine streaming over unruly white hair, laughter illuminating wrinkled faces, gnarled hands holding simple puzzle pieces. *Beautiful.*

He paused. How many years had he photographed elders in distant lands, but never considered his hometown as a place where the lost could be found?

Minnie turned from the table and met his gaze across the room. Habit made Jackson refocus the camera on her. The photo he snapped caught her with her arms folded, the corners of her mouth lifted, a smile in her eyes. With sunlight spilling over her, the moment was bright and unexpected. *Gotcha!*

She turned away to speak to a staff member, and he returned the camera to its case with a satisfied grin. Grandma Em would love a copy of that.

After the morning rush the next day, Jody spoke up as Minnie passed the front desk. "Hey boss, you've gotta see this."

Minnie detoured from heading to her office and joined Jody behind the desk. "You have time to surf the web?" she teased.

"I don't have time to breathe some days," came the quick retort. "I saw this last night." She leaned back to let Minnie get closer. "Isn't it beautiful?"

Minnie's eyebrows shot up. "It's Bertie!"

"In amazing living color. I love how the boa highlights her eyes."

"But...why is there a picture of Bertie online? What site is this?"

"It's a photo contest. Bertie's photo is front and center."

Expertly framed, the photograph focused on the woman's smiling face, the feathers of her ever-present boa adding a blurry contrast to her wrinkled, powdered skin. Minnie spun away, stormed into her office, and yanked her purse from her desk drawer. As she passed the now wide-eyed Jody, she said, "I'll be back."

The short drive to Em's house barely gave her enough time to formulate an opening sentence. She thrust the car into Park and strode up the sidewalk. Flinging open the front door, she stomped into the familiar home.

Jackson emerged from the kitchen and stopped, coffee mug halfway to his mouth. Hair tousled, barefoot, dressed in gray sweatpants and a wrinkled white t-shirt, he obviously hadn't been up long.

"What gives you the right?" she demanded.

His brow lifted. "To have coffee?"

"To use my seniors to further your career."

"Umm...I haven't?"

"I'm not amused."

"Neither am I." He set the mug on the dining room table and moved into the living room, running a hand through his hair. "What are we talking about?"

"You know exactly what we're talking about."

He lifted his hands and shoulders, looking genuinely confused. "Sorry. Maybe you've been up for a while but I'm still trying to get my brain in gear."

"Obviously living off Em allows you the luxury of sleeping in."

His expression darkened as he dropped his hands. "Is that what this is about? You're mad that I'm staying here?"

The truth of his question pricked her. "We're talking about Bertie's picture in the photo contest."

Jackson's morning-stubbled face pinched into a frown as he started to shake his head. Then he grew still, his gaze focused inward. His expression shifted, and he gave a small nod. "Bertie's photo."

"So that does ring a bell. Now that Bertie is splashed across cyberspace, you might find it difficult to feign ignorance."

He met her gaze. "Well, I am a photographer."

"I don't care if you're the personal photographer of the king of Siam." She jammed her hands on her hips. "These seniors deserve respect and dignity, not being made into a photo op."

He rolled his eyes. "The photo is beautiful, and you know it."

"Of course it is, because you're the world famous Jackson Young."

Pain flashed across his face.

"These are people I care deeply about," she continued, "not a means for you to win more awards. I won't let you use them for your own gain."

"Despite what you obviously think of me, I didn't put the photograph out there."

"It made its way from your camera into cyberspace without your knowledge or approval."

His mouth flattened. "Something like that," he said through clenched teeth. "So what? You got some free publicity. That's not a bad deal."

"We don't need publicity."

"Right. Because the center is doing so great on its own. From what I hear, you're on the countdown before the doors close."

Fire flared in her chest and she turned away to look out the front window. Cheryl's constant whispering in his ear had even included details.

"I'm thinking a little publicity could dig you out of the hole you've gotten yourself into and maybe, just maybe, keep the center open."

She whirled back. "So now you're the Open Circle savior? You don't bother about your grandmother until she almost dies, but now that you're her new BFF you decide you'll throw some magic photo dust around and make everything right?"

He stood his ground as she approached. Stopping a foot away, she pointed a finger at him. "News flash, Mr. Celebrity. I'm on my way to having the center running the way it should be with no help from you, so feel free to go back to wherever you came from and continue being famous. Lawton was in fine shape before you graced us with your presence, and we'll be fine when you're gone."

She spun on her heel and let the front door slam behind her. Throwing herself into her car, she yanked the door closed and flinched, hoping it wouldn't fall off.

"He's the most arrogant, self-important, *irritating—*" The tires spun on gravel as she roared away from the house.

It didn't help that he spoke the truth.

By Friday afternoon, the chill emanating from Minnie seemed to have affected Em. Settling his unusually quiet grandmother in the car, Jackson closed the door gently and glanced back at Open Circle before climbing behind the wheel. Grandma Em sat silent, her brow pinched.

Once in her driveway, as he helped her out of the car, she paused to look up at him. "Is there something I can do. To help?"

He managed a smile and offered his arm. "I don't think you can fix this one, Grandma. She's still pretty mad at me." The earlier reprieve had been great. Almost a whole week without her shooting blazing arrows at him or studiously avoiding him. Bertie's photo had ended that.

"And you won't tell me what happened?"

"A misunderstanding."

She nodded and remained quiet until she'd settled in her easy chair. The frown she turned toward him tweaked his heart. "You will work things out with her. Soon?"

He squatted beside the chair and took her hand. "I'll try. You know we're like oil and water."

"More like chocolate and vanilla. Complementary."

He gave a short laugh. "I don't think she'd accept a compliment from me wrapped in ribbons and lace."

She squeezed his fingers, a wan smile on her face as she rested her head back and sighed. "You can try. That's all I ask."

"I will. I promise." He stood and pressed a kissed to her forehead. "Now you rest while I make some phone calls to New York. Lots of details still to get ironed out."

He talked through the afternoon on teleconferences, approving publicity ideas for New York and then for Minneapolis. He'd designed the Minneapolis show around the gallery specs and information Dave sent. Added to the humanitarian series, he'd included photos of Open Circle, Grandma E, and Minnie with Elwin that worked perfectly in the local show. Although none would appear online, he probably should have asked for permission first.

"That's not gonna happen now," he sighed, leaning back from the design specs. He rolled his head and then stretched his arms overhead. She'd probably have been fine with the photos if he'd asked last week. Now he'd have to hope she didn't find out until after the show. Maybe by then she'd have cooled off.

He could give the center some decent publicity if she'd lighten up. He swiveled the chair toward his computer and clicked through the photo gallery, slowing as he reached the Elwin photos. A couple more clicks and he leaned closer. Minnie looked back at him, arms folded, brown eyes sparkling. For that one moment, when he snapped the photo, she'd allowed him a glimpse of the side she kept hidden. At least from him.

Noah had recognized it right away. Jackson chewed the inside of his cheek, studying the photograph. With dark hair in waves around her face, sunlight picking up red and brown highlights, pink flawless cheeks, freckles dusting her nose—she was darn pretty. The right side of her mouth curled up slightly more than the left, creating a tiny dimple. She looked relaxed. Happy.

"Why doesn't she act like that around me?" He lifted his gaze and let it roam the room, stopping on a collection of photos on a shelf he'd paid little attention. Pushing out of his chair, he moved around the table and studied them. Em and Minnie with their heads together, smiling over fluffy pink cotton candy. Grandma and four other ladies laughing together at a picnic table. Minnie sitting by a Christmas tree, holding a sweater. Grandma with a younger-looking Minnie, and a dark-haired woman, all with their arms around each other.

He lifted the frame. The dark-haired woman was an older version of Minnie. Her mother? He focused on Minnie's wide grin. Probably late teens—young, pretty. Happy.

Looking back over the six weeks since he'd arrived, he could count the times she'd warmed up to him. It always had to do with Grandma Em or the seniors. And the times she'd been angry...the same. Their first meeting, at his grandmother's bedside in the hospital, had ended on a sour note. When he'd introduced himself...

The realization crystallized. He'd blasted into Lawton, excited to claim his grandmother without considering she'd had a full life without him. She'd become someone else's grandmother in the intervening decades. Someone who loved her deeply.

He closed his eyes, shaking his head. What an idiot! Why hadn't he seen it before now? When he arrived, he'd crammed himself between them under the guise of being a loving grandson.

"Talk about a pompous jerk," he groaned. He'd been so eager to reunite with his grandmother, and then so shocked to find her in the hospital, he hadn't stopped to consider how the stroke and his sudden appearance had affected Minnie.

He looked at Minnie's photo on the laptop screen and nodded. A few changes were in order. If it wasn't too late.

CHAPTER NINETEEN

When the doorbell rang, Minnie set the book aside and crossed the room to the front door. Finding Jackson waiting on the other side pinched her eyebrows together. Now what?

Hands in his pockets, he lifted his shoulders slightly. "Hey."

"Hey." She waited, hearing an inner clank as her defenses slid wearily into place.

"I, um…" He glanced behind him then dropped his gaze to his feet. "It's such a nice night, I thought maybe you might…want to go for a walk."

"A walk." Her frown deepened. "With you."

He scratched his reddening ear and shrugged, still not looking at her. "Yeah. So we could talk. Away from work and stuff. If you want."

Talk? They couldn't seem to do that. "Jackson, I'm too tired to argue—"

Lifting his hands in his usual gesture, he shook his head. "Arguing is off limits while we walk."

"But once we're done walking, all bets are off?" A faint smile touched her pale face.

He smiled back, lowering his shoulders. "I'll leap back into my car before we can start."

As she hesitated, Em's words floated to mind. "Give Jack a chance." Might as well start now. "Let me put some shoes on and I'll come out."

"Great!"

The relief in his response tweaked her heart as she turned away. They should be able to walk around the block without fighting. Unless he had some bombshell to drop on her—like he'd decided to move Em to California.

"Don't go there," she whispered, tying her shoes too tight. She retied them. "For Em's sake, give him a chance."

Pulling the front door closed behind her, she jogged down the steps and joined him at the end of the driveway. He fell into step beside her as they started along the sidewalk in silence.

Minnie filled her lungs with fresh evening air. "What a beautiful evening."

"Yeah. I'd forgotten how clean the air is here. Even as far north as I live in California, it's not quite like this."

She glanced at him. "Have you lived there long?"

"About ten years. After college, I moved out there with my friend, Noah. When he moved to Chicago, I stayed. It's only an hour from Lake Tahoe, which is one of my favorite places in the world."

"Is it pretty there?"

He stopped and looked at her, eyes wide. "You've never been to Tahoe?"

She shrugged, feeling every bit the country mouse to his city mouse. "I haven't traveled much."

"Well, I'll have to get you and Grandma Em out there for a visit." A smile playing around his mouth, he started walking again. "You'll love it. Sacramento is only four hours north of San Francisco, so it isn't far from the action, but far enough that it feels like its own little world. Rolling hills, horses in green pastures, mountains an hour away. It's a great place to live. But then, so is Lawton."

She bit her lip. A few more weeks here and he'd be bored stiff.

"Do you think Grandma would be able to handle a three-hour flight?" he asked.

The question pinched like a rubber band around her heart. Once he got Em out there, he'd convince her to stay. She shrugged. "Maybe. Not anytime soon, however."

"No, not soon. Maybe next summer. Or next winter, for a break from the cold. You could come out to get away from the snow."

"Sure." She would never willingly take Em out there, knowing his intention would be to keep her. "Someday."

The crunch of gravel under their shoes filled the silence as they turned at the corner and headed into town. Visions of life in Lawton without Em made Minnie's eyes burn. Why hadn't he stayed away?

Em's words haunted her now. Why try to like him when his plans would ruin her life?

"Minnie, there's something I wanted to talk to you about."

Her fingers curled into fists. Finally—the real reason he'd come by. She wasn't going to lose Em without the fight of her life.

"Go ahead." The words squeezed past the tightness of her throat.

He remained silent for another half block, then he pointed at a picnic table at a little park up ahead. "How about we sit for a minute?"

Lips pressed tightly together, she angled toward the table. He settled on top; she chose the far end of the bench.

Jackson cleared his throat. "So I realized...I mean, I hadn't thought..."

She looked sideways at him. He stared straight ahead, his profile pale, hands clenched.

His gaze met hers. "I'm sorry."

"For?"

"For being such a jerk. And for not thinking about your feelings."

The words knocked her breath away.

"I blew into town like I owned the place and ran right over the top of you. And my grandma. I was so excited to see her, I never stopped to think that maybe she had a perfectly good life without me, and that my showing up like that might upset her."

Exactly. "So why *did* you blow into town? And why now? Where've you been all these years?" The questions she'd held onto the past two months tumbled out, colored with accusation. "She watched you build an amazing career but only from afar. You never once tried to contact her."

She jumped to her feet and faced him, hands on her hips. Now that the dam had broken, a riot of bottled emotion flooded out. "While you became a celebrity, your grandmother lived alone in this tiny town, telling everyone how proud she was of you. Your silence broke her heart. So saying you're sorry now doesn't really cut it for me. Or for her."

He stared at her, mouth open, eyes wide. Silent.

His lack of response strengthened her need to protect Em from the pain he could inflict fueled her anger. "So, tell me, *Jack*. Why now after all these years?"

Blinking slowly, he shook his head and looked away, still silent.

Minnie waited. They weren't leaving this park until she had an acceptable answer.

"Wow. I knew you didn't like me," he said quietly, "but I didn't know how much."

She flinched then lifted her chin. "I don't like anyone who hurts Em."

He climbed off the picnic table and took a few steps away, hands shoved into his pockets. Looking up at the trees, he exhaled and then turned to face her. Instead of the defensiveness she expected, his shoulders sagged.

"I doubt you'll believe me," he said, "but I only found out a week or two before arriving here that she was alive."

"You're right. I don't believe you."

They stood silently facing each other before he motioned with his head. "Let's keep walking and I'll explain."

Minnie hesitated then followed. She wouldn't let him out of her sight until she had her answer. They completed another block before he spoke again. "I'm an only child of an only child. Growing up, my parents were... Let's just say there were issues. I spent a lot of time with my grandparents. Probably more time with them than with my folks. I didn't find out about a lot of the stuff that went on until years later, not that I would have understood any of it as a kid."

His words were flat, his gait slower than when they'd set out. Minnie pulled her anger back up from where it had sagged, determined not to believe his story. Or his apology. He'd probably rehearsed this.

"My dad and grandparents had a fight when I was ten. I still don't know what about." He released a slow breath. "It changed my life. Without warning, we left Lawton and moved to Chicago. And then Detroit. And a number of other places."

"They didn't tell you why you were moving?" Sounded pretty far-fetched. Yet Em had said she didn't know where they went.

"They'd said for a new job. But I guess my dad wasn't very good at holding down jobs, so odds are it had more to do with losing one and needing another."

Memories of growing up in her parents' grocery store crowded her mind. Playing hide and seek, stocking shelves, finally getting old enough to run the register. Hardly glamorous, but still fun. "Did you come back for visits?"

"Not even once, no matter how much I begged. I tried to convince them to let me come back for the summers, but Dad wouldn't even talk about it."

Minnie studied his profile, looking for his usual smirk, a hint that he'd made this up. The downward tug of his mouth looked sincere. "So when did you see her again?"

He glanced at her. "The day I met you. At her bedside in the hospital."

She stopped, staring up at him. "They never came back to Lawton? Ever?"

"Ever." His half-smile faltered. "Hard to understand, isn't it?"

"Very." She shook her head. "What would be so awful they would sever the relationship completely?"

He lifted his shoulders then let them drop. "I still don't know. I'm hoping Grandma can explain it to me once she's stronger."

They looked at each other for a moment, then Minnie dropped her gaze. The sadness in his eyes made her want to hug him. "But that doesn't explain why you didn't come back once you were grown."

"When I turned 15, they told me she died."

"What?!" What kind of parents did something like that? "That doesn't make sense. Maybe you misunderstood."

"Oh, they were very clear." His eyes glittered beneath his frown. "They made sure I understood."

"Jack, I'm…" She blinked against the burn in her eyes. "I'm really sorry. That's awful."

His expression softened. "Thanks. I begged to come back for the funeral, but Dad said I needed to move on."

She reached out and touched his arm as they stood in the waning sunlight. "I can't believe they'd do that to you."

"Since finding out she's actually been alive all this time, I'm struggling with it myself." He continued walking. "So much lost time," he mused quietly.

"Have you asked them why?" She fell into step beside him, her heart aching.

"My dad committed suicide awhile back. My mom… well, we aren't in touch anymore. She remarried and moved overseas. I'm not sure I could find her if I tried. And I haven't."

"But…" The knot in her throat made it hard to speak. "How did you find out Em was alive?"

"I got a letter from Daniel saying there were some family things that needed attention."

"Family things?"

"I haven't found out what they are yet. Must not be too pressing." He glanced at her, a corner of his mouth lifting. "He never mentioned family money or an inheritance, I can assure you."

Em hadn't mentioned any issues or loose ends to tie up. She certainly never said anything about trying to contact Jackson. If she had, maybe it wouldn't have been such a shock when he showed up.

"Hey." The upbeat note in his voice startled her. "There's the ice cream store. Want some?"

She lifted her head. The Creamery lights beckoned from the opposite corner. Engrossed in Jackson's story, she'd paid little attention to their path. "I didn't bring any money."

He grinned. "I think I can spring for a cone." They crossed the street and he held the flimsy screen door open for her, then followed her inside. "I'll even treat you to a double."

She laughed. Laughed! After being spitting mad at him an hour ago. "The last of the big spenders."

Minutes later they retraced their path, cones in hand. At the counter, they'd debated the "best" flavors before accepting the server's challenge. They left the shop with each other's favorite atop sugar cones and returned to the park. Resettled on the picnic table, they tried to keep ahead of the drips, chuckling as they nibbled and licked furiously at the ice cream.

Jackson glanced at her as he turned the cone. "So how is it?"

She debated the wisdom of admitting how much she liked his choice. "Well…"

"Be honest."

"It's…yummy."

He tilted his head, eyebrows raised.

She rolled her eyes. "Okay, it's almost as good as my favorite. Happy now?"

He pumped a fist into the air. "Yes! I knew you'd love it."

"I didn't say that. How do you like my choice?"

He studied his half-eaten treat then lifted a smiling gaze to hers. "Almost as good as my favorite."

They looked at each other for a moment then burst into laughter.

"That's as close to agreeing as we're going to get on this topic," he said.

An unexpected sadness pulsed in her chest. Possibly any topic. It seemed a shame.

"So, here's what I came over to say." He pulled in a deep breath. "I didn't mean to crash into your lives and take over. I'm sorry for being such a jerk."

She paused mid-nibble. Jackson Young was apologizing?

Pink filled his face. "You don't have to look so surprised."

"Well, I never expected..." She relaxed into a smile. "Thank you. I appreciate the apology."

Your turn. Her stomach clenched. *She* had to apologize too? A montage of their disagreements marched through her mind. She popped the cone into her mouth and chewed slowly.

"Okay. Along that line...," she said finally. "I wasn't exactly warm and welcoming. I didn't give you much of a chance to get your bearings once you got here." She looked at him. "I'm sorry too."

The corners of his eyes crinkled. "Sounds like we're even." He stuck out his hand. "Friends?"

She accepted it and grinned. "Friends."

He kept hold of her hand for a moment. "Thanks, Mindy. Grandma will be thrilled that we've buried the hatchet."

"She will," she agreed. Her cheeks warmed under his gaze. "I'm glad too."

Releasing his grip, he climbed off the table. "Now that we're friends, let's talk about the photo I took of Bertie."

Minnie groaned as she stood. "Do we have to get right back to arguing?"

"Not if you'll agree that her photo turned out great."

"Does everything have to be about how wonderful you are?"

"Only when it's true."

She shook her head with a snort. "Whatever."

"So? You thought it was a great picture, right?"

Bertie's family had immediately asked for a copy when Jody showed them the photo. And the thought had surfaced to get a framed version for the Center.

He gave her a gentle shove. "Right?"

The teasing in his voice made her smile, despite not wanting to stroke his already inflated ego. "Okay, fine. Yes. But that doesn't excuse you for putting it online."

"I didn't." When she opened her mouth, he lifted his hands. "Honest. I happened to show those and a few others to my friend, Noah, when we were in New York. I didn't know he did anything with it."

His hopeful expression remained guilt-free. Did she have to forgive him for everything all at once?

"We have beautiful seniors at Open Circle. That should be celebrated, Mindy, not hidden."

He had a point. And somehow, his calling her Mindy made him almost likeable. How had she gone from seeing him as the enemy an hour ago to agreeing with him? Ice cream had helped.

"Nobody wants to celebrate Lawton's seniors more than me," she said finally. "But I want to be careful how we do it."

"I agree. They deserve that."

"Nothing on the web without checking with me first?"

He stopped and faced her, opening and closing his mouth as if he wanted to say something more, then he nodded. "Nothing on the web. I promise." A half-smile touched his mouth. "I'm on your side, Mindy. I want what's best for Grandma, and for the rest of the seniors. But you're the boss so I'll respect that. Put me to work—taking pictures, serving lunch. Whatever you need to keep Open Circle going, I'm your man."

The declaration made her eyes sting. She blinked quickly and looked away, folding her arms. *Can I trust him, Lord?* The turmoil in her chest faded and she turned her gaze back to his. She hadn't noticed the dimples on either side of his mouth before. A smile wobbled to her face. "Thanks, Jackson. That means more than I can say."

He winked, and they started home.

I'm trusting you in this, Lord. I sure hope it doesn't come back to haunt us later.

CHAPTER TWENTY

Jackson sat at the dining room table studying the photo on his computer screen. In Friday's sunshine, he'd caught Chief and Ruth sharing a laugh on the Open Circle patio. He could hear Chief's deep, gravelly voice followed by Ruth's teasing.

Pushing out of his chair, he stretched and then set his hands on his hips as he stared down at the screen. He'd traveled the world in search of photos like these. Climbed long mountain paths, ridden rickety jeeps down rutted roads to villages hidden in valleys. If he hadn't been so busy running from his own pain, he'd have seen the need in his own backyard.

He refilled his coffee mug, then returned to his chair and stared out the living room window. Mindy had seen it all along, which explained why she protected them so fiercely, willing to fight anyone or anything that threatened their wellbeing.

Since their walk, she greeted him with an unexpected shyness each morning. He enjoyed watching her come to life as the seniors entered the building. The more he watched, the more her laughter did something weird inside his chest.

Turning back to the computer, he sent her an email with a handful of the photos he'd taken the last few days, the ones he thought showed the best of the seniors, and of Open Circle. She worked tirelessly to keep the Center open, and he wanted her to step back and see the beauty in her hard work. Hopefully she would, in the photos of Chief, Moses, Bertie, and especially Em.

Anxious to hear her reaction, he shut down the computer and headed to his car.

～ero

Minnie settled in her chair and pulled off the yogurt container lid. With most of the group out for a stroll around the block, she could finally eat part of her lunch. The long hours were starting to fray her emotions, but at this rate she'd have to schedule a time to fall apart.

Em remained vigilant about making sure Minnie ate, and always somehow knew when Minnie wasn't truthful. At least now she could say she ate her yogurt and blueberries. Savoring the first bite, she opened her email. Jackson's name popped up at the top, and her heart did a funny shimmy as she hovered over the email. Since their walk, she'd lost her earlier irritation toward him. She felt exposed somehow, ripe for him to swoop in and decide to take Em back to Sacramento with him.

She opened the email and read the brief text explaining the photos he'd attached. Yogurt forgotten on the desk, she clicked on the first one. Chief and Ruth sitting on the patio last Friday, sharing a laugh. His cheerful expression squeezed Minnie's heart. *Perfect.*

Next, Bertie posing with her ever-present boa, Moses

slightly out of focus where he grinned in the background. Then Frances, then Em studying her Bible. Each click brought tears closer to the surface.

"Beautiful," she whispered when the last photo, of her and Em smiling at each other, filled the screen.

Jackson saw beyond the exterior to the soul within. He'd captured each person's essence in exquisite detail, from Bertie's childlike openness to Chief's heart behind his stern, bushy-browed expression.

She wiped at a tear as she clicked through the photos again, stopping on the photo of her and Em. The fear of losing her rushed to the forefront again. The stroke, Jackson's sudden appearance, the weeks of rehab, the looming threat of Open Circle's closing. Months of being unsettled, afraid, unsure what to do or who to trust. What a gift to have these photos, to see life in such vivid detail. To *see* the love she shared with Em—

"Knock, knock."

Startled, she spun the chair at Jackson's voice and their gazes locked. His brow dropped as he stepped into the office. "What's wrong?"

Minnie shook her head and turned away, brushing at her cheeks. "Nothing." She waved a hand to ward off his concern and her embarrassment. "I was…being silly."

"About?"

"The photos you sent."

He stood at her desk. "They're so bad they made you cry?"

A strangled laugh slipped out. "Of course not. They're beautiful."

Lowering into the chair, his dark eyes searched her face. "You like them? Really?"

The unexpected question surprised her. "Yes, really. It's classic Jackson Young."

He rolled his eyes. "Whatever that means."

Minnie leaned back and clasped her hands in front of her. "It means your gift is seeing the real person, beyond what the rest of us see on the outside."

She looked at the screen, the smile in her heart lifting her mouth. "The photo of Em and me is more than two women of different ages. It shows us as true friends."

"And family."

Her gaze swung back to his. For a moment, she couldn't speak. "As family," she echoed softly.

He grinned. "Wow. I didn't know you saw all that in my pictures. Sometimes I can see it. Other times I think I should look for something else to do, something I'd be good at."

"I don't know a single artist who doesn't think their work stinks at least half the time." She shrugged. "I guess you'll have to take my word for it this time."

"Hmm. Not sure you can be trusted when it comes to your seniors. I think you're a little biased."

"I think you're right. Would you print these off for me? I'd like to hang them around the center."

He leaned back in the chair and cocked his head. "On one condition."

She raised an eyebrow.

"You tell me why people call you Minnie."

Warmth crawled up her neck as she rolled her eyes. "It's short for Mindy Lee."

"Not buying it."

"That's my story and I'm sticking to it. When can you get the pictures back here?"

Their gazes held in challenge for a long moment before he sighed noisily. "Fine. But I want the real story one of these days."

She turned toward her computer and clicked the mouse. "One of these days I may tell you."

He left the room, chuckling. Minnie sat with fingers resting on the keyboard, staring blindly at the computer screen. This new and improved Jackson Young had thrown her off-balance. Smug and egotistical, then shyly uncertain. A know-it-all who loved his grandmother without reservation. A gifted artist who questioned his ability.

She rubbed the back of her neck and sighed. If she weren't careful, she'd let her guard down too far and start liking him. And there were far too many uncertainties to allow that. For starters, she needed to verify his story about why he'd been absent the last two decades.

Opening a new email, she shook her head. She'd find time this week to check it out with Em. *Lord, don't let me open old wounds for her. She's been through enough.*

CHAPTER TWENTY-ONE

"No ketchup? Mustard? Relish?"

"Just the dog." Jackson handed the New York street vendor a five-dollar bill and accepted the paper-wrapped hot dog, then settled on a shaded bench to enjoy his short lunch break. Last evening's rain had cooled the city considerably, enough to allow him to get out of the studio for a few minutes to clear his head. His lack of concentration had raised Noah's eyebrows more than once.

He popped the last bit of hot dog into his mouth, wiped his hands and pulled his phone from his pocket. His fingers gave an odd tremble as he dialed.

"Open Circle Adult Day. This is Jody."

"Hey, Jody. It's Jackson Young."

"Jackson! I hear you're out in the Big Apple for a week or so."

"Yup. Ironing out details for an event in September. Say, is Minnie around?"

"I think she's in her office. Let me see if she's available."

As muzak filled his ear, an inner debate raged over the

need to make this call. He'd only been gone a few days. What could have gone wrong since Sunday? And he'd talked to Em last night—

"Hi, Jackson." Minnie's voice replaced the muzak, snapping him out of his turmoil.

"Hey, Mindy. What's going on?" *Smooth.*

"Not much. Between meetings right now so you caught me at a good time. What can I do for you?"

All business. Not unfriendly but not encouraging conversation.

"Well, I uh…" Why had he thought this was a good idea? "I wanted to see how Em's doing."

"She's great. They're on a field trip this morning to the Farmer's Market. She was raring to go."

He chuckled. "I'll bet. We went every week and made a day out of it."

"She loves her fresh veggies. And don't be surprised to find flowers all over the house when you get back. She can't resist those."

"Yeah, she loves flowers."

Silence stretched between Lawton and New York City as he searched his empty head for something else to say. What a dumb idea.

"How's New York? The weather report said you're in the middle of a heat wave."

"The rain last night cooled things off, but it's been a bear all week."

"How goes the show planning?"

"Really good." Paper rustled in the background. He could picture her at her desk, phone propped on her shoulder as she sorted paperwork. "We've got most of it laid out now, prints ordered, publicity lined up. It's been a productive week."

"So you'll be home soon?"

Home. "Unfortunately, I've put off some projects while Em was recuperating so I've got a couple jobs to finish before I can come home."

"Photo shoot jobs, you mean?"

"Yup. One in Chicago and one in Atlanta. I should be back next Tuesday."

"Tuesday. Okay."

He searched for disappointment in her simple response. It sounded more like 'whatever.' "I talked to Em last night and told her it'll be a few days longer than I thought."

"Thanks for giving her that heads up. She's gotten used to you being around."

The thought warmed him. "I'm glad she doesn't think I'm a nuisance. I should probably stop living off her generosity and move to the Country Inn."

"Good luck convincing her that's a good idea." A smile colored the words.

"I figure you can do that for me."

"Nope. You're on your own for that battle. She's happy having you there."

He'd expected her to jump at the idea of his moving out. "Well, I guess I'll worry about that when I get back. So…you're doing okay?"

Silence at the other end. Was that the wrong thing to ask?

"I am, thanks. Busy. Jumping through financial hoops to keep Open Circle from becoming a closed circle."

"However I can help, Mindy, let me know."

Another pause. "Thanks, Jack. I appreciate that." Her words were soft, genuine. "Well, Mary is here to go over a few client health issues, so I'd better go. Good luck with the shoots."

"Thanks. I'll call you later." He clicked off the call and

stared blindly across the busy street. Call her later? Like this conversation wasn't awkward enough.

He pushed to his feet and slid the phone into his pocket. Well, next time he'd be sure to have something to talk about. A smile pushed across his face as he jogged across the intersection.

After a productive meeting with Mary, the center's nurse, Minnie moved through her afternoon appointments, a question mark floating at the back of her mind. Apparently, Jackson had needed assurance about Em. There hadn't seemed to be any other reason for his call.

Sharing a chicken salad dinner with Em that evening, she relayed the conversation. "He must think you're too much for me to handle while he's away. Or he's worried about being away from you too long."

A smile grew on Em's face as she studied Minnie. "Or maybe it's *you* he's worried about."

Minnie snorted. "That would be the day."

"Perhaps it is," Em mused, returning her focus to the food before her.

Minnie watched her a moment, her heart fluttering strangely against her ribs, before changing the subject. "I want to bounce something off you. What would you think of creating an Open Circle calendar that we could sell to the community? As a fund-raiser and a way to share who we are, what we offer."

Em patted her mouth with the napkin. "Tell me more."

"Well, I've been thinking about this since seeing some of Jackson's work. We'd include whoever wants to be part of it. I'm hoping Jack would be willing to organize it. He's obviously more artistic than I am."

"So we'd be pin-up models?"

Minnie laughed. "I hadn't thought of it that way. What do you think? Want to be a pin-up at age 82?"

"Darn tootin' I would." Her smile lit the room. "But no swimsuit for me."

Minnie waved a hand. "The swimsuit idea's been overplayed. How about photos of people doing what they love? Like gardening, playing cards, baking, singing."

"I like it. What does Jack think?"

"I haven't brought it up to him yet. I wanted to pray about it some more, get your opinion, see what the staff thinks."

"What do they think?"

"Everyone I've talked to loves it. Well, almost everyone."

"Not Cheryl."

Minnie bit her lip against a surge of frustration at the woman's continued resistance. "Since it's my idea, of course not."

"Don't let that stop you."

"Not for a minute. If you like the idea, then I'm moving forward with it."

She gave a resolute nod. "I like it."

"Great!" Minnie gathered their plates and silverware. "I'll talk to Jackson when he gets back. Without him, it won't be nearly as nice as I'm envisioning. Photography isn't my strong suit."

Em trailed her into the kitchen, carrying their glasses. "You like him now."

Minnie glanced over her shoulder and shrugged. "We've found a way to not be at each other's throats."

"I see."

Without looking, Minnie felt the knowing smile stretched across Em's face. Life was far easier not living on edge, prepared to do battle with him. Rinsing the dishes, she allowed her own secret smile. She'd never admit it to Em, but Jack had grown on her. And that afternoon's phone call, while awkward, had been rather sweet. Maybe he was setting her up for a fall later, but for now she'd relax and enjoy not waking up with a headache.

CHAPTER TWENTY-TWO

Crickets chirped a welcome as Jackson climbed out of the rental car he'd parked next to Minnie's old Buick. He stretched, pulled in a deep breath, and smiled. After a productive ten days away, he needed to slow down and find out what his girls had been up to.

He retrieved his carry-on from the backseat and hurried up the walk. The evening air was warm, filled with flowers and fresh cut grass. Bouncing between Lawton and New York City, he'd discovered plenty of small-town boy left in him.

With the front door open, he peeked through the screen door. Grandma sat at the dining room table playing cards, humming. No sign of Minnie. He pulled open the door and met Grandma's startled expression with a grin. "Is there room at the inn for a tired photographer?"

She pushed away from the table and hurried toward him, arms outstretched. "Welcome home, my dear Jack."

He held her close for a long minute, then leaned back. "Have you been behaving?"

"Mostly," she said with a wink. With a finger to her lips,

she turned and motioned toward Minnie's still form stretched out on the couch. "Let's go to the kitchen."

Jackson set his carry-on by the door and followed slowly, studying Minnie's peaceful face where she lay on her back, one arm over her head. Cheeks pink, dark hair tousled, features relaxed, she bore no resemblance to the defensive young woman he first met.

"She's working too hard," Grandma said as he joined her. She turned on the heat under the teapot then went to the refrigerator. "Are you hungry? After that long flight?"

"Not really." He dropped into a chair with a contented sigh. "Unless you have any cookies?"

"Minnie baked some last night. We didn't know when you'd arrive."

"I wiggled my way onto an earlier flight. Man, it's great to be home."

She set a plate of chocolate chip cookies in front of him, a glass of milk beside it. Her face creased into a smile, she lowered into a chair. "It's good you are home."

After a bite of cookie, he motioned toward the living room with his head. "How long has she been asleep?"

"An hour or so. Budget work."

He snorted. "That would put me out too."

"I'm worried, Jack. She's exhausted. Working too many hours at the center, then every evening."

"She's got a tough job, trying to show how valuable the center is while people are trying to close it down."

"You talk to her."

"Talk to me about what?" Minnie stood in the doorway, yawning.

She looked young and vulnerable where she stood rubbing her eyes. She'd never looked prettier. Jackson smiled. "Good evening, Sleeping Beauty. Do you have your days and nights mixed up?"

She rolled her eyes and joined them at the table. "It's all starting to run together," she admitted. "I was just resting my eyes."

"You need more rest," Grandma scolded. "You will get sick."

"That's better than being unemployed." She took a cookie and turned toward Jackson. "Welcome home. Tell us how the shoots went."

"Great. In Chicago, I spent time with some vets at the Veterans Center, highlighting their stories, taking pictures of their families. Really impactful stuff." He nodded slightly. A productive time, but also humbling. The selfless determination of people in the military always astounded him.

"I'd lined up the Atlanta job a while ago. There's a youth shelter there doing interesting work with skills training, job placement, cultural identity. It needs publicity so other cities can try putting their plan into place."

Minnie studied him across the table. Was he babbling? He bit into a cookie.

"How do you find out about programs like that?" she asked.

"A number of ways. Sometimes someone calls with a request. Or I see something online and figure it would make a compelling story. And word of mouth. I've developed contacts all over the country who let me know when they see something that should be highlighted."

His grandmother patted his hand. "All over the *world*."

"But how do you live on sporadic paychecks like that?"

"It all works out somehow. I make decent money on some shoots which carries me over while I do the other ones."

"God provides," Grandma Em said with a serene smile.

But He's not doing the hard work. Jackson kept his

expression neutral. She never failed to give God credit. He turned his gaze from her peaceful expression and encountered Minnie's narrowed gaze. She looked away but not before a questioning frown creased her forehead.

～

Minnie watched Jackson's jaw tighten after Em's comment. He obviously had an issue with God, but was he anti-faith or simply not interested? She finished the cookie. That would be hard for Em to accept, her only grandchild having drifted from the faith of his childhood. Em had told countless stories of taking Jackson to church, teaching him Sunday School songs, praying with him, reading Bible stories at bedtime. How she cherished those memories.

Reaching for another cookie, Minnie watched the two of them chat. Perhaps he'd seen so much pain and misery through his camera lens, his faith had taken a beating. Or after the story he'd told her about his parents, maybe he was mad at God. She couldn't blame him for that.

"Don't you think so, Mindy, dear?"

She blinked and raised her eyebrows. "Sorry. What did you say?"

"Like you, Jack has too many things on his plate. I told him he needs to slow down. Now he's been asked to speak at a college."

Minnie looked at Jackson. "You do presentations?" Along with traveling all over to take pictures? And have shows at big name galleries? Her calendar idea suddenly seemed small and insignificant.

He shrugged. "More like talks to photography classes, media groups. Stuff like that."

Em sat straighter. "Don't pooh-pooh that, Jack. It is a compliment."

"I guess it is." Pink stole into his tanned cheeks. "I love talking photography whenever I get the chance."

No doubt he got requests all the time. "Em, I don't think he's going to slow down anytime soon. He's in demand." Minnie met his gaze briefly. While he was recognized and lauded around the world, she worked every spare minute trying to keep Open Circle from disappearing into oblivion. "He definitely won't have time before the shows."

"That's for sure." He chuckled. "When the show closes, I plan on spending a week in a hammock on a beach somewhere warm. I'll need it."

Minnie offered a partial smile even as she mentally kicked herself. No way could he add her project to his schedule. She'd either settle for someone else or scratch the idea. She wouldn't make him feel like he couldn't say no.

She brightened her smile. "That hammock idea sounds wonderful."

"Then I'll find a place where we can get three hammocks in a row somewhere."

"If I got in," Em said, "it would take both of you to get me out."

Jackson's wink warmed Minnie's drooping heart. "I'm sure we can figure something out, Grandma. We won't leave you hanging."

Em laughed. "That's funny."

"He's a funny guy," Minnie agreed. As his schedule grew more hectic in the coming weeks, taking him away more often, Em would miss him.

Minnie would miss how happy he made Em.

"I surrender." Jackson leaned back in his chair Sunday evening and rubbed his face. "Getting beat six to two is hard on my ego."

Em chuckled and patted his arm as she stood. "Cribbage is difficult. You are getting better."

"Not fast enough to keep from getting trounced." He set their coffee mugs in the sink. "Why don't you go up to bed? I'll clean up here. Monday morning always comes faster than we expect."

His grandmother stifled a yawn. "It will be a busy week at Open Circle. Maybe you'll get started on the calendar."

He paused wiping the counter. "What calendar?"

"For Open Circle." She struck a pose, one hand on her hip, the other behind her head. "We'll be pin-ups."

"The seniors at Open Circle are going to be pin-ups? Huh." He faced her, folding his arms, and grinned. "Somehow I can picture Bertie doing that, but the rest of you? You'll be in swimsuits and the whole bit?"

"No bathing suits. I told Mindy Lee I'm too old for that." She hung the dishtowel on the hook and looked up at him. "Didn't she talk to you about it?"

"She's been running like crazy at the center all week. What did she want to talk about?"

Em hesitated. "She has a good idea. To make money for the center."

"By creating a calendar?"

"Of the seniors. Doing what we like to do. Showing off what a wonderful group we are," she added with a smile.

"That shouldn't be hard," he agreed. "How can I help?"

"She hoped you would take the pictures." She frowned. "But she knows you are busy."

"Not too busy for Open Circle. Think I should bring it up to her?"

"I don't know. If she hasn't mentioned it. Maybe not."

"Let's see what this week brings. Maybe she's been too busy to think about it."

His grandmother moved closer and reached up to pat his cheek. "You care about her. That makes me happy. Goodnight, dear."

In the quiet of the kitchen, long after Em had gone up to bed, Jackson sat at the table, turning her words over in the silence. Of course he cared about Mindy. She was devoted to his grandmother, and to all of the seniors in Lawton. Bright, creative, and determined to succeed. And she had a great smile, when she allowed it to surface. It had appeared more often since their walk weeks ago.

He watched fireflies dance across the backyard. And she was tough. She hadn't backed down from him at his most pompous, holding her ground when she thought it best for Em. A smile touched the corners of his mouth. They were connected by their love for Emily Young. Whether Minnie liked it or not, he was a permanent fixture in Lawton now. In Em's life, and, by default, in hers.

So yeah, he cared about Mindy Lee Carlson. And he would make sure that calendar got done.

⁓

From the moment she logged into the computer, Minnie's day raced ahead of her, beckoning her to keep up. Emails, requests from Nick, family inquiries. A decision had to be made about the roof. New forms from the state health department demanded attention. She'd pull her hair out if she had time.

"Good morning, Madam Director! May I enter?"

The boisterous greeting made Minnie turn with a snort from her computer. Jackson stood in her office doorway, a white bakery box in hand and a grin on his face. She didn't have a spare minute to chat, but his mischievous expression refused to be ignored.

She bit back a smile. "Yes, you may. What can I do for you, Mr. Young?"

He chuckled and moved to her desk, setting the box down with a flourish. "An offering for her directorship."

Leaning forward, she peeked through the clear window on the familiar box cover from the bakery down the street. Fresh pastries from Wyler's were her downfall. She released a sigh and looked up.

Jackson's smile disappeared. "What? You're gluten free? Can't eat sugar? Hate sprinkles?"

"Nothing so simple as that. Have you tasted their pastries?"

"No." His eyes went wide. "They aren't any good?"

She lifted the cover and forced herself not to inhale too deeply. "Well, you'd better try one."

Their gazes held over the box she held out to him, then his eyes narrowed and he reached in, choosing a fluffy glazed doughnut. Minnie pressed her lips together to keep from salivating on her desk.

Gingerly he took a bite, then closed his eyes, shoulders relaxing. "Mmmm." Pained pleasure crossed his face. Licking his fingers, he opened his eyes. "Thanks for scaring the pants off me since I already put a box of these in the activity room."

She giggled. "You're welcome."

He selected another doughnut and settled back. "These have to be the best doughnuts I've ever had."

"Mr. Wyler has baked his whole life. His grandparents started the bakery. The Mayo Clinic orders pastries from him for some of their high-end guests and sends a special courier to pick them up."

"I can see why." He chewed with reverence. "I think I

could eat the whole box."

"I'm not sure the cardboard is as tasty as the doughnuts, but you could try it, I guess."

He rolled his eyes. "Aren't you the comedian this morning."

She grinned, wiping her hands on a napkin, then took a swig from her water bottle. "So what brings you in here bearing gifts? Need to make amends for something?"

"It's Tuesday. What other excuse could I need?"

Minnie studied him. "Something's up."

He held his hands up in a familiar gesture, blinking innocently. "I'm just here to share some fun. And to see if there's anything you need help with."

"You aren't busy enough?"

"I have some down time now," he said with a shrug. "I thought maybe...you know, you might have some filing to get done, or a special project. Or maybe you need some more photos taken."

An image of him wallowing in her files lifted a corner of her mouth. Then the smile froze. Special project. Photos. Em! She swallowed back the rising irritation. She'd take care of the calendar on her own time, in her own way. He didn't need to come running to save the day.

Folding her arms, she leveled her gaze on him. "Jackson, if you have something in mind, just say so."

"Well, I thought...You've been so busy, and maybe I could help..." The laughter faded from his eyes, replaced by a dark frown. "Never mind. I thought I could be useful, but you've got it all under control. As usual." He got to his feet and gave a curt nod. "I'll remember that. Enjoy the treat. I've got phone calls to make."

The door shut with a resolute click and Minnie dropped her head back against the chair. *What is wrong with me?*

CHAPTER TWENTY-THREE

Over the next few days, it became clear Jackson was avoiding Minnie whenever possible in the crowded center. When they encountered each other in the hall or during lunch, he hurried past with a short nod. He laughed easily with Cheryl, Jody and the seniors, yet rarely smiled when she was nearby.

During the Friday morning coffee hour, Minnie watched Bertie press a kiss to his cheek and Moses give him a high five. Chief even let him wear the coveted police chief hat. A cold sense of invisibility washed over her but when his gaze lifted to hers, she turned away, determined he wouldn't see the hurt.

A deep sigh escaped as she dropped into her chair and massaged her temples. Invisible or not, she had a center to run. Nick waited for those reports. And she had three family meetings after lunch. Her email inbox remained full, as usual, so she waded into them methodically. One requested her to bring her Alzheimer's presentation to a senior center in Rochester. If complete strangers thought her capable and intelligent, why couldn't Jackson? Her fingers rapped out the staccato rhythm of her frustration as she agreed to the presentation.

She jabbed the Send button and continued down the list. Nick requesting the reports that were late. A family inquiring about an opening. The new bank statement. The words blurred as her thoughts spun into a knot. The financial situation of the center stayed deep in the red. She blinked rapidly and tilted her head back to keep the hot tears from escaping. Sure, this was a hard time, but no harder than losing her father unexpectedly, and then the grocery store. Or her mother to a heart attack. And almost Em to a stroke.

"I can do this." The fierce whisper vaporized as it left her lips. "No, I can't. But if you're with me, Lord…"

The fear receded, and her shoulders lowered. It didn't matter that Jackson thought her incompetent. Em remained in her corner, and God directed her steps. Jack could go back to his other life. She'd take care of herself like she always had.

Friday afternoon, Jackson watched Minnie hover at the periphery of the sing-along. The pinch to her eyebrows and the downward tug of her mouth were a sharp contrast to the jokes she'd shared with the seniors.

Since practically kicking him out of her office on Tuesday, she'd kept to herself, far from him. What was it with her need to do everything her way, even when people offered to help? He'd thought they'd made some headway the last few weeks. Obviously not.

His gaze followed her out of the activity room. Apparently he hadn't been as smooth as he thought when he gave her an opening to ask for his help with the calendar. Her prickles had appeared almost before the words were out of his mouth.

While they no longer argued over everything, she still didn't like him. She was nice for his grandmother's sake. He looked over at Grandma Em who shared a hymnbook with little Frances. But wasn't that what he'd been doing, being nice because she asked him to?

With a muttered oath, he stood and went to the coffee pot on the serving counter. Maybe at first. But then he'd realized she could be funny. And that he enjoyed hanging out with her. He took a quick sip and grimaced as the brew seared his throat.

Well, she'd made it clear she didn't want him hanging around, so he'd honor that. If she wanted help for anything, which was doubtful, she'd have to ask him. He wouldn't give her another chance to kick him to the curb. He'd be there for his grandmother, but Minnie? Not anymore.

He took another punishing sip and went back to his chair. That was fine with him.

⁊

"You are your father's daughter."

Enjoying a light supper together Saturday evening, Minnie smiled at Em over her sandwich. "Well, thank you."

"The stubborn part."

"The stubborn part made the grocery store successful."

"It also kept him from going to the doctor. When he should have."

Minnie flinched as the direct words pricked her heart. If he'd taken his symptoms to the doctor, he might still be here.

Em's soft hand covered hers. "Dear heart, I don't say that to hurt you."

"I know." Minnie offered a half-smile. "I'm just tired, Em. I never gave Dorothy credit for how much work it takes to run the center."

"Pish. You are three times as capable. It's not your job. It's your heart I'm worried about. You need to stop being mad at Jack."

"I'm not."

"That's not what I see."

"He doesn't think I can run the center and that irritates me."

"Did he say that?"

"Not in so many words. But it's obvious." She carried her plate to the sink. "We get along best when we do our own thing and stay out of each other's way. He'll be leaving soon anyway and then I won't have to deal with it."

"He's leaving?"

The alarm in Em's voice made Minnie pause. "You know he's got the upcoming shows. And he has to go back to work eventually. He can't stay here forever, Em," she added more gently.

"I know. But he will visit often. He promised." A smile lifted one side of her mouth. "And I can go visit him. We'll go to Sacramento."

Air left Minnie's lungs in a whoosh as she turned the water on to rinse her plate. "That will be great, if he's ever there long enough for you to visit."

In the silence, she glanced over her shoulder. Em looked so small and frail, it sent an ache through her heart. "We aren't enemies, if that's what you're worried about. We just...bug each other. So as long as we keep our distance, everything remains calm. It's better this way."

Em's blue eyes met hers across the room. "What about the calendar?"

Minnie shrugged, wiping her hands on a dishtowel.

"It's a good idea," Em insisted.

"Maybe. It also might be a bust and cost us money instead." She released a breath that set her bangs fluttering. "I've got enough to worry about right now, so the calendar is on the back burner." Where it no doubt would stay. Caring for her seniors was her priority.

CHAPTER TWENTY-FOUR

"Funding is a priority, Minnie." Nick's brow furrowed as he studied the report she'd sent last week.

Minnie nodded. She'd spent the weekend pouring over her budget in preparation for this dreaded Monday morning budget meeting in Nick's office. "We added three full-time clients this past week, so that additional income isn't well-represented in the report. They're already acclimated and doing great. I'm hoping to bring on another staff member later this month."

He ran his finger along the spreadsheet. "Full or part-time?"

"Part-time to start." Her fingers tingled where she clenched them.

Nick leaned back in his chair. "How do you plan to fund that?"

She hadn't figured that out yet. "I have a few ideas."

His dark eyes rested on her in the silence. She held in a squirm and met his gaze.

"Minnie, you're doing a great job as director. I want you to know that."

"But?"

"No buts in that area. The atmosphere in the center is a thousand times better. Ratings from the families have skyrocketed. You're a born leader."

She pushed a smile to her face. "Thanks. That's nice to hear."

He studied her for a long moment. "Now here's the 'but.' I can't guarantee all that hard work will keep the center open. I want you to keep that in mind when considering a new hire."

Sweat trickled down her back as she nodded. "I knew what I was getting into. Our seniors deserve every ounce of focus and energy I have."

"And that attitude is yet another reason we're grateful to have you running Open Circle. So, looking at the budget..." He looked down at the spreadsheet. "Any ideas on how to do a little fundraising in the time that remains?"

She bit her lip. Had Jackson brought her idea to Nick? "I'm noodling on one. I'll get back to you in the next few days."

"Great." He stood and extended his hand. "Minnie, it's always a pleasure meeting with you, even when the news isn't great. You are highly valued around here."

She stood and took his hand. "Thanks for your support, Nick."

His phone rang so she slipped out of the office and hurried down the hall, throat tight. Not valued enough if they were still considering closing the center. She'd work her tail off for these four months and still be out of a job.

Thrusting open the care center's front door, the bright morning sunshine stung her burning eyes. She turned away from Open Circle. Right now, she didn't need disdain from Cheryl, or requests from the staff, or Em's searching gaze. She needed a walk and answers.

She covered two blocks in silence, afraid to release the frustration that had built in the meeting. Once the questions started, she doubted she could stop them. Another block down she reached the community park, grateful for the solitude.

Plopping onto a swing, she lifted her face to the cloud-dotted sky. "Okay, God. What's the point of adding new clients if I'll just have to send them away when Nick closes the center? I can't help them if the doors close."

The clouds blurred, and she blinked quickly. "What will happen to them?" she whispered. "You know these seniors need Open Circle. They deserve to be cared for, loved. Respected in their final years."

She pressed a fist against her aching chest. "That's what you called me to do. Show me how to keep the center open. I can't let them down." She swallowed over a lump of grief. "I promised Frank."

Heart aching, she set the swing in motion, pumping her legs as she had decades earlier at this park, face lifted. A tear slipped down her cheek, followed by another. She let the breeze and the warmth of the sun dry them.

Quiet chirping filled the answering silence, along with the rhythmic squeak of the swing, and the distant rumble of a semi. As the pain in her chest lessened, she dragged her feet to slow the swing.

While there'd been no clear answer to her plea, a quiet determination reignited deep within. She would do whatever she could for as long as she could; there'd be no giving up until she'd poured every ounce of herself into keeping the center going.

She stood, straightened her shirt, brushed the hair from her face, and set out for the center with a purposeful stride. As hard as she'd tried to come up with other ideas, only one had potential.

If Open Circle closed, it wouldn't be from her holding onto her pride.

ello

Jackson looked up from where he stood beside Jody admiring photos of her son, and locked eyes with Minnie as she returned to Open Circle. He'd watched her leave the adjacent care center an hour earlier, hands in her pockets, looking as if she'd been fired. Now chin up, her expression calm, she offered a tiny smile.

He gave a pleasant nod before returning his attention to the photos.

"Hey, boss." Jody held several pink messages slips over the counter. "These are for you."

"Thanks, Jody." Minnie took the papers, then looked at Jackson. "When you have a minute, will you stop by my office, please?"

"Sure." The sudden butterflies reminded him of being called to the principal's office, although the Mouse was more intimidating than any principal.

"Thanks."

After she disappeared into her office, he whispered to Jody, "Uh, oh. I think I'm in trouble."

The young woman laughed, silver hoop earrings dancing. "She doesn't bite, you know."

"I don't plan on getting close enough to find out."

He left her giggling at the desk and moved to the director's doorway. Pulling papers from a file drawer, Minnie had her back to him. He took that moment to set his shoulders, prepared for a scolding of some sort although he had no clue what he'd done to deserve one lately.

"Knock, knock."

She glanced over her shoulder. "Come in. I'm getting files for a meeting this afternoon."

He approached her desk but remained standing, determined to make a fast exit if she got back on her high horse.

She piled the folders beside her keyboard then motioned for him to sit. "Thanks for coming in so quickly."

He settled in the chair and waited.

She bit her lip and pushed her hair behind her ears. She glanced at him then looked away, her jaw set. "Well, I..." She cleared her throat. "I have an idea for some fundraising and I could use your help. However, I know you're busy, so you're free to say no." The words picked up speed and ran together. "I can certainly look elsewhere for a photographer, but the seniors are pretty fond of you. And so is the staff. But that said, I don't mean to pressure—"

"Whoa." He held up a hand to cut off the momentum. "Tell me what your idea is, and I'll be honest about my time."

Their gazes held for a moment, then her shoulders lowered, the edge leaving her face. "Okay. So." She folded her hands on her desk. "Em mentioned the calendar idea to you?"

He wavered a moment then nodded. "Briefly."

"Well, I'd like to figure out a way to incorporate who they are now with who they've been. The whole package, so to speak."

"I like it." Em hadn't mentioned that part. "So, for instance, we'd do something around the fact that Bertie owned a store?"

"Exactly." A spark lit her eyes. "Every one of them has such a rich history. Obviously, we couldn't cover all of it in a photo or two, but you're so good at capturing who they truly are, you could pull off something like then and now."

STACY MONSON

Her enthusiasm, and the unexpected praise, made him smile. "What if we took photos of them here at the center and then went on a field trip, taking them out into the community to where they lived and worked? Like with Bertie, we could get a few shots of her here beating people at Bingo and giving Chief a hard time, then visit her shop."

Minnie's widening smile faded. "Her store's been closed for a decade. The building is pretty run down." She sighed. "I think that would be depressing actually."

"Pish, as our favorite Emily says," he responded, waving his hand.

She laughed.

"It wouldn't be depressing if we do it right. I'm sure someone has photos of the store in its heyday, right? We could incorporate those into the shoot somehow. Make it a montage using black and white for then, and lots of color for now."

Her eyebrows lifted. "You could do that?"

"Sure. We can play around with it and see what works." He leaned back in the chair. "What's your timeline?"

"Wait—do you even want to do it?"

"I'd be offended if you asked someone else. I'd be honored to be part of this." He rubbed his hands together. "The sooner we get going, the more time I'll have before the shows."

Her brow slid back down. "It's okay to say you're too busy. Honesty, remember?"

He held up three fingers like a Boy Scout. "I'm being totally honest. I do have time right now. It'll get a little hairy when we get farther into August, but I can get a lot done in the next week."

"There's one more thing we need to talk about." She swallowed. "How much would you charge?"

"Nada."

Folding her arms, she leaned back and lowered her chin. "Nope."

As stubborn as Grandma. "Mindy, if you pay me, it takes money away from the fundraising."

She cocked her head, holding his gaze.

He blew out a breath. "Okay, how about this. I'll write up a bill, an honest bill of what I'd charge another client. But when it comes time to pay, I'm going to write it off." He held up a hand when her mouth opened. "That's the only way I'll do this. I need write-offs for my taxes, plus I'd see this as a gift for Em. For all of you. And it's something to add to my portfolio."

They looked at each other in silence before a smile inched across her face. "You drive a hard bargain, Mr. Young."

"Some things are worth fighting for, Miss Carlson. Deal?"

She grasped the hand he held out. "Deal."

"Good." He tightened his fingers. "Thanks for including me in this, Mindy. I think it's going to be great."

Pink rushed to her cheeks and she glanced away. "I think it will be too, now that you'll be part of it."

A knock at the office door broke up the moment. Cheryl's solid frame took up most of the doorway. "Sorry to interrupt but we need Jack for the trivia game."

Minnie pulled her hand away and shooed him out of her office. "Hurry up. Don't keep your adoring fans waiting."

He stood with a chuckle. "Yes, ma'am. Let's talk some more about this tonight. Ideas are already chasing around my empty head."

"Okay. I'll stop over after supper."

Jackson followed Cheryl down the hall, grinning.

Hopefully he didn't mess this up. Like by opening his mouth.

"Thanks for being part of the trivia game, Jack."

He smiled down at Cheryl. "I'm happy to. It's fun."

They stopped in the back of the activity room, watching two of the aides lead singing. Arms folded, Jackson leaned back against the wall, that stupid grin still tugging at his mouth. Life felt better when he and Mindy were getting along.

"Have you met Nick Butler, our administrator?"

Jackson glanced at Cheryl. "Once. Back when I first got here. I've seen him in Minnie's office now and then."

"He's a nice guy. Everyone thinks so. And most of the girls have a crush on him." She leaned toward him, whispering out of the corner of her mouth. "I know Minnie's had her eye on him for a long time."

The grin froze.

"I'm thinking he's got his eye on her too," Cheryl continued with a wink. "He's been visiting here more often lately. Not," she added hastily, pink spots emerging on her round cheeks, "that I'm keeping track. It's none of my business, of course. But they do make a cute couple, don't you think?"

"Sure. Cute." *What an idiot! Acting all stupid because we're getting along again. Obviously, it doesn't matter to her. She's got her big brown eyes on a much bigger prize.*

"Music time is over." Cheryl's cheerful tone grated on him as she clapped her hands and moved into the group. "Let's play some trivia. Our favorite photographer is here to join the fun."

Jackson's feet moved him forward. His hands took a trivia card and his voice read the clue. But his heart had stuck in his throat.

CHAPTER TWENTY-FIVE

Minnie climbed out of the car humming the last song on the radio. She rang the doorbell and let herself in. "Anybody home?"

Em shuffled from the kitchen. "Nobody but us chickens."

The old saying made Minnie laugh. "Well, I hope you chickens like brownies fresh out of the oven."

"You know I do, dear heart." She took the warm plate, patted Minnie's cheek, and turned back to the kitchen. "I'll get the milk."

Minnie set her purse on the floor and slipped out of her shoes before trailing Em. "We'd better get ours quick before your grandson swoops in and eats them all." She glanced around. "I'm surprised he hasn't come dashing downstairs already."

Em waved a hand toward a stack of papers with a folded sheet on top on the kitchen table. "He had to leave. But he left you that."

Ignoring the abrupt drop of her heart, Minnie

sauntered to the table. *Mindy, had to go out. Here are a few ideas. Talk soon.*

She lifted her head and encountered Em's sideways glance, shrugging off the disappointment. "Oh well. All the more brownies for us." She retrieved two plates as Em unwrapped the dessert. So much for planning the calendar tonight.

They settled at the kitchen table and savored the first few bites before Em leveled her attention on Minnie. "Did you fight?"

"No. Why?"

"He seemed upset. About something."

Minnie leaned back in her chair, hands raised in defense. "Don't look at me. Those artist types are pretty temperamental."

Em's eyes twinkled. "Artist types?"

"You know. Painters, sculptors, photographers."

"I see." She turned her attention to the last of her brownie. "Not just artists."

"Hey, I'm not the one who left in a huff about something. You'll have to ask him what his problem is. We were going to plan the calendar."

"Really? You talked to him then."

And practically swooned over him simply because he said he'd be happy to help. Of course he would. He'd do anything for his grandmother. Even spend time with his least favorite social worker.

"We talked a bit." She shrugged and finished her milk. "I guess something more important came up." She gathered their plates. "Now, how about a few rounds of gin rummy?"

They played for an hour and then chatted over coffee in the living room before Minnie declared it their bedtime. It would be humiliating for Jackson to find her still here when he'd obviously made himself scarce.

Em walked her to the front door, concern clouding her gaze. "Don't be angry at Jack."

She busily searched her purse for her keys. "Why would I? He's got important shows coming up. Squeezing in time for the calendar is way down on his priority list."

A gentle hand rested on her arm. "Mindy Lee. He knows it's important. For you and the center. He will make time."

"We'll see." She hugged Em, then wagged a finger at her. "The last thing I want is for my project to make his life more complicated, so don't you nag him about it. He's only got so much time and energy, and it needs to be directed at you and his shows."

"He loves his family." A smile softened Em's face. "All of his family. Good night, dear heart."

Minnie went out into the cool evening shaking her head. That woman had to be the most single-minded person on the planet. She'd badger poor Jack into making time for the calendar.

Poor Jack? The Buick started with a rattle and cough. *Poor me! I'm the one that'll get the brunt of his burnout.* Exactly what she'd wanted to avoid.

Jackson slipped into the center during Morning News, hoping Minnie was in her office or tied up elsewhere. He'd been a chicken last night, unable to face her with Cheryl's latest revelation still rattling around in his head. Instead, he'd wandered around town taking pictures of sites and landmarks that might be useful for the project. No doubt she wasn't happy he'd been a no-show.

He pulled his camera from the bag and attached a lens, then slid the strap over his head and yawned. He'd been unable to turn off his thoughts even after turning off the lights. Either they were or they weren't dating. He started out of the room. If they were, then the guy never bothered to take her out. Ever. If they weren't—

He crashed into someone passing by the doorway, sending them stumbling into the wall. As he caught his balance, he met stunned brown eyes. "Mindy! I'm sorry!"

She straightened and adjusted her sweater. "Where in the world did you come from?"

He waved toward the meeting room. "I just put my camera together. Sorry, my brain wasn't engaged. Are you okay?"

"I'm fine, despite your side tackle move. You? Your camera?"

"It's all good. I'm really sorry."

She offered a polite smile and continued toward her office. "No problem. Have a good day."

Her door closed. Yup, she was ticked. *Great job, Young. You're back to square one. Again. You'd better come up with some amazing photographs or you can kiss that friendship goodbye.*

He headed toward the buzz of voices in the activity room. He'd get some solid shots of each senior today, hear a bit more of their story from them and the staff, and get busy pulling it all together. This would be a project she could be proud of. The *town* could be proud of.

She had a lot to prove to the Suit, and he'd do everything he could to help her. When it came to her job, anyway. He wasn't helping when it came to the relationship part.

ماره

Two nights later, a knock at the front door made him check the saucepan. He'd better get the gravy finished or dinner would be late. Minnie's voice blended with Grandma Em's as they greeted each other. Laughter dotted the conversation floating into the kitchen. His grandmother perked up so quickly when Minnie came around. Their bond went deep, and it still pinged his heart that he'd missed out on creating a similar bond with her over the past two decades. At least she hadn't been alone.

"Jack is cooking?" Minnie's disbelief reached the kitchen before she did.

"Pork chops and potatoes and gravy. Vegetables and even dessert." Grandma's words rang with pride as the women approached.

He glanced at where they stood in the doorway. "Dinner will be served in ten minutes, ladies. Make yourselves comfortable and I'll ring the bell when it's ready."

"You have a dinner bell?" Minnie asked.

"It's to let the wait staff know when it's time to serve," he replied, shooting a wink at his grandmother who chuckled.

"Well, haven't you two gotten all fancy. Em, let's look through your albums for photos of you when you were on the City Council."

Their voices faded. Apparently she'd read the notes he'd left for her the other night; he'd suggested including Grandma's years serving the community as the backdrop for her piece in the calendar. A smile lifted the corner of his mouth and he finished stirring the gravy.

Around the dining room table, conversation centered on news at Open Circle, the new bridge at the other end of town, and the refurbished restaurant offering crazy Happy

Hour deals. Grandma was still in the know about everything Lawton.

As he cleared the dining room table, he suggested they move to the kitchen with coffee and slices of the pie he'd bought. Pork chops he could handle. Making a pie? Not hardly. Settled between them, he booted up his laptop and positioned it so the women could see. "Grandma has already seen these, and given her opinion," he told Minnie. "Now it's your turn."

She turned a dubious expression toward him. "My opinion on what?"

He grinned, nerves making him fidget in the chair as the photos loaded. "Gimme a minute and you'll see."

The slide presentation lit the screen. "Okay. Here's what I've got so far for the calendar. You can let me know if it's even close to what you were envisioning. If not, we'll change it."

Minnie leaned back, cradling her coffee cup. He alternated between watching the slideshow and gauging her expressions. At the photo of Helen and Frank, a tiny sigh escaped and her chin quivered.

"Well," Grandma Em said as the last photo faded, "I think they're even more wonderful the second time. You have a gift. Jack."

Praise from her meant more than a great write-up in a major magazine. "Thanks, Grandma."

Minnie pushed away from the table and went to the counter. She took her time refilling her cup, then held the carafe up toward them, eyebrows raised. They declined, and she returned to her seat.

Jack bit his lip to hold in the barrage of questions that surged. He scratched the back of his neck, then folded his arms and studied the last photo. Bertie and Chief leaving the Center. A wide smile on her profile, her ratty red boa caught in a breeze behind her. Chief prodding her out the door, his expression focused and grim.

"It's perfect." Minnie's voice broke the silence.

The sheen of tears in her eyes surprised him. "You like them?" He sounded like the anxious ten-year-old he was inside.

A smile blossomed as she looked at the screen. "Frances in the kitchen. Moses watching the weather. And that last one is exactly how I think of Bertie and Chief. He's always trying to corral her here or there. It's who he is at his core, a caretaker, the chief overseer of Lawton. And Bertie, the consummate shopkeeper of her day, always dressed in wild, crazy outfits, a smile on her face."

Her gaze became distant. "She could sell you the shirt right off your back, and you'd be happy to buy it. She loved her customers, loved to provide what they were looking for."

Grandma Em chuckled, nodding. "Bertie and your parents were quite the team in Lawton," she said. "They were never afraid to send customers to each other if they didn't carry an item." Her sigh went deep. "That's what people did back then."

"I want the calendar to show that," Jack said. "It's not just about Open Circle, Mindy. It's about Lawton." Their gazes connected. "This is a great idea, and I think you'll be amazed at the response."

Her cheeks flushed. "Thanks to your photographs."

"It's a team effort. I went out the other night, and the last few mornings, taking pictures around town of the different landmarks, places of interest. Anything I thought you might want to use. Do you have an idea of the layout?"

"I hope you two don't mind," Grandma Em said, pushing to her feet. "I am ready for bed."

Jack stood abruptly. "Of course we don't mind. Would you like some help?"

"Pish." She waved a hand at him, then steadied herself against the table. "Thank you, dear, but I can manage. I am tired. Not helpless."

He laughed. "No one has ever used helpless and Emily Young in the same sentence." He pressed a kiss to her cheek. "Have a good sleep. We'll clean up in here."

She patted his chest. "Thank you. You two do good work." She accepted Minnie's hug, then added with a twinkling look, "Together."

Minnie's semi-stern look morphed into a smile. "That's enough out of you. Sleep well. I'll see you at Open Circle tomorrow."

As she shuffled away, Minnie refilled her cup and then settled at the table. "We've got work to do, hmm?"

"We do," he agreed. "Together."

They shared a grin and then focused on the computer. Jack hoped the dance inside his chest didn't show on his face. *She's interested in someone else, Young. Get over yourself.*

He would. Tomorrow.

CHAPTER TWENTY-SIX

Minnie and Gail gathered a handful of seniors in the meeting room the next morning after Morning News and encouraged them to share their memories of life in Lawton.

"Those were happy days." Bertie tossed the boa over her shoulder and blew against the feather that fluttered at her lips. "So much to do."

"Being mayor isn't a walk in the park," Jerry said. "This is a fine town, but it can always be finer. Lots to do. Everybody has an opinion, but nobody wants to do the work."

Minnie set a fresh cup of coffee in front of him, then glanced at Gail. Their memories were so clear of that time in their lives, so many years ago.

"Jerry," Gail said, "what do you like most about being mayor?"

He folded his arms, nodding. "Good question, young lady. You must be a reporter. I don't remember seeing you at a news conference before."

Gail winked at Minnie where she stood behind Jerry.

"I'm new on the beat. So tell me what you enjoy about your job."

Though emails and phone calls waited in her office, Minnie leaned against the wall and listened to the rambling conversation. Jerry loved meeting the people in Lawton and making sure Chief did his job. Chief scowled at the remark and said he was always ready to defend their town, no matter what cockamamie scheme the mayor came up with.

Bertie adored her customers and enjoyed making sure they had what they needed. She'd loved her years as a storeowner and missed knowing the town gossip now that she couldn't get there very often. She didn't remember the sadness of having to close the store over a decade ago.

"We all knew each other," Em said from her spot next to Bertie. "When the town was smaller, people knew who needed what, who'd been injured or gotten sick. Who had a baby when."

"Not to mention whose love life needed a boost, which kid had had detention, and who entered their pie in the county fair," Minnie added with a wink.

Em smiled and nodded, then seemed to deflate. "When we're young, we have purpose. As we get old, it's harder to find reasons to get up in the morning."

Minnie straightened at the defeat in her tone. "I didn't know you felt like that."

"Once in a while." She looked around the table at her friends, nodding. "We all do."

As the conversation continued, Minnie slipped out of the room and returned to her office where she stood at the window. She'd never heard Em sound depressed, not even right after the stroke. Did she truly feel she had no purpose? Maybe she didn't feel well today.

Gnawing her bottom lip, she ran through the

conversation. Each of them had found joy and purpose in their chosen careers, felt part of the community. Had a reason to get up in the morning, as Em said. Now what did they have?

Much as the staff tried to keep the activities interesting and challenging, and offered nutritious meals to help them stay healthy, it probably still felt like the same old routine day after day. They had no say in the planning, no job they needed to do.

A knock at the door made her turn. Gail stood in the doorway, her mouth pursed to one side. "You get the same feeling I did?"

"Definitely." She sat at her desk and motioned for the young woman to take a seat. "Things need to change. Anything come to mind?"

"Actually, yes." Gail's face glowed. "Not sure how or if we can pull it off, but it's worth a try."

Minnie leaned her elbows on her desk. "Let's hear it!"

$\sim$

After a quick dinner, Minnie headed to Em's house. Parking in the driveway, she chided herself for the fleeting disappointment that Jack's car didn't sit in its usual spot. He'd mentioned running up to Minneapolis for the day to check on plans for the show, which was probably a good thing since she had so much to tell Em.

"Come in, dear heart." Em removed her reading glasses and set them aside with the newspaper. "I'm so curious about your phone call."

Minnie settled onto the couch, pulling her legs up under her. "There are so many ideas bouncing around in my head, I knew I wouldn't stop talking if I started on the phone."

Em's face lit with interest. "We've got all evening."

"It might take that long." Minnie recounted her hour-long conversation with Gail. "So that led us to this idea. Let me know what you think." She leaned forward. "We'd like to start the Open Circle Boutique and Café. It would be open to the public maybe two days a week. Bertie could run the clothing part of it, from donations we'd get. Frances could oversee the café part which would be coffee and donuts. Chief could offer security. Jerry could help spread the word. And there would be other things people could do like sort clothes, clean tables, welcome people. You'd be best as the greeter, since you know everyone in town."

Ideas continued to form as she talked until finally she pressed her lips together and leaned back. If Em didn't approve, they wouldn't go forward with it. "What do you think? Too crazy? Too complicated?"

Em reached for Minnie's hand, holding it between both of hers. "I think you have a heart bigger than Minnesota, Mindy Lee. I am so proud of you."

Tears blurred the beloved face. "What you said made us realize we needed to do something different, change things up."

"What *I* said?" Em frowned slightly.

"About having a reason to get up in the morning. It made us realize that life for seniors changes dramatically when everything gets planned for them instead of with them. I hadn't realized we'd taken away your choices, your purpose." Minnie squeezed Em's hand. "I'm sorry and I want to change that. Will you help me?"

Em, not as hardy and strong as six months ago, offered a glowing smile. "I would love to."

"Thank you," she whispered.

From his car parked down the block, Jackson watched Minnie's battered Buick rumble and cough its way down the street. Much as he'd wanted to be spend the evening with his two favorite women, they needed that time to themselves.

He'd done what Grandma asked and taken the time to get to know Minnie. No doubt she'd asked the same of Minnie. Unfortunately, he'd taken that suggestion and run with it, while Minnie seemed fine with simply getting along.

He thumped his head against the headrest, eyes squeezed shut. While she'd never given any indication she thought of him as more than a co-worker, he hid out here like an idiot, avoiding her so his growing feelings wouldn't be on display. Grandma Em hadn't meant for him to like her like *that*, but somehow his respect for her work had morphed into more. He enjoyed making her laugh, listening to her insights, sharing a meal with her and Grandma.

A long breath filled the car. Yup. He'd been such a dutiful grandson he'd gone above and beyond Grandma's request. And now sat hiding down the block like a thirteen-year-old with his first crush.

With the Minneapolis show looming, and final prep being made for New York, he'd be away a lot more. Minnie would be here doing what she did best—keeping an eye on Grandma Em as she had for the past 20 years. And he'd be out there doing what he did best—capturing life through the lens of his camera. Surprisingly, it didn't thrill him like it used to.

Minnie stood on the front step of the center, watching the sun peek over the bluffs. Its rapid rise mirrored her desire to get the day started. She'd hardly slept as ideas for the boutique tumbled through her head. At first light she'd been up and dressed. Giving her seniors purpose, a reason to *want* to come to Open Circle, had renewed her energy.

"Whatever it takes, Frank," she murmured, then unlocked the center. "We're going to do everything we can to make them see how important this place is to Lawton."

She strode through the quiet building, turning on lights, looking for items that could be used in the boutique. Moving the meeting room to where the storage room sat in the back would free up space to put the boutique right by the front door, allowing people to come and go under Jody's watchful eye. And it would force her to clean out the storage room and keep only what they truly needed.

The flood of ideas could only have come from God, filling her mind as she prayed for guidance. She was beyond grateful, and more excited than she'd been in months. In the thirty minutes before the morning staff arrived, Minnie moved storage room items to outside the back door, and made numerous trips from the meeting room pulling chairs, the table, and odds and ends to the storage room. Breathless and a bit grimy, she greeted Cheryl and the others from the boutique doorway.

"So what's going on?" Cheryl's cautious tone did nothing to dampen Minnie's excitement. She'd expected nothing different. The other women looked around with growing smiles and questions.

"You'll all find out once Gail gets here. We have some exciting news to share, and a fabulous idea that will require everyone's energy and brainpower. We think it will make a huge difference for our seniors."

Cheryl folded her arms and pursed her lips, studying

Minnie with a raised eyebrow. Couldn't she be excited just once about trying something new? *I'd even accept mild interest.* Minnie turned away to hide the smile that threatened. It had to be a God-thing for her to find *anything* amusing about Cheryl.

During Morning News, Gail and Minnie stood before the clients and staff, trying unsuccessfully to harness their excitement. Their energetic silliness had everyone laughing. Nearly everyone.

"And so, thanks to those who shared wonderful memories and some of their current struggles recently, here's the plan." Gail gestured to Minnie to take over.

"You've probably noticed a number of things out of place around here this morning." Minnie flexed her muscles which garnered laughter. "We're making room for our new venture at the front of the building. We're going to start the Open Circle Boutique and Café where people can stop by to enjoy a cup of coffee and a treat, maybe do a little shopping."

Several of the seniors, including Em, smiled and clapped, while the staff shared excited whispers. Cheryl stood stiffly in the back of the room. Minnie regained their attention and outlined the ideas, and how it required everyone's help to be a success.

"It's certainly not something only the staff can do," she said. The seniors responded with surprised enthusiasm tinged with hesitancy. Minnie exchanged a hopeful smile with Gail. It would take a lot of effort from the staff to keep the seniors focused, but setting up and running the boutique would also keep them engaged and stimulated. Most of all, she prayed they'd realize they were needed to run the boutique.

Unease fluttered at the edge of her heart as she looked at the beloved faces, their voices filling the room. *Is this too much? What if I make things worse for the center? What if it's too confusing for some of them?* Her gaze connected with familiar blue eyes that smiled back at her from the middle of the group.

Em nodded and Minnie released the fear. She could do this for them. Nobody would ever be able to say she hadn't given it everything she had. Even in the face of eventual, inevitable defeat.

CHAPTER TWENTY-SEVEN

It was true. New York City never slept. Jackson climbed out of the cab shortly after midnight and headed into the hotel. More activity hummed along the street now than at midday in Lawton. He chuckled to himself as the man at the counter checked him in. He'd thought he'd left country life behind when his family left Lawton, but after getting reacquainted with the town, he preferred the slower pace. With meetings and interviews lined up for the next three days, this country boy would be itching to get back to Lawton, and his family, by Friday.

Tossing his duffel on the bed, he kicked off his boots and dropped into the desk chair. Minnie had been impossible to connect with before his flight—in and out of the center, in meetings, on the phone. He'd resorted to leaving a note under her windshield wiper before heading out of town.

He chided himself as he checked his email, rolling his eyes as his heart jumped when he saw her name. Even knowing she and the Suit probably had something going, he was happy to at least be on her radar.

"You've been out of circulation too long, Young," he muttered, clicking on her email.

Jack, sorry I missed you. It's been wild getting the Boutique and Café ready to open on Friday. I must be nuts to take this on. (no comments from you on that thought.) Anyway, I'm praying you have a really productive time in New York. I can't believe the Minneapolis show is next week, with the big shindig only two weeks after that. Speaking of crazy... I'll try to keep Em out of trouble while you're gone. Take care and see you soon! -M

Not exactly a love letter, but more than just "see ya." He shook his head and closed out his email. She would no doubt prefer to smack him with a blunt object than consider a date with him. He settled onto the bed, punching the pillow into a ball. Good thing he wouldn't have much time to think this week. He'd been spending far too much time focused on a pretty girl with freckles and a sweet smile infrequently directed at him. He needed to be focused on the show.

This was his chance to re-establish his reputation, to prove the Blunder didn't define him. Assuming the meeting with the magazine exec went as he hoped, he'd be back on top. He stared at the shadows playing across the ceiling, cold dread stealing into the corners of his mind. If it didn't go as he hoped, he'd need to find a new career. He couldn't maintain the pace of the past three years. He didn't want to.

He rolled on his side. He wanted to spend as much time as possible in Lawton, not crisscrossing the world. There seemed so little time left with Grandma Em, even if they were blessed with a decade together. Panic slid in beside the lurking dread.

The work he'd done these past years had to stand on its

own merit. If the magazine exec resigned him to the deal he'd lost in the Blunder, he'd make Lawton his home and travel from there. If he lost the deal again... With an oath, he reached for his phone and scrolled through photos, squinting against the light.

Propping the phone on the bedside table, he scrunched the pillow several more times and settled down, looking at the photo of Grandma and Minnie sharing a laugh. He'd make this a show New York City raved about for months, and prove he hadn't simply been a flash in the photo industry. He'd grown up. The photos he produced had too. But this wasn't just for him. It was also for Grandma and Minnie. He glanced again at the photo as his eyes fluttered closed. He wanted them to be proud of his work. And of him.

From a final review meeting right after breakfast, to two radio interviews, to a photo op with Noah, Paul, and Pierre, Jackson's every thought was laser focused on what needed to be done for the show. Except when Noah poked him as he stared after a dark haired young woman who looked a lot like Minnie.

The first radio interview finished with no hiccups. The second also went well until he literally got the hiccups. Which reminded him of the time Minnie suggested he drink water while upside down to get rid of an earlier bout. He'd decided she was trying to drown him. He chuckled through the remainder of the interview like a lunatic.

Over dinner at the hotel restaurant, Noah and Paul studied him with growing smiles.

"What is your problem, Russell?" Jackson demanded.

"I'm not the one with a problem." He elbowed Paul. "And you don't have a problem."

Jackson looked from one grinning friend to the other. "So apparently I have the problem."

Noah leaned back in his chair, chuckling. "A big one, it seems."

"Definitely a big one," Paul added then drained his soda.

"And that would be?"

"Well," Noah said, "you're either distracted by being away from your ailing grandmother—"

"She's not ailing."

"Or from the pseudo-granddaughter. Mary? Margaret?"

"Mindy. And she's been more of a granddaughter than I've been the last 20 years."

Paul laughed. "Haven't seen you in a skirt, but I'm pretty sure she'd make a better granddaughter than you."

Jackson couldn't stifle a grin. "Funny, Branton. Things could have been a lot worse for my grandma if not for her."

"Seems to me you thought she was a pain when you met her," Noah said.

"I did. But I was one too. We've worked it out."

The waiter set platters of sizzling steaks before them. Jackson sliced off the first bite, savoring it, then redirected the conversation. "What are you hearing from Pierre? Is he happy with the way things have shaped up?"

"Ecstatic would be a better word. Weren't you listening in today's meeting?"

"You know him better than I do. I just wondered if he'd said anything different." He shrugged. "Like if he's worried I'll repeat the Blunder and mess this up too."

Paul looked up from his platter. "Young, people are excited you're back. Especially Pierre. Your exile was self-imposed, remember."

The bite of meat didn't go down easily. "I needed time

to get my head back in the game. By the time I did, everyone had lost interest."

"Maybe it felt like that, but we heard only praise and excitement when your photos started surfacing again."

"And maybe some jealousy from those happy not to have to compete with you." Noah added, chuckling.

Jackson's mouth quirked. No doubt. "I don't want my past messing it up for you guys."

"It won't," Noah assured him over a mouthful. "We're happy to be in this with you. We all want the show to run perfectly."

"That we do, my friend. That we do."

Noah shot a wink. "Just don't forget to show up this time."

Hiding a wince, Jackson nodded. "Front and center." Nothing would keep him away this time.

CHAPTER TWENTY-EIGHT

Frenzied. That would describe her life. Minnie coaxed her shoulders away from her ears as she settled into her office chair, coffee in hand. Organizing the Boutique required every free moment. The city planner had outlined the steps required before the Boutique and Café could open. She, Gail, and Jody had split the list and tackled the paperwork in what had to be record time.

She sipped the steaming brew and smiled. The biggest surprise had been her assistant director's attitude. Several times, Cheryl had stepped in without being asked, telling (more like ordering) Minnie to get those details ironed out while she took care of the daily activities. The first time, Minnie had asked her to repeat the offer, and then worried that Cheryl had an ulterior motive. When there didn't seem to be one, she accepted with overwhelming relief.

On her already packed calendar, she'd penned in nightly dinners with Em who seemed to be missing Jackson a great deal. Most days her mind was clear, her humor sharp, her eyes as bright blue as the summer sky, especially after Jackson's daily check-in phone call. But there were others when it seemed her thoughts tangled more easily, and her attention drifted. Those days sent a tremor of unease through Minnie.

Her too-brief coffee break over, Minnie prepared for a care conference at Crosswinds, then on her way out paused to remind Mary, the nurse, to let her know of any changes she saw in Em. And then she apologized, yet again, for being overprotective. The nurse simply hugged her and shooed her off to the meeting. Crossing the parking lot, Minnie whispered a prayer of thanks for the amazing people around her.

Opening Day for the Boutique and Café arrived with clear skies and glittering sunshine. A gentle summer breeze set the neon balloons waving from the sandwich board Jerry had created. Gail's artful lettering invited the town to stop by the Café for free coffee, along with donuts from Nelson's bakery, and to check out the craft items and clothing in the Boutique.

Minnie glanced at the clock behind Jody, and prayed again for someone, anyone, to visit their new venture. Bertie tinkered in the Boutique arranging and rearranging items, her fuchsia boa fluttering behind her. Chief sat stoically in a chair by the door, ready to peruse anyone who dared cross the threshold. Jerry's cheerful meandering presence offset Chief's stern expression.

"Stop looking at the clock," Jody ordered, focused on the spreadsheet on her computer. "It won't make people come any faster."

"What if *no one* comes? They'll be crushed." *I'll be crushed.*

"People will come. Gail and Jerry covered every inch of town. I saw posters in the bathroom stalls at Ed's Bar and Grille."

Minnie snorted. "Really?"

"Yep. And Eric Nelson said they'd send bakery customers over for the grand opening. The mayor will be here in an hour for the ribbon cutting, which always brings people around."

The receptionist's gentle scolding calmed Minnie's nerves. "You're right, as usual. I'll go focus on something else for a few minutes. Holler if you need anything, like if Bertie starts packing the Boutique back up." The woman had unpacked and then repacked the boxes delivered from the thrift store the other day, giggling and fluttering her boa each time someone reminded her it was an *unpacking* day.

In her office, Minnie plopped into her office chair and gave it a gentle spin. *Focus on something else—ha.* Since the idea first developed, she'd thought of nothing else. Well, maybe she'd wondered how Jackson fared in New York and Minneapolis. More than a few times. But mainly it had been all about making the Boutique work. Her seniors had worked as hard as they could doing their part.

They'd suffered so much loss in their lives. Maybe she'd just set them up for another one. She lowered her head. *Lord, for their sake...* The plea echoed in her suddenly aching heart. Blinking against the sting of tears, she pushed out of the chair and stood in front of the window. Hands on her hips, she set her shoulders. She wouldn't let this opportunity fail without giving it everything she had for them. "No way."

"No way what?"

She spun at the unexpected male voice. "Jack!"

His familiar grin reached across the office to warm her. "I hear there's quite the shindig going on around here. Can I crash the party?"

Silly joy swept through her as she approached where he stood in the doorway. "You'd better. You're the photographer." Folding her arms over the dance in her chest, she raised an eyebrow. "Got your camera?"

"I might." He shook his head. "A coffee shop *and* a store? Where do you come up with these ideas?"

"I might be a little impulsive," she admitted, heat crawling up her neck.

"More like creative," he corrected. "Jody said it opens at 10:00? The parking lot was getting crowded when I pulled in."

"Really?" The tears were back in an instant and she pressed her fingers to her mouth.

He frowned. "Wait. Is that bad?"

She shook her head, swallowing over the knot in her throat. "I thought maybe..."

"Ahh." A knowing nod relaxed his frown as he reached out and wrapped her in a reassuring hug. "You figured no one would come."

Startled by his unexpected gesture, Minnie stood quietly for a moment, drawing strength from his embrace. With a deep breath, she stepped back and lifted her shoulders. "It's just... Jack, they've worked so hard. I don't want them to be disappointed."

"I'll bet working together toward a goal is more valuable for them than the number of people who show up."

His words wove through images of their work. Bertie teasing Chief with her boa. Frances counting trays and doilies for the café. Em leading prayer over the group and their endeavor. Laughter. Lots of it.

A smile grew in her heart and spread across her face. "I think you're right."

"Of course, I am." He winked and motioned her out the door. "Now let's get out there and celebrate. You can fill me in later on how you pulled this off. Maybe over dinner."

The smile didn't leave Minnie's face for the next half hour as people crowded the Boutique, ate donut holes, and drank coffee. At ten o'clock, she stepped into the reception area where the mayor waited with oversize scissors in hand. Jerry stood proudly beside her. Gail and Jody stretched a purple ribbon across the boutique doorway, and Jackson positioned himself beside the Lawton newspaper photographer to capture wide smiles and cheers as the satin ribbon fluttered into two pieces.

Gratitude sang a chorus of thanks in her heart as Minnie laughed and chatted with her seniors who glowed with life, a sparkle of purpose lighting their weathered faces. Whether her motives had been pure or not, God had answered her plea. There was no disappointment to be found, at least for today. The community had poured love and energy into the old building, honoring the elders as they deserved.

Her heart overflowed with sweet, unexpected joy.

Over a celebratory dinner at Grandma Em's dining room table, with steaks from the grill he'd managed not to burn, Jackson listened to the women's recap of the day's events. So much had happened in the two weeks he'd been gone, a part of him felt cheated he'd missed the planning and the fun.

He peppered Minnie with questions. Between bites, and compliments on how perfectly he'd cooked the meat, she described the process. Brown eyes glowing, cheeks flushed with excitement, or perhaps exhaustion, she talked and gestured, laughed, and mused over how perfectly God put the pieces together.

Em watched her and smiled, inserting an occasional

comment. But while Minnie exuded life, his grandmother seemed pale and tired. After barely touching her favorite raspberry sherbet, she opted for bedtime. When Minnie offered assistance, Grandma waved her off.

Minnie placed a gentle kiss on her cheek. "We couldn't have pulled this off without you, you know."

"I know nothing of the sort," came the reply. "You are using the gifts the Almighty gave you, and part of that is encouraging everyone to work together. Which you did beautifully. Didn't she, Jack?"

He nodded. "As she always does. Lawton and Open Circle are lucky to have her."

The flush of Minnie's cheeks deepened as she shot him a grateful smile.

"Luck has nothing to do with it." Grandma reached up to pat his cheek. "I'm glad you are home, Jack. We missed you. Now good night, you two."

As she shuffled away, Minnie started clearing the table, her brow wrinkled. Jackson collected glasses and silverware and followed her into the kitchen.

"I think all the excitement today wore her out," he commented.

"I don't know." Minnie rinsed plates in the sink. "I'm worried it's more than that."

"Like what?"

"I'm not sure." She paused and lifted a thoughtful gaze to the window. "Something's off. She seems so frail."

"Since the stroke?" He ran back over the evening's conversation. Grandma had been quiet, but she'd still contributed.

"No. More recently." She glanced at him before returning her focus to the dishes. "I'm keeping an eye on her. So tell me how everything went in New York. All the details. Are you ready for the shows?"

By the time he'd finished recounting two weeks' worth of activity, they'd settled in the living room, coffee in hand. She asked insightful questions about planning, interest lighting her face. He itched to capture her smile, the sparkle of energy, the intelligence in the gaze that rested on him. Two weeks away with sporadic conversations had made him wonder if he'd imagined the Mindy Lee he'd been getting to know before he left.

He bit back a grin. He hadn't.

"Sounds like you've got everything under control," she commented. "I'm excited for you. This will be great for your career." The career she'd sneered at when they first met.

She studied her coffee for a moment, then looked up, eyebrows tented. "Em has always been so proud of you. She has a lot to be proud of."

"Oh. Wow. Thanks." *Great response.* "That goes for you too. I guess she has a lot to be proud of all the way around."

Minnie smiled and sipped her coffee.

"Hey, there's something I wanted to talk about before I head up next week for the Minneapolis show." He set his empty mug aside and settled back against the couch. "I'll need help with the logistics."

"I'll do what I can."

Maybe she'd consider coming along. It could be a weekend away for all three of them. Then he wouldn't worry about Grandma while he was busy at the show. The unexpected idea made him smile. That would be the perfect solution. And he'd get to spend more time with both of them.

"Okay, so I'm thinking it would be really nice to have family get to experience the shows with me." Her interest faded into wariness. "You know. See what it's like, be there for the speeches and stuff."

She seemed to have stopped breathing as she waited.

His heart climbed up his throat. *I guess I have to spell it out.* "I'd like to take Grandma with me to Minneapo—"

"No."

No? "I think she'd enjoy it. And I'd really like to have her there to meet people."

"She's not up to that, Jack. She barely made it through today."

"But this would be a lot less stressful. Just riding in the car to the Cities, and then hanging out at the studio."

"That would be *more* stressful than today. Traveling is hard work, especially for older people. Unfamiliar surroundings like a hotel can be disorienting, not to mention the noise of the city as you drag her around."

The old defenses shot into place. "I won't be dragging her around. She can sit in a chair in the gallery. All day if she wants."

"While you're busy doing whatever it is you people do."

You people?

"It would be exhausting for her, stuck in a strange place all by herself, no one talking to her."

"*I'd* be talking to her!" He threw his hands in the air. "I'd be right there, for Pete's sake. Do you really think I'd take her up there and expect her to fend for herself?"

"Well, you'll be extremely busy. You said so yourself."

He wanted to shake that condescending look off her pretty face. How did she switch from pleasant to prickly so easily? So much for thinking they'd made progress in their relationship. "You must think I haven't learned anything from all the time I've been here."

"I don't know what you've learned," she said, "but what *I've* learned from years of working with seniors day in and day out is that change can be very difficult for them."

"For the more fragile ones, maybe."

"*She* is fragile!"

He pushed off the couch and walked a few steps away. "Today was a big day after weeks of hard work," he said, forcing a calm that he didn't feel. "My grandmother isn't fragile. She's tired."

"Tonight she's both."

"I'm not asking her to move to Minneapolis. I want to take her up there for a weekend."

"And I want her to stay here where she's comfortable in her home. Not traipsing around the state and sitting alone in a chair in a cold art gallery for who knows how long."

He held back a snort. "A few hours. I'd like her to be part of *my* life, see what my career is all about. You know, the one you just told me she's so proud of. Is that so much to ask?"

"Well, we can't always have what we want, Jackson."

He spun away and crossed his arms so tightly it felt like he cracked a rib, lips pressed to stop the torrent of words building behind his clenched teeth. In the cold silence, he drew a slow breath. Why had he ever thought they could have a rational discussion about this? Two weeks away had dulled his memories.

"After living with her this summer," he said finally, turning back, "I think I've gotten to know her pretty well. And one thing I've learned is that making decisions for her is a bad idea. I thought we could have a civil conversation about this, come up with a few ideas that would make the trip fun and as easy as possible before I mentioned it to her. Obviously I haven't learned *that* lesson very well."

She flinched and looked away.

"So I'll ask her in a day or two and see what she wants to do. If she doesn't want to go, I'm fine with that." He narrowed his eyes. "Contrary to what you think, I really do want what's best for my grandma."

The Mouse got slowly to her feet, releasing a deep breath as she straightened her shoulders. "I know you do," she said quietly. "So do I."

She gathered her purse from its usual spot by the door and walked out.

CHAPTER TWENTY-NINE

The weekend felt unbalanced after the exchange with Jackson. Or maybe *she* was unbalanced. Minnie leaned her head back as she rocked, Bible in her lap. Stunned by his unexpected plan, she'd reacted poorly. Em seemed so frail lately, the idea of even a short trip wasn't a consideration. But that didn't give her the right to be rude and self-righteous, exactly what she'd disliked about him when they first met.

She flinched as her response came back in all its ugliness and pressed her hands against the Bible as if it would erase her words. How many times would she have to seek God's forgiveness, and Jack's, for her uncensored responses? Would she forever make the people around her suffer because of her lack of control?

Eyes closed, she bowed her head. She was exhausted from months of running like a hamster on a wheel. No, past exhaustion. She was the hamster gasping for breath beside the wheel. There were only weeks until the final decision would be rendered. Could she hold it together that long? Even if she did, she'd have no friends or family left to care.

"I can't do this, Lord." A sigh trembled within her ribs. "I'm so tired. And cranky, and scared, and confused. Am I doing anything right? I just want what's best for the center. And especially for Em."

Come to me all you who are weary and burdened.

The familiar verse stung and soothed. What would she do if the center closed? If something happened to Em? If Jack never spoke to her again?

I will give you rest.

A tear burned down to her chin. "I need rest," she whispered. And she needed God. She wasn't doing so well on her own.

Take my yoke upon you and learn from me.

The turmoil calmed, and she relaxed into the chair. She could learn, right? It might take forever, but she could learn to tame her temper and hold her tongue. She'd start with Jackson—an apology first, and then maybe they could talk about finding another time, when Em was stronger, that she could visit one of his shows.

Jackson dropped his grandmother at Open Circle Monday morning, then returned home to work on the calendar. In the confines of the cramped center, it would be impossible to stay out of Minnie's line of fire, and he wasn't up to going another round with her about the Minneapolis show. Her stinging comments from their run-in stuck like a burr.

He'd talked with Grandma Em at length on Saturday about going along to his show in Minneapolis, and she'd seemed delighted. Last night he'd had to remind her they'd be going on Thursday, but she'd waved off her memory lapse in typical Grandma Em fashion.

"Pish," she'd said. "I've got a lot on my mind, Jack, that's all. It's been a busy few weeks." She'd smiled across the kitchen table at him. "You worry too much. I'm looking forward to it."

He hadn't figure out how to tell Minnie, but they were bound to bump into each other, literally, at the center, so he'd tell her then. No reason to elicit another tirade by bringing it up days ahead of the event.

The Minneapolis show. His first in more than three years. He leaned back against the couch, his stomach a knotted mess, and rubbed the kinks from his neck. The calendar formatting had kept him from a constant dwelling on all that could go wrong. In his early years as a photographer, his rapid, upward trajectory had made him oblivious to the idea of failure. Since the Big Blunder, it required focus to not imagine every dark possibility.

That first show in Minneapolis had fallen into place with little effort from him. People lined up to offer help, money, encouragement, and praise. Lots of praise. He'd had more job requests than time. Years of great assignments followed. Then he'd blundered—big time. He had blown not just one major opportunity but two.

Everything had dried up like an old photo. Instead of lauded as the next big thing in humanitarian work, he was labelled incompetent, pompous, unreliable. The job offers stopped, income vanished, and silence blanketed adulation. His amazing life changed from clear, vibrant color to blurry black-and-white.

Three long years later he stood on the edge of regaining at least some of what he'd had. He'd honed his craft and earned this opportunity, and he took none of it for granted. If he were a praying man, he would prayer that nothing went wrong this time, but that was the one thing he'd lost for good after the Blunder.

If God couldn't be trusted with what he'd had before, he wasn't about to trust Him with it now. He'd worked torturous hours, logged thousands of miles, ridden jeeps and donkeys, climbed worn paths up mountainsides, and inched across rickety bridges to find his subjects. He'd invested all of himself into rebuilding his career.

No. If he succeeded, or failed again, it would all be on his shoulders, where it belonged.

⁓

Thursday afternoon, Minnie's call to Em's house went unanswered. For the third time. She pulled her purse from the drawer and told Jody she'd be back in thirty minutes. *Barring a crisis.* The short ride across town seemed to last an hour as she replayed the morning activities. Em had participated in Bible study, called numbers for Bingo with Gail, ate half her donut and sipped at a cup of coffee. She still seemed tired, but her mood had been upbeat.

Minnie's fingers curled around the steering wheel as she pulled into the driveway, her chest tight. Much as she prayed Jackson hadn't been stupid and taken Em to Minneapolis, she'd prefer that to finding her collapsed on the floor. With no answer to her repeated knocks, she unlocked the front door. "Please, Lord," she whispered.

"Em? Jack?" Heading toward the kitchen, she passed Elmer Fudd draped over a dining room chair, uninterested in her midday appearance. No lunch leftovers or dishes in the sink.

She clambered downstairs, praying Em was doing laundry although the silence told her otherwise. A check of the bedrooms on the upper floor revealed no one, nothing out of place. Jack's room, surprisingly neat, gave her pause. Although they'd barely spoken all week, she remembered his plan had been to head to Minneapolis this morning. Em had been at Open Circle until lunchtime. Where had she gone after that?

On her way back down, she called the center. "Hey, Jody, it's me."

"Hey, boss."

"What time did Emily leave today? Before or after lunch?"

"Right before. Jack picked her up about 11:45, when you were on the conference call."

The truth hit her square in the chest. "Okay, thanks," she said through clenched teeth. "I'll be back soon."

Phone clutched in a white knuckled grip, Minnie stood in the silence of the kitchen and marveled, as if from a distance, that her rising blood pressure didn't blow the hair off her head. Who did he think he was? She'd told him Em wasn't up to traveling or being left sitting alone in an art gallery while he ran around being Mr. Bigshot Grandson.

"But did he listen to me?" she demanded of Elmer Fudd who now sat in the doorway blinking at her. "Of course not! *He* knows what's best for her, even though he hasn't been in her life for twenty years. I'm just some hysterical female who doesn't know up from down."

She squeezed her eyes shut against the sting of angry, frightened tears. "Lord, what do I do?" Every inch of her tingled with the desire to race up to the Cities to rescue her beloved Em. She'd have a few choice words for Mr. Grandson before buckling Em into the car and driving out of his life for good.

Stomping out of the kitchen, determined to make sure he never did something like this again, the 8x10 photos on the dining room table stopped her. Bertie and her boa. Frances holding a coffee pot. Em with her Bible in hand during Bible study. The fight drained as she lifted the picture, studying Em's peaceful expression. Em wouldn't fly off the handle and race two hours north without knowing all the details. She'd pray first, an actual prayer rather than self-righteous muttering. *Boy, it didn't take long to go right back to my old self.*

Sinking into a chair, she closed her eyes. "Sorry, Lord. I'm making a stink about his attitude while mine's no better. But...I'm afraid." She rested her forehead against her clasped hands. "Keep her safe. Give her whatever strength and endurance she'll need. Help her have fun with —" she swallowed, "him. And bring her home soon."

Wanting to cling to the anger and fear, she consciously uncurled her fingers one at a time, and lifted open palms. "It's not about me, Father. Or Jack. It's about her."

In the quiet of the moment, she pulled in a long breath and slowly released it, unclenching her jaw, her neck muscles, the crease in her forehead. When she told Jackson what she thought of his behavior, which she would do when they returned, at least she wouldn't do it at top volume. Lucky for him God had hold of her temper—at least for now.

Jackson shifted his weight, watching his grandmother study each photograph carefully. After a nice nap on their drive up to Minneapolis, she'd been anxious to get to the studio. Now she took her time with each photo, stepping back then moving close, her expression neutral.

It mattered what she thought of his work, like it had when he'd taken his first pictures as a child. She'd lavished

261

praise on him along with honesty then, but now she said nothing. Anxiety had a stranglehold, cutting off his breath. Did she know she was killing him with silence?

"There's water in the backroom," Dave Emerson, the gallery owner, said as they waited for Grandma Em's response.

"I think I'll get some and step out back for a minute." Grabbing a bottle from the small fridge, he shoved open the back door. In the shade of a scraggly elm, he guzzled the bottle empty.

He'd been taking photographs the majority of his life, and received dozens of awards and accolades from prestigious places, but no one's praise meant more than his grandmother's. And, if he were honest, Mindy's. She'd no doubt discovered they were gone by now. Amazingly, he hadn't received a blistering phone call. The police hadn't shown up with a missing person's report. He deserved both, sneaking out of town like that.

She'd made it perfectly, condescendingly clear what she thought of his capabilities when it came to caring for his grandmother. And while he'd fully intended to tell her they were going, while reminding her he didn't need her permission to go on a trip with his own grandmother, he'd chickened out. He'd convinced himself it would be better to slip away without a fuss, but his conscience continued to poke at him. Minnie deserved better.

The plastic bottle crumpled within his grasp as he turned back to the studio. He hadn't noticed it earlier, but Grandma did seem frail now. He'd been so preoccupied with final show details, he hadn't noticed. Maybe Mindy had been right.

Well, she was here and doing well, so Mindy's opinions were irrelevant. At least until he had to face her again. He shook off the guilt and returned to the studio, the cool air a welcome change from the humidity outside.

"There he is." Dave stood with Grandma Em in the middle of the showroom. "Your lovely grandmother has some comments for the artiste."

Jackson joined them. "My toughest critic."

"And your greatest fan," she said with a smile. She held out her arms and he hugged her. "You have a heart for people, Jack. We see it in your photographs. In the focus you give to each subject."

His heart leaped in his chest.

"You aren't photographing their plight," she continued, moving to stand near one of his favorites. She gestured at the wizened old man squatting before a fire, bushy brows over black eyes that were focused on the camera. "You show their dignity. The light of the Creator in them despite their circumstances."

Standing beside her, he could smell the smoky air of the tiny village, hear the clang of cow bells and the laughter of children. Even there, in the harshest of settings, he'd encountered love and hope, joy, resilience. Acceptance. "I'm glad that's what you see," he told her.

"And I, for one," Dave interjected, "am stoked that Minneapolis gets to experience it this weekend."

Jackson smiled, grateful the opportunity had materialized. His life seemed governed by coincidences like this lately. "I'm excited to open the show tomorrow."

His heart took up a disjointed beating as he steered his grandmother toward the last grouping of photos. He'd told Dave he wanted to be there when she saw them. "There are a few more back here. These are my favorites."

They moved around the column and her breath caught, a hand going to her mouth. "Oh! Jack!" She stared up in amazement at the larger-than-life photos of her Lawton friends. "It's Bertie! Chief! There's Moses. Oh, and dear Helen. Oh, Jack—I love this one most."

He did too. Minnie crouched beside Elwin, her hand on his arm, the two generations sharing a smile. The bright colors, the clarity of the subjects with the blurred background of others in the activity room. Minnie's young, flawless profile as she looked up into Elwin's craggy, weather-worn face.

Grandma turned a tearful smile to him. "As beautiful as all the others. Thank you for including them." Her smile faded as she studied him. "Does Minnie know they're here?"

Did he look as guilty as he felt? "She's seen them, but I didn't have time to..." The lame excuse trailed.

"You were afraid of how she'd react."

He lifted his shoulders. "Stupid, I know."

"You need to tell her." She set a hand on his arm, the corners of her mouth twitching. "After the show."

His shoulders relaxed as he smiled. "I will. After." Always easier asking forgiveness than permission. Although this might prove that old adage wrong. But she was right. Minnie deserved far better than he'd given her.

"So," Dave said, "can I treat you two to dinner tonight to celebrate?"

Jackson put an arm around his grandmother's thin shoulders. His gut told him to take her back to the hotel, but he'd learned the hard way to ask first. "Which would you prefer—dinner out or room service at the hotel?"

"Why don't you young men go out and enjoy yourselves? This old lady would like to go back to the hotel."

"Then room service it is." He lifted his gaze to Dave. "Thanks for the offer, but I'd better take my best girl back to the hotel and make it an early night. Big day tomorrow for all of us."

"Gotcha. How about I see you back here around 4:00 tomorrow? I'll have dinner for us in the backroom, and a buffet at that end of the studio for our guests."

"Perfect. We'll be sightseeing tomorrow, so that will give us time to get back to the hotel for a quick nap and shower."

They said goodnight and Jackson led his grandmother slowly out to the car. She leaned against his arm, her steps not as steady as they'd been. He pushed Mindy's warning from his mind and focused on getting Grandma Em settled in her room, feet up, with a hot meal before her.

As they ate, she asked about the photos, how he'd met Dave, and how long they'd be staying in the hotel. Most of her questions and responses were clear, but the confused ones unsettled him. He'd make sure someone stayed with her every minute tomorrow evening.

After helping her into bed, where she drifted off immediately, he sat on the edge and watched her sleep, her hand relaxed in his. This shouldn't be the very first show she attended. She should have been at all of them over the years. So much time lost, memories not made.

Why? He turned the question on her God. *Why did you keep us apart? I needed her in my life. Maybe I wouldn't have screwed up so bad if she'd been there. You knew she wasn't dead, so why didn't I?*

Uttering a quiet oath, he went to the window as an old memory swept over him like a cold breeze—a ten-year-old on his knees looking out the back window of the car as they left Lawton, tears in his eyes. He'd known a broken heart at that young age, and again at fifteen when they'd told him she died. And he'd known anger at a God who hadn't seemed to care.

He returned to her bedside and listened to her gentle snore. And his heart broke again at the realization that their time together was limited. She believed so deeply in God, her faith unshakeable despite their separation. He shut off the light and went to his adjoining room, leaving the door open between them.

If believing gave her strength and courage, he wouldn't argue. But she'd never convince him that God cared one whit about his life. Too many events proved otherwise. She could have her faith. He'd continue doing fine without it.

CHAPTER THIRTY

From dropping her toast buttered-side down on the carpet to the handle breaking off the coffee carafe, Friday morning seemed to conspire against her. She stubbed her toe while making her bed, closed her scarf in the front door as she left the house, and dropped several files before reaching her desk at Open Circle.

Once the lights were on and the coffee pot had started perking, she returned to her office and reached for the morning devotional beside her computer. Moses led the people out of Israel but day after day they complained. They were sick of manna. They were bored. Why had they even left Egypt? Hardly reassuring.

She leaned her head back against the chair, staring at the water-stained ceiling tiles. *Moses was obedient and look where that got him. Stuck in the desert trying to make everyone happy. That's how I've felt, Lord. No matter what I've done, it hasn't changed the fact that they're going to close the center. Why am I trying so hard?*

"Morning, Minnie!" Gail passed the office door with her usual upbeat greeting.

"Good morning, boss," Jody echoed from the reception area.

"Morning, ladies," she called back, straightening in the chair.

That was why she tried so hard. For this amazing staff. For the seniors who deserved her best. And that's why Moses had kept at it. For the people who needed his guidance, his leadership. She closed her eyes and raised a prayer of thanks filled with praise. She might still be feeling off-balance today, but focusing on what she was called to do, following the path God had put her on would put life back in perspective.

Clients filtered in and the building filled with chatter and laughter. Cheryl presided over donuts and coffee with a surprisingly cheerful expression. Gail's infectious enthusiasm during morning exercise made even Chief crack a smile. When the group broke for program activities, Minnie went to Mary's office to discuss client progress, med changes, and new issues that had surfaced.

"Minnie!" An aide appeared in the doorway an hour later, beckoning. "Moses is having a heart attack!"

In a motion eerily reminiscent of Em's stroke, Minnie dashed down the hall to the activity room, Mary close behind. Moses sat in a recliner, head back and eyes closed, Gail kneeling beside him. Minnie knelt on his other side and took his hand, relieved when his fingers wrapped around hers. Mary spoke softly to the elderly man, checking his pulse and listening to his heart.

Cheryl and Gail kept the seniors calm and occupied as the paramedics arrived. The men chatted quietly with Mary as they took the elderly man's vitals and gently transferred him to the gurney.

Clasping Moses' gnarled hand, Minnie walked beside him to the ambulance. She leaned close before they lifted him in, and said firmly, "You'll be just fine, Moses. They'll take good care of you, and you'll be back here very soon."

The oxygen mask muffled his response, then he squeezed her hand weakly and closed his eyes. Moments later she stood alone in the parking lot, watching the ambulance pull away. "Lord," she whispered, "let him feel your presence. Keep him strong."

Inside, she paused at the front desk to confirm with Jody which incident report she'd need to fill out. The front door opened, and she greeted Bonnie and her therapy golden retriever with smiling relief. Gentle and attentive, three-year-old Muffin was a favorite at the center. Bonnie brought her every Friday, which never failed to close out the week with wide smiles on seniors and staff alike.

As Bonnie and Muffin made their way toward the main activity room, Minnie exchanged smiles with Jody. "Perfect timing," they said in unison.

Chuckling, Minnie returned to her office. She took a sip of coffee and grimaced. Lukewarm. At the serving counter, she refilled her cup and watched Muffin in the activity room. Former mayor Jerry couldn't work a room better. The dog moved patiently from person to person, giving tail-wagging, undivided attention to each. Bonnie did the same, setting a hand on a stooped shoulder, sharing a joke, complimenting the bright colors of a ragged sweater or favorite piece of costume jewelry. What a delightful team they were.

As Muffin moved to Helen, Minnie started back toward her office, then paused. Alice, their sweetly confused newest client, shuffled her walker with purpose toward Muffin as Helen leaned down to pat the dog's head.

"Alice, not too close," Minnie called, her voice lost in the noisy room. Most of the seniors knew to let Muffin come to them so no one crowded the dog.

Minnie started forward as Alice moved closer to Muffin. The walker's front wheel rolled across the dog's feathery tail and Muffin yelped and jumped up, sending Helen teetering backward with a startled cry. Hot coffee splashed across the back of Minnie's hand as she set the cup down and dashed toward the falling woman.

In slow motion, she watched Bonnie reach for Helen as other staff did the same, but the tiny woman landed on her backside then bumped her head against the thread-worn carpet and lay still. Heart pounding, Minnie shook the liquid from her stinging hand and dropped to her knees beside Helen.

Mary raced from the nurse's office, phone already at her ear. With practiced efficiency, she urged Helen to remain still while they waited for the ambulance. Minnie held Helen's cold hand, smoothing the gray curls from her forehead and chatting quietly about upcoming activities, Em's escapades in Minneapolis, and the calendar that was nearly complete.

Again, Minnie watched the paramedics take gentle care of the woman, then walked beside her to the ambulance. As it pulled away, she folded her arms tightly against the urge to burst into tears. With her emotions already at the surface, Helen's frightened, confused expression had stretched her control to the breaking point.

She looked upward and pulled in a shaky breath. "Thanks for helping me hold it together," she said, then offered a broken laugh. "Or more like holding *me* together. What a day."

Lunch passed uneventfully, the atmosphere of the seniors subdued after two disruptions to the morning's routine. Even Cheryl stepped up with a few jokes, parading through the dining room with Bertie's red boa wrapped around her neck. Minnie delivered meals, reassured those looking the most confused or concerned, and wished yet again for Em's stoic presence for them. And for her.

Once the afternoon activities were underway, she debriefed with Mary and Cheryl, and completed reports for both incidents, then mailed off a card to Bonnie assuring her they couldn't wait to see Muffin again. When Gail had walked her to her car, the poor woman cried and apologized yet again.

Glancing at the clock, Minnie breathed a deep sigh of relief that the programming day would end in the next hour. The staff would need a debrief, right after she applauded them for their professionalism in the face of two events within hours of each other. Heart filled with gratitude, she penned quick notes of thanks for each person.

Her intercom buzzed. "Minnie?"

"What can I do for you, Ms. Jody?"

"You need to take this call. It's the police department."

Minnie sat frozen, unable to breathe. Em.

"Minnie?"

"Yes. Send it through." When her phone rang, her trembling hand bobbled the receiver. She cleared her throat. "Minnie Carlson."

"Hey, Minnie. This is Mitch Griffin at the police department. I'm calling about your van."

She sagged against the chair. It wasn't Em. "The center's van? Did we forget to renew the tabs?"

He gave a short chuckle. "I'll have to check on that. It was in an accident about thirty minutes ago."

"Oh, no! How's Manuel?"

"A little shaken up, but he's okay. Sounds like the brakes went out. He wasn't going fast, but his quick reaction kept him from hitting anyone. Unfortunately, he hit a tree. The front of the van is pretty banged up."

"We can fix that." *No, we can't. There's zero money for van repair.* "I'm just glad he's all right, and there weren't seniors on board." *Thank you, thank you.* "Does he need me to pick him up?"

"I said I'd give him a ride home. Stu is towing the van to his repair shop. That okay?"

Sure, why not? Stu could take whatever he could use off the old vehicle. and they'd sell the rest for scrap metal. "Yes, that's fine. Thanks, Mitch. I appreciate you taking care of all that. Do I need to sign anything?"

"Nope. Give Stu a call later so he can give you the bad news."

"Is there any other kind coming out of a repair shop?" Lame but the best she could do as the center's future faded to black.

"Good point. Take it easy, Minnie."

Receiver still in her hand, she stared at the computer screen, devoid of emotion. It didn't matter anymore whether the Boutique and Café brought in money, or if they sold even one calendar. If any of the board members were on the fence about closing the center, today's events would—

The blare of the fire alarm lifted her to her feet and propelled her into the hallway. Cheryl and Gail were already herding the seniors toward the front door, grabbing armloads of coats and sweaters from the closet.

Minnie squeezed past them to check every room and bathroom for people and for the threat. No burning smell, no smoke or heat. She scanned the kitchen and activity room with narrowed eyes, turning in a slow circle. Nothing.

Pulse pounding in her temples, she brought up the rear of the group as the staff led the anxious seniors out the front door and shepherded them to the far end of the parking lot. Sirens approached as Minnie, Cheryl, and Gail did head counts. All accounted for.

"There's no fire," Jody told her moments later. "Hector accidentally pulled the alarm while putting his jacket on."

The pent-up air left Minnie's chest in a whoosh that made the scenery lose focus for a moment. *Really, God? Like we haven't had enough excitement for the day?*

The fire chief's SUV and two fire engines pulled into the parking lot, engines rumbling and lights flashing but thankfully without sirens blaring. Minnie met Ron, the fire chief, as he climbed out of his vehicle. Three fire fighters hurried past and disappeared into the building. Moments later the alarm went silent.

Ron, the fire chief, questioned her and Cheryl about the event. After the earlier fiascos, there had actually been a brief period of calm and quiet in the center. "Apparently one of the client's caught his sleeve on the handle," she said.

An imposing man with broad shoulders and a thick neck, Ron frowned down at her. "There's supposed to be a cover over the handle. It shouldn't be that easy to," he made air quotes, "accidentally catch it."

Minnie tried to picture the alarm near the main closet. "I thought—"

"It was old and cracked, and it just fell off last week," Cheryl said from beside Minnie. Hands on her hips, she frowned up at him. "The fire department said they'd replace it. We put a request in for a new one weeks ago."

Minnie fought a sudden urge to laugh. All 5'2" of her assistant director standing up to the 6'4" fire chief. She coughed and nodded, thankful for Cheryl's keen memory. "She's right. The plastic had cracked. We were told it was on the list of repairs to get done soon."

Ron looked momentarily confused, then his frown

deepened. "The inspector didn't mention that to me. We'll make sure it gets done Monday morning. Now, is everyone accounted for?"

"Yes. The evac went perfectly." Minnie shot a half-smile at Cheryl. "We have an outstanding staff."

"I see that," he nodded. The fire fighters emerged from the building, and he stepped away to talk with them, then returned to Minnie and Cheryl. "It appears everything checks out. They've reset the alarm. Good job on the evacuation, ladies."

"Thank you," Minnie said. "I'm assuming we won't be charged for this call?"

He grumbled and nodded. "I'll charge the inspector, instead."

"That's fine with us," Cheryl said, arms folded. Her steely gaze remained fixed on Ron.

Minnie's lips twitched. Hysterical laughter bubbled under a thin blanket of control. "Thank you for your prompt service, Ron."

As the fire engines lumbered out of the parking lot, Cheryl turned to Minnie. "Manuel is late again."

Manuel. In the excitement, she'd forgotten their dilemma. "He's not coming. Right before the alarm went off, I got a call from Mitch Griffin saying the van brakes went out. Manuel wasn't hurt but the van sounds totaled."

Cheryl stared at her, mouth open. "So how do we get a dozen seniors home without the bus?"

"Well..." Few of the staff were certified to drive clients anywhere. "I guess you and I will be driving them."

The woman's eyebrows leaped up, then crashed down. "I only have room for three. And your car isn't even safe."

Nice reminder. "I'm open to suggestions."

Gail walked past leading the clients back to the building, an eyebrow raised. Minnie nodded. "I'll be right in." The group shuffled past, their posture stooped, exhaustion in their movements.

"There must be someone we can call." Cheryl's voice pulled her attention back.

"I don't mind driving—oh!" Over Cheryl's shoulder, Minnie stared at the St. Edwards Childcare bus pulling into the parking lot.

Stopping beside them, the door swung open and Manuel grinned. "You ladies need a lift?"

"Manuel! What are you doing? Are you okay? How did you get this?" Questions spilled out. She was beyond making sense of anything now.

"My wife, she runs the daycare at St. Edwards. When I told her about the van, she said we can use the church bus until we get ours fixed."

"That's wonderful!" Minnie exclaimed. "Give your wife a great big hug from me when you get home."

The young man chuckled. "My pleasure. Now, I have some seniors to get home so I'd better get parked."

As those seniors needing the ride filed back out of the building, Minnie stood beside the bus, reassuring each person as she helped them step onto the stool, climb into the unfamiliar bus and get settled.

When the last of the clients departed an hour later, Minnie gathered the remaining staff at the front desk. "Well, this was a day for the record books, don't you think?"

Tired smiles, muted chuckles.

"First, I want to say that it's truly a joy serving with each of you. I've never been prouder to be part of Open Circle. You met each crisis with professionalism, putting the needs of our clients first. Because of that, we made it through without anyone falling apart, which we know can happen all too easily."

"You kept us all focused," Gail said. Heads nodded.

Minnie smiled. "Thanks, Gail, but today took all of us working together. We should be proud of what we did. Now, get out of here and enjoy the weekend. You've earned it."

What she'd earned was a shortcut to closing the center.

CHAPTER THIRTY-ONE

"This is delicious, Jack. What a lovely idea." Grandma Em smiled at him over her leafy salad where they sat on the trendy Uptown restaurant patio. "And a perfect day too."

"You're not too warm?" Despite the stifling August humidity, she'd insisted they sit outdoors. He'd asked for the shadiest seating available.

"Not at all." Her eyes twinkled. "Old folks have bad circulation."

Jackson laughed. "That might be true, but since you're hardly what I'd call 'old,' that doesn't necessarily apply to you."

"I'm two years into my eighties. That's old," she stated, then sighed. "Although how it happened so fast, I'll never know."

"Time goes faster and faster the older I get," he said. "I can't imagine you're 82. You're the same as when we left Lawton so long ago."

"Older, wiser, and slower." She reached across the checkered tablecloth to pat his hand. "And you are the man I knew you would be."

The bite of hamburger went down hard. She'd said something similar right after the stroke. He'd fallen far short these past two months, especially with Minnie. Not only had he snuck off with Grandma, he'd "forgotten" to bring up using the photos in his shows. Yeah, not doing so well on that good man thing.

He wiped his mouth and leaned back. "Grandma, I still don't know why we left in such a hurry."

A shadow crossed her face as she picked through her meal. Finally, she set her fork aside and met his gaze. "It's my fault, I'm afraid."

"What could you possibly have done that would make my parents pick up and leave, and never return? Did they ever speak to you again?"

She studied him silently. "What do you remember most about your father?"

He shrugged. "Man of few words, to me or even to Mom. I don't know what he actually did for a living. We never talked about it. He'd come home from work, we'd eat dinner, and he'd lay on the couch watching sports until I went to bed. We left Lawton for Chicago, then Detroit, but even then I didn't know why."

"You paid the greatest price," she said softly, sorrow creasing her face.

"For what?"

"Can I get you folks anything?" The pompadour-styled waiter smiled courteously. "More water? Coffee?"

Jackson glanced at Grandma Em before shaking his head his head. "Nope. We're good. Thanks."

"I'll check back in a bit to see what you'd like off our amazing dessert menu. No rush."

Grandma Em refocused on her salad. When she didn't continue her earlier thought, Jackson prompted, "So what went wrong?"

"When?"

He blinked. She looked at him, eyebrows raised, and an alarm rang in the back of his mind. "We were talking about why we left Lawton."

"Oh, yes. I'm sorry." She waved her fork. "I get distracted so easily now. You left because your father was angry with us. We'd told him we wouldn't continue paying their mortgage if he wasn't going to work harder at holding down a job."

What? "He didn't have a job?"

"He couldn't stay with a job longer than a year. Due to his depression, I believe."

"He was depressed?"

She pursed her lips and nodded. "It runs in the family, I'm afraid. Your grandfather dealt with it his whole life."

"Grandpa Richard?" He had that parrot thing going again. Memories surfaced of a soft-spoken, occasionally morose grandfather who only came alive when they talked photography. How often had he brought his camera to Grandpa with some made up issue simply because then the man would talk to him? His father hadn't had the same interest, so he'd never been able to engage with him. Not that he would have been allowed to, anyway. Silence reigned when Dad was home from "work."

"Jack?"

He shook the memories away. "Sorry. How long had you been paying the mortgage?"

"We helped whenever we could. After they lost the babies, he lost interest in even looking for a job. We thought we could light a fire under him." Her brow pinched. "We lost you instead."

The knot in his throat made it hard to respond. So much new information to take in. "We all lost," he managed finally. "So...I had siblings?"

"She had four miscarriages after you were born." She closed her eyes briefly. "They never got over it. We hoped that the stability of a new job would help, but he stopped trying."

"Instead of leaving, you'd think they'd want family around during that time."

"Most of us would. Depression alters how people think. Behave. How they perceive the world."

A city bus lumbered by as they sat quietly.

"I suppose that explains why we up and moved, but not why they told me you died."

She drew back as if he'd slapped her with his words, eyes wide, a hand at her throat. He reached toward her. "Grandma, I'm sorry. I thought you knew."

"Any dessert for you two?" Could the waiter have worse timing? "Or a box for—"

"The check," Jackson snapped, not looking away from her pale face.

"Yes, sir. Right away."

Grandma stared at her half-eaten salad, fingertips pressed to her lips. His stomach churned. If she didn't know... *Oh, God. Minnie was right.* "You thought I'd just forgotten about you all these years," he whispered.

He leaned toward her. "Grandma, you know I would never have stayed away from Lawton if I'd known you were still there, right? I'd have come back as soon as I could drive." Desperation drove his words. "I begged them to let me come back for Grandpa's funeral, to visit you in the summers. I tried a million different ways to get them to let me go. But we moved farther and farther away instead."

Tear-stained eyes lifted to his, dark in a face that had suddenly aged a decade. "What were their reasons?"

"There weren't any. Just the same answer over and over.

It won't change anything. Move on." Even then he'd wondered how people could be so unfeeling. "They said that that part of my life was over." He blinked hard. "Like I could forget my childhood, and the people who'd loved me most."

The waiter returned, and Grandma collected her purse as Jackson stuffed cash in the check folder. He helped her up from the chair, keeping a firm arm around her shoulders as they returned to his car.

The short trip back to the hotel was silent. Much as he wanted to pepper her with more questions, the stunned sadness on her face silenced him. He helped her settle in for a nap, then went back out for a walk.

The little she'd told him explained a lot. Like why there'd always been a cloud over their home. Other kids' homes were noisy and fun and filled with light and energy. The curtains in his home were always drawn. The only sound came from the muted television. He'd always had fun with Grandma, occasionally with Grandpa, but never at home. Never with his own parents.

He started across the street, then pulled up short when a car raced by, horn blaring. He stepped back up on the curb and waited for the walk signal. Being killed before tonight's show would be bad press, not to mention a repeat of the Big Blunder.

His mind whirled faster than his pace, thoughts tangling with questions. He'd have had siblings, if not for the miscarriages. Maybe that would have changed the atmosphere. Apparently, he wasn't enough. Dropping onto a bench, he stared across the busy street, vaguely aware of people hurrying past. Understanding dawned slowly, like the sun peeking over the mountains near Sacramento.

With parents who rarely spoke to him, and even less

frequently to each other, he'd escaped into a childhood world of his own design, speaking through pictures. He'd used his camera to give himself a voice, and he had searched for other forgotten people to make them known, shining light on beauty amidst unbearable pain and loss. Unable to make sense of his own life, he'd spent the past decades trying to bring attention to the plight of others as bewildered by the world as him.

He had answers now to some of his questions, but he was also more confused. The angst of his parents had colored his life, and the choices he made. Like his need to keep moving, and his lack of commitment to any one place or person.

Mindy's smiling face leaped to mind. Her devotion to his grandmother had irritated him. Threatened him. She had what he'd been missing all his life—a place to belong, people who loved her, a home. He wanted that same relationship with Grandma Em. And now he wanted it with Mindy as well.

The buzzing in his pocket jolted him from his musings. The calendar reminder set him on a return path to the hotel. Only two hours until he needed to be in place for the opening. He realized now he had a lot to say, and this show was essential to making the world take notice of issues around the world. He couldn't mess this up.

Having Grandma Em at his side as the show opened would prove something else. He wasn't a nuisance, nor unwanted. He had family, a place where he belonged. Jackson Young did indeed have something to say, and tonight would be the start of a whole new conversation.

"The seat of honor," Jackson said, sweeping his arm toward the wingback chair he'd bought on his last trip to Minneapolis. He had tested at least fifty before deciding on this one for her. "You'll be able to see everything that's going on from this VIP section."

"Pish." Grandma Em waved a hand at him before settling in. "*You* are the VIP. My, this is very comfortable."

He winked. "Not too comfortable, I hope. I don't want you dozing off. Now, Nanette here is usually Dave's assistant, but for tonight she's all yours."

The woman stepped forward with a bright smile and shook his grandmother's hand. "Miss Emily, I'm here to do your bidding, so you let me know what you need. I'll be sitting right here with you for the evening."

Grandma Em chuckled. "I guess it's good to have friends in high places. I'm perfectly capable of getting whatever I need, but I'll be happy to have you tell me all the gossip."

Jackson tugged at his tie. "The biggest gossip is that Jack Young is wearing a sport coat and tie."

"You look so handsome," Em declared. "Nanette, would you take a photo of us? I want Mindy Lee to see how well he cleans up."

The last thing Minnie would want tonight was an in-your-face photo of the two of them. He still expected her to show up with a SWAT team to save Grandma Em from the villainous grandson. The image made him grin and Nanette took the picture.

"Jackson," Dave called from the other end of the small gallery. "Need your expertise over here."

He waved back, his stomach doing a two-step. "And we're off and running. At some point I'll be giving some remarks, so I'll let Nanette know when to bring you up front." He pressed a kiss to the top of his grandmother's head. "Thank you for being here, Grandma. I love you."

"I love you, Jack." She patted his cheek. "Thank you for bringing me. I'm so proud of you."

His heart singing, Jackson headed toward Dave. How the evening went hardly mattered now that he had his family back. But deep inside he wanted it to be wildly successful so she'd have a true reason to be proud.

Greeting the early attenders, he autographed prints, spent a few minutes in a live interview with a local news station, and marvelled at how the studio filled with laughter and conversation. He wandered from one photograph to the next, chatting with admirers, and adding details to the printed materials. There were countless stories about each subject, their location and plight, and what had been done—or still needed to be done —to ease their situation.

As the crowd grew, so did interest in the Open Circle collection. It seemed people were accustomed to seeing photos of Third World countries, but to be faced with the aging and dementia in their own backyard made them pause. He fielded as many questions about the adult day program as he did about the man in Guatemala and the children in Ukraine.

"Ladies and Gentlemen, may I have your attention?" Dave stood at the podium mid-gallery. The chatter quieted as guests turned toward him. "I'm Dave Emerson, owner of the Emerson Gallery, and I thank you for joining the celebration tonight. Isn't this an amazing collection of humanitarian work by one of Minnesota's own?"

Standing beside his grandmother's chair, a hand on her shoulder, Jackson acknowledged the enthusiastic applause with a nod.

"I know you're not here to listen to me," Dave said, "so

let's hear from the photographer himself. Jackson, how about a few words?"

Dave motioned, and Jackson forced his feet toward the microphone. He cleared his throat. "I'm thrilled to be here tonight, sharing photographs from around the world. This gallery holds a special place in my heart because I had my very first show here many years ago, so it's good to be home again.

"These photographs are a tiny glimpse of a very big world. Even within a small village in Nepal, no two stories are the same. I use my camera as best I can to showcase who they are, and their corner of the world, but so often..."

In the quiet gallery, he steadied his breath. "So often, my attempts show only the first layer. One thing I've discovered is that people are people are people. We all have dreams—for ourselves, our children, our home. We hate injustice and unfairness. And we all have riches. For some, it's money. For others, it's the determination to have a better life. And for still others, it's a desire to care for others in need."

He smiled. "And for others, like those of us here tonight, it's the willingness to raise awareness. My hope is that photographs like these will encourage us to work together to make this a better world."

Applause sent heat crawling up his neck. Usually he said something simple like 'thanks for coming and enjoy.' But now he understood the significance of his work, that it was a calling far beyond taking photos because he was good at it.

"There's a collection here tonight of which I'm especially proud, and I want to take an extra moment to tell you about it. Over here," he gestured to his left, "is a collection called Open Hands, Open Hearts, Open Circle.

The photos are of some very special people I've had the absolute privilege to spend time with this summer."

He pulled the mic from its stand and moved toward the collection. The audience shuffled along behind him. "I was born in Lawton, a speck of a town outside Rochester, and spent the first ten years of my life there. My grandparents were born and raised there, as were their parents. My grandmother still lives there now. Actually, she pretty much runs the place." Amidst the laughter, he looked over at her, and she waved a hand in dismissal, smiling. He gave a quick nod at Nanette before turning back to the gallery guests.

"These people are the backbone of Lawton and of society in general. They raised generations, built a community, managed farms, ran stores, kept the town safe, taught the children." Minnie's voice rang in his soul. "But what I've learned over this summer is that once they're older, they are often shunted off to nursing homes, or they live alone and lonely in tiny apartments. At Open Circle Adult Day, however, the amazing staff is determined to shine a light on the joys and concerns of aging. On the value of each person, even in the face of dementia. The photographs in this collection represent some of the seniors who take part in that program."

Nanette had brought Grandma Em to his side. "I'd like to introduce you to the single most influential person in my life, and the rock of Lawton, Minnesota—my grandmother, Mrs. Emily Young."

Through the applause, he hugged her warmly, laughing when she reached up to pat his cheek. Then he turned back to the crowded studio. "Thank you all for coming tonight. If you enjoy the photos, tell your friends. The show will be here through the weekend, then I'm taking it to New York for a show that starts in two weeks. Thank you."

With Grandma Em at his side, he couldn't be prouder of how opening night had gone. No major blunders for this show. He would cross his fingers and toes that all went as smoothly in New York City.

Before that, however, he'd have to face Minnie. Of the two events, that was the most frightening.

CHAPTER THIRTY-TWO

After endless hours of tossing and turning, Minnie rose with the sun, drained. Desperate to stop reliving Friday, she cleaned every corner of the kitchen, then changed bedding and did a load of laundry. Unfortunately, keeping her hands busy didn't stop the chaos in her brain. One disastrous event after another battered her with what ifs.

The battle followed her into the yard where she puttered in the garden, deadheading flowers and pulling weeds. If only she could pull the condemning thoughts out of her head as easily. She tried humming but couldn't keep a melody straight.

Tires crunched over gravel and she turned where she knelt, swiping at her forehead with the back of her glove. Jackson's car, Em smiling and waving in the passenger seat. Minnie pushed slowly to her feet and started toward them, pulling off the gardening gloves. If they were boxing gloves, she could give Jackson the punch he deserved. But after yesterday, she didn't have the energy for even one swipe at him.

She mustered a smile and opened the passenger door. "So the prodigal grandmother returns!"

"Hello, dear heart." Em hoisted out of the car and wrapped Minnie in a familiar hug. "It's good to be back."

"Did you have fun? How was the show?"

"Wonderful. There were so many people there last night, they were standing outside." The breath she blew out sent strands of red hair waving upward. "But I am tired. Can we sit?"

"Wouldn't you rather go home? I'm sure you need a rest after such a whirlwind trip."

"Pish." She leaned on Minnie's arm as they strolled toward the shaded lawn chairs. "I will nap soon. I want to hear what's happening here." She paused and motioned at Jack who stood beside his open door. "Come sit with us."

Minnie looked back without meeting his gaze and gave a short nod. He shut the door and followed, settling in a chair slightly away from Em's side, as if to give them privacy. His cautious, sideways glance gave Minnie a moment of satisfaction.

She turned toward Em resting in the lounge chair, gratitude swelling her chest. Em was home, safe and sound, weary but smiling. "Now, tell me all about this latest adventure of yours."

As she recounted their activities, Jackson quietly supplied an occasional detail or clarification. Clearly, she'd loved the time with him, gushing over the gallery, the photos, and how kind everyone had been. When she ran out of words, Minnie excused herself to get them something to drink.

In the kitchen, she set tall glasses of lemonade on a tray beside a plate of cookies and a few flowery napkins. The screen door opened, and she turned to scold Em for following her in, then stopped.

Jackson held the door open behind him, as if ready to run. "She dozed off," he said.

Minnie nodded and unloaded the tray. Their snack could wait.

"Mindy...I'm sorry."

She nodded again, looking out the window.

"Could we talk for a minute? I want to explain."

Eyes closed, she prayed for calm, then turned to face him. Crossing her arms, she leaned back and waited. He stepped inside, letting the screen door latch quietly behind him.

"We had a really great time," he said. "I didn't know how much I'd missed her until she stood there with me on opening night."

No surprise that it was all about him.

"But I realized, Friday morning actually, that you were right. She's a lot more frail than I wanted to believe. I've been determined to believe she's come back 100%, but when the two of us were alone, I could see she hasn't."

He stuffed his hands into his pockets, studying her worn but clean linoleum floor. "Getting to know her this summer has been amazing. It's filled a hole in my life I'd covered over with activity, and awards, and rarely staying in the same place longer than a few weeks. Trying to be somebody, to be noticed. Getting my grandma back has made me realize I already *am* somebody. I don't need the accolades, although they're nice," he added with a fleeting grin. "What I've needed were answers to my weird childhood."

He nodded absently. "We had some good talks. I learned...lots of things. But what I learned most is—" Their gazes met, and he swallowed. "I'm not always right. In fact, most of the time I'm wrong, especially when it comes to relationships. Simply because I wanted her there didn't make it okay to disregard what the professional said."

Turning, he looked out at where Em slept in the shade. Minnie watched his shoulders drop, surprised that the fury of several days ago had been replaced with compassion.

"I missed out on two decades with her. I can't get that time back no matter how hard I try, so I need to savor every minute we have going forward. And," he faced her again, "be thankful for how well she's been loved all these years. By this town, her friends. Especially by you."

Minnie stared at him. Was he being serious, or simply trying to get back in her good graces? She bit back a snort at the idiocy of such a thought. He'd never cared if he were in her good graces or not.

"I was a coward," he admitted, stepping closer. "I should have talked about it more with you, but my, uh…ego wouldn't let me."

Now *that* was honest.

"I'm sorry, Mindy. I wanted to be the most important person in her life, the one who knew her best, but I'm not. And I didn't want to face the truth that the stroke changed her, probably forever." He pulled in a deep breath, lips pursed. "I wanted to pretend that nothing had changed, but it's been 20 years. Everything has changed."

Minnie carried two of the glasses to the table, motioning with her head. He grabbed the plate of cookies and followed. She took a long sip before responding. "I want to pretend the same," she admitted. "I'd even be happy to go back six months, to when I wasn't running Open Circle and the stroke hadn't happened."

"And I wasn't here."

She studied him across the table. "No. I'm glad you're here. You make her happy. And I think your being back in her life gives her some closure to the past."

He relaxed against his chair, a smile playing at his mouth. "So, I'm not quite the thorn in your life that I was?"

"Not *quite*," she said, "but don't push it. I was so angry when I realized you'd taken her to the Cities I'm surprised *I* didn't have a stroke."

Jackson nodded, dark eyebrows tented as he lifted a shoulder. "I'm glad you didn't. I was stupid and selfish."

His sincerity splashed water on the last smoldering embers. "With my mom gone, Em has been my family. I didn't want someone taking my place in her life. Even the grandson she adores. But that's as childish as you sneaking out of town."

They sat in silence, looking out the window at the sleeping woman they loved.

"How about," he suggested, "we start seeing her from a grown-up perspective, and work together to take care of her?"

She chuckled. "Are either of those possible?"

"Well…" He wiggled his eyebrows. "Even though I didn't act like one, I'm really trying to be a grown-up."

Their smiles connected. "Me too."

"Okay, then. We're co-captains on Team Emily. I'm going to take her home now for a nap and start focusing on the next show. And I promise I won't sneak her out of town for that one."

Minnie stood, rolling her eyes. "I would hope not."

She followed him toward the door but before pushing it open, he turned back to her. She stopped before bumping into him.

"Mindy, I—" His silent perusal brought a rush of warmth to her face. "I don't know how to thank you for being her family all these years. She loves you, and I know when I act like a jerk to you, it hurts her as well. I'm gonna do better for both of you."

Words failed as she looked up at him. This Jackson, with a sweet smile and sincerity in his eyes, was a nice surprise. She bit her lip and nodded.

His smile widened and he opened his arms. "C'mere."

She rested within his friendly hug, the tension of the last few days evaporating in the security of his arms. More than wanting to clobber him for scaring her so bad, she wanted to stay right there, with his arms around her. A safe place to hide from the world.

That was a far scarier thought.

Jackson studied the calendar proof. Each page highlighted a different aspect of Lawton, featuring those seniors most closely tied to it. The Town Hall page featured Chief and Jerry in their public servant careers, and Grandma Em in her Town Council days. Retail and Business stood out brightly with Bertie. Education and Learning featured Frances, and the teachers Joyce and Marg. Moses grinned from the Farming page. Family and Community had six other men and women.

He nodded, satisfied, and propped his feet on the coffee table. The final design revealed Mindy's creative eye woven into his photography. They made a good team— eager to showcase Open Circle's importance in the community, as well as their delight in each senior.

They were a team in other ways now too: working together instead of against each other for their grandmother's benefit. He chuckled. He'd come a long way if he could concede Em was as much Mindy's grandma as his. Who'd have thought that would be possible?

Fingertips tapping, he stared out the window. In his earlier life, he'd have given God the credit. But if he did that now, he'd have to give Him credit for the Minneapolis show. With a snort, he went into the kitchen for a cup of coffee. He'd leave the faith bit to Grandma and Mindy. He had enough to think about. Like making sure he'd covered all the details for New York. It wasn't only his reputation on the line this time. Russell and Branton would be forever linked to him if he messed up. His stomach flipped. And, of course, Pierre Guillaume, who'd thrown open the doors of his studio to welcome him in.

At least in the Big Blunder it had only been him going down in a flaming wreck. Now he had a chance to not only redeem himself, but to shine light on the amazing talent of his colleagues.

There was no room for error, no excuses this time around. Everything had to run smoothly. A lot of people were counting on him.

CHAPTER THIRTY-THREE

Jackson leaned into Minnie's office. "Well, you look very professional and in charge this morning. Like someone heading to a board meeting."

Or a firing squad. "Looks can be deceiving, but thanks."

He set a brown box on the edge of her desk and dropped into the chair. "You're not nervous, are you? Mindy, you'll blow them away with everything you've done in just four short months."

"I needed more time. What we've done won't be enough."

"It will be," he insisted.

His firm response calmed the jitters dancing in her chest.

"I've brought something that will be icing on the cake." His dark eyes sparkled. "It turned out great."

"The calendar?" she squeaked, pulling the box close and lifting the cover. A hand went to her open mouth. The cover photo of the center bathed in sunshine somehow made the old building look impressive. How did he do that? "Oh...Jack."

He grinned in response, then motioned her to go on. "It gets better."

The simple image she'd had in mind paled compared to the final product. She carefully lifted a calendar from the box and settled back in her chair. Jackson's pictures breathed life into the center, into Lawton. She saw the town she'd grown up in, then and now, in brilliant color and breath-taking sepia tones. And there at the end, a summary page of activities, celebrations, everyday life. Even the Boutique and Café. The back featured a group of seniors and staff wearing plastic leis and hoisting cups of pineapple juice.

"I hope those are happy tears."

She lifted her gaze at his quiet comment and nodded, lips pressed together. If she opened her mouth, she'd make a fool of herself, and probably wreck the calendar clutched against her chest. He'd done so much more than simply take photos. His creative genius was evident in the combination of old and new, the quiet beauty of wrinkled skin and gray hair, and in the polish of the finished product.

Pushing to her feet, she set the calendar back in the box, then moved around the desk. He stood, and she went into his embrace, thanking God for sending this man into her life. He'd put up with so much from her yet continued to offer his help and friendship.

"It sorta made me want to cry too," he admitted, his breath warm against her forehead.

Her giggle sounded more like a snort. Mr. Bigshot Grandson had a soft heart. And a warm hug.

"Okay." He reached around her, then handed her a tissue. "Time to put on your Director face and give them a presentation they don't expect."

She mopped her face and returned to her chair. "That's

the plan. And you're right—this calendar is icing on the cake." She ran a hand over the cover page. "It's really beautiful, Jack. Thank you."

"You're welcome. I enjoyed working on it with you. Now, what can I do to help you knock their socks off? Want to practice your speech?"

"That will make me *more* nervous," she admitted. "How about serving lunch with me?"

"Sure." He glanced at his watch, then pulled a calendar from the box. "But since lunch isn't for thirty minutes, let's admire our handiwork."

She laughed and eagerly opened her copy. His chuckle slid between her ribs to warm her heart.

Minnie smoothed her blouse and adjusted her skirt, then checked her folders one more time. Financials. Staffing. Past and Current Comparisons. Future Plans. Calendars for each board member. She drew a steadying breath, lifted her chin, and entered the noisy meeting room.

Nick approached with a welcoming smile. "Good to see you, Minnie. I've been looking forward to this meeting. I'm glad the board will get to see the full picture of what you've accomplished."

"I hope it's enough," she said.

"I'll do my best to help."

She shot him a grateful smile before depositing her materials at the far end of the table. Connecting her laptop to the projector, she breathed a prayer of thanks when the opening slide jumped to life on the screen. As more board members wandered in, laughing and chatting with each other, she distributed handouts around the table. Praying over each item, she set out a comparison report, and the financials she'd spent hours laboring over.

She'd hand out the calendars toward the end of her presentation.

Nick called the meeting to order and they covered several business items regarding the care center, then she was on. Pulling the feel of Jackson's arms around her, she opened her presentation with a story close to her heart—Em's stroke and how it had affected everyone at Open Circle. As the presentation unfolded, she chatted through each slide, sharing stories to illuminate the numbers, figures, and facts.

Lastly, she handed out the calendars and invited them to take a few moments to look through it. She returned to her seat, praying that Jackson's vibrant photos would bring the center to life for them. They looked through each page, pointing out photos of interest, exchanging smiling comments. Every person at the large table praised the effort that had gone into such a quality project. She savored their positive response, eager to share their comments with Jackson.

As she moved into the financial portion of the presentation, she prayed for calm. The numbers spoke for themselves, sadly, and she had no desire to belabor the point. But the questions seemed relentless.

"So how did you have the funds for printing the publicity materials for the grand opening?"

"When did you take a cut in pay?"

"Who pays for the extra coffee and bakery items for the café?"

Minnie answered the inquiries carefully, honestly, wanting to disclose as little as possible about how her own money had been used. She didn't elaborate unless they probed. By the time the inquisition had died down, she felt like she'd run a marathon. She'd have to zip home for a shower before heading back to her office.

Finally, Nick drew the presentation to a close, giving her a hearty handshake with an extra squeeze as he smiled down at her. "Well done," he said quietly as the board members applauded.

"Great job, Minnie," several people said.

"Best presentation I've seen in a long time," another added. "Thanks for all you've done for the seniors."

When she finally stepped out of the nursing home and into the sunshine, her emotions were a tangled mess. Relief. Sadness. Joy. Fear. She'd done all she could except thank God for the calm and focus that had gotten her through the longest ninety minutes of her life. She paused in the parking lot to do that with a full heart.

"So you knocked their socks off?" Jackson's voice came from behind.

She jumped. He relaxed against the back of his car, arms folded as he grinned at her.

"Unfortunately, they were all still wearing them when I left," she said, "but I think it went well."

He shrugged. "Socks are over-rated."

"I agree. I need to run home for a couple of minutes. Is everything okay in there?"

"All's quiet, especially with Bertie at a doctor's appointment." He opened the passenger door with a flourish. "Limousine service at the ready. Hop in and I'll run you home."

"Thanks, but—" He could probably smell the residuals of her boardroom workout even now.

"Get in. I'll have you home and back in a flash."

Unable to muster a good argument, she approached. "Fine, but you might want to leave the windows open."

He chuckled. "I just had my own firing squad experience in Minneapolis, remember? I can sympathize."

On the short drive across town, he peppered her with

questions about the presentation, their reactions, how they liked the calendar. She happily recounted the praise they'd showered on his work. When he offered his palm for a high five, she laughed and slapped it with her own.

After she'd changed, they headed back to the center. When Jackson took a left instead of a right, she raised an eyebrow. "You forget where we're going?"

"Funny. I need to pick something up." He parked outside the ice cream shop, hurried in, and then returned with a large bag which he deposited in the backseat. Minnie hid a smile at his smug expression.

She stopped in her office to deposit her computer and presentation materials as Jackson moved on toward the activity room.

"Come on down when you're ready," he said over his shoulder.

When she entered the room moments later, a cheer erupted.

"Three cheers for our fearless leader," Jackson exclaimed, leading them in successive "Hip, hip, hoorays" that left her laughing.

Every senior wore a party hat, many holding glasses of punch that they lifted in a toast as they cheered. With his own party hat set at a jaunty angle, Jackson stood behind a table covered with bowls, spoons, and several containers of ice cream along with toppings.

As she approached, his wide grin set her heart spinning.

"We're glad you could join us for a little celebration to thank you for everything you've done for Open Circle. And for delivering a presentation that showed what a great place this is, and how amazing we all are."

She accepted the bowl heaped with her favorite Peppermint Bon Bon. "The last part being the most important, of course." Her smiled faded as she poked at the ice cream. "Not so sure the presentation will sway any opinions."

Em slipped an arm around her. "God will take care of that," she said. "We are called to do the best we can. Which you did."

Minnie rested her head briefly against Em's. "The easy part was talking about all of you." She looked around at the dear faces smiling back at her, blinking quickly. "I did what I could, but I can't guarantee it will be enough to keep the center open. So when you think of it, pray for the decision makers, and for this program. Now, we'd better enjoy Jackson's treat before it's ice cream soup!"

Savoring her first bite, she sighed. What would life look like without seeing these people every day? She swallowed with difficulty, praying she wouldn't find out.

CHAPTER THIRTY-FOUR

Jackson came down the stairs and joined his grandmother in the living room. "Grandma, I meant to ask you about something." Packing for New York, he'd discovered the letter that changed his life.

Settled in the rocking chair, glasses perched on her nose, she looked up from her book. "What's that, dear?"

He sat on the edge of the couch closest to her. "Remember I said I'd gotten a letter from Daniel asking me to come to Lawton? That's how I found out that you were still living here."

"I remember. What did the letter say?"

He held it out and watched her read it. She lifted a confused expression, then understanding filled her face. "Wait here."

She handed the letter back, set her book aside, and pushed out of the rocker, pausing to get her balance.

Jackson thrust a hand out in reflex.

"I'm fine, thank you." She went through the kitchen and he heard the door to the garage open and close.

He waited, foot tapping, fighting the temptation to see

what she was up to. Then she came shuffling back carrying a box. He stood to take it from her.

She lowered back into the rocker with a satisfied sigh. "This is for you. From your grandfather."

"Grandpa Richard?" He lifted the cover and gaped at the contents. "His cameras!"

"One is his," she affirmed. "The other was *his* father's. Your great-grandfather's."

"Wow." He reached in and gingerly lifted out the camera he remembered his grandfather using as he shared his knowledge and passion. "This is amazing."

She smiled at him. "I knew you would think that. I didn't want to send it through your parents. I was afraid you'd never see it."

"I'm glad you didn't." He set the box on the floor and stood to hug her. "This is so much better anyway."

She patted his cheek when he leaned back. "I think so. Now, you should get both cameras appraised. I don't think Richard's is worth much, but your Great-grandfather Young's might be."

Through the viewfinder of the vintage camera, Jackson looked around the room, memories spiraling. Walking through the woods, traipsing through fields, in blazing sun and icy winters. He'd loved every minute Grandpa had spent with him.

Turning his attention to the other item in the box, he carefully lifted out an old 35mm. In pristine condition. "Wow. It's a Leica III with a range finder."

"You know old cameras?"

He grinned. "I'm a camera geek. This one is amazing. Do you know if it still works?"

"It did when your grandfather was alive, but it's been many years."

Returning it to the box, he hugged her again. "Thank

303

you. I'll take great care of them."

"I know you will, dear. He'd be so happy to know you have them now."

Jackson stood on Minnie's front step that evening, one hand behind his back, and a box at his feet. He swiped the sweat from his lip. Maybe the flowers were too much. She'd appreciate the cameras, but it might look like—

The front door opened, and a surprised smile lit her face. "Jack! Hi. Come in."

When she pushed the screen door wide, he produced the flowers with a self-conscious flourish. "I have something to show you."

"They're beautiful."

"Oh." His face flamed. "I don't mean the flowers. Well, I do, but..." He cleared his throat. "These are to say bravo for a job well-done yesterday."

Her smile deepened along with the flush of her cheeks. "Thank you. Come in and I'll put them in water."

While she went into the kitchen, he set the box on the coffee table, muttering. "What a moron, Jack. Can't even bring a girl flowers without—"

"There." Minnie set the vase on the mantel and stepped back, hands on her hips. "They're perfect. Thanks, Jack. That was sweet."

He nodded. "You're welcome. Before I head off to New York, I wanted to be sure you know how much I appreciate everything you do for Em." The words ran together.

"I do. You've told me."

"I know, but I'm telling you again." Like any reasonable idiot would. "Anyway, what I wanted to show you was what Grandma gave me tonight. This is the reason I came back to Lawton." He handed her the original letter. "When we first met, I mentioned getting a letter. I wanted you to see I didn't make it up."

She flinched. "Jack, I'm sorry—"

He cut her off with a wave of his hand. "I know. But I wanted to show you what changed the direction of my life and brought me here to Lawton. To Grandma and," he lifted his shoulders, "you."

Biting her lip, cheeks a pretty pink, she turned her attention to the brief paragraph. Her eyes widened. "I can see how this came as a shock if you thought she'd died years ago. Did you find out what the family matter was?"

He pulled out his grandfather's camera. "Cameras. This is the one I learned to take pictures with. It's my grandpa's Yashika."

"Wow. How cool that she wanted you to have it."

"*He* did, I guess. He wasn't much of a talker without a camera in his hands."

She examined it with a careful touch. "The apple doesn't fall far from the tree, hmm?"

"Yeah, except sometimes I don't know when to shut up."

"Well, there is that." She laughed at his mock frown, handing him the camera. "Can you still use it?"

"I hope so. I'm going to take them in for an appraisal and get them checked out."

"Them?"

He pulled out the other camera. "This one belonged to my great grandpa."

"Really? Jack, this is amazing!"

He nodded, watching her study the old Leica. Somehow he'd known she'd appreciate the gift, its sentimental value. "Having generations of cameras really ties me to my family. It's a shared connection that sort of affirms what I do for a living."

She glanced at him. "You needed the affirmation."

Hands in his pockets, he shrugged. "I guess I did. Sounds childish."

"No, it doesn't. We all need to be affirmed in what we do." She handed him the camera. "Aside from wanting to keep Open Circle going for my seniors, it would also affirm that my work is important. That it matters."

Their gazes met and held. Apparently, they weren't that different. "You know it matters even if the center closes, right?"

She looked away. "Sure."

He set the camera in the box, then stood and gently pulled her to her feet. Grasping her shoulders he said, "Mindy Lee, look at me."

She complied reluctantly. Man, she was pretty. "You've made an impact on the seniors, but also the town. People see your passion and hear you talk about showing respect to every age, and it changes things. They come by the café because they know it's good for the seniors to have people to visit with. They're buying the calendar."

Her brow lifted. "They are?"

"I checked with Randy at the drugstore this morning. They're nearly sold out. We'll need another printing soon."

With a shriek, she threw her arms around him, bouncing with excitement. He laughed, happy to hug her for any reason.

"But," he said, leaning back with a serious expression, "even if they weren't, the calendar will keep their memories alive. Whether Open Circle stays open or not, you've provided dignity, and joy, and care for people who have thrived because of it."

Her mouth trembled. "But what if..."

He set a finger against her lips. "No what ifs. You've done all you could the past few years, right up to the presentation. Now it's up to God whether it stays open or not." *Up to God? Since when?*

"Yeah, you're right," she agreed with a sigh, relaxing in the circle of his arms. "Thanks for the reminder."

He smiled. "You're welcome."

In the silence that followed, he studied her upturned face. From her freckles, to the slight curve of her dark eyebrows, and the pink brushed across her cheekbones. He drew a finger along her jaw, a smile lifting a corner of his mouth.

The ring of her phone made them jump, yanking them from the moment, and she stepped away as she pulled it from her back pocket. "It's the hospital," she said, frowning. "Hello?"

Though Jackson had left Grandma happily reading in her rocker, his heart leaped into action as he listened to Minnie's side of the conversation.

"When? Is she stable? I see. Would you like me to come now? Okay. That's fine. All right. I'm praying for her. Thanks for letting me know, Roberta."

She clicked off the call, shoulders slumping. "Bertie fell at home this afternoon. Her daughter called 9-1-1, and they took her to St. Mary's in Rochester. Broken hip."

He felt a twinge of guilt at his relief. "She'll be okay?"

"It's hard to say." She dropped onto the couch, obviously not rushing to the hospital. "Broken hips are especially dangerous for seniors. The trauma to their bodies, and the difficult recovery period can lead to pneumonia. Many don't recover. It's what eventually took my grandma ten years ago."

He sat beside her. "They can die from a broken hip?"

"It can be a death sentence for some, especially the very frail," she said. "But Bertie is tough, and though her memory is iffy, her body is strong."

Jackson scooted closer and wrapped an arm around her shoulders.

She leaned against him, resting her head on his shoulder. "My head knows this is part of working with seniors," she said quietly, "but my heart doesn't like it."

He tightened his arm. He couldn't imagine flirty, funny Bertie in a hospital bed, in pain. "We'll pray for a quick recovery. She's a tough old bird, like our Em." What was with all this God and prayer talk?

"Thank you. I'll go see her later tomorrow. Her daughter, Roberta, said the surgery went well."

"That's great. See? She's already on the mend."

"Yeah." The noncommittal response suggested there would be more to the story than Bertie simply recovering for a few weeks and then bouncing back to her old self.

Maybe praying wouldn't be such a bad thing—at least for Bertie.

After a long, peaceful silence, she sat up, giving him a shy smile. "Thanks, Jack. I'm glad you were here when I got the call."

"Me too. I suppose I'd better get on home and let you get to bed." He reached for her hand, studying the slender fingers resting in his. "I'm heading out first thing tomorrow for New York. I'll be gone at least a week. After that, I have to head Botswana for a shoot I've had on the calendar for months."

Gnawing her bottom lip, she nodded slowly. "How long do you think you'll be there?"

He'd never thought in terms of time before. He'd simply left for a shoot and gone where it took him. How long had never mattered to anyone, including himself. "A couple weeks maybe. I'll come back as soon as I can."

Her smile lacked energy. "You do what you need to do. We'll be here."

"You won't miss me? Even a little?" Hopefully the teasing tone would cover the fear behind the words.

She looked down at their lightly clasped hands and tightened her fingers before meeting his gaze. "Maybe more than a little," she admitted, a corner of her mouth lifting. "You'll be careful?"

No one had ever asked that either.

"Of course. I have family who needs me to keep things running smoothly."

She laughed and pulled her hand away as she got to her feet. "Oh, that's right. How *ever* did we manage before you?"

"Good question." He stood and stretched, then settled the box under his arm and followed her to the door. "Thanks for watching out for our favorite girl."

"Always."

He looked down at her with the oddest sense of rightness. This place, this girl. *This* was his life. He pressed a gentle kiss to her forehead, then tapped her nose, enjoying her shy smile. "Be good," he whispered.

"I'll try," she replied, a sheen in her brown eyes. "Good night, Jack."

"Good night, Mindy. I'll call when I get settled in New York."

She stood at the front window, waving as he pulled away from the curb. He imprinted the image deep into his mind. He couldn't wait to come home.

CHAPTER THIRTY-FIVE

The days following Jack's departure dragged for Minnie, despite his daily check-in calls. With Bertie missing from Open Circle, the other seniors were cranky, expending little energy to participate despite the staff's best efforts. Chief was especially obstinate without the job of herding Bertie in and out of the building. The eccentric, eternally cheerful Bertie was missed by everyone.

Em half-heartedly encouraged the others to join in the activities, though she sat quietly during the singing and offered little to the Bible study discussion. Several times she mentioned going to see Bertie, and Minnie agreed she'd drive her, Joyce, and Marg over soon.

After dinner at Em's each night, they played cards and talked. Mainly about Jack. The only time Em truly smiled was when Minnie blushed in anticipation each time her phone rang. Since it brought Em some element of joy, Minnie didn't scold her.

Jack's late-night calls, separate from his daily calls to Em, were the highlight of Minnie's day. It seemed easier to open up over the phone, to share her concerns and get his advice. He always ended the conversation with a joke or story that left her smiling.

Late Thursday evening, snuggled under her comforter, Minnie smiled at Jack's nervous chatter. After a week of interviews, meetings, and last-minute decisions, Opening Night was now only 24 hours away.

"So it's probably a good thing the big night is almost here," she mused. "I think one more day would send you babbling off the cliff."

"Hey, I resemble that remark."

She giggled. "I know." His answering chuckle warmed her. "After all the interviews and planning stuff, I'm surprised you aren't tired of talking."

"I need to focus on something other than the show. I like knowing how things are back there. It keeps me sane amidst the craziness out here."

"Well, I wish you were here to liven things up. Everyone is still upset about Bertie. It's funny how one event can change the dynamic of a group."

"How is our favorite flirt, anyway?"

"They moved her to rehab. New Life in Rochester."

"Already? That's great! I've heard that place has quite the reputation."

"Whatever," she laughed, grateful they could joke about it now. So much had changed. "It will take her longer than it took Em, but this is a whole different issue. What surprises me is that she's not more confused than her normal state."

"Maybe it helps if you're already confused," Jackson suggested.

"Hmm. That could be." She sighed. "Thanks for calling Em every day. Bertie's fall really shook her up. I think it helps to hear your voice. She wants to take a couple of the ladies to visit Bertie, so I promised I'd drive them next week, once Bertie's had a chance to get a routine going."

"She's brought it up every time I've called. I'll call her twice a day starting Sunday, at least until I get to Botswana. Once we get past opening night, I'll be able to breathe."

Minnie rearranged the pillows behind her and settled back, content to talk as long as he wanted. "Are you nervous?"

"More than I thought I'd be. I screwed up really bad a few years ago, so this is my chance to restore my reputation. It doesn't help that both Noah and our friend Paul are counting on me to pull it off."

"What happened?"

"It's a long, boring story about stupidity. Wouldn't you rather be sleeping?"

"If it's that boring, I'll doze off," she assured him, relieved he laughed.

"About three years ago, my agent set up a show for me while I was in the midst of some major assignments in Africa and India. Along with the show, she scheduled a meeting with the head of a major magazine. She worked months to set it up. It was a major coup so early in my career, and I was scared stupid."

"Uh oh."

"Yeah. So stupid that I missed the show."

Minnie's hand went to her heart, feeling his pain. "Not the meeting too."

He released a long, noisy breath. "That too. Somehow, I got so involved in the shoot, I blanked on the show. Missed my flights and everything. I was in a remote village, out of cell phone range, so I had no contact with the outside world. No access to my calendar. And apparently no brains in my head."

"You were so busy doing your job—"

"I messed up the biggest opportunity of my life." The words were heavy with regret.

"They didn't cut you some slack? No chance to reschedule?"

"Nope. And I lost my agent, as well. Can't blame her. Like I said, she'd put in tons of work getting the meeting arranged, and it looked like I blew it off."

"But...but..." She frowned at the injustice. "If she knew you at all, she'd have known you wouldn't do something like that."

"But it was up to me to keep track of my life, and I didn't. The good news is I have a meeting Sunday morning with the guy who's the new owner of the magazine, so I have another chance. That's why I can't mess this up, Min. I need everything to go perfectly, especially the meeting. It could mean some amazing assignments with solid pay, rather than me peddling my photos to whoever will look at them."

"That's great, Jack! I'll pray that everything goes perfectly, and that he loves your work *and* you."

"Thanks. I'm trying not to be as scared, but it's not working."

Jackson Young, scared? And willing to admit it? "You'll do great, and the guy will buy every photo you've ever taken."

He laughed. "I'll be happy if I get to sign a contract."

"Well, contract or no contract, your Minnesota fan club will welcome you home with open arms."

"I have a fan club? Cool. Who's running it?"

"Your grandmother, of course."

"Who's in it?"

She giggled. "Your grandmother."

"Oh." He was silent a moment. "That's it?"

"Well...I might be a charter member."

"Don't sound so excited." His chuckle returned. "There might be a few surprises in store for certain members of my fan club."

"Really? Like what?"

"Hmm. Well, maybe tickets to a show at the Guthrie Theater and dinner at a nice restaurant when I get back."

"Jack, she'll love it."

"Not her. You!"

Me?! A smile flooded her heart. "Really? I've never been to the Guthrie."

"Good. We'll get it on the calendar as soon as I get back."

Fingertips pressed to her mouth, she closed her eyes, enjoying the tingle racing through her. *We have a date!* "I'll look forward to it. And on that note, we'd better hang up, so you can get some sleep before your big day."

"I suspect I'll do more staring at the ceiling than sleeping. Wish me luck tomorrow."

"No need for luck," she said. "Everything is in place. Your photos are fabulous. And you're right there for the meeting. I think God is blessing all your hard work with a flood of good things that will take your career to the next level."

"Thanks, Mindy," he said softly. "That means a lot. I'll call you after the show tomorrow, if it's not too late."

"Call me no matter what time it is," she insisted. "I want to hear all the details."

"Yes, ma'am. Good night."

Minnie clicked off the call and lay quietly smiling into the darkness.

⁓

Friday afternoon, Minnie waved goodbye to Frances, then noticed the bus still waiting in front of the building, Manuel standing beside the open door. Only three of the usual five seniors were aboard. Minnie stepped out and waved at him. "Who's not on yet?"

"Joyce and Marg."

"Really? I'll go find them." She returned to the front desk. "Jody, have you seen our favorite teachers? They're usually first on the bus."

"They left with Emily right after lunch."

"What?" She searched her mind for an appointment she'd forgotten they had, or an activity they were going to. "Where did they go?"

"Emily said they were going to run over to see Bertie, and they'd be back," she glanced at the clock, "right about now."

Minnie bit her lower lip, willing herself not to panic, and returned to the waiting driver. "Apparently they're not here, Manuel. A little miscommunication. Sorry you've had to wait. I'll make sure they get home."

"We don't mind waiting another few minutes."

"No, go ahead. No sense in making everyone late. Have a good weekend."

As the bus pulled away, Minnie perused the parking lot, hands on her hips. Wait—Em's car sat its usual spot. She sucked in a sharp breath and pivoted. Her old Buick was missing. Em had taken her piece of junk? No!

She raced inside. "Did Emily tell you she was taking my car?"

"She said she'd forgotten to fill up, so she'd take yours." Her penciled eyebrows pinched together. "I thought you knew."

"No. I didn't. And I'd never have agreed. Mine's been acting up more than usual lately." She paced before the counter. "I told her I'd take her and whoever else wanted to go next week, but we'd have gone in *her* car."

Lord, what do I do? If I call the police and it turns out she's fine, she'll be so angry. But if I don't, and they're in trouble— No, she wouldn't go there. Couldn't go there.

"Do you want me to call the police, Min?"

Jody's voice broke into the disjointed thoughts and prayer. "No. Well, actually I do," she admitted, "but our independent Emily will throw a hissy fit if they're fine and I've treated her like a child."

"But it's three fairly frail older women…"

"I know. That's the part that scares me most." She gnawed her lip for a moment, then set her shoulders and gave a firm nod. "If she said they'd be back around now, let's give them a little more time. I'll call the rehab center to find out when they left. I should have *made* her carry a cell phone," she grumbled.

"I think I'll stick around a bit longer," Jody offered, "to make sure everyone's okay."

"Thanks, Jods. Would you call the housing unit and let them know Marg and Joyce will be back a bit later than usual? Oh, and ask them to call us if the ladies show up. Em might avoid me by dropping them off and then going home. With *my* car."

Minnie called the rehab center, relieved to learn the three women had indeed arrived and had a lovely visit with Bertie. Em had mentioned they were leaving later than she'd planned, and that she'd be "in big trouble" when they got back.

She'd be in bigger trouble than she imagined, but that would come after a long hug. The war of emotions making her nauseous, Minnie debated a call to Jackson. It might make her feel better, but it would only worry him right before the show.

She glanced at the clock and turned to her computer. Em had one hour.

⁓

Jackson wandered through the gallery again, stifling the urge to laugh out loud. They'd done it. He, Russell, and Branton had made it to New York. Together. In Pierre Guillaume's gallery, no less. After three long years of fighting his way back, he stood on the edge of his future with a stupid grin on his face. And tomorrow morning he'd have breakfast with the person who could fully restore his reputation.

He stood before the photo of Em and Minnie, the silly grin now tinged with warmth. The conversation with Minnie last night had done wonders for his peace of mind. He'd never have thought they could be friends, let alone have a date when he got back. He hadn't been planning anything of that magnitude, but when the words popped out and she agreed, he'd nearly whooped into the phone. He couldn't wait to get back to Minnesota. Maybe he'd buy new clothes before leaving New York. To take Mindy out on the town, he needed to dress better than his usual attire.

Still grinning, he returned to the backroom where Russell and Branton sat sharing beers and a laugh. He'd barely settled in the chair before Pierre swept into the room in an expensive grey suit and silk tie. Jackson glanced down at his twill pants, button-down shirt, and sport coat. He should've shopped before the show. At least he wore his decent shoes.

"Gentlemen, the time has come. All of your hard work has paid off, eh?" He nodded at each of them. "You have good gifts, and I am happy to share them with the world. I am sure the turnout will be amazing. We will be in top form tonight, no?"

"As long as the star of the show stays front and center," Noah said with a wink at Jackson. "Paul and I are the icing on the cake of Young's work."

Even Pierre laughed at the ridiculous analogy. "I believe each of you is a layer of this exquisite cake, while my simple gallery is the showcase for all to enjoy it. But we will have a last walk through before the doors open wide. Come. Let's review our setup one more time."

Jackson followed them back to the gallery, a hand at his stomach. He should have asked Grandma to pray for a perfect show, for all of them to receive the recognition they deserved. He squared his shoulders and strode after them, head up. He deserved this night.

When the gallery doors opened, the initial trickle of guests grew to a steady stream, keeping them busy with greetings, introductions, and discussion about their varied photographs. Jackson enjoyed a third bottle of water from Pierre's assistant whose job, it seemed, was to keep him hydrated and introduce him to various guests. Feeling exposed without a camera around his neck, he gratefully accepted the young man's cheerful, knowledgeable presence.

He caught Noah's eye across the room and they exchanged winks and grins. To be holding this show with his best friend gave the evening an added spark. Having Grandma Em and Mindy here would truly be the icing Noah mentioned earlier. He turned to greet another guest, determined to make his family proud.

At eight o'clock, Pierre took to the small stage and welcomed all who were now crowded into the gallery. His accent, more pronounced than usual, gave the evening a European flair, as did his grand gestures as he briefly described each photographer's work. Then he called Noah to the stage. As they exchanged a hearty handshake, Pierre's assistant produced an extra microphone.

"Noah Russell has produced marvelous works," Pierre gushed, "particularly in zee areas of South America and zee Pacific rim. Noah, *si'l vous plait*, tell us a bit about what inspires you to take such special photographs."

Jackson folded his arms and leaned against a display wall, crossing his eyes when Russell looked his way. Whatever grief he gave, he'd no doubt get back times twenty, but he'd enjoy being on this side for now. His phone vibrated in his pocket and he pulled it out.

He slipped around the wall and out the door into the cool evening. "Hey, Mindy!"

"Jack, we can't find her!"

The terror in her voice stopped him. "What? Find who? Grandma?"

"She took my car to go see Bertie at the rehab center. And she took two other women with her." The high-pitched words muddled together with hiccupping tears. "But no one's seen them since they left the center hours ago. Jack, my car isn't reliable. What if they're lost—"

"Min, slow down. Take a deep breath." He took an exaggerated breath to help her breathe, and to slow his own heart that had kicked into high gear. "Good. One more. Okay, now start from the beginning."

As she related the details, her voice wobbled. "The police have been looking for them for the last few hours. On the ground, even in a helicopter. What if... if—"

"Sweetheart, don't go there. We'll find them." At least it wasn't the dead of winter. "She must have taken a wrong turn. People are looking for them, professionals who will know how to find them."

"I can't believe she snuck off with my car."

"We both know our girl wouldn't ask for permission. This isn't your fault, Min." He glanced back at the glittering lights of the gallery. "Do you want me to come?"

"No. You need to be there." A sharp breath. "They'll find her. I just wanted...I thought you should know. I'll call as soon as we hear something."

It didn't feel right to be celebrating in New York, but she'd probably show up before he could even get a flight. To leave now would mean destroying what he'd worked years to rebuild. Worse, leaving would damage Noah and Paul's reputations.

Jackson held the now silent phone in his hand, eyes closed. *God? Please help them find her. Not for my sake but for hers. And Mindy's.*

He returned to the gallery, his heart two thousand miles away.

CHAPTER THIRTY-SIX

Minnie stood in the middle of Em's living room, silence squeezing the breath from her as she glanced at the mantel clock. Eleven-thirty. The women had been missing for nearly nine hours; she closed burning eyes against the realization that they might not return at all.

Sinking into the rocking chair, she clasped the well-worn Bible to her chest, letting the tears fall. She'd had the nerve to be mad at Jack for taking Em to Minneapolis, yet she couldn't even keep track of her at home. Wrapped up in her own issues, she hadn't listened to Em's concerns about Bertie, hadn't heard her fear and anxiety.

She rocked in short bursts. *You should have known she'd do what you kept putting off. You, in all your great wisdom, decided she'd have to wait until next week.* The recriminations poked at her from all sides, stabbing into her aching heart.

She pushed out of the chair and retrieved her phone from the dining table. No messages. No missed calls. No news. Sliding the phone into her back pocket, she moved through the main floor, turning on every light, pushing curtains wide, opening blinds. Em would scold her for wasting electricity, but she wanted the brightest welcome possible.

On the second floor, she hesitated in Em's bedroom doorway, soaking in the familiar lavender scent. Not a wrinkle on the chenille bedspread, items arranged neatly on the dresser. From the photos lining the table beneath the window, Minnie lifted her favorite and smiled, running a finger across her mother and Em's smiling faces. Her twelve-year-old self sandwiched between them, grinning over a blazing birthday cake. Beside the weathered frame sat a new one, sparkling crystal, holding a recent photo of Em and Jackson.

She set the frame down, turned on the lights, and returned to the living room. She could call Jack again, but with no news, it would only make him feel worse being so far away. She dialed the police department. The sergeant kindly told her people were still looking, covering every country road, checking farms. She would receive word the minute they knew something.

Clutching her Bible, she paced and prayed with disjointed words that made no sense except to express the fear pounding against her ribs. The minute hand on the clock over the fireplace barely moved, inching its way around again.

In the kitchen, she started a fresh pot of tea. Em would enjoy a cup when she returned. And probably a cookie. She set out plates and napkins on the kitchen table, Em's favorite china cups and saucers at each spot, then gazed at the lonely setting through tears.

The front door opened, and her heart leaped into her throat. "Em? Thank God," she exclaimed, racing around the corner, then pulled up short. She frowned, blinking rapidly. "Jack?" Without pausing to make sense of his sudden appearance, she dashed across the room and flung herself against him. Strong, secure arms enveloped her.

"I couldn't let you do this alone." His familiar voice at her ear soothed the edge of hysteria.

She burrowed against him, eyes squeezed shut. If she opened them, he might disappear.

When she finally loosened her grip, he leaned back. "You holding up okay?"

Not so much. "I'm trying."

"I called the police department when I landed. Nothing new."

"Jack, where could they be? She's made that drive a thousand times and never once gotten lost. Any season, any time of day or night. I should have taken her when she first asked. She been upset by Bertie's fall, but I was so focused on keeping the center running, I didn't see how much. Why didn't I—"

"Mindy, stop." He put a finger to her lips and she stilled. "You do a fabulous job every single day caring for so many people, running an adult day program, keeping everyone happy. And above all, you love Em in a way no one else can. This isn't your fault, and you couldn't have stopped her."

With an arm firmly around her shoulders, he steered her to the couch and settled beside her.

Tears filled her eyes yet again as she leaned against him. "It will kill me if something happens to her," she whispered.

"I know." He pulled her close. "We'll pray nothing does."

After a silence, she asked in a tiny voice, "Really? You'll pray for her?"

He chuckled and pressed a kiss to the top of her head. "I have been since you called."

She sighed and relaxed against him. *Thank you, God.*

Jack slowly propped his feet on the coffee table, careful not to jostle Mindy where she slept nestled against him, and rested his head back against the couch. Getting her call, hearing the fear in her tearful voice, had set off a collision of emotions that still had him reeling.

He glanced at the clock. In a few hours, the new owner would discover he'd been stood up for the breakfast meeting. Blowing off that relationship was professional suicide, but what did his career matter compared to finding his grandmother? He'd sent a text and an email apologizing profusely for leaving New York before their meeting, and prayed the man had some semblance of a heart.

"You're *what?*" Noah had stared at him. "You can't leave! What about your meeting tomorrow? What about *us?*"

"You guys don't need me here." He'd stuffed papers and meeting notes into his bag. "The show is a success, and people are pushing each other out of the way to get interviews with both of you."

In the tense silence that hung between them, Jackson zipped his bag closed.

"After all these years of rebuilding," Noah said, "and you're going to throw your career out the window."

Jackson flinched at the sting of his words. "It's my family, Noah. I have to go. Pierre understands."

"So you're racing back there in the middle of the night to do what? Drive around the state of Minnesota in the dark until you find her and save the day? Isn't that what police are trained to do?" Noah followed him to the back door of the gallery. "At least wait until after your meeting tomorrow. You'll be more help in the daylight."

Hand on the doorknob, Jackson had paused. "And then

I can fly back for the funeral? Maybe I can't find her tonight, but I need to be there. For her. For Mindy. It's where I belong." He motioned with his head. "Now get back in there and be the man of the hour. I'll call you in the morning."

Minnie's restless sigh pulled him back to his grandmother's living room, and his arm tightened reflexively. *God? She's out there somewhere with her friends. Keep them safe. And help us find them before... Help us find them soon.*

He closed his eyes, letting the prayer fill his chest, and rested in the strange peace that blanketed them.

A persistent ring brought his head up. Early light was filling the livingroom. Minnie scrambled off the couch and grabbed the phone where it vibrated on the coffee table. "Hello? Yes, it is."

He sat up beside her, a hand at her back.

"You did? Where?" She glanced at Jackson and nodded, then pinched the bridge of her nose. "Okay. Yes, we'll be right there. Thank you. Thank you so much."

She clicked off the call and stared at him, chin trembling. "They found them. They're okay."

A flood of gratitude brought tears to his eyes. *Thank you.* "Where are they?"

"Being taken to the hospital in Rochester. We need to go."

⁓

Minnie and Jackson left the rising sun behind as they hurried through the sliding doors of St. Mary's Hospital, then down the hall to the Emergency Room. The receptionist gave them visitor passes and directed them to the rooms where the women were resting.

Sending Jack ahead to Em's room, Minnie stopped first to see Joyce. The woman greeted her warmly, her smile twinkling with mischief as she squeezed Minnie's hand. "Such an adventure for us old ladies. And to be saved by those handsome police officers was so exciting."

Minnie laughed, shaking a finger at the woman. "You're a stinker, Miss Joyce. Don't you go having more adventures without telling your family, all right? You scared us half to death."

"No more adventures anytime soon," she agreed. Her smile faded. "Especially overnight. It's not comfortable sleeping in a car."

"I wouldn't think so." Minnie patted her hand. "I hear your son will be here soon to take you home. Get some rest and I'll see you Monday."

In the next room, Marg wasn't quite as enthusiastic about the adventure but managed a laugh about the young men who'd come to their rescue. She vowed not to let Emily talk her into another drive. Minnie left her with a hug.

Minnie greeted and thanked the two police officers standing outside Em's room, then asked for details.

"It seems there was a slight detour that confused your grandmother," one explained. "They should have gone only a few blocks off the main road, but a wrong turn sent them down a few roads until they hit a dead end. That's when the car broke down."

"Good thing you keep a survival kit in your trunk," the other added. "The candy bars and water kept their energy up, and the blankets kept their body temperatures fairly regulated."

"How did you find them?"

"The farmer that owns the adjacent property was checking fences when he found the car. Got quite a surprise when he discovered three older ladies sleeping in it."

The men exchanged smiling glances. "Mrs. Young is a feisty one. Very unhappy that we called for an ambulance."

"She insisted she could get them home. We insisted otherwise."

Minnie managed a short laugh. "Thank you for overruling her."

"We're glad everything turned out okay. Well, we've got reports to write. We'll check in on the ladies later today. Oh, and we had the car towed back to Lawton," the first officer added. "It's at Stu's service station."

Probably parked right next to the Open Circle van. A towing charge on top of repair costs. She'd face that later. She paused at Em's door and pulled in a calming breath, then pushed it open. Jack stood beside his grandmother, holding her hand in a scene eerily reminiscent of the stroke. But this time Em was smiling—with a tinge of regret, but smiling. And this time, Minnie's response to Jack was completely different.

After a hug and an exaggerated once-over to make sure Em was okay, Minnie perched at the foot of the bed. "I can't wait to hear how this whole thing transpired."

"I didn't realize my tank was empty until I got to Open Circle." Em lifted thin shoulders. "You were on the phone so I didn't bother you." She lowered her chin, looking genuinely contrite. "I should have asked."

"Yes, you should have." Minnie patted her leg. "I'd have gladly filled your tank for you. So, you had an uneventful drive to the rehab center?"

"Yes. And a nice chat with Bertie. We headed back a little bit late, but we were doing fine until the detour. I hate road construction," she declared. "We were on roads I didn't recognize."

"I didn't know there were any roads you haven't driven on at least once," Jackson teased.

"Pish. They add roads to confuse us. And then the roads don't lead anywhere."

Minnie watched them interact, noting the dark circles under Em's eyes and her ashen coloring. While she downplayed the gravity of the event, Minnie knew she didn't take it lightly. She'd never knowingly endanger someone else. They'd discuss it later, when everyone had recovered.

Jackson said something that made his grandmother laugh, and Minnie smiled despite her exhaustion. He must have taken the first flight he could find after she called. And though she'd told him not to come, she couldn't imagine getting through the night without him. Her eyes narrowed. But that meant...

She frowned. He'd up and left his show. On opening night. He'd been living for this event, intent on restoring his career and reputation, thrilled to have the meeting with the magazine guy. She checked the clock over Em's bed. A meeting that should be happening right about now.

He glanced toward her as he laughed with Em, then sobered, lifting an eyebrow. She blinked the realization away and offered an awkward smile, turning her attention to Em. "So, did the doctor say you can go home, Miss Emily?"

"As soon as they bring in some papers. I'm ready for a bath. And a nap."

"I'll see if we can get things moving," Jackson offered. "How are the other ladies?"

"Fine," Minnie said. "They have family coming to get them." No doubt ready to sue Open Circle for endangering their senior. As Jackson left the small room, she reached for Em's hand. "You know I want to be angry with you, which I always fail at doing."

"You have every right." Even her wild red hair was subdued. "I am sorry, dear heart. I didn't mean to frighten so many people."

"Of course, you didn't. And I'm sorry that I didn't take you to see Bertie when you first asked. I should have."

Em rested her head back against the pillows and managed a partial smile. "We are a pair. Both taking blame. I won't let this reflect badly on you, Mindy Lee."

"It won't, silly goose." She'd already made a mess of everything. This would simply be one more thing added to the list. "Just a couple of ladies going to visit a friend," she wiggled her eyebrows, "and having an adventure along the way."

CHAPTER THIRTY-SEVEN

Leaving Em tucked warmly in her bed, lightly snoring, Jackson guided Minnie into the living room, and brought her a cup of coffee. She settled silently into Em's rocking chair, focused on the fire he'd built. Since that moment in the ER when he'd caught her frowning at him, she'd been quiet. He had no idea what he'd done wrong this time.

"I'm glad she's home safe, sleeping in her own bed," he commented.

"Mmhmm."

The fire crackled and popped. "You were great during all this, Mindy."

A faint smile relaxed the pinch to her brow. "I'm glad you couldn't see the mess inside. God got an earful the whole time."

"I think He's okay with that," he chuckled.

She shifted in the chair, her full attention on him. "I've always had the impression you weren't interested in God."

His turn to study the fire. "Yeah, well... We had a sort of falling out a few years ago." *We?* "Okay, I'm the one who fell out. When my life imploded around the Big Blunder, I needed someone to blame, so rather than look at my own behavior and choices, I blamed Him for letting me mess up. Lately I've thought maybe I was wrong."

He'd have to call it BB1, now that he'd added a BB2. There'd be no opportunity for BB3. *Loser.* "I messed up all on my own."

"But that was a combination of an overpacked schedule, traveling, being out of communication…"

He shrugged. "Excuses."

She rocked quietly for a long moment. "This time you made a choice."

"Yes, I did." Professional suicide.

"Because your family needed you."

Doubtful that would matter to the man who'd made a special trip to New York City to meet with him. He'd avoided his phone this morning, afraid to have that sentiment confirmed by text message.

"Jack."

He looked up at her firm tone, surprised by the tears shining in her eyes.

"You chose your grandmother over something you've worked every minute for over the past three years," she said. Awe colored her words. "You made an amazingly difficult decision that put her needs over what you've wanted so badly. No matter what else happens, she'll never forget that."

He forced a nod and tried to absorb her assurance. Once he recovered from intentionally trashing his career, he'd be happy about that.

"Neither will I," she added softly.

Their gazes held in the silence, a shy smile lifting a corner of her mouth. "When you showed up last night, I was so surprised. And so glad."

Breath stuck in his throat, he slapped his heart back

into rhythm. "Even though you told me not to come?"

She bit her lip. "Because of it."

"Oh. Good. That's good. Right?" His insides did cartwheels.

Her smile widened. "Yeah. It's good."

He stopped the growing puff to his chest. "Well, nothing is as important as my girls. Both of them."

Pink touched her cheeks. "You'll try to fix things in New York, right? At least explain what happened? You aren't irresponsible, Jack. You're the opposite, and they need to know that."

"I can't imagine it will make a difference."

"You won't know if you don't try, right? You came back for Em. Now go back there for you. You deserve it."

The earnest light in her eyes touched him. Strangely empowered him. What did he have to lose? He nodded. "I'll try. For us."

She relaxed with a satisfied smile. "Good. Now go find the earliest flight to the Big Apple."

Hours later he walked out of JFK Airport and hailed a cab, praying Pierre would let him back into the gallery. Too quickly, the cabbie pulled to the curb, then Jackson stood on the sidewalk scrounging for courage.

He hadn't known how to make things right the first time, hadn't thought he deserved a second chance. But there, in the tall gallery windows under soft spotlights, were photos that said he did. Brilliant colors. Poignant expressions. Powerful emotion in each one.

He had to try again, for himself and for the women in one of the photos hanging in the gallery. The two women who meant the most to him. Shoulders squared, he jogged up the steps and let the bells announce his entry into the gallery. *Here goes nothing. Or everything.*

Minnie slid a slice of apple pie onto the plate, added a scoop of ice cream, and handed the plate to Em in her rocking chair beside the fire. She freshened their coffee, then settled in her corner of the couch. "Yum!"

"Audry's apple pies are the best," Em agreed. "She's won many ribbons at the county fair over the years."

They ate in companionable silence. "Jack is very good at building fires," Em said.

"Is there anything your precious Jack doesn't do well?" came the teasing response.

"I don't believe there is."

Minnie laughed and set her cleaned plate aside, then raised her eyebrows at Em's perusal. "What?"

"At one time you wouldn't have thought that funny."

"True." She sipped her coffee and watched the flames. "He turned out to be okay."

"Just okay?"

"You already think he hung the moon. I don't think you need me to recite his many virtues."

Blue eyes twinkled. "I don't need it, but I think you wouldn't mind." She set her empty plate on the nearby table. "I have seen how he looks at you."

Minnie focused on the dancing flames, refusing to acknowledge the heat in her cheeks came from Em's declaration. She certainly hadn't seen it, although she'd wondered if her own growing feelings might be displayed that clearly. His swift return home Friday evening cemented those feelings.

"He said your words made him go back to New York. That if you could believe in him, he should too."

"Well, he can't give up without a fight," she said. "He's

worked too hard to get back to this point. I'm praying they'll hear him out."

Em released a deep sigh. "I caused such trouble. I'm so sorry."

Minnie slid to her knees beside the rocker and set her hands firmly on Em's arm. "You only wanted to see your dear friend. You just shouldn't have taken my junker of a car. But I totally understand you and the ladies wanting to see Bertie. If I had a decent car, this wouldn't have happened."

A wrinkled hand rested atop hers. "We're going to buy you a new one this week. I've been setting money aside for that purpose for a while. Consider it an early Christmas present," she added, a hand lifted to cut off Minnie's protest. "We *will* buy a car this week."

Tears smarted as Minnie gazed up at the beloved face. "Thank you," she managed. "And on that surprising note, we won't talk about your adventure again, all right?"

"Except to say how touched I was that Jack would leave his show and fly home for his crazy old grandmother."

"You're not so old," Minnie countered, and they shared a laugh. She returned to her spot on the couch. "He'd do anything for you, you know. He adores you. And he's heartbroken that the two of you lost so many years together."

"He is a good man," Em said, nodding. "I always knew he would be. His parents...they were misguided. And my son's untreated depression affected all of us. I didn't know they had told Jack such lies."

Minnie propped her chin in her hand. "Why did you send the letter about the urgent family matter, if you thought he'd forgotten you?"

"I always hoped there was a reason he stayed away,

something more than being too busy. If he didn't respond to the letter, then I wouldn't have tried again." Firelight danced over the tiny wrinkles created by her distant smile. "I prayed and prayed before we mailed the letter."

"But you never mentioned it to me."

Em glanced at her. "You would have tried to discourage me. To keep me from being hurt if he didn't return."

"Probably."

"We can't protect those we love from every possible hurt, dear heart. Much as I tried to do so with my son, I realize now I should have been more truthful with what I saw. I waited too long."

She looked every one of her eighty-two years. Minnie's heart creased. Em and her family had suffered in so many ways, but God had wrought a miracle for her when he returned her grandson. *Thank you, Lord, for bringing Jack home. And for forgiving my stubborn selfishness.*

Em met her gaze and smiled. "Now we will pray that Jack's dream comes true with that big magazine guy."

Minnie nodded. "He deserves it."

When she headed home, she tried to ignore the warring emotions in her chest. When Jack's dream came true, Lawton would become a place he visited when he had time. She pulled into her driveway and turned off the car, resting her forehead against the steering wheel. She'd miss him.

ее

Jack's phone call to Minnie that evening flowed with happy chatter. He'd had a conversation with Pierre that had "knocked his socks off."

"He wasn't happy that I left, of course," he said, "but he

understood why I needed to. Tonight I got an hour's worth of stories about his grandmother in Paris when he was growing up."

"So he didn't kick you out of the show?"

He chuckled. "Nah. I didn't think he would. Bad for business. But I hoped I wouldn't be banned for life."

"Now *that* would be bad for business. How about the other guys? Were they mad?"

"I think if it had been for any other reason, they would have been, but it seems like everyone has a soft spot for their grandma. And once I left, they both got more face time with the guests." He blew out a short breath. "Wow. That sounded egotistical. I didn't mean that the way it sounded. Like, since I wasn't there they could... Stupid comment, sorry."

"It didn't sound stupid," she assured him, then added, "maybe a little arrogant." When he remained silent, she burst into laughter. "Kidding! I'm kidding, Jack. Pierre gave you top billing for the show. It makes sense that when you weren't there, everyone circulated more."

"Not funny, Carlson," he grumbled. "Anyway, I feel so much better after talking to them."

"Good." She tried not to sound smug. "Have you talked to the magazine guy yet?"

"I had called from the airport before I left but had to leave a message. And I also emailed a quick explanation. I asked if he'd be willing to reschedule, and said I'd go wherever he wanted to meet, since he made a special trip to New York to see me and the show."

"I'm sure he'll reschedule."

He sighed. "I'm glad one of us is optimistic. My realistic side is winning right now. Remember, my reputation isn't stellar when it comes to these meetings."

"For very good reasons," she insisted. "I'm praying God works it all out perfectly, so you get the opportunities you deserve."

"Thanks, Min," he said quietly. "I'm not so sure I deserve much of anything, but I'm willing to grovel my way back into his good graces."

"Groveling is hardly befitting of Emily Young's renowned grandson."

His chuckle returned. "How about I send you in as my PR person? You'd end up running the mag."

"No thanks. I'm having enough trouble with my own little corner of the world."

"Heard anything back from the Board?"

"I'm assuming I will this week. I'm almost afraid to answer the phone, especially if it's Nick."

"Now who's being the pessimist?" he challenged. "The presentation went great, Mindy. They loved the calendar, and everything you've done in only four months, right? People are trying to get into the program, not running away from it. They'd be stupid to close it down now that you've turned it around."

His passionate words reached across the miles and wrapped around her. "How about you go to my meeting and I'll go to yours?"

"I'd prefer that. But you were right. We have to be willing to defend our best work, and trust God to take care of the details."

"You and God seem pretty tight lately," she mused, smiling at the memory of his earlier defensiveness.

"Yeah. Me and God. Thick as thieves," he said. "Whatever that means. Watching you and Grandma helped me look at everything, including my life, in a different light."

"I'm glad you've worked it out, Jack."
"I'm glad a lot of things have worked out, Mindy Lee."
Me too, Jack.

CHAPTER THIRTY-EIGHT

Minnie checked her voicemail after Morning News, her heart stuttering when Nick's pleasant voice invited her to his office after lunch. Would he sound so cheerful if he were about to ax her job, and the center? When the afternoon activities started, she made the short walk across the parking lot.

"Hey, Minnie. Come on in." Nick motioned her into his office and indicated the chair where she'd sat when he appointed her director.

She sat and smoothed the wrinkles from her pants as Nick settled behind his desk and pulled a green folder from the stack, then folded his hands and smiled at her.

"I have to say again that you gave an amazing presentation, Minnie. Great visuals, the perfect mix of information and stories. I didn't know you were so adept at presenting."

"Neither did I," she said. "I'm glad everyone enjoyed it."

He flipped the folder open. "The board members couldn't say enough about how blessed Open Circle has been to have you as the director."

She waited as he shuffled through the myriad of papers, notes scribbled in the margins of some, others on official letterhead. Her life, her seniors' future, were in that pile.

"I heard about your day from hell." Nick looked up, a sympathetic lift to his brow. "Sorry you all went through that."

And here comes the ax. "In the end, everything worked out. Moses didn't have a heart attack, and the fire department got the cover installed over the fire alarm the following Monday without charging us for the call."

"I also heard how professional you were through every crisis."

Until she got home, anyway. "I have an amazing staff."

"Yes, you do. That wasn't an easy task cleaning house, then hiring and training new staff." He grinned. "I knew you'd do well as director, Minnie. I just didn't know how well."

Her face warmed under his approval. "I guess jumping into the deep end made me learn how to swim."

"And now you're Olympic-caliber."

She forced a smile, her stomach churning.

He looked through the papers, then cleared his throat. "I'm always happy to talk about the good stuff you're doing for the organization."

"But?" His discomfort sent her blood pressure zinging upward.

"But it comes down to the numbers."

Her spine weakened.

"We can't figure out how to make it work financially, Minnie." He met her gaze, sympathy shining within his administrator's expression. "I've spent hours looking at everything from different angles, but... The board voted to close Open Circle and combine the program with the existing opportunities in the care center."

With the final decision before her, a strange calm settled her pounding heart. She'd known this was the probable outcome four months ago, when Nick first asked her to fix five years' worth of issues in a summer. She'd vowed to do what she could, knowing it would take a miracle to be successful. It seemed this wasn't the year for miracles.

"We've been on the upswing the last five weeks," she pointed out in a clear voice. "Would the board consider extending the grace period for three more months?"

"I suggested that," he said, "but the concern is that if the upswing doesn't continue, we'll be that much more in debt."

She'd grovel if she thought it would change things, but his grim expression stopped her. The last bit of hope evaporated, and she nodded, strangely calm. "It makes me sad, but I understand. I appreciated the opportunity, and especially your support and encouragement along the way. Do you have a closing date?"

"September 8th. Does three weeks give you enough time to close things up?"

Another impossible deadline. "I hope so. My priority will be getting all of the seniors settled in new opportunities."

"I'm confident you'll get that done in your usual, efficient manner."

That made one of them. *How do I tell Em? The staff? Chief, Bertie, sweet Frances?* "Do you want me to make the announcement to the staff and the seniors, or do you want to?"

"Which would you prefer?"

"I'd rather speak to everyone myself." Letting him do it would be a cop-out. They deserved better from her.

"That's fine." Relief tinged his response.

341

Minnie pushed to her feet and stiffened her knees so she didn't wobble, then offered her hand. "I'm sorry I didn't do a better job, but I'm grateful to have had the chance."

His fingers closed arounds hers. "Minnie, I gave you an impossible task, and you did far more than I ever could have expected. Every member of the board wrote letters of recognition for you."

"That's kind of them."

He stacked the papers together, closed the folder and handed it to her. "Mine's in there too, of course. Whatever I can do to help you in your job search, you let me know."

Minnie left his office on wooden legs, green folder clutched against her chest. She'd failed Frank and Helen, her seniors. Em. What would happen to all of them? How could she say goodbye?

On the short walk back to Open Circle, she struggled to steady her breathing, blinking hard against pulsing tears. Tonight she'd figure out how best to tell the seniors and the staff, but for now she had to hold it together. Somehow. *God, help.*

Jackson wiped his palms on his jeans, and retucked his shirt before entering the downtown Chicago restaurant. He'd hopped a red-eye to get here for this breakfast meeting. *Don't blow this, Young.* The hostess pointed toward a table in the back, and Jackson walked toward his future on wobbling legs.

In a button-down shirt and sport coat, the middle-aged man at the table looked up and smiled, reaching out a hand. "Jackson! Trent Garland. Glad you could make it."

Jackson shook his hand, then settled across the table. "Thanks for rescheduling our meeting."

"I'm glad you were able to meet here instead of New York City." He spread his hands over the white tablecloth. "I'm much more comfortable in my hometown. Let's get something ordered and then we can talk."

When the bubbly waitress bounced away from their table, Trent leaned back in his chair. "So, you flew home because your grandmother was missing. That must have been a frightening experience for everyone involved."

"With a happy ending. Again, I apologize for leaving town before we had a chance to meet."

"It says a lot about your character, Jackson. We can reschedule a meeting, but we can't reschedule a family crisis. Now, your grandmother is still driving, which is good news. Tell me about her."

Jackson relaxed into his chair as he launched into stories about his amazing grandma. From his early years with her, to the lengthy break, to their reuniting, his stories kept his breakfast companion nodding and chuckling.

As they ate, Trent asked questions and shared his own stories about growing up with two somewhat overbearing grandmothers. Clearly, he'd loved his grandmothers like Jackson loved Grandma Em. Jackson's earlier apprehension faded.

"I've had an idea that keeps pestering me." Trent drained his cup. "And after seeing your work in Pierre's studio, you're the person I want to partner with."

Jackson tempered the surge of excitement with a casual nod, hoping he didn't look like a Christmas-morning four-year-old.

"While I told you about my grandmothers," Trent continued, "I didn't mention my grandfathers. One died many years ago, but the other was my best friend. Unfortunately, he was diagnosed with Alzheimer's at 66. In the ten years that followed, he went from being the most brilliant, energetic, and interesting man I knew to a shriveled shell who didn't talk for the last year of his life."

"Wow. I'm sorry to hear that." What if Grandma Em hadn't recovered from the stroke?

Trent fiddled with the straw wrapper. "We were fishing buddies. I could talk to him about anything. I was devastated when he died. When my dad got the diagnosis last year, it all came back. He's still in good shape and they're trying new treatments all the time, so I'm hoping things progress a lot slower."

A double whammy. "That's really rough."

"Yeah." He straightened and lifted a determined gaze. "In light of that, I've wanted to do some major fundraising for Alzheimer's research, as well as educating the general public. That's where you come in."

"How can I help?"

"You can do what you do best—take amazing photographs. Here's what I'm envisioning." As he outlined his ideas, the initial butterflies in Jackson's stomach multiplied to a swirling horde of nauseating movement. A traveling photography exhibit, presentations, fundraising and special events featuring Jackson's work around dementia and Alzheimer's. Trent's plans were so beyond what he'd hoped for at this meeting, he couldn't decipher the emotions banging around in his chest.

"So what do you think? I'm open to ideas, suggestions, whatever."

Jackson grasped the arms of his chair to keep from leaping to his feet and dancing around the restaurant. He forced a calm nod. "I think it has great potential to reach a lot of people. I love the traveling exhibit idea, bringing the information right to the people. Photographs tell a great story but having someone there to give the presentation will have a stronger impact."

"So you'll do it?"

"I'm not the person you want for that."

The enthusiasm in Trent's face faded. "Jackson, your show is exactly what I'd envisioned."

Jackson held up a hand and smiled. "I'll do the photography and the exhibit, but you need someone else up front. I'm a storyteller with pictures. The person I have in mind is a storyteller with words. Someone who can charm money out of any sponsor with heart-breaking stories that people will identify with."

"That's exactly who we need. Would they be willing to be part of this? Can they travel with the show?"

The million-dollar question. "Right now, she runs an adult day program in my hometown in Minnesota. She's committed to that program and those seniors, so I doubt I could convince her to step away. Maybe for short periods of time." That would be a miracle.

"Do whatever you need to, to convince her. We'll start with financial backing from the magazine, and me personally, but I know we'll be able to bring on other supporters who will make it worth her while financially."

"It won't be about the money for her," he said. She'd pour the money right back into Open Circle. "Her passion is about preserving the dignity and individuality of people as they age."

"I want her!" Trent declared.

Get in line. "I'll see what I can do."

CHAPTER THIRTY-NINE

Minnie stirred the soup absently, staring across the room.

"Dear heart, tell me what's on your mind." Em's voice broke into her thoughts.

Blinking her attention back to the kitchen table, she forced a smile. "Sorry. I'm lousy company tonight."

"Considering I had to bribe you with chocolate chip cookies to get you to come over, I know something's wrong."

The hand that rested atop hers brought a sting of tears to her eyes. She swallowed back the lump and met Em's concern, chin trembling. "They're closing the center."

"I suspected as much. You were distracted this afternoon." She tightened her grasp. "Mindy Lee, it's not your fault. You inherited a failing institution and did wonders in such a short time. If you'd been the director these past years, Open Circle would be a thriving community. Instead, old Dots didn't leave you anything to work with after she drove it into the ground."

Minnie nodded. "My head knows that, but my heart is broken." She flinched against the stab of pain. God had called her to do this work, gifted her for it. She didn't want to do anything else.

She rested her head back against the chair. "I prayed so hard that I could keep the center open. I tried everything I could think of. None of it mattered."

"It mattered a great deal," Em declared. She collected their plates and took them to the sink. "Your prayers are what kept the program running, kept people involved, and safe, and happy. And it has helped Jack get his career back on track."

Minnie released a snort. "I think he came around eventually to understanding what I do, but I doubt I had anything to do with his career."

Em returned with a plate of cookies. "Time will tell," she said. "Now eat a cookie. Then we'll talk about what comes next."

While they ate and chatted, self-pity waned, and focus returned. Minnie jotted notes for the staff meeting. Em had always been her rock, and this was no different. She soaked in the calm wisdom, even managed a laugh as they reminisced about Open Circle. Back home an hour later, Minnie sat in the quiet darkness, wrapped in the prayer shawl, and thanked God yet again for the gift of Em.

As the next day flew by, Minnie reveled in the ordinariness of it—the teasing and laughter, an uneventful lunch, activities to challenge and entertain. And hugs. Why had she never noticed how many hugs she received every day? Who would smile and hug her simply for bringing a cup of coffee? Where would she find such satisfaction from showing up to work each day?

When the last client had gone home, Minnie stood before the staff with her chin up, clear-eyed and focused. She'd had time to process the news. Now she needed to be strong for them.

"Thanks for staying late," she said, "and for coming in, those of you who weren't scheduled today. I'm amazed we could pull together this meeting on such short notice."

"Didn't sound like we had a choice." Though Cheryl grumbled quietly, the words carried to where Minnie stood.

"As I believe you all know, Open Circle has been on a mission to regain our financial footing these past few months. Every single one of you," *with one major exception,* "has risen to the occasion and given 110% to not only our seniors but the program as well. I can't begin to express how that's touched my heart and encouraged me."

She smiled. "You guys rock. This is the best staff ever."

Gail whooped from where she sat in the back of the room and clapped. Others joined in and they cheered for themselves for a full minute. Minnie laughed and clapped along. As they quieted, she grew sobered.

"You deserve an ovation like that every day for the amazing work you do, and for the love and respect you offer every person who walks in our front door. Thank you."

She'd spent part of the morning preparing the letter she now handed to Mary in the front row, asking her to send the copies around the room. As the stack passed from person to person, Minnie watched the reactions as they read the brief missive. Disbelief filled their eyes as they looked up at her, some already shiny with tears.

Heart aching, she waited until the sheets had reached the back row. "Writing this letter was the hardest thing I've ever done. Since meeting with Nick yesterday, I've been heart broken, angry, ashamed, and frustrated. I expect you may be feeling some of the same now.

"Although highly impressed with our work, the board

of directors decided to close Open Circle effective three weeks from now."

Muffled conversations broke out around the room and she waited, allowing them time to absorb the news. "So what questions do you have?"

"The financials don't look that bad," Kim said, her face pale. "Couldn't they give us a few more months?"

"I suggested that. They chose not to let things run any longer in case there wasn't the change we hoped for."

"What will happen to the seniors? And to us?" another asked.

"The care center will be ramping up their activities, so if our seniors would like to participate in those, they'll be welcome. And they'll be hiring a few new staff to help with that." When she'd looked through the folder Nick gave her, her heart sunk at how many of her staff would soon be unemployed.

"Nick would like to meet early next week with whoever is interested in making the move. There will be a sign-up sheet with Jody at the front desk if you want to talk with him."

The rumble of conversations continued, and she held up her hands to quiet them. "I don't like it either, but we'll need to work together to make it a smooth transition for the seniors."

As the questions dwindled, Minnie invited them to stop by her office anytime to process the news, and said she'd spend time with each of them during an exit interview. After she dismissed them, most stayed to talk with her and each other, sharing hugs and tears, and funny memories.

The last to leave, Cheryl gathered her belongings with jerky movements. She approached Minnie at the front of the room. "Figured this would be how things ended."

"I prayed it wouldn't be, but I saw the writing on the

wall from the day I stepped in." Cheryl's attitude grated more severely than ever. Even a simple "You gave it your best shot" would help. Minnie busied herself putting papers into a folder to keep from lashing out at the woman.

"Maybe if you'd stuck to doing your visits and little community classes, things would have worked out differently."

Enough already! Minnie faced her. "You know, Cheryl, I always thought you'd be the one to step in if something happened to Dorothy. I know you did too. But that's not how it worked out. I understand disappointment at not getting a job, but to hold onto it, even nurture it to the point of harassment is beyond my understanding."

As she moved closer, Cheryl stepped back, mouth open and eyes wide.

"You know what saddens me the most? Your wasted potential." Shaking her head, she gathered her folders and strode away, adding, "Please lock up when you leave."

Head up, tears in her eyes, Minnie walked out the front door and climbed into her car. She'd wanted to say those things, and so much more, for months. So why didn't she feel better?

~~~

She'd barely gotten the teakettle on the stove when the doorbell rang. For a moment she stood still, eyes closed, praying it wasn't Cheryl with some biting response. Blowing out a short breath, she went to the front door. No one waited on the front step.

She pushed the screen door open and looked around. A vase of wildflowers waited on the front walk, colorful blooms waving in the breeze. Jackson was in Chicago, hopefully lining up a job with the magazine guy. Em wouldn't sneak around leaving flowers. Nick certainly wouldn't offer her a new job via wildflowers, no matter what Em hoped for.

Retrieving the vase with one last glance around, she brought it in and set it on the coffee table in the living room. She returned to the kitchen for her tea, jumping back when she realized Jack sat at the table, a grin on his adorable face. She gaped at him, a hand at her throat. "How did you get in here?"

"You country folk never lock your doors. The back one was open." He stood and approached.

"But...why aren't you in Chicago? Or Botswana or Ethiopia, or wherever you're supposed to be."

"Because I'm here." He opened his arms. "Not even a welcome home hug?"

The emotions churning just below the surface flooded down her face as she rushed into his embrace. With his arms tight around her, she released the tears she'd held back all day. Jack had come home.

Jackson held Minnie close, stunned by her welcome. A hug *and* tears? Between the meeting yesterday in Chicago and this welcome tonight, life couldn't get sweeter. *Thanks, God.*

"Wow. Now this is a welcome home hug." Her hiccupping breaths spoke of more than happiness. He leaned back. "Hey. What's wrong?"

She shook her head and pulled out of his embrace, wiping her face. "I've been...a little..."

"Lonely for your favorite adversary?" he supplied.

She managed a half-hearted laugh as she went to the counter and pulled two mugs from the cupboard. "Coffee?"

"That'd be great."

She nodded toward the table, her breath still uneven. "Sit while I get it ready and tell me why you're back early. Did you get to meet with the owner editor guy?" She stuck a K-cup into the machine.

"I did. I had to come back to tell my favorite girls all about it. You were right about me needing to fight for what I wanted." He shook his head, grinning. "It was definitely worth it."

She set the mug before him, then settled into a chair with her tea. "Sounds like good news. I'm all ears."

He took a sip, studying her through the steam. The forced smile, dark circles under eyes that held pain. Much as he wanted to blurt out every detail of this new opportunity, something was very wrong. "It can wait. I want to know what's been going on here the last few days. How's our favorite Emily?"

"She's great. She seems stronger. There's more color in her face."

"That's good." After a silence, he prodded, "So what else is going on?"

She drew a slow breath through her nose and met his gaze, her pretty face clouded with pain. "They're closing the center. In three weeks."

"No." Air left his lungs in a whoosh. "Min, I'm so sorry. I can't believe they're going through with it, especially after all the changes you've made. They won't reconsider? Give it a few more months? You're right on the edge of something great."

Eyes shiny, she shook her head. "I asked. They're afraid of going further into debt if it doesn't actually get better."

He stood and pulled her to her feet and into a hug. As

she melted against him, his heart raged. *Why, God? She's done so much more than they asked for. She's put her life into these people, this place.*

"I've failed everyone." The broken, whispered words pierced into him.

"No." He tightened his arms. "You didn't fail, sweetheart. You stepped up and hit a grand slam. Open Circle is in much better shape than before you took over. You couldn't make money appear out of thin air. Just because something doesn't work out the way we want doesn't mean it failed."

He leaned back to smile at her. With gentle fingers, he brushed the hair from her forehead, heart pounding crazily. "I'm not the same guy who blew into town ready to take over. I've learned about compromise, putting others first, sticking with something no matter how hard it is—all from you. And I've discovered that no matter where I go in the world, Lawton is my home. You and Grandma are my family. I belong here."

Color seeped into her cheeks. "Yes, you do," she said softly. "I hope that's always true."

He pressed a kiss to her forehead, then enfolded her in his arms again. "It will be."

CHAPTER FORTY

Minnie spent the next morning crafting the right letter to send to the Open Circle families. When she finished, she took copies to the Bible Study group to begin sharing the news with the seniors. As they read the letter, she studied each beloved face, imprinting them on her heart. Everything was about to change, for all of them.

"We're not surprised," one of the men said. "We may be old, but we can still read the writing on the wall. There've been rumors for months, before you replaced Dorothy."

Minnie frowned. "But you continued coming." She wouldn't have faulted anyone for abandoning a sinking ship.

"This is family," Em said. "Whether we knew it would happen or not, there's no place we'd rather be."

The blasted tears filling her eyes yet again, Minnie looked around the group. "I'm sorry I couldn't keep the doors open," she said.

"The doors have been wide and welcoming all these months," Helen said. "You've done wonders for me since

Frank died, and I know it's true for others, as well. You can't blame yourself, Minnie. We won't let you."

Dear Helen. "Thank you," Minnie said. "I'll be working with each of you to figure out what's next, where you'd like to spend time, and how we can make sure your needs are met. Please don't hesitate to ask questions of me, the staff, or Nick. We'll get through this together."

"That's the best way to face a challenge," Helen said.

Minnie nodded and sighed. *Lord, how do I do this?*

Making her way through the center to share the news, Minnie encountered Jackson around every corner. He offered jokes, hugs, and encouragement that kept her moving, and kept a smile in her heart. He'd become her second biggest fan, behind Em.

Around Em's dinner table that night, she sat quietly as Jackson shared story after story with Em about his New York exploits. He still hadn't given any details about the rescheduled meeting, though they'd had little quiet time together. Exhaustion sitting on her like a weighted blanket, she closed her eyes to simply enjoy their voices.

The scrape of a chair startled her. Jackson motioned for her to stand. "Come on. I'll take you home. You're practically sleeping in your chair."

When he'd insisted on picking her up, she'd been too tired to argue. She nodded now, relieved she didn't have to navigate the short distance back to her house. "Okay."

Em hugged her warmly. "It will work out, dear heart. Believe that. God has a plan."

"I know." But did His plan have to be the opposite of hers? "Things always work out."

"Usually better than we expect." Em patted her cheek, blue eyes smiling up at her. "A good sleep will give you a different perspective in the morning."

That would be good. Maybe she'd even discover it was all a dream.

Jackson remained silent on the ride, leaving her to her thoughts as she looked out the window. So much history in this little town. So many good people. What a gift she'd been given to do her part in honoring them.

He walked her to the front door, taking her key to unlock it, then ushered her in. Facing her, he took her hands in a gentle grasp, his smile warm and tinged with... something that made her insides a little wonky.

"Grandma Em is right, you know." He smiled. "Life has a funny way of working itself out. Look where I am now after totally bungling my career a few years ago."

She cocked her head. "You haven't told me how the meeting went."

"All in good time. Now, go to bed."

She studied him a moment, tempted to wrangle the news out of him, but fatigue won and she nodded. "Yes, sir. Thanks for chauffeuring me around tonight. I didn't realize I needed it."

He chuckled and hugged her, then turned her around and prodded her forward. "Off to bed."

She glanced back as he pulled the front door closed behind him, blushing at his wink before the door clicked. For a long moment she stood in the middle of the living room, heart still fluttering, a smile on her lips, her mind too fuzzy to make sense of anything.

Turning the living room lights off, she climbed the creaking stairs to her bedroom, his familiar grin warming her deep inside. Maybe her perspective would be different tomorrow, like Em said, but hopefully some things would stay the same. Like the way a certain photographer smiled at her.

By Friday morning, Jackson couldn't wait to put the plan into action. He'd spent the last few days on the phone with Pierre in New York, Noah on a shoot in Mexico, and Trent in Chicago. Everything was in place.

Standing on the front step of Open Circle, he focused down the street as he waited and let his mind wander. When Minnie told him the center would be closing, he'd been hit with both sadness and relief. He'd grown to love these seniors and truly wanted the best for them. But without the center, she'd be free to join him in creating and implementing the traveling photo and lecture show. However, watching her grieve even as she encouraged both staff and seniors through the week had changed his perspective.

She needed this place, these people. And they needed her. Trent would arrive soon to provide what she needed to keep Open Circle running for at least six more months, which would postpone, perhaps permanently, his chance to help Trent make his dream come alive. Strangely, the thought hadn't hurt nearly as much as he expected. He wanted Mindy Lee to be happy doing what she did best. And he would be beside her every step. Though he wasn't her top priority right now, she was his.

A rental car pulled into the parking lot and he waved at Trent. They shared a warm handshake, went over the plan one last time, and then entered the building. Jody, only a week from her due date, greeted Trent cheerfully before directing them to the activity room.

Jackson gave Trent a tour as they made their way through the center, surprising himself with all he knew about programming, dementia, and the ins and outs of running the center. Trent asked thoughtful questions, stopping to greet the seniors they passed in the hallway. His genuine interest shone through his ready laugh and hearty handshakes. Jackson marveled at how God had brought them together.

In the busy activity room, they stayed off to the side watching Gail and Minnie lead a Minnesota trivia game that had everyone laughing as they shouted out answers. Jackson folded his arms and leaned back against the wall, scolding himself for not having his camera handy. It never failed—when he didn't have it, he had to watch the best photo ops go by.

Minnie acknowledged him with a nod as she leaned down to listen to Chief's answer, sharing a laugh with him before returning to her place beside Gail. Jackson admired her strength and resiliency. Several times throughout the week, camera in hand, he'd captured the pain in her eyes while she smiled with a staff member or reassured a confused senior. She rarely stopped moving, no doubt trying to absorb every minute she had with them.

The activity ended, and she made her way toward him. "I didn't hear you shouting out answers," she teased.

"I figured they were tired of hearing my voice during trivia," he said. "Mindy, I want you to meet a friend of mine. He's here to see how you run Open Circle. Trent, this is Mindy Lee Carlson. Mindy, Trent Garland."

She offered a warm smile as she shook his hand. "Welcome to Open Circle. Do you run an adult day program?"

"Not yet, but I'm interested in the nuts and bolts of how they're work. Is it sort of babysitting for seniors?"

"Not at all. Adult day programming is designed with the senior in mind." She directed them toward her office as she explained the premise behind the adult day concept.

Jackson shared a glance with Trent when she paused to

speak to Jody, then they settled in her office. As the conversation continued, he looked around the small room. The dingy, disastrous office he'd first encountered now glowed with light. Framed inspirational quotes filled the walls, photos lining the shelves.

He turned his gaze back to her. A change much like the woman herself, from suspicious and defensive to inviting and loving. He'd shied away from the Mouse but continued to be intrigued by Mindy Lee.

"You're the editor of the magazine?" Minnie's question pulled Jackson back to the conversation. "World Aware?"

"The owner, actually. I thought—Ahh. I didn't realize Jack hadn't shared that detail." Trent looked at him, eyebrows raised. "I'll let him take it from here."

Minnie shifted her attention, a tiny crease between the question in her eyes. Dang. He should have been paying attention.

"Trent is who I met with in Chicago. We discovered a shared interest in seniors, the impact of aging, and how dementia impacts people. Turns out Trent has had plenty of personal experience with all of it and made me an offer I don't want to refuse. However, for it to be effective, it will take both of us."

"You and Trent?"

"You and me."

"Me?" she squeaked. She glanced at Trent, eyes wide. "I'm no good at taking pictures."

"I know," Jackson agreed, laughing when she harrumphed. "I'm talking about my photography skills and your knowledge about dementia."

She frowned. "I don't get it."

Trent stood. "I hate to leave the party when it's just getting interesting, but I could use a restroom."

Jackson pointed him down the hall, then turned back to

Minnie. "The idea we have has two parts. The first is creating a program, using both photos and lecture, about dementia, especially Alzheimer's. It will travel around the country to raise money for research, and to share information about the disease, options for care such as adult day programming, and all that."

Her expression relaxed. "That sounds amazing. Using your photos?"

"And your expertise."

"What!? I'm not a lecturer, Jack, I'm a social worker." Fear colored the words. "You need someone far more knowledgeable than me. Someone with—"

"Passion? A deep love and respect for the elderly? Someone who's been in the trenches designing programs, serving lunch, creating opportunities for the community to be involved?"

"Well...yes."

He smiled. "Who better than you, Min?"

"I... This is..." She lifted her hands. "Wow."

"Part two of Trent's idea may take part one out of commission."

The frown returned.

Jackson moved around the desk and pulled her gently to her feet. "Trent is committed to being part of the solution for the issues facing the elderly, one of which is meaningful interactions." He tapped her nose. "Adult day programming."

"So he's here about that? Or the traveling program?"

"Both. He wants *you* for the program, but he also wants to help you keep Open Circle going, at least for the near future."

Her mouth opened and closed.

"He wants to provide the extra funding needed to keep it running, at least for the next six months. By then, it should be operating in the black. I've already talked to Nick, and it's a go as far as he's concerned."

"Funding from where?"

"Him. He has an inheritance from his grandfather that he wants to use for this."

"Oh, Jack." Fingertips pressed to her mouth, she stared at him. "Really?"

"Really. Funding would also cover roof repairs, and other structural updates."

Tears spilled over as she threw her arms around him. After enjoying her hug for a long moment, he leaned back. "That's where part two may eliminate part one. I'm assuming you'll want to continue working with Open Circle."

"Of course."

"But that makes traveling around the country a little difficult."

"You don't need me. *You* can do the show."

He shook his head firmly. "No, I can't. I'm not a speaker, Mindy. And I don't have your knowledge base. You're a natural storyteller. You can share experiences, best practices, industry news in a way I can't."

Hands resting lightly against his chest, she shook her head. "Jack, there are lots of far better qualified people who could help you make this an amazing program. I can give you a list of names."

"But I'm not interested in doing this with anyone else. I won't." He shrugged, offering a crooked smile. "It's bad timing right now. We can take the show on the road in a year or two."

"No. That information needs to be out there right now," she insisted. "People need to know what their options are, what adult day programming can do for their senior. As you travel around, you can talk to health care professionals and social workers about how to start a program."

She glowed with excitement. "Think of it. Open Circles across the country! Maybe some of the fundraising could go toward getting programs up and running. And your photographs would be perfect illustrations for how it could look. Jack, you need to do this."

An overpowering urge to hit the road with her right that moment surged through him, He shoved it down and linked his hands behind her back. "Let's back up a bit. The first question is would you even consider working with me on something like this? It would mean a lot of togetherness as we created the program, designed all the pieces, and then traveled around with it.

"And," he added, "I haven't always been your favorite person. I'm not the easiest person to work with."

"Like I am?" She grew quiet as she studied him, and he held his breath, heart pounding. Humiliation was a word away. Her expression remained unreadable.

"Am I interrupting?" Trent's voice came from the doorway.

Yes! Jackson nearly pushed him out of the office. Rotten timing!

Minnie stepped away from Jackson to hug the man she'd only just met, and Trent chuckled. "I hope this is a yes to our ideas."

"It's a totally inadequate thank you for partnering with Open Circle."

"It's my pleasure, Mindy. From what Jack told me, and from what I've seen today, it's exactly what I want to get involved with. You are one impressive lady."

She glanced at Jackson, face pink. "Thank you."

"I'm looking forward to being part of the team. So what do you think about the other idea? Taking Open Circle on the road to share your innovations with a wider audience? Making a change in how seniors are cared for across the nation?"

"I think it's a fabulous idea, but there are plenty of highly qualified people out there who would work beautifully with Jack. Trained speakers with connections and influence."

"Jack says you're the only person he'll work with."

"Because I'm the only one he knows. When you put the word out there about this opportunity, you'll be inundated."

Jackson shook his head. She could protest all she wanted, but he meant it when he said she was the only one. "Trent, we need to get across the parking lot to meet Nick, the administrator, to iron out the funding details."

Trent nodded, still looking at Minnie. "I hope we can continue this conversation later."

"How about dinner at my grandmother's tonight?" Jackson suggested. "That work for you, Mindy?"

"Tonight? I'll have to check with Em first…"

"I'll take that as a yes," he said with a grin. "See you over there about six? I'll let her know we're coming. We'll keep it simple."

He left her with a wink, then directed Trent out the door and across the parking lot. Once they got things figured out with funding for Open Circle, he'd convince her to work on the new project with him. She hadn't given him a flat-out no. *That's promising, right, Lord?*

His future did indeed look different than what he'd plan, or even hoped for. He was one lucky man.

CHAPTER FORTY-ONE

As Minnie hurried into the kitchen, Em turned from the stove with a welcoming smile. "Dear heart, this is exciting."

"Is it?" She hadn't been able to string a full thought together since the extraordinary meeting in her office. "I'm still trying to make sense of everything. And I'm afraid to believe any of it will actually come true."

Em hugged her. "Faith comes from believing what we can't see. Don't be afraid. God will put it all in place."

Minnie pulled the comforting words into her heart, letting them still the chaos. She released a slow breath and lowered her shoulders. "You're right. Now, what can I do? Whatever you're cooking smells heavenly."

"The roast has been in for a while, potatoes are cooking. Pudding is in the cups. Why don't you make a salad?"

Half an hour later, the doorbell rang, and Minnie's heart resumed its earlier speed.

"Anybody home?" Jackson entered the kitchen. Trent followed with a bottle of red wine. "Hey, Grandma. Mindy. It smells great in here."

"Dinner's almost ready," Em told him.

"Grandma, this is Trent Garland. He visited Open Circle today while you were at your dentist appointment. Trent, my grandmother, Emily Young."

She welcomed him with a hug, accepting the wine with a pleased exclamation. "Jack has told me about your ideas. I'm praying you'll make a great impact."

"Mrs. Young, we'll gladly accept those prayers. I'm looking forward to what God will do by uniting our respective talents. Including Mindy will bring even more impact."

"Since she hasn't actually agreed," Jackson said, "we have some convincing to do."

"Mindy Lee will make the right decision," Em said with a nod.

"Right now, Mindy Lee thinks it's time to eat," Minnie said, salad bowl in hand, smiling as they laughed. "Gentlemen, let's head to the dining room while Emily's meal is hot."

After a blessing, food was passed, wine poured, and conversation kicked into high gear. Em asked questions about Trent's work, what he did before owning a magazine, how many children he had. She was at her most charming as she interrogated him. Minnie hid a smile and passed the potatoes to Jackson which he accepted with a knowing wink.

Minnie listened with interest to the conversation, eager to learn about the man who had appeared out of nowhere with a boatload of money, ready to bail her center out of imminent closure. With four children, mostly grown, and a physician wife, his commitment to doing what he could to preserve families, and to keep aging parents as active participants in life was a major priority for him.

His easy banter with Em, and relaxed responses in the

face of her pointed questions, set Minnie's hopes soaring. It seemed Open Circle wasn't simply an investment for him, but a cause to support, even promote. He believed in utilizing top-notch staff who used their gifts and passions to do their best work.

"After all," he added, "with people like Mindy in charge, what could I possibly add to make Open Circle better?"

"Money," Em said as she took another slice of bread.

"Em!" Minnie scolded, but Trent lifted a hand to stop her, laughing heartily.

"She's exactly right, Mindy. That's one of my gifts and I'm more than happy to share it with the right causes."

"What are your terms for repayment?"

"This isn't a loan. Think of it as a grant. Repayment for me comes from seeing progress, growth, change. Improvement in people's lives. Advancement in research and treatment." He smiled reassuringly. "I enjoy finding and investing in those causes. That's what I've found in you at Open Circle."

She blushed under his admiration, stunned to be included among such noble ideas. "What we do won't change the world, but hopefully it will change one life at a time. Our primary focus is on the individuality of seniors, what we call person-centered care. It's important to us to know who they are, where they come from, what their specific needs are. And how we can help their family members."

Em and Jackson quietly cleared the table as the conversation continued.

"What I don't understand," Trent said, "is why there aren't more programs run like yours."

"Not everyone is sold on this type of care. It requires constant planning, involvement of everyone on staff, and ongoing evaluation of what works and what doesn't. It's not a one-size-fits-all program, and some places don't have the staff or funding to accommodate that."

"I did a little research on you and Open Circle before I came. I'm impressed with what you've done, and I believe it needs to be shared with the wider community of aging services." He leaned on his elbows, focused on her. "That's why I want you to work with me and Jackson to develop a program that will go where the people are. Your voice, your ideas and innovations, need to be heard to benefit the greatest number of people."

Jackson set a cup of coffee before her, then a slice of peach cobbler, as Em did for Trent. Minnie smiled her thanks, trying to gather her whirling emotions. With the new funding of Open Circle, how could she possibly walk away now? There was so much to be done, new ideas to implement, staff to hire. She wanted to—

"Mindy, I can see how much Open Circle means to you," Trent said. "And with the surprise of being able to keep it open, even improve it, I understand we're asking a lot of you to shift your focus to a broader audience."

She nodded. "The people at Open Circle mean the world to me."

"As you do to all of us," Em interjected. "But that doesn't mean we'd expect you to give up an opportunity like this."

Minnie looked from her to Jackson who focused on his slice of pie. Leaving seemed disloyal. New funding comes in and she jumps ship for a 'better' opportunity? No, that didn't sit right. They deserved more from her.

"How about we enjoy our dessert for the moment," she said. "Jack, what else happened while you were in New York and Chicago?"

He followed her lead and shared a few stories about the hazards of riding in a cab that made them laugh. Several times he set his hand over hers as he made a point. The warmth of his touch, and the comfort of the gesture danced along her arm and into her heart, leaving her momentarily unfocused.

"Well, I'm a bit worn out after all this fun," Trent announced. "I think I'll head back to the hotel."

He pushed back from the table and stood. "Mrs. Young, thank you for the most delicious home cooked meal I've had in a long time."

She rose, steadying herself against the table, and smiled. "You are most welcome. Please do come back before you leave town. This has been simply delightful."

"It certainly has." He extended a hand toward Minnie. "And Mindy Lee, it's been a pleasure getting to know you and Open Circle. I'm grateful you've allowed me to join the team."

"That makes two of us. I won't disappoint you."

"You couldn't possibly. We'll talk more about our next venture when you're ready, all right?"

What a nice man. No pressure, just friendly warmth. "All right. Thank you."

As Jackson walked him out to his car, Minnie and Em cleared the dessert plates in companionable silence, filling the dishwasher, storing leftovers.

"I'm tired, Mindy dear. I'll do those last dishes tomorrow."

"It was absolutely delicious, Em. Thank you for going to all the trouble." Mindy wrapped her small frame in a hug. "And thank you for all you do for me, Jack, Open Circle. You're amazing."

"Pish," came the muffled response. "Now, I'm off to bed. Tell Jack goodnight for me. I'll see you tomorrow."

"Good night. Sleep tight."

Em shuffled toward the stairs, then paused and looked

back. "Think about what I said, Mindy Lee. God has placed a wonderful opportunity before you to reach many more people, to make a difference just as you have in Lawton. Don't pass it up out of a sense of duty and loyalty." She gave a tired smile. "We know you love us. Now it's time to share that with the world."

Minnie stared after her as she made her way up the stairs. How could she leave? Who would take over for her? Certainly not Cheryl. Thoughts bouncing like errant ping-pong balls, she washed the remaining dishes.

Don't be afraid. God will put it all in place. Em's words from earlier slid back to mind, calming her, chastising her for how swiftly she let fear take over.

"Up for a stroll?" She startled when Jackson set his hands on her shoulders.

He chuckled. "Sorry. I thought you heard me come in."

She shook her wet hands at him, laughing as he ducked away from the splattering drops. "That's what you get for sneaking up on me." She dried her hands and faced him. "Cool enough for a sweater?"

"You might want to grab one."

She grabbed an old cardigan from the front closet, then followed him into the quiet evening. Stars winked from a black sky. A sense of autumn edged the night air, the faint aroma of a bonfire over the chirp of crickets.

"Trent seems like a very nice man," she said eventually.

"I've enjoyed getting to know him. He's serious about changing the landscape for seniors, raising awareness of Alzheimer's. It's personal for him. He lost his grandpa to it, which affected him deeply. Now his dad is dealing with it."

"He didn't mention that." The revelation explained a lot. "I'm still speechless that he's keeping Open Circle running for another six months."

"I told him about you and Em, and the center when we

met. He asked a million questions and seemed really interested. When I let him know about the funding issue, hoping he might know someone who could help, *he* offered. Insisted on it, actually."

Minnie nestled her hands in the pockets of her sweater. "Thank you," she said softly.

"God worked that one out," he replied. "I put the issue out there and wham, a solution. Pretty amazing."

They walked another block, their matched step the only sound in the quiet neighborhood.

"Do you think we could work together without fighting?" As the question left her lips, she wanted to clap her hands over her mouth. Where had that come from?

He stopped and faced her, the corners of his mouth twitching. "After what's happened with Open Circle these past few days, anything's possible."

She giggled. "I'm serious, Jack."

"So am I. Do I think we can work together? Absolutely. I wouldn't have suggested it if I thought we'd be miserable." He reached for her hands, holding them loosely. "Min, I know there are lots of people who would do fine with this project, but I want more than fine. I want fantastic. Amazing. Beyond expectations. And I think you and I together can offer that."

"Nothing like setting the bar out of reach before we even start."

"It's not out of God's reach," he said, then his grin faded. "The question is do *you* think we can work together?"

Lips pressed together, she nodded thoughtfully. "I wouldn't have thought so months ago, but now I do."

Jackson started them walking again, holding her hand snugly. "What about Open Circle? The programming you've created?"

Much as her ego didn't want to admit it, Open Circle

had existed before her and would continue after her. It wasn't about or for her. It was all about the seniors. "Before Nick told me the center was closing, I'd thought that Gail would make a great co-director."

"Not Cheryl?"

"No." She slid her gaze away. "Especially after I told her off."

His mouth dropped open. "No kidding?"

"I'm not proud of it, but I'd had enough." She chewed her lower lip for a moment, eyes narrowed. "Maybe..." Ideas crashed together in the most beautiful rush of sound. "Maybe now that we've got the program running smoothly, I could do quarterly training for the staff. I've wanted to develop that idea but there's been no time."

"Could Gail run the program?"

"If I helped her get up to speed. I'm not sure we'll find another activities director as good as her, but I guess since God sent her to us, He could send someone else." The decision was being made as she released her grasp of Open Circle and placed it in God's hands.

There, at the end of the block, sat the building that housed the program she loved. They stopped on the opposite corner, studying it in silence.

"It needs a coat of paint," she mused.

"And landscaping. Definitely."

"A new roof will make a huge difference."

When Jackson remained silent, she lifted her gaze. A smile of warmth and wonder filled his face, his eyes shining as he looked at her.

"What?"

He gathered her gently into his arms. "Would you have believed, when we faced off over our favorite girl in the hospital, that we'd be standing here now, ready to set out on an adventure together?"

"Not for a minute."

He laughed. "Me neither. But do you believe it now? That we're being called to do this as a team, and that God will make it happen?"

This moment, this *decision* felt absolutely right. A peaceful calm, tinged with joy, had replaced her earlier fears, and a smile filled her chest, lifting her mouth. This was exactly what she needed to do, and the man she needed to do it with.

"Yes," she said with a firm nod. "I believe it now."

"Then let's call Trent and get this tour idea rolling."

She reached up and lightly kissed his cheek, then slid her arms around him, nestling against his solid presence. She'd come full circle and found a purpose far bigger than she could ever have imagined. Others believed in her; it was time she did as well. She'd go forward now believing God would provide whatever she needed to step into the unexpected future stretching before them.

MY PERSONAL STORY

Having lost both my mother and mother-in-law to Alzheimer's, I know the heartache of watching someone you love fade away, replaced by someone you don't recognize. So it was especially heartbreaking to learn my husband (of 39+ years now) was diagnosed with dementia at age 66 in early 2020. Being a spouse/caregiver to him has been a roller coaster of emotions.

Since the first edition of *Open Circle* was released, our lives changed in ways we couldn't have imagined. Even before his diagnosis, I knew things weren't right but hadn't considered dementia as the issue. This man who taught elementary physical education for 40 years (and loved it) no longer had patience for children. He was an avid woodworker but could no longer finish a project. After decades of enjoying the results of his love of gardening and caring for the lawn, I realized our yard was no longer one to be envied. So many things I couldn't make sense of just three years ago I now see as pieces to the puzzle.

We sold our home in the metro area and live with our daughter's family in the country which has been a blessing in so many ways. There are more eyes to keep watch over him, people around which allows me to get an occasional break, others who can see where changes need to be made to keep him safe.

We're on a journey I didn't expect, nor did he. Without faith in a God who sees all and provides what we need, I can't imagine trying to navigate the cruel, strange world of dementia. God and I have lots of daily conversations that help me persevere, giving me strength and wisdom beyond myself. It's a frightening, lonely journey that should never be attempted alone. Family support is crucial, as is finding a support group of others on the same path. I thank God I've had both.

Please know that if you are currently dealing with the issues of aging or perhaps the effects of life-altering illness or disease either yourself or as a caregiver, YOU ARE NOT ALONE. While no two people travel the dementia journey in the same way, many have gone before you and are waiting to lend a hand, a listening ear, respite care, and information. Please check the Resources page that follows for just a few of the many, many options available, then take that step and reach out for help. There *is* help for you.

RESOURCES

There are many agencies, associations, and foundations across the country that offer support, education, daily cares, expert advice, and financial and legal information for not only senior citizens but also people of all ages coping with the effects of TBI, stroke, and other life-altering issues, and their caregivers. Through these national organizations, you can find local resources to meet your needs. This is by no means an exhaustive list; it's a sampling of the many options available. Consider it a starting point to guide you as you look for help, advice, and encouragement.

AgingCare.com – Helping caregivers of elderly parents find answers on senior housing, home care, elder care, caregiver support, senior financial and legal information.

Alzheimer's Association – Information on Alzheimer's disease and dementia symptoms, diagnosis, stages, treatment, care and support resources.

Community Aging Services and Senior Centers – A *nationwide* infrastructure that provides a wide array of home and community-based *services* to over 8 million *elderly* individuals each year.

Eldercare Directory – Free *elder* care resources for *senior citizens* and care givers. Complete guide to the *senior* care *assistance* programs and *services* in all 50 states.

Eldercare Locator – A public service of the U.S. Administration on Aging connecting you to services for older adults and their families.

National Alliances for Caregiving – *Caregiving* is truly an international phenomenon. No nation is without family *caregivers*, and the ways in which nations support the needs of *caregivers* are many.

National Family Caregivers Association – The National Family *Caregivers Association* (NFCA) supports, empowers, educates, and speaks up for the more than 50 million Americans who care for a chronically ill, aged, or disabled loved one.

Senior Services Organization – This site offers all kinds of information relevant to caregivers and their loved ones. Many of the websites listed include assessment tools, expert advice, directories of local resources, and links to public health organizations and services.

Volunteers of America – *Volunteers of America* has helped America's most vulnerable for over 120 years. Get help, find local offices, give support, and learn more about us.

ABOUT STACY MONSON

STACY MONSON is the award-winning author of The Chain of Lakes series, including *Shattered Image, Dance of Grace,* and *The Color of Truth,* as well as *Open Circle*. As a member of The Mosaic Collection, she has also released *When Mountains Sing,* book 1 of the My Father's House series. Her stories reveal an extraordinary God at work in ordinary life. She's a founding member of The Mosaic Collection, and is active in ACFW and the MN Christian Writers Guild. Residing in the farmlands outside the Twin Cities, she is the wife of a retired juggling, unicycling physical education teacher, mom to two amazing kids and two wonderful in-law kids, and a very proud grandma of 5 (and counting) grands.

TITLES BY STACY MONSON

THE MOSAIC COLLECTION: NOVELS
When Mountains Sing

THE MOSAIC COLLECTION: ANTHOLOGY STORIES
"Mountaintop Christmas"
(in *Hope is Born: A Mosaic Christmas Anthology*)
"A Summer of Reckoning"
(in *Before Summer's End: Stories to Touch the Soul*)
"The Sweetest Sound'
(in *Song of Grace: Stories to Amaze the Soul*)

THE CHAIN OF LAKES SERIES
Shattered Image
Dance of Grace
The Color of Truth

Open Circle

UPCOMING
When Valleys Mourn (2022)
Book Two in the My Father's House Series

LET'S CONNECT!

For news about upcoming books, contests, giveaways, and other fun stuff, stop by www.stacymonson.com and sign up for my monthly newsletter. You can find information about my speaking ministry there, as well.

My ultimate goal as I write is two-fold: to glorify the mighty God I serve, and to share inspiring, encouraging stories that point people to the Source of all goodness, the One who can and does redeem everyone who seeks Him.

I would love your help to spread the Good News. Please consider 1) writing a review, and 2) sharing this book. One of the best ways to spread the news about a book you've enjoyed is to write a few sentences sharing your thoughts. The other way is, of course, to tell your friends and family! If you know someone dealing with the effects of aging, dementia or other issues, they could use the encouragement.

May the Creator of all that is good, bless you and keep you until we meet again!

Stacy

GRATITUDE BEYOND WORDS

With the experience of each book comes the joy of new friends, and discovering fresh ideas and new resources. I am beyond grateful for those who've friended me, taught me, and shared their expertise.

My heartfelt thanks to...

Gail Skoglund who daily lives out her heart's passion to preserve the dignity, honor, and respect every elder deserves. You are my soul sister, my inspiration, and a dear friend to seniors everywhere.

The amazing staff of Augustana Open Circle Hopkins, Apple Valley, and Heritage Park who shared their time and expertise with me, and whose collective heart for the elderly inspired this book: Both paid and volunteer who daily do the hard, often thankless, and always invaluable work. You continue to raise the bar for adult day programs. What a privilege to know you.

My family who continues to encourage, inspire, and love me through every book.

The **Moms Group**, the **Marriage Group**, the **Tuesday Bible Study** gals, our **PCC Small Group**—your encouragement means the world to me.

The Alzheimer's Association Minnesota-North Dakota Chapter. A simply amazing organization.

Thank you, Sweet Jesus, for the privilege of serving you through writing.